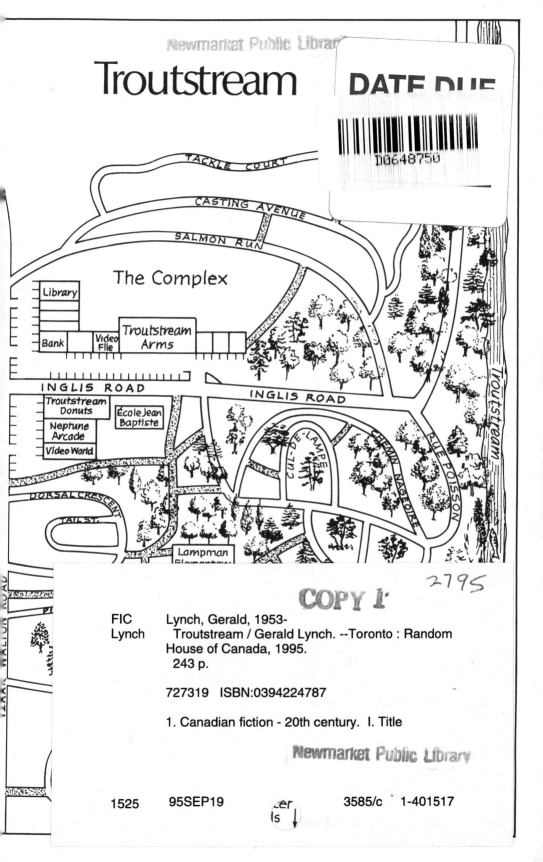

Troutstream

The Complex

Library

Bank | Video File | Troutstream Arms

INGLIS ROAD

Troutstream Donuts | École Jean Baptiste

Neptune Arcade

Video World

INGLIS ROAD

CUL-DE-LAMPE

CHEMIN NAGEOIRE

RUE POISSON

Troutstream

TACKLE COURT

CASTING AVENUE

SALMON RUN

DORSAL CRESCENT

TAIL ST.

Lampman Elementary

•

Troutstream

•

Troutstream

Gerald Lynch

Random House of Canada

First published in 1995 by Random House of Canada Limited,
Toronto, and simultaneously in Great Britain by Fourth Estate
Limited, London.

Lyric excerpts of "Trouble," pages 236-7, by Jerry Leiber and Mike
Stoller, copyright © 1958 by Elvis Presley Music. Copyright
assigned to Gladys Music (administered by Williamson Music for
the world excluding the U.S.). International copyright secured.
Used by permission.

Lyric reproduction of "Are You Lonesome Tonight," pages 238-9,
by Roy Turk and Lou Handman by kind permission of
Redwood Music Ltd.

Canadian Cataloguing in Publication Data
Lynch, Gerald, 1953-
Troutstream
ISBN: 0-394-22478-7
I. TPS8573.Y43T7 1995   C813'.54   C95-931139-4
PR9199.3.L95T7 1995

Printed and bound in the United States of America

10 9 8 7 6 5 4 3 2 1

for
Bryan, Meghan, and Maura

• ACKNOWLEDGEMENTS •

Portions of this book appeared originally in *Canadian Fiction Magazine, Dalhousie Review, Event*, and *Wascana Review*.

Evil is easy, and has infinite forms.
(*Pascal*, Pensées)

• CONTENTS •

• THE PRINCIPAL CHARACTERS •

Jake: resident of Troutstream, a civil servant, the prefacer and implied author answering, after long silence, a call.

Alice Davies: resident of Anglers Court in Troutstream North, mother of two, and incoming President of the Troutstream Community Association.

Eugene Davies: her husband, employee of the National Research Council of Canada, and outgoing President of the Troutstream Community Association.

Jack Kavanagh: resident of Anglers Court, employee of the National Research Council, husband of **Marla**, and father of four.

Norman Gray: a renter on Anglers Court, an unemployed house framer, husband of pregnant **Dorothy** (**Dot**), and narrator of 'Movement'.

Cathy Fogel: new owner of the house in which the Grays rent the ground floor while she occupies the upper, and mother of **Tommy** (10).

Iris O'Connor: elderly resident of the Complex (Salmon Run), a tea-leaf reader and reluctant clairvoyant, wife of **Fred**.

Dennis Ames: resident of the Complex (Tackle Court), a graduate journalism student at Carleton University, and narrator of 'The Needs of Others'.

Les Mellanson: resident of the Complex (Tackle Court), and a part-time handyman.

Linda Mellanson: his wife, a part-time special education teacher at Holy Family Separate School in Troutstream.

Wes: the Mellansons' German Shepherd.

• The Principal Characters •

Frank O'Donaghue: resident of the Complex (Tackle Court), a middle-aged teacher at Holy Family, and narrator of 'Shall I Come Back Again?'

Paul Arsenault: resident owner of the Troutstream Arms on Inglis Road, editor of *Current Affairs*.

Anne Cameron: resident of the Project, cashier at Home Hardware, and single mother of **Leslie** (12).

Mark Macdonald: resident of the Project, moving to the Complex, a technical writer at the National Research Council, and narrator of 'The End of Jokes'.

Sherman Wills (**Shitbag**): Macdonald's fellow technical writer at the NRC, husband of **Sara**.

Sam Blank: resident of the Project, occupation unknown, and unnamed narrator of 'Peeking Man'.

Big Jacques: the last male dinosaur, a brontosaurus, the fantastic projection of Sam Blank.

Nigel Withers: resident of the Project, part-time language teacher, and Sam Blank's only real friend.

John Sheridan: resident of Troutstream North (Jonah's End), employee of the National Research Council, husband of **Martha**, father of **Michael** (12), **Margaret** (10), and **Marion** (3), and narrator of '*L'Envoi*'.

Amusing Myself

•

I am showering, breathing deeply as the steaming water, failing to numb the nerve bundle at the base of my neck, sprays a scalding reminder upon my scapulae. Hanging out flat-palmed on the turquoise tiles of my phonebooth-sized shower, I am a nobody whipped by pale fire waiting for a call. That's what I am without you, a waiting nothing, with a sore throat.

Then you called.

I had little to answer at first. With chin on chest I cleared my throat and whispered, 'Yes,' and felt a chill, and watched a fat drop splat in cinematic slow motion between my spidery big toes, which I wiggled at myself.

My end of our talk proceeded typically, if hoarsely:

'Yes.

'We'll see.

'I prefer not to.'

You signed off with lugubrious regret, 'A *public* man now? *Ja-ake*,' giving my name two syllables.

I didn't reveal that I had felt your immanent presence here in Troutstream.

There is something about your proximity that makes me want to appropriate the real world, possess it fresh and fearlessly again.

1

When you are nearby I want to point to things: the November sun like a calcifying eyeball, like macular degeneration in some old imaginary world, someone else's failing vision; the low grey sky that plants us, kindly keeps us from colder space; the serrated brick corners of the Toronto Dominion Bank, ragged edges inviting us to risk our wrists, wanting to be touched; snub-nosed boots that nuzzle the earth. Things like that.

We have not seen each other for years. When we were together last you displayed a face more exacting than provocative, your eyes like single quotation marks enclosing the undisclosed, parenthesis-like furrows holding your nose and at their base pinching a thin mouth forever withheld. You were dark-haired then, with a brush-stroke of silver like feathers. In the intervening time we have communicated periodically, distantly, and politely about impersonal things.

A public man now? No. Over the past decade I've grown as silent and pale as untouched liquid paper. And I fully expect that if you won't take me back the way I am now, I'll just die quietly.

I am breathing irregularly and shallowly. Let us take up some topic while there is still breath in us. Fortune-telling? The possibility of Canadian life on Mars? *Betrayal?* The media? Politics? Armageddon? The weather generally? With you returning, no subject is without its rewards, the obscene its bouquet, the profound its slick surface, the trivial its black depths. With your homecoming the lethal becomes the vital disguised, the living the slowly dying.

Or something more topical? Something from the very dumpsters of Troutstream? Say, the sexually mutilated body of a prodigy?

Ah, you were always the one for mysteries.

Already I can hear what you'll say first when you materialise and I wrap loving voice around you: *Where are we now, Jake? It's cold here.*

Cold? Cold here in Troutstream? Colder than a witch's stiffest nipple! A cold that cuts like something intentional through mere layered clothing. A cold like some famished *wanting* hungry for marrow. And that *wanting* fixes an ice-bite on brittle bones and twists and snaps and thrashes like an Arctic shark after a year's diet of algae. Until we make some artificial warmth, my love, my only life.

Why *did* you stay away so long this time? Without you everything I touch turns to harangue in my hands, everything I think becomes rant on my tongue. If you do not take me back, all the way back, what will become of me? What will be my subject? You? Only you? Always you? *This?* Then more of this? All preface to your face only?

You must save me from that, only you can save me from that . . . that *decadence*.

I was a mere self of an incapable boy when we first made acquaintance. Each wet green morning distinguished a moist mossy world like a floodlit aquarium, a wet green world. Before you I viewed life with adolescent clarity only, with that post-pubic view that distorts everything to a simple calculus. And even after meeting you I could declare, We will live in Truth! . . .

But why this sudden drop of the gaze? Love? Love too? And devotion? Absolute love? Total devotion?

You made life so complex. I found myself confused, then unsure, then viewing even the hateful from behind and awakening to a body of raw sympathy like compassion's newborn daughter. By the time I knew what was wanted, you had gone for the first time.

I have failed you so often, betrayed you so many times. Why have you returned now? Why bother with me?

After years of failure as a poet, rejection as a novelist, poverty as a freelance journalist, nervous breakdown as a technical writer, I sought refuge in the federal civil service and the great indifference of these my middle years. Here I am: a mid-level employee in the Ministry of Failure, Department of Compromise.

So yes, do come and get me, come promise me promise again. Give me mystery, even a murder mystery, or leave me alone.

★

I have walked through the stripped greenbelt that surrounds Troutstream and come to this rise overlooking what in winter becomes a toboggan run and skating pond. I have been here once before. Last New Year's Day I stood here as dead as the dead when something vibrated the ground (a Mann Quarry explosion, I'd thought). Then faintly a sound like a death rattle, then silence; then a hum that became a nightmare's whisper issuing from below, and dark shouting skaters streamed blindly from the base of the rise for a black hole in the ice. They encircled it, leaving a dazzling border of skate-chipped ice between themselves and the opening with its inner border of shards like a shark's double teeth.

An explosion *in* the pond? Has someone fallen in? Or can holes just open?

'It was an old man!' a girl shouted.

'I saw a mother and a baby!' a man wailed.

'I saw a polar bear!' a boy gasped.

'A girl!' cried someone. 'I saw it happen! A girl my age!'

'It *was* a girl!' someone else shouted. 'And she was pushed by . . . by him!'

From my vantage point *they* appeared only as human forms of relatively the same shape and size, and human only because I knew them from their alarmed voices. Otherwise they could as accurately be described as a dark mass of hysterical noise pulsating teasingly about a black opening. Like an ink blot, that hole, or what happens when paper tears in a printer and the roller shows through.

I took a shallow breath of pure sub-zero air.

And noticed just ahead of me at the mid-point of the rise a young fiery-haired girl pointing at the scene and laughing, 'I'm he-er!'

But no one noticed her, all continued to alternate their attention between the hole and me.

Showing no embarrassment at my approach, she alternated her glances between me and the frozen scene. And I caught coyness teasing from her slightly slanted eyes, a nymphetic allure in those almond eyes fanned by coarse red lashes below coarser red eyebrows, those eyes above apple cheeks like two great red dots. In truth, I sensed a something very full of you, a something that made my breath come shorter still.

Northern wind blasted the rise.

'This is as cold as she gets!' I think she shouted out at the accident, but she was shaking her head rapidly now and already moving off in the icy air.

I leaned into her and shouted, 'What – what happened?'

She smirked indulgently across her shoulder, but I could barely hear what issued from her parted lips.

'My *what*? Lose my *what*?'

She laughed and flitted off.

'Huh?' But already I was talking more to myself than to her.

The hole in the ice was eventually abandoned by all save a couple of uniformed investigators of such mysteries. One of the officials cordoned it off like the restricted area of a theatre lobby. The other raised his arm and pointed at me, crooked his forefinger.

I raised my eyes and a flurry of crystals filled my lashes, my nostrils united, and for a moment I saw nothing and didn't breathe. This is as cold as she gets indeed. I threw back my head and stared blindly into the swarming air and opened wide my mouth to shout some curse, and my silence was a moist vain hole in the storm. My raw throat tickled, as if by a feather, scratched as if by a quill, and a growing and scraping till I could contain it no longer and out of my mouth flew a tiny crow of a visibly indivisible perfection, out over that other hole it flapped, but instead of diminishing as it receded it grew larger, circled the hole once, twice, three times, and three times three, and filled the sky as it bore down on me. But it stopped and hovered upright, peered into my vacant eyes, and whispered harshly, 'Kiss me,' stuck the tip of its beak into my mouth, parted us both as its body elongated into a slippery grey fish and slithered in. Then the words of warning and praise issued keen and clear:

'Troutstream! Troutstream!'

·

GARDEN
HOMES

·

Anglers Court

•

Right where Jack and Marla Kavanagh stand, unfashionably early, wouldn't you know it . . . or maybe not, it is exactly one, but *really*. Anyway, right where they stand watching the kids playing in the hedge at the bottom of the yard, *that's* where Alice would like to build the solarium. Through white French doors to *café au lait* and a view of the park. The oak sapling at Jack's shoulder was just a stick in the mud anyway . . . like Jack and Marla lately. It had leafed in May, shed, then *fffft*. Acid rain. To get the right view, they'll have to take out the cedar hedge along the back, and the big corner maple, though she wouldn't want to lose the birch, and she won't. Conserve, conserve. Jack secretly runs his fore-finger up and down Marla's bare biceps, Marla smiles at him. Why can't Eugene master that act? . . . Poor Gene. But how does Marla image herself anyway? As a piece of meat to be pawed? Here come the Andersons, silly Karen, she's dressed Kitty up as if for a recital. Those wild Kavanagh kids will take care of that outfit, doesn't Alice know it. But Kitty doesn't run to the hedge. And the Burroughs right behind them. Poor little Paul, he looks so perfectly . . . normal (note: Helen Burroughs hates that word). There he goes, straight to the corner, where he'll sit by himself in a pile of earwiggy old leaves till somebody moves him. Autistic (and *that* word). The sink ledge depresses Alice's abdomen – she's

9

getting paunchy again, she weighs one hundred and ten pounds – as she leans towards the window and calls out, 'Hi Bill, Karen, Ted, Helen! Make Jack show you where the juices are, I'll be right out!' She waits for the oven timer and removes the last, thank God, tray of scones (Marla Kavanagh still calls them tea biscuits, though she's been told the proper name). She tilts the tray to slide the scones into a wicker basket lined with a green-embroidered linen tea-towel, but she has to reach into a drawer for a knife to dislodge some of them. F-ing timer. She wraps them. She fills her kettle full, surprised at its weight, and sets it on the element. From the cupboard over the fridge she takes the pretty tin of loose tea Eugene had insisted she buy at some smelly little store in the Byward Market. The big mystery. They're having a garden *tea* party and Eugene has invited some witch from the Complex (of all places) to read their cups. *Invited?* Not likely, he'd had to pay her fifty dollars. And their guests are supposed to make her a *donation* too. Let Gene explain *that* to Bill Anderson. Though who knows, maybe they'll have some fun. And the pretty tea tin will be useful afterwards. A dark olive green, its borders festooned with black leaves, a silhouette of a woman standing in a gondola and poling herself towards a dark sun. Probably something out of Tennyson. Or maybe Charon's kid sister, she smirks. Who out *there* would get that reference? *Allusion.* She pries off the lid and with her eyes closed bows over the tin more than brings it to her face. An aroma of dark places . . . of echoing breathing . . . trailing into groans – she snaps open her eyes, for the briefest moment she's unsure. The loose leaves inside the golden mirroring tin look like the charred remains of some document. But I guess that's what they are sorta, she smiles, burnt leaves. Too bad it's against the law to burn garden leaves. Showing her age. She will anyway. Shit, there's Gene with his witch. Does anyone know how to make this stuff? All the tin says is Tea Time. Don't these foreigners have to list their ingredients? Gene, Gene, the obsessing machine, more and more about the explosions at the Quarry. Now, on top of everything else, she has to assume the presidency of the Troutstream Community Association, just to get him out of it. Oh, she's getting herself all worked up over nothing. Out! Out!

Through a hurting blue sky the revitalised October sun bombards the Davies' yard with ultraviolet rays, so all the adults stand about in sunglasses. Leaves lie everywhere, yellow, brown, black, slick underfoot, in spaced moderate piles, stuffed into burnt-orange bags along the cedar hedge with twigs sticking from the plastic like the bones of small animals; some are still falling, even touching down softly on heads; while others cling to the densely stark branches of the trees that loom in the parkway at the bottom of the yard.

At the side door Eugene introduces Alice to the woman, Iris O'Connor, who, though taller than any woman Alice knows, is absolutely pathetic in her shy silence and black cardigan, like some Italian widow with the evil eye. But Alice places her fingers on the woman's forearm and tells her she simply must show her how to make the tea, don't move, and moves off.

'You *brew* tea,' Iris smiles, hugging herself.

There are some people you just couldn't make feel at home. Alice moves along to Bill and Karen Anderson, her next-door neighbours.

She had put out a baby's bathtub full of juices, and the gathering, standing around in their shades and holding small plastic containers with the foil coverings peeled back like tiny radio-wave receptors, looks like some space-age solar cult. Eugene waits by the tub in his baby-blue National Research Council sweat shirt – 'Canada's Bestest and Brightest' – inadvertently picking at the wisps of plastic on the tub's lip, estimating what concentration of laser would cut it neatly without melt, wondering where Alice had found the big basin. Such free-fall thinking had sometimes led him to discovery or innovation at the Council. Jack Kavanagh was a linear one-tracker. *Was that a detonation at the Quarry?* . . . No. His legs are weak from overwork and lack of sleep. He pats the tub and moves along to the tight group formed by the three Wier sisters in flip-down shades and straw hats. It had been hell convincing the old douchebags to come. But they were among the charter members of the Troutstream Community Association, and if *they* weren't here, what kind of community was this anyway?

'Still,' Alice says to Bill Anderson, 'we're lucky to get such an Indian summer as this. Though it's only fair after the summer we've had.'

11

'It's about the *only* good thing the Indians ever did for this country,' Bill laughs. His wife, Karen, slaps his shoulder and shakes her head. 'Well it's the truth,' says Bill.

'You're *so* right,' Alice whispers. 'If more people were like you, Bill, this would be an even better community.'

'Damn right it would. Or it could've been if Euge – if we'd stopped the Project.'

'Karen, didn't you say Kitty was entering j-k this year?'

'I am,' Kitty answers, needlessly straightening her green plaid skirt and looking out from beneath a red visor and dark pageboy like a helmet. 'But I'm not going to Holy Family 'cause Daddy says Catholics are nuts.'

'Well, I didn't put it quite that way, sweetheart,' says Bill. 'Now run along.' He pushes her between the shoulder blades and she stumbles a few feet, stops, clenches her fists and without turning back shouts, 'You did so!'

'Oh, it's all right,' Alice says, flapping her hand. 'We lapsed long ago. But what's all this about not going to Holy Family?'

'The real reason's that they don't have French immersion,' Karen says. 'And though we don't agree with forced bilingualism, you know what living in Ottawa – '

'Tell the truth, honey,' Bill says in an exasperated drawl. He often pictured himself as someone struggling through a sea of bullshit with his resistant wife in a life-saving headlock. 'The real reason's that the Catholics *are* nuts, they'll hire any pervert. Alice, don't tell me you didn't hear about that O'Donaghue character, the old bachelor who's been teaching there since the school opened. First off, he went into the Whites' at their last open house, put his feet up and decided he was moving in with them. They had to call the *cops* to get him out! Now he's talkin' about putting on one of those karaoke Elvis shows right in his class for Christ's – '

'Bill,' Karen says sharply, secretly pinching his triceps and causing Bill himself to do something of an Elvis twitch.

Alice, unnaturally wide-eyed, moves over to Jack and Marla Kavanagh, and says generally, 'Politically correct, Bill ain't.'

Jack, who towers above the women, is cramming the aluminum cover of his grapefruit juice inside the container: 'Alice, when did Gene give up beer?'

'Beer, Jack?' I'm sure we have some somewhere. I'll get Gene – '

'No-no, for God's sake, it was a *joke*.'

'Jack, this is no time for jokes.'

'Don't I know it. What's with him lately?'

Alice smiles about the yard.

Marla draws a deep breath and speaks in the tone that betrays preparation: 'Alice, Jack and I were just remarking on how long it's been since we had one of our old get-togethers, and we were wondering if perhaps you and the family would like to join us at the soccer fields for a picnic some day soon?'

'Oh, okay . . . Marla. We'll have to talk.'

Alice moves off to where her husband is talking to the three Wier sisters, who stand close to the tall cedar hedge between the Davies' and the Andersons'. The Wier sisters, triplets actually, live together in the only bungalow on Anglers Court. Shoulder to shoulder they stand, at exactly five foot, with some two hundred and seventy pounds divided equally among them, with their identical straw hats nearly touching and their backs right up against the hedge, as though Eugene Davies were fiercely lecturing them.

Of course *they* would know this Iris O'Connor, Alice smirks, they'd all waved to each other. Three retired school teachers who take no real part in the Troutstream Community Association. She and Gene keep praying they'll sell and move into Safe Harbour down at Walton and Inglis. It's not like they don't have the money.

'Is this lame duck bothering you dear ladies?'

'To tell you the truth, honey, Melissa . . . *here* was just telling me that they've all been coming down with migraine headaches. No, seriously. Even worse, she says they've developed ag . . . aggrava . . . What's it called again, Melissa?'

'Agoraphobia,' Melissa mouths carefully, and looks to her sisters, who nod. 'We had to pay Debbie extra to come in and do our hairs.' They nod again. 'It isn't just imagination.' They shake their heads.

'You look just darling,' Alice says to no one in particular.

Eugene hoists his cloudy plastic container: 'Oh well, anyway, here's to my last meeting as president of the Troutstream Community Association.' Though he'd begun saluting only the Wier sisters, Eugene swivels to address the small gathering. 'As your outgoing president – and I am a sociable sort' (Jack Kavanagh hoots) – 'I can report that although we lost on the Project, we did get the Bypass. We controlled the size of the Jonah's End development, and I also got Troutstream taken off the list of potential incinerator sites. Thanks to increased interest from . . . well, let's just say from some newcomers to Troutstream, we were able to initiate our own T-ball league, and next summer Troutstream girls will have their own soccer league. *And*, without mentioning any names, *honey*, wink-wink nudge-nudge, we almost got the Crown to prosecute that hate-monger who owns the Troutstream Arms. We'll get him next time. Anyway, here's to our new president, *Ms* Alice Davies, I promise to work closely with her in making a smooth transition.'

'Hear-hear!' Jack Kavanagh shouts. 'Gene, you old smoothie!'

Eugene holds up his hand. 'Nonetheless, what grieves me still as outgoing president is that I leave with a job unfinished.'

Hush.

'Oh honey, please.'

'No-no, dear. As you all know, the subterranean blasts at Mann Quarry have been growing increasingly violent and numerous. An engineer friend at the Council agrees with me that there could well be foundation cracks in our houses, either ones so fine as yet that we can't see them, or buried faults. Although we'd all hoped the Quarry administration was complying with our agreement, it turns out they've been setting off even more explosions at night when we're all sleeping the sleep of the naive. I suspect that, like me, many of you have been waking up in the middle of the night to find your house rattling like the Devil himself had taken the foundation in both his hands and shaken it. And I promise – '

'Gene, Gene,' Jack Kavanagh moans loudly.

'No-no, big guy, Troutstream is being *undermined*, I tell you! By some*body*. Or some*thing*. This is the new enemy, and I have a new battle plan. What we need – '

'All right, honey,' Alice says through her teeth, then hides what she says next by turning her back to the gathering. She faces her neighbours again and, smiling like the victim of an ambitious face-lift, moves a half-step away from her husband.

Red-faced and sweating, Eugene places his left arm around Alice's waist, pulls her near and presses a kiss to her cheek. Some grape juice sloshes from his container. 'You old smoothie!' she shrieks. And everyone laughs nervously.

Everyone but Iris O'Connor, who stands outside the semicircle of neighbours, thin-lipped and head shaking slightly as though someone had described a dirty job – chicken plucking and cleaning, say – and no one volunteering to do it. She is just taking a step towards the bottom of the yard, where children are popping in and out through gaps in the hedge, and where that quiet boy sits facing the corner, when she feels Alice's hand on her forearm, more firmly than before.

'Mrs O'Connor, would you be a dear and please come into the kitchen and show me how you like the tea done. I bought the brand you told Eugene to get, Tea Time.'

Iris blinks down at the shorter woman, knowing she would feel even more awkward in the kitchen. 'You don't know how to brew tea, Mrs Davies?'

'Alice, please. No, it's just that I'm not sure how much to measure out.' The effrontery!

And though she's known all along that the leaves will show nothing here and she'll have to make up the lot of it, Iris smiles pleasantly, if guardedly, in acquiescence. Known all along, yes, but something had made her come still. Though she will *not* mouth the silly fortunes Mr Davies had hinted he was paying for: future success in badgering the Quarry people, love in the offing for everybody, by which he meant adultery probably, a miracle for the dumb boy in the corner. Oh well, at least it can't be as bad as two weeks ago with the Wier sisters, the last time she'd made a house-call, and they'd simply slit open Red Rose bags. Sure nothing would come of it, she'd begun reading and unintentionally slipped into deep trance and scared the matching stirrup pants off the triplets with talk of darkness, madness and murder, so much so that they were afraid to leave the house now. So it's with some misgivings that she allows Alice to link her arm and lead her into the kitchen, where the kettle is shrieking like a banshee, the window ledge is weeping steam onto the biscuits . . . and she can feel vibrations from the tin on the counter.

15

Iris goes cold. 'Are you sure, Mrs Davies, that you want to go through with this?'

Alice smirks and smiles too brightly: 'Oh, there's no use being melodramatic with me, Iris dear. Although I'm probably the only one here who can appreciate the ancient and honourable tradition of *wick* to which you belong, I do not believe in spiritualist mumbo-jumbo. I'll play along, though, for Eugene's sake, don't you worry your head on that account, dear.'

'This doesn't need your belief . . . dear. Only your willing participation.'

'*How* much goes into the pot?'

Iris grinds her teeth. 'You don't make it in the pot, dear. Set out the cups and put three pinches in each cup.'

Alice already has her second-best cups on a large rectangular wooden tray. She snatches a teaspoon from a drawer and reaches for the dark green tin.

'No, Mrs Davies, you must pinch the leaves with your fingers.'

'Oh why don't you do it then.'

'No. *You* must do it. As I said, you must willingly participate.'

When she wishes to intimidate a snotty salesgirl, Alice insinuates a hint of British accent: 'Come, come, woman.'

As if ordering about a washerwoman. But before Iris can turn and leave, both women freeze. The sound is a distant rhythmical boom-ing, three times, like timpani being tapped in the basement cold storage; the window shakes and the cups rattle, Iris's legs weaken.

Alice compresses her lips and shakes her head in smiling con-cession: 'I guess Gene isn't exaggerating, those Quarry explosions *are* getting more powerful, closer too. My first task as incoming president of the Association will just have to be organising another delegation to the Mann people. Why, it sounds like . . . like . . .'

'Like something walking towards you underground? . . . But it's Sunday, dear, don't forget. And as far as I know – I mean, living south of Inglis and all – the Quarry people have stuck to their promise not to operate on Sundays. Even Arsenault at the Arms concedes that.'

'Then we should call the police on them.' She removes the lid and puts her hand into the tea tin.

Iris opens her mouth to speak and leaves it hanging when the booming sounds again, three times, louder this time, like an old furnace oil-canning. 'Now, don't laugh at me, dear. But something tells me this isn't a problem that can be solved by the police.'

'What are you talking about, woman?'

'Make the tea.'

'It's just the Quarry.'

'Perhaps you're right.'

More than the third repetition of the three booms, distant again, it's the tears sliding down Iris's cheeks and her dilated pupils that make Alice's fingers fly to her mouth, where she deposits a small moustache of tea leaves like someone's comic Hitler.

Iris's eyelids flutter, she shows whites as if seized by the *petit mal*, and whispers, 'It's on the way.'

'What? The police?'

'Yes, here.'

Troutstream, designed in 1958 by a graduate student on an Izaak Walton Foundation Fellowship in urban planning at the University of Ottawa, and constructed in the early 1960s, represents the epitome of the 1950s suburban dream. Its plan had won a competition organised by Foster City Council, which had convinced Ottawa's National Capital Commission to permit the construction of a model suburb in the treasured greenbelt that protects the capital from suburban sprawl. In tribute to the sponsor of his Fellowship, the winning student had named his community and all its streets in honour of the author of the seventeenth-century fisherman's bible, *The Compleat Angler*, though there remained no fish of any kind in the stream that slid northwards to the west.

Semi-rural Troutstream, threaded through with parks and paved walks, displays space lavishly. There, some twelve models of houses originally dubbed Garden Homes repeat distantly to avoid the impression of sameness that colours so many latter-day developments in their tempered pastels and earth tones. Here and there, individual contractors were licensed to build custom-made houses. Here, a triple-gabled house rests not too close to a modestly deceptive backsplit of equivalent square footage; there, two identical bungalows sit side by side in the kind of sameness that distinguishes twins. Everywhere in the development trees were saved by design, mature trees were planted at great expense, and saplings have grown into flourishing thirty-year-olds. A good number of the homes back not onto other yards, but onto those evergreen and maple-shadowed walkways which are generously interrupted by small parks and the more open fields of schools. Circular by design and self-contained by greenbelt, Troutstream will eventually deliver walkers back to where they began, conveying the impression that, in the pictorial sense, the setting has no real background, only a foreground of garden homes and a midground of parks and trees.

Unfortunately, and in violation of the spirit of its permit from the National Capital Commission, Troutstream has sprawled southwards in a complex of town houses which appropriated the name Garden Homes; and most recently a subsidised housing project has reared up in the south-east, despite the furious opposition of the Troutstream Community Association. What local business would survive the scared-off customers and shoplifting that comes with subsidised housing? Paul Arsenault, proprietor of the Troutstream Arms, had asked in his bar's newsletter, *Current Affairs*. None would, given those conditions, just as later no one would concede that receipts had increased, only marginally in most cases, true, but by double for the Troutstream Arms, from where the nastiest criticism of the completed Project continued. What self-respecting community, Bill Anderson had inquired in an open letter to *Current Affairs*, wants dope addicts and teenage hookers? None did. So no drugged young perverts had dared materialise, as Bill was proud to point out publicly. And who wanted all that extra traffic? Eugene Davies, the Troutstream Community Association's president, had demanded at a series of town hall meetings and in a flurry of flyers. No one did. So in a naive bid at compromise the Association had dropped its opposition to the addition of a few new houses on the north end, to be called Jonah's End, but finally had to settle for the Troutstream Bypass in trade-off for the Project.

Although the Project spoiled one's idea of Troutstream as the ideal suburb, ironically it was the only place stocked with enough old men and fatherless boys to pursue the philosopher's pastime. Increasingly they were doing so together, and trying their luck in the actual Troutstream. Rumours had begun circulating that fish had returned to the deep northernmost end of the stream, where it emerged from the sewage treatment plant on its way to the Ottawa River, though an angler was yet to land one.

Anglers Court itself is a cul-de-sac surrounded by Troutstream North's renowned walkways and parks, off a large crescent, Piscator Drive, which is off the main artery, Izaak Walton Road. Those 'in the sac', as they say, comprise a club of sorts, referring to themselves as 'la famille de sac'. The most recent census figures describe Troutstream as seventeen per cent Francophone, which makes it a microcosm of Ottawa itself. Those living on Anglers Court are all Anglophone, however, and their use of French in labelling themselves, with the exception of the Kavanaghs and Wiers, is intended ironically, if not derisively. Nonetheless, the majority send their children to French immersion and French schools, knowing that bilingualism is a prerequisite for employment in Ottawa; and besides, the three English schools in Troutstream are filled now with kids from the Complex and riffraff from the Project. Those living on Anglers Court, nucleus of the Troutstream Community Association, always use the word 'community' when referring to Troutstream generally, though they mean that part of it north of Inglis and, even more specifically, their immediate neighbourhood, if not exclusively their near neighbours in the sac. The seven families living on the large bulb of Anglers Court know they live in the most expensive houses Troutstream has to offer. Only one house has changed hands in fifteen years, and that was five years ago when the Davies moved in, paying a quarter of a million dollars for a house that had quadrupled its price in ten years. Sometimes those at the bottom of Anglers Court exclude from la famille de sac those living on the stem of the thermometer-shaped street. Ultimately, Eugene Davies and Bill Anderson believe that they, and they alone (with the infrequent exception of Jack Kavanagh), constitute the crème de la crème of Troutstream and its Community Association. In their meanest moments they even exclude each other and think of Jack as useful.

But this afternoon's garden tea party had been planned by Eugene as an inclusive affair. Thus the Wier triplets and the nasty

Burroughs with their retarded son. Iris O'Connor is there because Eugene wants his fortune told and could think of no other way of doing so acceptable to himself. If Alice knew that he hadn't slept a wink for days, she'd make an appointment with some shrink, as she'd done during their last year in Toronto. But he's under a hell of a lot of stress at work again; the boys upstairs are growing tired of waiting for his next big thing. Ever since he and Jack had made the fibre optics breakthrough, the pressure had been on, though of course no one has said so in as many words. One of the things that had queered his friendship with Jack was the big guy's pretending not to notice the pressure from above. So this party's also useful because it fulfils an awkward social commitment to the Kavanaghs. And when Eugene looks around the garden at his guests sipping tea from delicate cups and making displeased faces, he feels the elation of insomnia-inspired mania. This was why they'd moved to Troutstream: friends, family, home. Community.

Jack Kavanagh throws back his tea in one swallow and shouts at him, 'Hey, Gene, isn't there anyone in the Stream reads beer bottles?'

Eugene smirks, looks for Iris to see if she's offended, and finds her heading towards the bottom of the yard where the children are playing in the hedge. All the children, that is, but the idiot Burroughs kid, who sits backwards in the corner like some offensive yard ornament, like some nigger kid without a lamp. There's nothing organically wrong with that kid, all the best doctors have said so.

Alice Davies takes Jack by the forearm and leads him to a card table, where she tells him to place his cup on his name card. She leaves him there. Jack smiles back at Marla, who goes over to talk with the Wier triplets. One of the old girls soon has her hands fluttering about like moths, and to Jack's bewilderment Marla is frowning. He looks towards the bottom of the yard, where Iris now stands facing the green wall of cedar. He would like to follow, to shoot the breeze, but there's something about her that spooks him. Her height maybe, or that dark-eyed smile. She might tell him something he doesn't want to know. Yet when Bill Anderson comes alongside and fastidiously sets his cup on his name card, Jack decides he will go to her.

'Fucking Project people,' Bill whispers loudly. 'Someone told me they're eating carp from the stream where it comes out of the sewage treatment plant.' He lowers his whisper: 'Eugene-you-genius did his best to stop it, I'll grant, but it just wasn't good enough. He knows sweet fuck about city hall.' Bill rubs his fingers under Jack's nose like he's balling enormous snot. 'And where the fuck did Gene get the idea he could anoint his fucking successor?'

'Bill, I've heard business is way up at Home Hardware, that the Project people work like hell and need lots of materials to make those small apartments liveable?'

'Who told you that? Anne? She's not supposed to talk to customers about the business. And it's lousy anyway.'

'No, it wasn't Anne.'

'Hey, did you see the shit the Davies were selling at their garage sale yesterday? People selling shit's what hurts my business.'

'I believe you,' Jack smiles. Then frowns: 'You hear anything about the Burroughs moving, Bill?'

'Not a moment too soon far as I'm concerned, the way they've shut us all out and mishandled that kid of theirs. It's a disgrace, I say. If it was me . . .'

But Jack is worrying that he's got Anne, Bill's cashier, in trouble. He and Anne have developed a kind of friendship over the years, ever since he'd been refitting the bathroom. He'll have to make things right. He should have Anne and her daughter out to the house some time . . . now that Eugene and Alice seem to be finished with them.

He says, 'No, it was an old man, Martin somebody, from the Project, in your store looking for a fishing net. Said he never saw such a well-run hardware.'

'Really?' Bill smiles. 'Hey, big guy, why don't you and me have a talk with Eugene and Alice about going easy on Arsenault over at the Troutstream Arms. He's really not a bad guy. And besides, a lot of what he says in *Current Affairs* makes pretty good sense to me. Funny too. Did you see that one about the two Irish queers?'

'Yes.' Behind Bill's back two-thirds of the Wier triplets in matching hats, white cardigans and navy sundresses have arrived with their tea cups. The other sister still engages Marla intensely.

21

Bill says loudly, 'Patrick Fitzgerald and Gerald Fitzpatrick!' and roars. 'Get it? *Fits?* Like they're cornholing each other!'

Relieved that the two Wiers are genuinely befuddled, Jack says, 'Talk to you later, Bill.' He speaks loudly and slowly: 'And you girls don't let this gentleman sell you any subscriptions to *Current Affairs*. Your cards are right here, ladies.' He swings by the corner of the table and out onto the lawn, feeling he should save Marla, where she stands gaping at the old girl who has pulled her lower lip down from the gum to display surprisingly dazzling teeth, but he wills himself onward to the bottom of the yard.

Iris stands in the hedge's deep shade with her back to the house. Children weave in and out of the hedge, the younger squealing playfully after the older. Some notice the big man approaching and, screaming 'He's after us, he'll kill us,' they all scoot through to the park on the other side. In the right corner sits Paul Burroughs, as still and erect as a meditator, with his back to the yard and his hands flat in the grass as if buried to the wrists.

The last Iris remembers is wandering to the back of the Davies' property, and being tempted to keep going, through the hedge and on to a path back home. There was nothing here for her, they were set on playing her the fool. Except for that nice Jack Kavanagh . . . and here she's looking slightly up into the fleshy face of Jack Kavanagh. This has happened before, this daydreaming, at the Wiers' that time, and other times lately, only it's not the same because in a daydream you don't really have to be called back. And something else different this time, a sound in the dark, like the call of a peacock, which she'd heard only once in her life that time the zoo passed in the night by the farm back in Depot. A peacock . . . or a child, in pain, and then that other sound, like huffing. She's cold, clammy.

'Mrs O'Connor, are you all right? You look like you've just seen a ghost.'

'Oh, I'm just daydreaming, Mr Kavanagh.'

'Jack, please . . . Iris.'

'Jack, am I here to be made a fool of by this crowd?'

Iris's expression remains pleasant, though suspended, a face caught between self-recognition and anger. Recognition wins out, but she won't give these people the pleasure of showing hurt feelings. Tight-lipped and staring, she will keep her resolve, even as she feels the clown's big tear roll across her cheekbone. Old fool, what did you expect?

'I'm no fraud, you know.'

Jack whispers, 'Nobody's making a fool of anybody, Iris.' Without thinking he takes her hand. Her eyelashes flutter, she wavers, and Jack is afraid.

She squeezes his large fingers: 'Why does your friend sit up all night waiting for the worst to happen, when it will soon enough? Why is your friend no longer your friend?'

Had Eugene spoken to *her*?

From the head of the yard Alice Davies shouts, 'Ja-ack, would you please return our guest of honour. It's time to do the voodoo!'

Laughter.

Iris's grip tightens, she trembles, a dark maple leaf brushes her forehead, sits on her nose, slides down, and her eyes roll up, showing bluish whites like the ends of two hard-boiled eggs.

'Desire. Sick and self-loving. Blue – '

'Iris, Iris,' Jack insists. 'Stop it already, you're spooking me.'

And Iris relaxes, her eyes return, though she looks again like she's just wakened.

'Jack,' Eugene calls. 'No private readings, eh big guy?'

More laughter.

Bill Anderson shouts, 'Let's get this show on the road for Christ's sake!'

Screaming children come tearing through the hedge, some through gaps, but others springing from the green wall itself, and go running to the top of the yard – 'He's back! He's back!' The adults smile warily, not knowing that these are screams of real terror, but Jack knows, and to his shame he realises that he's checked to recognise the backs of his own kids only. He registers that all the kids are present, and that Paul Burroughs has not moved a jot.

He steps into the largest hole in the surprisingly deep hedge, not feeling the scrapes on his arms and neck; he pushes through to the other side, feeling Iris tagging along on his shirt-tail. Despite the nearly bare trees, he is suddenly in deep shade, chilly, a place as different from the Davies' sunny yard as midnight from noon, and silent. He looks to the right and spots what has frightened the

23

children: a large dark dog finishes cocking his leg against the mossy side of a trunk, then it's moving along the walkway with just a clicking of paws, not quite bounding, but moving through the air as if propelling itself by contraction and extension. Looks like a Shepherd, and Jack is relieved. But Iris moves closer to his back, all but clinging. Soon the dog is out of sight without having noticed them. Jack is turning back to the hedge when he hears a clomping sound, and looks again to find the stocky man stumbling along.

'He went thataway!' Jack shouts.

The man stops opposite them, places his hands on his hips and exhales heavily, dips his chin and shakes his head at some private joke. He turns towards them and walks over. He's been running in untied workboots and a pair of overalls, no shirt. His hair is long and wild, but his eyes are friendly brown. When he smiles largely his face crinkles, and Jack smiles in return. The man giggles like a girl.

Iris steps from behind Jack: 'You're from Tackle Court, aren't you? You sometimes help my Fred with the maintenance.'

'Iris! How are ya? It's me, Les, Les Mellanson.'

Jack extends his hand and shakes Les's, says, 'Les, you're not supposed to let your dog run loose in here. You scared the wits out of the children.'

'*Gee*, I'm sorry, Mr. But I'm not out walking ol' Wes, like. He got away from me and I been lookin' for him for days. 'Sides, ol' Wes wouldn't hurt a fly. He's nine parts Shepherd and one part chicken.' He giggles.

Jack stiffens: 'Looks to me, buddy, like you've been having maybe one too many somewhere.'

Les smirks: 'Yeah, well, I'm having trouble with my old lady, and now I find out some sicko's been beating my dog.' He giggles again.

'Okay, buddy. I don't see what's to laugh about. And like I said, he went that way. But if he's your dog, it's funny he won't come to you, eh?'

Les turns and jogs off sideways: 'Like *I* said, somebody's beat him bad. And it's your shades, man! Shades in the dark!' And giggles.

Jack snaps up the clip-on shades, turns to the hedge and almost bumps into Iris, who has her own sunglasses folded in her fist and her forehead on the back of her hand.

'Iris, Iris, it was just a dog and a drunk. I'm surprised *anyone* would let that old hippie work for them. Now let's go up and join the others, you do the readings and everything'll be okay.'

Iris straightens, stiffens and sniffles. She says without emotion: 'The reading is over, Jack.'

'*What* are you talking about, Iris?' he says as he steps past her. 'God Almighty.'

When he emerges from the hole in the hedge he has to shut his eyes against the glare. He's startled to find Gene standing right there, smiling idiotically and holding his tea cup in joined palms like a chalice. Jack squints towards the top of the yard and senses the subdued atmosphere before he sees the policeman. He runs.

The policeman spots him and jerks his hand towards his holster, recognizes Jack, grins and shouts, 'Easy, Jack, easy, it's me, Mark Fournier,' gesturing with both palms pushing downward.

'Whew, Mark,' says Jack walking. 'What's up? Too much rowdiness here?' He laughs alone.

Marla places a hand on his forearm: 'Jack, there's a young girl missing.'

'From where?' Jack asks the policeman.

'From Troutstream.'

'He *means*, officer,' Bill Anderson says, 'from what *part* of Troutstream? As in, *another Project problem?*'

'I *mean*,' Jack says, 'is it serious? How long's she been missing? Maybe she's just run away for the day, or something.'

'Serious enough, Jack, or I wouldn't be here. She lives on Piscator. The Archer girl. Teresa.' Some gasp. 'Circumstances indicate foul play, sorry to say.'

The Wier triplets are already sniffling, the children are grinning. Helen Burroughs runs to the back corner and lifts her son into her arms. 'He's not a baby,' Ted Burroughs whispers harshly. Jack looks around for Iris and sees she's still at the bottom of the yard . . . and that Gene is there, gesticulating wildly, threateningly almost?

'Look, folks, I stopped here for a couple of reasons. Number one,

I was tailing some wild man who's chasing a big black dog that looked to be foaming. I don't suppose any of you've seen them?'

Jack says, 'They just ran along the pathway at the back, twice I think. Why, is *he* a suspect?'

The policeman cocks an eye at Jack: 'And two, Jack here's a friend.' He laughs nervously: 'Buys my coffee every morning at Troutstream Donuts. I wanted to warn him, and all of you, to talk to your children, keep them close over the next while, but don't alarm them unnecessarily.'

Some of the children are crying now and clinging to their parents. Eugene is returning alone from the bottom of the yard, his tea cup still held in two hands like a boy's frog, and with no sign of Iris behind him. Grinning he shouts from halfway up, 'Jack, the witch predicts big things in our future! Another breakthrough! Her very words! And soon!'

• 2 •

Movement

•

I was about to start the old Dart when the front screen door whined like a cat in heat. I smiled indulgently at my lap: Dot was coming out to remind me about the pre-natal class later that afternoon, which is her way of needlessly telling me one more time to drive carefully. But it was the boy, Tommy, who now lives above us leaving for school. He stood on the large cement stoop and looked stealthily about, in that furtive way of a ten-year-old boy sniffing trouble. Though he may simply have been searching for the neighbourhood girl he'd recently made friends with. When he spotted me behind the reflective windshield he crouched to fiddle with his mother's bike, which had been chained to the purely decorative wooden post for six days. He leapt to the ground and scatted down the side of the house.

Gone to check something in the back yard? Or maybe he's already found the short cut to Holy Family. It's a long way round by Piscator and Izaak Walton, much shorter as the crow flies.

Still, I started the car and waited to see if Tommy would return. Poor Dot must have suffered from my idling. With her knitted fingers cradling her big belly, or with palm circling rapidly and lightly, working some kind of expecting spell, she'd indeed have been battling her worst instinct to come out and call, 'Now drive carefully, Norman!' But I *am* careful, very careful. I don't know

27

what it is lately, why she's so stressed at my absences, or why she's skittish in my presence, or why those quizzical looks. I've taken to meeting her endless cautions with a smirk, and she to saying in a singsong, 'I don't know you any more, Norman.'

Well, I don't know nothin' any more, Dot.

So I backed out and drove off. The list of addresses lay face down on the seat beside me, where Tommy now felt disinclined to sit. Although I sympathised with the boy's dilemma, I hated his mother so much I wanted to feel vindicated, pure and simple. You cannot live as she does and your progeny not suffer the consequences! The sins of the father . . . or the mother, as in this instance of sin. I strongly suspected that Tommy ignored my implied offer of a ride because he was ashamed of his mother's recent betrayal of Dot and me and our coming child. As if a ten-year-old boy could have done anything to save us. I then felt pleased that *my* first impulse had been to offer him another ride.

We had formed a friendship, Tommy and I, a secret friendship. I'd given him a ride to school the week before and complained man-to-man about 'the wife' eating gobs of spooned peanut butter dipped in sugar first thing in the morning. I'd lit a cigarette and sighed as I exhaled out my window: 'Sickening . . . ruins my first smoke.'

He'd frowned, brightened, turned away and giggled like an imp.

'Sometimes I eat peanut butter on toast for breakfast,' he'd said, the first he'd spoken to me since they'd moved in three weeks before. He had the voice of a choirboy, not a trace of the crack that was coming as surely as death and taxes. 'Sometimes my mom forgets to fix me anything before she leaves for work at the university! And she won't let my dad smoke any more in the house, and she says he's gotta stop drinkin' now 'cause we're living in the city! But he drinks *more!*' He crammed his hands between the knees of his brown corduroys. 'Hey, how come cigarettes don't catch fire?'

'Who knows? What a question.'

I suffered the most helpless compassion for him, in his dark greasy corduroys and clodhopper shoes, when all the other kids are wearing brightly coloured sweat pants and expensive runners. So I reached across and tousled his rich auburn hair, the car swerved a bit on rush-hour Piscator, but he didn't shy away or look worried.

We waited at a beeping orange crosswalk light, comfortably silent for a spell.

'Your mom's preg – ' He snorted and squirmed. 'Your *wife* is pregnant, ain't she?'

'Why yes. That means we are going to have a little baby.' I didn't know what a ten-year-old knew.

'I know *that*. I seen lots of animals born on the farm. What's it like to be goin' bald, Mister? Does your hair fall out all over or just from your head? Does your head get tougher? Or are you worried all the time that something'll hurt ya? My dad gets real mad if I ask him.'

'That's right. You were a farm-boy, weren't you?'

'Huh? You talk funny, Mister.'

'You can call me Mr Gray.' Nothing. 'But you like it upstairs, eh?'

'I'll bet you were scared Mom was gonna make you move sooner . . . *before* those old people that were living in *our* house.'

'Uh, for a while there, yeah.'

'Mom says *she* was living in a little room at Dad's parents when she had me. She says people *pamper* themselves nowadays.'

'You mean they wear diapers?'

'Huh? Hey Mr Gray, the light's stopped now.'

'*Pampers*. They're disposable diapers.'

'Oh yeah, like my aunt Ina who lives in Montreal uses, you just use 'em and throw 'em out!' And he laughed like a mad imp, though I don't think he got it. I eased on the gas.

'But like, what I really meant to say was, you guys can live in our house for a long as you, uh . . . *for as long as you so choose*.'

'My-my, aren't you the articulate little fellow.'

'Huh?'

'Smart.'

'But like, if you *had* to move, your mom could still have the baby, right?'

'What?'

'Slow down please! The light's orange, you have to stop and turn right!'

We sat silently through most of the red light, both staring straight ahead.

'My mom simply *adores* our new house but I don't think my dad likes working in the government as much as the farm. He's going crazy! That's what he says.' He laughed with an ambivalence you wouldn't think possible in a kid that age.

We turned onto Izaak Walton and were soon in the parking lot of Holy Family. I kept him there with an unfair authority: 'So, your dad likes his liquor, eh?'

'He only drinks *beer*. My mom likes li . . . li-*quoor*. 'Cause now she has to work and unwind too. When she and Dad fight about things like the house and his new job, she says, "But what if *I* want to have another baby too?"'

Tommy had dropped his voice and given a good throaty impersonation of his mother. But he liked what he'd said about as much as I did: he slapped himself hard on the cheek, mugged dramatically, then again crammed his hands in his crotch.

'Anyways, I like sleeping on the couch. Hey, Mister, if *you* could choose, which would you rather be, hairy and poor or rich and bald?'

'Rich and bald, I guess, because then I could get hair implants.'

'Hairy pants!' He laughed with wild inappropriateness, and I laughed along; it was a joke designed to sound like a kid's joy in verbal nonsense, but I knew he was doing it intentionally, because he settled too quickly. We both knew.

'My mom says rich too, for Dad. She says if she was rich he could look like a fish for all she cares.'

He was in no hurry to get out. In front of us a group of boys were playing baseball. Not a proper game, but a pick-up involving only a batter against a brick wall and a pitcher at what looked like major-league distance. Not that there weren't other players available, but they stood around giving respectful room to the pitcher, who wound up big time and threw. I had to be seeing things, a pantomime of pitching, because I didn't see the ball, and neither did the batter, till it returned to the pitcher in one hop, a red, white and blue rubber ball. The batter did a comical triple take and gapingly touched his bat to a mark on the wall: perfect strike. The boys ooohed sarcastically, and before they'd stopped another bullet found the heart of the strike zone.

'You're outta there, Blago!' the pitcher shouted. A big bony kid, he removed his cap and wiped his . . . *her* brow?

'Good God,' I said, that's a *girl*.'

'Yeah, that's Teresa. Yesterday she showed me how to throw a curve.'

'*This* is phenomenal!'

'Yeah,' he said sadly, 'her and Michael Sheridan are the smartest in class too, and everybody's older than me, 'cause I accelerated.'

I didn't know what to say. I looked around and saw a tall man in a dark overcoat (I *think* a man) standing between parked cars with his back to us, watching the game, or the pitcher. He bowed his head and appeared to be writing. A scout, I smiled. I thought maybe I should report him to the office, but remembered my house-hunting mission.

'So you've made some friends already then?'

We sat silent, I in wonder, watching strike after rocket strike. A rubber ball, granted, but outside of the real thing (triple-A here in Ottawa), I had never witnessed such hurling. Literally, none of the boys saw the ball. They took turns at bat merely to mug amazedly, assured of not *being* hit.

'I hate her.'

'I thought she was your friend.'

He snorted and shook his head at his lap: 'Yeah, I guess so.'

'Well, Tommy, as much as I'm enjoying this, I really must get moving.'

Still he didn't make a move to leave. But after a silence he suddenly said, 'Knock-knock,' knocking on an imaginary door between us.

'Who's there?'

'Yo the lady.'

'I am not!'

'C'mon, Mister. Knock-knock.'

'Who's there?'

'Yo the lady.'

'Oh, come on in, Yo the lady. Won't you have some li-quoor?'

31

'*Mister! Knock. Knock.*'

'Who's there?'

'*Yo the lady,*' he shouted.

So I yodeled my heart out for him.

The next day we received an eviction notice. Tommy's mom must have discovered that he'd let the cat peek from the bag's mouth. On the official form she'd checked the one box that justified our eviction: 'Owners wish to occupy premises'. Sixty days' notice, which she'd delivered to Dot.

'On the dot?' I joked, but Dot didn't even hear me. Until she'd intruded I'd been in the shower worrying about what the government calls a further drop in housing starts, a drop which would adversely impact my job as a framer, to put it in bureaucratese. While I dried off, Dot sat on the closed toilet, the notice in hand, and sobbed – the baby! the baby!

Later she apologised, blaming the hormones.

I tried to joke her out of it: 'How do you make a hormone?'

'Beats me,' she said without interest.

'Kick her in the cunt.'

'That doesn't sound like you, Norman.'

We had fully expected the new owners to evict us and occupy the whole house. Instead Tommy's mom had bounced only the old couple who'd been living upstairs for ten years. Oh, she had been so accommodating when we'd first talked (if you'll pardon the pun). A lanky woman with pageboy red hair, she'd come alone to inspect the house and I'd shown her around our ground floor quarters. As I'd explained our situation – nine years resident, my wife pregnant – she'd looked directly into my eyes and blinked slowly. Assuring me that she needed the higher rent from our place, she'd proceeded to a particular inspection, all the while complimenting the absent Dot on the decor. She'd even cracked at the bedroom door, 'When the cat's away . . .' In the tiny shared foyer she'd insisted that I and Dot must come up for a drink when they got settled in.

I told Dot everything when she got home from work, even the sexual wisecrack, and we worried that the new landlady would be intrusive in her friendship.

'Could be interesting for you, though,' said Dot, eyebrows

raised, looking down her nose, working her circling spell, but as unable as ever to strike the right tone.

'*That* piece of sinewy gristle? Not my type.'

'So you'd be all over her if she was dumpy like me?'

See? She sounded serious.

'Norman, I want to stay where we are.'

'What are you talking about? We *are* staying where we are, I just told you.'

'Oh, I know. It's just . . .'

Where we are is Troutstream, Ontario, in the area called Old North, its most desirable neighbourhood, living on the street stem of Anglers Court in the deep west. We rent the main floor of a big house bordering National Capital Commission greenbelt and set among old maples just emerging starkly from full autumnal glory. The actual Troutstream flows within a hundred metres of our back door! The atmosphere is comfortable, so languidly smug even, it is a privilege to feel only slightly inferior. Middle-aged men in high-riding pants seem always to be standing about sucking steak from their teeth, or cutting their grass in Bermuda shorts, sandals and dress socks. (At least they're a good ten years older than me, which must be the generational dividing line between socks and no socks.) Dot and I had planned, when we learned she was pregnant, when I could still say that I'd recently been designated redundant and was hopeful of work soon – I never said 'between jobs', never – we'd planned to buy a small house here, not on Anglers Court, of course, but somewhere in Old North, maybe one of the houses in the new Jonah's End development. Now we're – now *I'm* – looking for a cheap town house in the Complex south of Inglis. And Dot will have to return to her landscaping job at the National Research Council as soon as her maternity leave ends.

So, I had been feeling displaced for a week now, out of sync with the familiar, at home with the strange. While the media go ballistic over the sexual slaying of a young girl from Piscator Drive right here in suburban Troutstream, I don't react with horror and disgust, because I don't feel them. But when the tv talks of a manned mission to Mars, I excitedly see myself comfortably outward bound, then at home in a biosphere on a red desert. As I stare at the kids coming home from school, scenes of graphic violence play uncontrollably in my head, involving dismemberment and the street running red. For the first time in twenty years I pray silently to God: Turn back the clock ten years or so, please. Okay, ten months . . . You see: I was being slowly driven crazy trying to accommodate that crazy stranger upstairs. *Why* is she so needlessly cunning? *Why* are people allowed to do such evil to perfect strangers? If I can't stop her, I can at least tell her what I think of her! I'll . . . I'll . . . I want to spend all our savings on lottery tickets. I had to resist urges to hurt myself, such as taking my right forefinger and breaking it sideways.

To top it all off, or bung it all up, I'd been constipated for a week. Even on a car seat my asshole itched like poison ivy and my abdomen felt like a ball of shit was cooking there like the planet's core.

I looked at eight town houses in eight different 'developments', 'complexes', 'blocks'. You know the places: the more decrepit and thoroughly paved the site, the more otherworldly or bucolic the name: Elysian Fields, Eden Lawns, and six other places called Country this and Country that, all flaunting Troutstream's fixation on fishy names. To qualify for the position of superintendent in one of those places, or 'Super' as they call themselves, you must have a belly and breath formed by canned beer, whether morning or afternoon, a predilection for sleeveless T-shirts, a disinclination for shaving. (Should I say, 'And the men were no better'? Too late. And normally I would never be so cruel a joker.) There wasn't a tree, flower, or shrub to be seen in the vista of concrete, only a view of more garish yet somehow colourless town houses. Toppled plastic toys – day-glo orange tractors, pistachio-coloured bats and balls – littered what packed bare earth remained. Yet for all the kiddy clutter, there were no children to be seen, all off at daycare, I suppose. Leaving a silence as of a vacuum. As if a spaceship had visited and whisked all children off to some alluring planet playground. Where they were actually being fatted for a galactic banquet. At the next turning I expected to see a lime popsicle melting in the dirt, a riderless horse still rocking to equilibrium. You could make love or commit murder in the open in such a place and no one would care.

At the nadir of my search I recognised what I already knew: that if we took this town house we would be neighbours to Trout-stream's subsidised housing project: The Project. And if I don't find work soon? If Dot is laid off in the ongoing restructuring at the NRC? Might we not one day be *lucky* to get an apartment in the Project?

Look around in flaring panic, sweat, gouge my asshole.

If it weren't for Dot and the baby-to-be, I might contemplate killing myself. With pills and whiskey. Maybe I will anyway.

All the chest-scratching Supers assumed an undeniably superior attitude towards me, while yet apologising for the filth of the vacated town houses they displayed. The last Super actually told me that if I stood on my toes and looked north-west to an area emanating a rainbowed nimbus of maple and money, I would be viewing the space above Anglers Court. I realised that I'd inadver-tently been working my way westwards and back towards Inglis, to within striking distance of my own home. This final complex of town houses – Valhalla Homes – which we probably couldn't afford anyway, had met with some Troutstream Community Association opposition. Dot's and my name were on that petition, though the Association's executive, our distant neighbours on the bulb of Anglers Court, were none too neighbourly otherwise. We'd not been invited to the Davies' tea party the week before, though our near neighbours, the Wiers, had.

'And they won't mind us living so near?'

'No-no, not at all, young fella.'

I looked him up and down: 'Obviously.'

He looked away and drew a hand down his bristled cheeks, then cocked a wry boozer's eye at me: 'Look, buddy, I'm just doing my job. And that doesn't include putting up with smartass – '

'Thanks, Fred,' I turned and walked to my car, shamed past apology and smarting from his familiar address.

That's what Tommy's mom was doing to me.

She had spent the first month renovating the upstairs apartment. 'Good,' said Dot. 'Owners on the premises have a vested interest in the place. Maybe now we'll get that oil-canning furnace fixed.'

'There's nothing wrong with the furnace.'

'You snore right through it – boom, boom, boom!'

35

We never considered that improving the upstairs was the only way she could justify a huge increase in its rent to the review board. An animal. That was the nicest thing I could think about her and the worst I could think about animals. In my transforming mind, she was assuming mythic proportions: the head of an orang-utan on a lanky rabid alley cat, with something serpentine for good measure.

Dot was packing the last of the pictures when I returned after six hours of fruitless town house hunting. Our place, which we had lived in for nine years, showed pale rectangular patches on the walls like the deprived flesh beneath a band-aid. Our familiar space echoed rawly when she spoke: 'I'll go back to work earlier, we can get Student Movers cheap, what a sneaky bitch! That's Mom when they moved here from Scotland with *six* kids and *no* place to live, and that's me the baby she's holding.' She smiled wanly at the framed photograph. She'd been going on like this for a week.

'Shouldn't you leave that stuff till the end?'

Still on her knees she looked down her nose: 'Any luck?'

'Yeah, if you want to live in a box that looks and smells like a dumpster.'

'No, I meant hmmm . . .?'

'No. And don't suggest a dynamite enema again.'

I hoped she was laughing into the back of her hand, but no, she was crying again.

'Don't worry, I'll be okay, we'll make out.'

She sobbed: 'I was just thinking of that poor Archer girl.'

'Who?'

'The girl from Piscator who was murdered.'

'Oh. I think the boy upstairs knew her.'

I looked at my watch and headed down the hall to our bedroom at the back of the house. I had thought briefly to bet Dot a cup of tea that she couldn't guess the time within half an hour. But the time wasn't right for our old game. And I was dead tired. I would lie down for a short nap before supper. Lazy, perhaps, and doubtless irresponsible, when Dot was packing the walls. But she would never accuse me, the way things are.

I lay on top of the covers, feet together, hands folded on my chest. I remembered Tommy's mom's sexually suggestive remark when I showed her this bedroom, and sleepily regretted that I was aroused. But dead tired, like a visitor after a long journey, I wasn't myself, slipping off . . . My cement head swelled till it filled the room. What day is it? Shouldn't I be at work? I remember a verdant odour like this, and the sound of wind in green leaves, and a deep bone-tiredness, once before, I was about thirteen, racked by growing pains, but momentarily comfortable on the big round brown couch on our screened back porch in the Glebe. Where am I now? The Red Planet, drifting deeper. We have messed this home place, we must move there, as a race, selectively, start over from – My stomach knotted and startled me awake. I licked salty sweat from the corners of my mouth. Did I vomit and swallow it? God, she's probably given me an ulcer! And piles! I'll at least tell her what I think of her! To hell with maintaining my humanitarian image! I envisioned myself urbanely brazen: You, my dear, are a rabid feline guarding its shallow-buried shit. You are lower than snail skitter! You're –

'Pull down your pants and *show* me.' A boy's voice, sounded a bit like Tommy imitating his mother again. But I distrusted my fevered senses.

'I'm gonna make *you* pregnant.' It was Tommy. That had been his own voice, if assured and commanding in a way I didn't recognise. 'Pull down your pants or you're chicken.'

'My chicken!'

I raised up on my elbow, afire in the pit, sticky with sweat and as enervated as a moth struggling from his old cocoon. I moved stealthily to the narrow back window and opened the blind slats a touch. They stood directly below me, my new friend Tommy and his new friend, beneath our weeping willow and hidden further in the corner formed by the house and tall cedar hedge. The late afternoon light in the green yard was like an aquarium's, the air amber. The new girlfriend was a touch shorter and slighter than Tommy. She was charmingly pretty: carrot hair to her shoulders, eyes like robin eggs, a kewpie's mouth, pale-skinned but apple-cheeked.

'No,' she whispered, endearingly feigning shock in a way she'd learned from tv. 'I haven't reached puberty yet, stupid.'

'I'll show you.'

37

Tommy lay on his back, unfastened his jeans and slid them to mid-thigh. He held his pale little penis in its full-hooded foreskin and wiggled it as if scaring her with some albino worm. He released and framed it with a hand flat on each thigh, letting the crown of his head rest on the ground so that his back arched slightly. He kept his eyes strenuously closed. If he'd opened them, he might have spotted me, though my room was dark.

The girl knelt and sat back on her calves, hands gripping her thighs. As she lowered her head closer to Tommy's penis, weak sunshine through the willow caught the thicker auburn hair at her crown. Normally at that point I would have disturbed them as you would two practising kittens. But as her head descended she held back her hair and revealed a dark wine-coloured birthmark shaped like a toothed hole. So I let them continue. And a forbidden vision of myself arose in almost material form. It stood beside me, or half beside me, occupying half of me. If I were a joker like Tommy's mom, I would say I was suddenly half beside myself at the prospect those curious children afforded.

Tommy cupped his hands over his penis like a boy possessive of a toad, and the girl snapped back her head. Hair fell across the birthmark.

'C'mon, let me look,' she whined.

Tommy wriggled into his jeans, left the buckle and fly unfastened. He turned onto his side and propped his head. 'Now you. Then I'll make you pregnant.'

'Well . . . okay, but I don't get a period yet. I haven't had *the change*, which means I'm not dropping eggs. I can't wait.'

'Huh?'

But she was on her back. Like Tommy she slipped her pale sweat pants to mid-thigh; unlike the furtive Tommy she kept her head up and watched as he slithered sideways till his head lay alongside her hips. Then she rested her crown on the ground and looked directly into my eyes, though she couldn't have seen me.

I had heard of 'playing doctor' only after I'd grown up, so I cannot reliably imagine what impelled the intent Tommy. To me the girl's unripened crotch looked like one of those coveted plastic change purses of my boyood. In my sorry state I felt nothing for the something pained I detected in Tommy's inspection. He frowned, his head jigging for position, looking for something. A hole perhaps? The hole he'd no doubt heard about and seen depicted in toilet art? The hole he'd expected would be on display like another smiling mouth to reward his explorations? Who knows? Who but a pervert *could* know these things?

I inhaled deeply, relieved at the incorporation of that disembodied vision of myself that had stood patiently half beside me. I'd never felt so impersonal, so empty. Is *that* what allows sickos to do what they do?

Tommy raised up on his elbow and, posed as in some old picture I half remembered, raised his forefinger and poked her gently on the bellybutton. They both giggled, Tommy not so freely.

'I *can* make you pregnant,' he insisted more to himself than to her. 'Then you can have a baby and we can live downstairs. It's much more spacious.'

'You're nuts, you said your friend lives there already.'

I left the window, ashamed for the last time of the slimy thing that would issue from the plot I was hatching. I was concerned at least that I should perhaps halt developments before his doctoring progressed to an internal. Anyway, I had to.

'C'mere,' I called softly to Dot from the doorway to the back hall.

She was kneeling over a box filled haphazardly with photograph frames, their corners poking up like contact points on some mine she was defusing. She showed me a rapid face of vulnerability, hopelessness, resignation, determination.

'C'mon, you won't believe what's going on outside.'

'Outside *where*, Norman?'

In the way she rose wearily, pinched her mouth, shook her head and came reluctantly, I could see the exasperated and patient mother she would be.

I stood behind her in the barred light from the slatted window and held gently to her firm sides. She gasped and put a hand to her mouth, her stomach shifted encouragingly, and for the last time I was touched by remorse. Tommy was poking the girl's vagina lightly, though frequently, like some pellet-obsessed rat. Then the

39

little pervert rolled onto his back and again slid his jeans down, this time to his shins.

'What the *fuck* are you doing, Norman?' Dot whispered. She turned and glared at me. 'You've gotta stop them, the girl will be hurt.'

I caught her wrist before her knuckles rapped the window: 'No! I mean, he'd only tell his mother and it would just be embarrassing. Go –'

'You care about *her*?'

'You're right, of course,' I said, ushering her out with hands on her buttocks. 'Go to the side door and slam it.'

She hustled up the hall in a state of unhealthy excitement. In the moment I waited, a gaseous sort of expectancy slithered about my empty insides, licking up to tickle the back of my throat, rifting a claim on the world. I needlessly consoled myself with the knowledge that I'd at least spared Dot the dirty work to come. The side door slammed, Tommy and his friend leapt like cartoon characters set afire and scatted round the corner of the house pulling up their pants. They'd known, of course, that they were doing wrong. Yet they'd persisted. I reamed my dry lips with the tip of my tongue.

Dot returned and, after an awkward moment, at her instigation we made love for the last time before the baby was born. She was very dry, like a tiny brass ring, but persistent, whispering that she needed to be held and loved. So I stopped and unsealed the lubricant whose scentless smell made the act feel even more mechanical. That was the first time I felt as if I were watching us do it.

Afterwards she told me of the time she'd played doctor with a neighbourhood boy. She claimed that kids playing doctor is perfectly normal.

'Yeah, natural, like the way dogs say hello to each other.'

'*Come on*, Norman, that doesn't sound at all like you.'

'*No?* Who *does* it sound like?'

After a moment she said quietly, 'That sneaky *bitch* upstairs.'

'Oh thank you, thanks a *fuck* of a lot. At least she gets what she wants.'

'I didn't mean *that*. I was just thinking.'

I questioned her to discover what she'd thought of her own

doctoring. She remembered feeling that the sight of a pre-pubescent penis was not nearly as thrilling as she'd expected from the monstrous drawings in girls' washrooms, and that the boy had made the whole game feel momentous and sick. But to my surprise I soon lost interest in how she felt. I let her continue simply because the remembering relaxed her, and that was good for our future child. Then she confessed she'd felt like she was going crazy for the past week. I affected drowsiness and yawned something about hormonal tyranny.

'No . . . it wasn't that. Just everything all at once – the move, the Archer girl, and I was worried about you.'

'*Me?* I'm all right.'

'Well, you do seem better now, more settled, for the first time since that sneaky bitch told us to get out. Anyway, I'm just confident now we'll get through it.'

'Why?'

'No good reason.'

'We're not evicted yet.'

'What?'

'Nothing.'

She turned away, propped her belly on a pillow, and slept for an hour and twenty minutes.

When she awoke, I pretended I'd slept too. She insisted we play our silly old game of guessing what time it is after a post-coital nap. The one furthest from the correct time must serve tea in bed. I let her guess first and she was short by only fifteen minutes. I selected a time five minutes closer, but magnanimously insisted on serving .

She drank her tea, ate her biscuit, washed up. Back in bed we turned on the news. The announcement of the day's stories ended with news that the Americans, Russians, European Community and Japanese were now talking about a joint mission to Mars some time early in the twenty-first century. Such unprecedented collaboration would cut the project time in half. Then the lead story: 'In Seoul last night, the US Secretary of State, just back from a fact-finding mission to the former Yugoslavia . . .'

'Getting harder and harder to tell the good guys,' I said.

'That's where we'll end up,' Dot yawned. 'Living on Mars.'

Though it was not yet seven, she curled away and was soon purring a snore.

Finally the tv showed some file footage of Mars taken by the Mariner spacecraft, and I realised I'd been waiting for this story. Stronger than ever I thrilled to the idea: over a year in space, the red desert landscape, and if all went well, another year in return. We *must* get off this earth we've messed, colonise space, start over from scratch. I drank straight scotch and didn't begin feeling the belly-warmth till three in the morning, when I unwrapped the pack of Craven A *Speciale douce* I'd shelved three years before. I was on only my second puff when I had to run for the toilet (if you'll pardon the pun). Such relief, such elation. Ah, the unchallenged hole. Then a sort of cold vacuum, like I wasn't there from the chest down.

That afternoon, numbly hungover, breathing Tictac-tinged alcohol, it was nothing to catch Tommy's mom in the foyer and tell her about what had gone on out back the day before while she and her husband were working.

'Little Julie with the starburst birthmark here?'

'Little Julie with the birthmark there.'

Flustered for once, she babbled that her marriage was in trouble, the boy confused. I suggested that it would be responsible to inform Julie's parents. Damage may have been done, psychological as well as physical, what with the things that have been happening to young girls right here in Troutstream. Though I saw no reason to be alarmed. She gripped my forearm with a hand of dazzling red nails and insisted I come upstairs for some welcome tiny glasses of raspberry schnapps, we had things needed calm talking over. She called me Norm and I called her Cathy. I mentioned offhandedly that I had been concerned for some time now about their leaving the boy alone for such long stretches, what with the sexual murder of that young girl right here in Troutstream and all. She shot back that I worried too much, that the boy knew right from wrong, that kids mature early on a farm, she'd give him a scolding and ground him.

'I have seen the evidence of his sophistication, Cathy,' I joked.

I then said plainly that it was illegal to leave a ten-year-old unsupervised.

'He's almost eleven! That's legal! Do you know what a house in this neighbourhood *costs*?' She was shrill.

'I have some idea, Cathy.'

I downed my sweet red drink and left.

The next day we received written notification that our eviction had been cancelled.

One week later Cathy's husband left, returning to his parents' farm near Smiths Falls and taking the boy with him. A week after that, Dot gave birth to a nine-pound boy we named Sean.

In the gentle Indian summer afternoons remaining to us, Cathy and I often sit out back and drink and smoke and chat beneath the old weeping willow. We analyse her legal position vis-à-vis custody and comment randomly on what husbands and wives do to each other. Mostly, though, we talk about the future, since neither of us likes to dwell on the past. When I want to, I will make her a quietly desperate kind of lover. Who knows, the cheating might even remedy my displaced voyeurism during the infrequent act with my wife, whose current favourite expression is 'Earth to Norman, earth to Norman'.

Nights I get drunk. I still have trouble sleeping, though I am getting better. In the meantime I woozily wander the circling sidewalks of this rich arboreal neighbourhood I really can't afford. I enjoy a clear or cloudy night equally. I am afraid of nothing, though another girl has been killed nearby. I don't think of Mars or suicide any more.

· 3 ·

Home Hardware

·

Eugene had no use for the tiny eyeglass repair kit he fingered like some poor sleight-of-hand artist a coin, but he realised too late that he'd picked it up simply to delay his stay in the air-conditioned store. Anne was watching him, with one hand resting on the cash register and the fingertips of the other lightly drumming the counter between them, her mouth set in that slightly disdainful pinch. But she had humiliated him too many times with her helpful knowledge of ballcock assemblies and such. He could give the repair kit to Veronica.

'I wear contacts,' he said softly, handing over his credit card. 'But sometimes first thing in the morning I bump about the house in glasses, so I could use this micro-mechanical wonder.' He had spoken simply, assertively; yet he was explaining himself again, and as usual he had to resist the urge to explain even further. He hadn't worn glasses in ten years, anywhere, they drew attention, if only his own, to his large ears. Why couldn't he just say the repair kit was for his daughter and leave it at that?

'That everything?' Anne asked.

'Yes, thank you, Anne. The tomato cages and earwig powder for next year, I think I've remembered everything. Like an elephant, eh? With *these* ears.' He pinched a lobe and wiggled it.

Anne said nothing till he was turning away: 'Get the computer?'

Eugene smiled round the store, which was empty of other customers, if thin-aisled with garden implements, green and white bags of peat-moss, clear plastic bags of grass seed, burnt-orange bags for fallen leaves, goods galore. Just like a town's general store. The air outside, even at nine in the morning, would lightly suffocate him. A heat wave in October. He turned back to the counter.

'As a matter of fact, Anne, I have. Thanks for asking. A Macintoch LCII. Little Vera has been spending day and night playing chess on it, or with it, rather. Ruining her eyes, no doubt. Maybe I'll give the repair kit to her.' He laughed lightly.

'*Chess?*' said Anne. 'Vera's only twelve, ain't she? Same age as that – '

'How's *your* computer course going?'

Another customer came in, an old man wearing a filthy white T-shirt and the dull green pants of construction workers, hitched high. Eugene hoped to recognise him, but didn't, so he wanted to leave.

Anne watched the new customer finger some decorative netting. She spoke offhandedly now: 'Well, don't forget to save everything before you shut down. Does Microsoft prompt you to save?'

Eugene's voice went softer when he was irritated: 'I'm sorry, Anne, but, as usual, I really don't know what you're talking . . .'

But Anne had moved from behind the counter and was at the old man's side. He knew what he wanted, an inexpensive reel, some cheap flies. 'Can't see to tie 'em myself any more,' he said. 'Fish can't be eaten anyway. That net wouldn't hold ostrich feathers.'

Anne returned to her station and straightened the collar of her brown Home Hardware uniform. 'I'm sure those'll work just fine, Martin. It's miracle enough you're spry as you are. But you're not the one spreading rumours about fish in the stream are you?'

The old man grinned challengingly at Eugene: 'You fish?'

Eugene smiled and spoke too loudly: 'Well, Martin, I used to with my father out east where I grew up, near Truro in Nova Scotia – '

'Live in a place called Troutstream and not fish?' He cackled once and turned away, grinning at Anne in a way Eugene resented more than a slap. The old man picked a harmonica from the stack in front of the eyeglass repair kits, a falsely old-fashioned package that showed a Huck Finn type sitting on a fence and playing a harmonica with the notes hovering like birds round his head. 'Better give me that for another young fella,' he said. 'He's crazy for the rock'n'roll, plays his guitar night and day, loud, and pretty good. You know, before they put me in the Project, I lived by a real river in Smiths Falls, and I ate real trout out of it till the day – '

Eugene took his last breath of artifically cooled air and exited. But it didn't matter – the humiliation he'd just suffered, another malcontent, or this heat. It didn't matter because he loved Trout-stream with such fondness and pride. And since the Bypass had been finished he loved its isolation more completely. In his love for the place he thought naturally of the Kavanaghs and the something that had soured between their two families. He and Alice did not talk about this something. They couldn't. What was there to say? Whatever had happened – *the falling away*, he'd named it only for himself – it was as incomprehensible, as inexplicable, and as unmendable as the unravelling meanings of anything important. Any effort to mend the messy affair with neurotic talk would drop them into yet more awkward gaps down a black hole of unravellings. That mad quantising of relationships and emotions, he'd had enough of it his last year in Toronto. Better end than try to mend. That's what *he* knew and Jack didn't. The mysterious lure, the surprising snag and necessary break of inti-mate friendship. As sure as entropy. That's what the big guy could never see. Jack had asked him point blank if something was 'wrong', if he or his family had offended them in any way. That sort of blundering only proved how impossible these situations were. And, of course, he was sorry to think, it just went to show the big guy's indelicacy, his intellectual limitations.

But now it looked like they were getting together for a family picnic today. Maybe things could be settled once and for all one way or another. Finished in a way even they would see, or start over from scratch, with no questions asked . . . *Family picnic*, Eugene shook his grinning head in wonder at the phrase.

On his way along to the IGA for charcoal and chips – *You can walk*

everywhere in Troutstream – he searched the parking lot for faces
. . . and who should he spot but Jack himself picking his way
among the cars. Jack wore glasses, yes, big clear plastic glasses he
was forever pushing up his nose. Loose arms. Perfect.

Jack loped recklessly along the lanes of the lot, concentrating on
his errand: *Home Hardware, croquet set.* He was tall and growing
heavy set, with overhanging eyebrows that seemed to have sprung
from his brow like freed mattress springs, and with the flesh of his
face falling to jowls. But he was often saved from a glowering
appearance by his large sad eyes, his smile, the roar of his laugh.

Eugene pinched the repair kit and dangled it at his chest: 'Whoa
there, big guy, I bought you a present.'

Jack hadn't noticed Eugene till he was on top of him, and he
was still collecting himself from having pulled up short. 'What?
Hey, Gene. I was just thinking about you. We still on for the
picnic today? Is it gonna be too hot?'

'It's an eyeglass repair kit. I bought it for you. And, yes, the
whole family has been looking forward to this picnic since I told
them about it. But if recent events – the Archer girl – have made it
uninviting, or if you guys have something else you have to do,
that's okay, we can do it tomorrow, or next weekend, or some
other time. The thing is, we all agree in principle to do it *some*
time.'

'No-no, we're on. Shit, we haven't gotten together in months.'
Jack snorted: 'Christ, Marla's been wondering, we both have, if
we've offended you guys in some way.' Jack glowered.

Smiling slightly Eugene gazed across Izaak Walton Road
towards Troutstream's tiny public library. At his request, it now
subscribed to *Nature* and *Gentleman's Quarterly*. He spoke softly:
'Come off it. You guys are paranoid. Really, you and Marla
should stop talking to each other.'

'What the hell did you buy me this for?' Jack took the dangling
kit and examined it. 'Is this supposed to be something symbolic?
You're so fucking weird, Gene, I don't know *what* you're saying
half the time. Even after five years.' With Gene, such talk was
going way too far. But Jack was pissed off now.

For too long Gene grinned up at him with his brow furrowed,
then said, 'You going in here?'

'Na, I gotta see if . . . if they got a croquet set at Home. See ya later.'

Walking away Jack pivoted and said loudly: 'Eleven o'clock, right? By the soccer fields, right? For a picnic lunch, right?'

Gene saluted: 'You got it, big guy.'

Jack twirled again and shouted, 'You guys play croquet, right?'

Without turning Gene flexed his shoulders like he'd been clubbed in the gut, then mimed a golf swing, and walked on.

Inside Home, Anne's solicitations were lost on Jack, and she assumed again that he, like his buddy Davies, could still be snobbish to people from the Project, even though she'd recently accepted his invitation to a barbecue. Jack stood at the counter with head bowed, brow furrowed and lips pursed, without the croquet set, unmindful of why he'd come in or, for that matter, why he was down at the plaza. Anne held up a huge metal funnel and suggested that maybe he'd come for a hat. Jack went blank, then roared, and Anne couldn't help giving him her winningest smile. Jack wanted to tell Anne that if she got another funnel she could be Madonna. After his joke the other day, he was almost sure she'd not take it the wrong way, that Anne, whom he'd known in this strange way for ten years now, would not say like Kristen at work, 'There is no *right* way, Mr Kavanagh.' But he merely smirked again, and left wishing he and the family were picnicking with Anne and her daughter that very day.

Back on the plaza's hot walk, he worried about his memory. And then again about relations between his family and Gene's, and Gene himself. Gene was acting nuts. Look at the way he'd carried on at the stupid tea party. *Had* he done or said something atrociously offensive to Gene and Alice? . . . He looked up and the sun was only a ball of fire burning his face for his lazy thick-headedness. He knew nothing. What *was* it about him, or his family, that Gene knew and remembered and he didn't? What had he, or they, done? *What was it?*

Jack sometimes worried about the paleness of his own spirit compared to Gene's, most often because he could never feel Gene's manic commitment to Troutstream life. Gene attacked everything with a gusto Jack could not match, and Jack wished he could. Gene's intense seriousness seemed the best way to live. Jack felt only half alive by comparison, with only a third of Gene's energy. Yet he, Jack, was the one who'd been living in Gene's beloved Troutstream for twenty years, there when the trees were not so 'mature', as Gene described them; there before Troutstream had its own little shopping plaza; there when the bare neighbourhoods looked no different from the Lego suburbs now spreading eastward like some alien thing without natural enemies. Like that purple loosestrife, or a thing that consumed vegetation.

Until the last half year – for five years, that is – Jack had believed that he and his family were just about the most important people in Eugene's life and the life of his family. How could he have thought otherwise? For five years Eugene had blatantly said so, or told *him* so.

Jack had been at the National Research Council for fifteen years when Eugene was hired seven years ago. Eugene's had been a move down from a managerial position with Ontario Hydro in Toronto, and though he was not the sort to explain himself, it became well known to everyone that he'd done so for the health and safety of his family, for their quality of life. His knowledge of fibre optics had impressed everyone at the NRC, to the extent that he was soon made a team leader, or co-leader with Jack, of the Council's most heavily funded area of research. Within two years Jack's and Gene's team had made a minor breakthrough in decreasing the resistance of a certain strand of fibre. They had spent every night for a year on Jack's computer writing up their experiments and findings, and rewriting tirelessly. That work had been fun, bestowing the unexpected reward of discovering complementary styles, and of finding friendship. The article was published in *Nature*; then the *Globe & Mail* had run a half-page story on its science page, and the *Ottawa Citizen* had published a feature, with a number of pictures of Jack and Gene at work and home. Although their work had as yet no practical application and was unrelated to such fields as laser surgery, Gene, and then Jack, had speculated for reporters on its potential medical uses. Gene had suggested that a laser therapy might eventuate that would help doctors reshape distorted eyeballs with even greater precision, thereby rendering glasses obsolete. 'Some day our work will make the Excimer look like a hacksaw,' Gene was quoted. 'But don't throw away your glasses just yet. This is years down the road.' Alone Jack and Gene howled over this attention and their performance.

Late in his second year in Ottawa, right after the breakthrough and promotion to greater responsibility at the Council, Gene had quit renting in Sandy Hill and bought the biggest house Troutstream had to offer. It was a five-bedroom executive home on Anglers Court, where Jack lived. Only the Andersons' home intervened between the Kavanaghs' and the Davies'. Two or three nights a week the two families got together, and though Marla and Alice had little in common they managed pleasantly enough. Gene talked tirelessly for the next five years: of things that could be done to make Troutstream even more of an oasis for family life, of Canadian writers and foreign films, of the benefits of working at the National Research Council. He always began their get-togethers with blatant talk of how wonderful Jack and his family were. If eventually he was going to reminisce about a distant place he and Alice had visited, or about a movie Jack and Marla had never heard of, in a language they couldn't understand, he would say, 'But you guys have probably seen it a dozen times,' and proceed rapidly and softly to explain what they must have liked most about it. Or if he wanted to talk about renovations he was having done to his house, he would say, 'We just want it to be more like your home, that's all. That's all we've ever wanted.' Gene openly admired Marla, Jack's wife, to an extent that implied he had made a big mistake in not seeking her out and marrying her years ago. If Marla drew back her head and smiled warily and said, 'Alice?' Gene would say disgustedly, 'Her? She's hopeless,' without a hint of humour. Jack's very average kids were 'precocious', 'amazing', 'little geniuses'. And when Marla pointed out that they had their faults, and that Peter and Veronica Davies were obviously gifted, Gene would brusquely brush off those qualifications more convincingly than could a contradicted granny.

Eventually, though, Gene had used their frequent get-togethers to talk about new projects. Never mind that their team had been funded for another three years to work only on fibre optics, Gene wanted to improve satellite communications, to work on a more sensitive signal for Troutstream's crosswalks, to make an industrial motion picture. At the height of these pitches, he would say, 'We have to recapture that ol' spirit, big guy!' That would always inspire enthusiasm in Jack, for Gene was referring to the year they'd spent writing up the breakthrough article, and Jack would remember the fun and friendship. Later he'd marvel at his own suggestions on schemes such as the marketing of a palm-sized video camera that would hook directly into a blind person's optic nerve.

And then, about six months ago, Gene and his family had begun to ignore Jack and his family.

At first Jack and Marla assumed that Gene and Alice were busy doing other things, family things, and they'd not taken offence when their invitations, their suggestions, and ultimately their pressing phone calls were met with Alice's flustered disorganisation that wouldn't permit her to confirm any planned rendezvous. Then Marla's calls were received with coolness. After a couple of months of only curt responses, Marla stopped calling. Soon afterwards she and Jack realised with a stab that they were, and had been throughout the winter, doing *all* the calling. Marla then recalled that at the IGA three weeks before Veronica Davies had behaved strangely when Marla asked her point blank why she didn't come over any more to play with Ashley: 'She asked me to phone them, if you please; not phone her mother, but *them*.' And Jack saw with dumbfounding clarity that at work Gene had begun eating lunch alone in his cubicle. Or no, not alone: he'd not been imagining lately that he'd sometimes heard Pete Donovan's voice from Gene's cubicle. Donovan from Personnel! The hated Donovan who hand-picked new administrators. And Jack and Marla began worrying obsessively about what had gone wrong. What had they done?

They could be doing anything, watching the youngest of their four kids learning to skate on the back-yard rink, or drinking tea and having a treat after the kids had gone to bed, or staring at nothing on tv, and one of them would say without turning to the other, 'It was that time they asked us over for a barbecue when Gene's favourite sister was visiting from the Maritimes and we didn't go because you said you couldn't stand Gene's divided fawning loyalties in such situations. I told you it was rude to refuse.'

'Possibly. But remember what I said last night: whatever we say, *if* we break our agreement not to talk about it, whatever we guess, must match the enormity of what they are doing. And that doesn't. They don't call any more! They're our near neighbours and we don't see them any more! Their kids look away on the street! He acts different at work! For God's sake, they didn't even send a card at Christmas! Don't forget that clincher. They'd insisted we eat Christmas dinner at their place the last six years for fuck's sake, before they even became our neighbours!'

'Don't swear, you've been swearing too much lately in front of the kids.'

For minutes Jack would seethe. And then, because the subject had been opened for the night, he would proceed in a whisper.

'It makes no sense, *no fucking sense*: the greatest mystery of human relations I've ever encountered. One: did we do something to offend them? No. Certainly nothing we can think of. But he's *so fucking* weird, who's to know? Though remember, I have asked Gene if we've offended them, and he's said we're paranoid, and I'll ask him again, if I ever get the chance. Okay then, two: they just don't like us any more, we grossly overestimated the friendship. Three: they've done something unspeakable and they're so ashamed they can't stand to be around us? Maybe. But if that's the case, you'd think he'd have the courtesy to say something, seeing as how I've revealed our hurt feelings by asking him point blank if we've offended them. Or how about four, five, and six: we know too much about them – remember when they lied to each other about the vasectomy and the tummytuck? – we *know* them, Marla, we're ruining that image of themselves they like to project, our presence makes them uneasy. Or am I being too much of a linear fucking one-tracker? He's said that in front of Donovan!' And he could cap this catalogue with neurotic non sequitur. 'Or forget that, let's just pretend they're not even aware of what they're doing, since that suits their style! Or better yet, say they've decided they don't like us: *they just don't like us any more!* Oh, shit this!'

'Sh-sh . . . How can you say *we* overestimated the friendship? *He's* the one's always acted like it's a privilege just to breathe the wind you pass . . . It's gotta be something you did at work.'

'Oh, thanks a *fuck* of a lot.'

Marla's mouth pinched. 'I mean, maybe you've *unintentionally* shown him up at work in some way.'

'Yeah, right, that's me, the Cro-Magnon of tact.'

As such marathon sessions of speculation, spite, and self-recrimination wound down, Jack would become lost in his own thoughts: 'Okay, let's say he did act that way, like I shit nickels. What I didn't see, stupid me, is he treats *everybody* that way, even someone like Donovan, who's the only person I've ever heard Gene wish dead! Now *they're* buddies!'

And Marla would inevitably conclude more to herself than to Jack: 'I should phone Alice, I said I would at the tea party, didn't I? Right this very moment. No.'

'Maybe you should.'

'I'm not phoning her again to hear the non-excuses.'

'Fuck 'em.'

They assured one another that it was impossible to figure out, they had no evidence, they lacked factors, they made another solemn pact not to speak of it again, and smiled to have it over with once and for all. But it would start up again getting into bed, or the next night, and, ashamed of their dismissive conclusions, once more they would commence turning the situation this way and that, contorting to see imagined things from the Davies' impossible point of view, straining credibility to find an action or word of theirs commensurate with the radical change in the Davies' behaviour towards them. Or, if deliberations had begun early in the evening and petered, they would sit staring dumbly at some show on tv that both of them hated, until the news came on.

'What does she see in that guy?' Jack would ask rhetorically. He had a crush on a reporter who had recently married the anchorman. 'He's smug and bald, with the mug of a mamma's boy.'

'He's tall and rich and powerful.'

'Oh, that.'

Then in the middle of October, the hottest October on record after the coolest summer, Marla had phoned Alice and commiserated with her over the disastrous tea party, then forced herself to gab like old times about ozone depletion and again having to smear the kids every morning with sunscreen, and reminded her that they'd talked about a picnic at the tea party and insisted that the two families meet near the Troutstream soccer fields. No excuses. And Alice, sounding distracted, had agreed.

Prized throughout the Ottawa-Carleton region, the Troutstream soccer fields lie opposite the mounds and mountains of Mann's Quarry north on Izaak Walton Road, nine full-size playing fields cut into official greenbelt land and kept lush at great expense. The actual Troutstream runs along the west of the fields, with a margin of sloping woods as buffer. A thinned wooded area with tables for picnicking lies to the south of the fields, though no one from Troutstream ever picnics there, only out-of-towners and people from Ottawa marooned for day-long soccer tournaments. Troutstream's teenagers also gather there in the evening to drink and cause a little trouble, most often among themselves, there being nothing for them in Troutstream once they've outgrown T-ball and soccer.

From elevated Izaak Walton Road, the goal posts look like staples from the misfiring gun of some frustrated giant trying to patch emerald sod to hard earth. It's only a fifteen-minute walk from his house, but Jack drove because that's still a long way for the youngest and too far to lug the picnic cooler. They'd been late getting away because little Nick had shit himself as they were leaving the house, and both Marla and Jack had scolded him. They were still silent as they drove down into the parking lot, ashamed of themselves for their impatience, anxious over the approaching meeting, feeling foolish for their social klutziness. As they walk towards the picnic area across the sunburnt margin of the soccer fields they move imperceptibly downward, for here the ground slopes most gently towards the stream. They approach across open ground, as self-conscious as in dreams of public nakedness. Marla carries Nick, who at three is really too old to be carried, with his legs scissoring her waist and his arms around her neck, and Jack carries the cooler with the air of somebody lugging home the food. They grin and squint against the blinding sun towards the woods. The Davies are there already.

The four Davies stop what they're doing and look out at them from the cool shadow of the fir trees, caught like some prehistoric family distracted from its daily chores by movement on the savannah. Veronica Davies, the same age as Mark Kavanagh, twelve, twists from her sitting position at a dark brown picnic table; her younger brother, Peter, pauses down by the stream with a switch in his hand. Veronica wears a brown sundress and a black ribbon in her blonde hair; she turns her back to them and bends over some book. Peter, in dark T-shirt and jeans, returns to whipping a blue oil drum for garbage. Alice, in jeans cut short and a close-fitting short-sleeved plaid shirt, with her hair pulled back by a red cotton band, remains bent over and looking out sideways at them. Eugene, in pale green shorts and white T-shirt, stands holding his chin and watching from the deeper shadow of his maroon Neighbourhood Watch cap. He turns and shouts something at Peter, who gives no sign that he's heard.

What natural grass there is in the field is like cropped straw. As they walk six-year-old Brenda keeps saying 'Ouch' and whining that the grass is hurting her. Smiling distantly at Eugene, who is coming towards them now in a helping attitude, Jack scolds her in a whispered hiss: 'Mr Davies hates complainers.' So when Brenda, the second-youngest, stumbles, falls and begins wailing, showing her scratched palms, Jack sets down his cooler and scoops the girl onto his shoulder. He leaves the cooler and ushers them along.

'Hey, you made it,' Eugene grins, walking past them and picking up the cooler. 'You guys are amazing coming out on a day like this. How do you do it, Marla?'

'Are we late or something?'

'Been here long?' Jack quickly asks.

'Oh, we came about an hour ago, just for the fun of it.'

Marla looks at Alice, who has sat beside her daughter at the picnic table and is reading a book. 'Where's your stuff?' Marla asks, eyes widening, her mouth remaining open.

Alice holds up an index finger and reads on.

'Oh, the kids were *starvin*',' Eugene says mockingly. 'We had a brunch before we left home.' He shouts down towards the stream, '*Now, Peter! And I mean, now!*'

Mark runs down to join Peter at the stream, and Eugene and Alice exchange a defeated glance. Jack and Marla and their other kids gather loosely around the picnic table where Alice and Veronica still sit.

Rubbing at the right thigh of her old black spandex shorts, thirteen-year-old Ashley Kavanagh says, 'Veronica, did you *see* how low-cut Terri Blackburn's dress was yesterday? Gross, eh?'

But Veronica tightens her lips and keeps reading the page she's been on since the Kavanaghs arrived.

Alice closes the hardcover book on her thumb, looks up and smiles: 'So, you made it. Well then, we're all here now.'

Marla says, 'Of course we made it. You're the ones who're early.'

'Oh, don't worry about that,' says Alice, smiling and placing a hand on Marla's forearm as if placating a child. She turns and shouts, 'Peter, if you don't obey your father right now . . .'

'What're you reading there, Madam Curie?' Jack says quickly to Veronica.

By way of answer, Veronica shows the cover of the green book while keeping her head averted.

'Chess and the computer,' Jack reads. He whistles how impressed he is and pushes his glasses up his nose: 'Man, or, excuse me, *woman* against the machine, eh? Surely the computer will never match the intuitive brilliance of a grand mm – mistress!' He touches his glasses again.

'They're programmed by grand masters,' says Veronica to her reopened book. 'Where's the glasses repair kit my Dad gave you, Mr Kavanagh?'

Jack gives Eugene a slightly surprised questioning look, but Eugene is glaring off at Peter. 'Gee,' says Jack, 'I don't really know. But if you want it, you can have it. I sure don't want it.'

Veronica makes a *hmph* sound and says, 'I don't need it either.'

A horn blares from Mann Quarry across Izaak Walton Road, and down at the stream Peter and Mark shout, 'Explosion!' They hook their little fingers and close their eyes. A rumbling, and the ground trembles. The boys disengage. Peter seems slightly embarrassed, as though having forgotten himself, and turns back to the stream.

The blood has drained from Eugene's face, he stands rigid.

Jack checks his watch: 'Right on the dot. And that warning horn isn't loud at Anglers. To tell you the truth, Gene, I don't see what grounds for complaint you have.'

56

Gene remains silent and pale, his head tilted slightly as if straining to hear.

Needles of sun through the pines play upon the crown of Veronica's head as she bows more closely over the same page of her book, and for a moment Jack feels the tenderness he associates only with his own family. He is a good head taller than those around him, so he looks up into the trees and takes a quick deep breath. (He'd not imagined it, paranoid or not, there is a whiff in the air of something rotten, but he'll not complain.) More and more lately, usually when he dozes on the couch and the kids are around him, laughing, playing, arguing, fighting, even with the tv on, it doesn't matter what, he finds himself in a strange state of tranquillity, of invulnerability for them all, of an intimacy that makes them distinct yet somehow indistinguishable one from the other, and from him. He has attempted to bring on this feeling by lying on the couch and trying not to think. But the state can't be induced, and he soon feels foolish. He has never before had the feeling nudge him in the outdoors, or among non-family, yet here it is, or the warm wet nose of it. He had wanted to ask that Iris about it. Maybe he just will.

A thought descends from the pines: Maybe it's a taste of the afterlife. Wouldn't that be great . . . The Davieses have suffered some unspeakable family tragedy involving an ugly self-discovery. It came crashing like a comet, one of those shattering horrors every family dreads. But they had a hand in its attraction, and the sacrifice of our friendship is partial atonement.

Jack exhales, smiles down and says to Veronica: 'You'd rather be home with your computer or out with your other friends on a Saturday like this, wouldn't you, Veronica?'

Eugene swings away from guardedly semaphoring Peter at the stream, and they all watch Veronica in silence. She stiffens: 'This part's about new software programs they're developing so beginners can learn to play the game with greater sophistication.'

'Don't waste your time on me, honey,' Jack grins.

'Anyone can learn,' she insists as if offended, and there's a catch in her voice.

'Not me, kid. I've owned a computer for years, work with them every day, and I still don't know the difference between hardware, software and underwear.'

Only Veronica laughs, despite herself in an unladylike snort, and sniffs. Jack's lingering grin is so defenceless that even Marla looks away with the rest.

Eugene laughs towards the stream and says, 'I'll have to remember that one for Donovan, Jack. That's great, hardware and underwear, ha!'

Down by the stream Mark Kavanagh shouts, 'Dad, Mom, c'mere, you won't *believe* it!'

All but Veronica walk down towards the two boys standing beside the blue garbage can. Before they arrive all are sniffing and wincing and saying 'What's that *smell*? What *is* that stink?' As they draw nearer they all pinch their noses in cupped hands. Mark, his nose covered, is alternately looking into the garbage can and at his father. Peter Davies stands quietly apart facing the stream, with the switch, a willow switch cut elsewhere, even limper at his side.

'What *is* that?' Jack says, still somewhat dreamily. But the stink, at first tantalisingly pungent, concentrates powerfully and jolts him down like smelling salts. Unlike coming gently back to earth in his family room and resting there in a lesser dream, the hard reality of the scummy stream, the bare ground, and the bludgeoning stink, shoves him lower and lower.

'Something dead,' Eugene replies.

Peter, the only one not covering his nose, twists and flicks his switch at the can, then turns back to the stream.

'Peter,' says Alice, 'what's the – '

But Peter pushes her hand aside as he bounds past. He doesn't stop at the picnic table, but takes the trail to the right that cuts back along the stream to residential Troutstream.

'I wonder what's got into him?' Alice smiles, uncovering her nose.

'I don't want the kids looking in here,' Eugene snaps, standing in front of the can. He has not looked in himself.

'It's only a dead dog,' Mark says. But when he steps towards the can for another look, Eugene blocks him.

'What!' says Marla, leaning forward wide-eyed then recoiling in disgust. She stares blankly at the can, and all is still as she's watched closely by Eugene and Alice. Brenda and Nick, the two youngest Kavanaghs, cling silently to her thighs as tiny insects buzz their faces. 'Let's get outta here,' she says in a mixture of urgency and resignation. 'It smells like . . . It must be what somebody who's been dead for days smells like. Yee-uck.'

'Yee-uck, yee-uck!' shout Brenda and Nick. Marla has trouble getting them by the hands and pulling them up towards the picnic tables. Halfway up she turns and calls for Ashley and Mark to come, and Jack has to nudge his son. Then Alice follows, still covering her nose. She passes Veronica alone now at the table, the Kavanaghs having continued on towards the parking lot.

'Come Veronica,' Alice sings, 'the picnic's over.' She takes the path to the right, but Veronica remains.

When Jack, expressionless, steps towards the can, Eugene says through his cupped hand like a kid doing a bombardier, 'Sure you want to see the physical evidence, big guy?' and stands aside.

Jack uncovers his nose and, holding his breath, squints down into the can. The interior is much darker than the shadowed air surrounding him, but his pale blue irises react. It is a much bigger dog than he'd expected, dark-coloured, a German Shepherd it looks, lean and muscled and curled upon itself to fit into the can. It's not the most recent addition to the garbage, for it lies on its side with its flanks covered by the stripped corrugated cardboard of a soggy beer case. Flies buzz the darkness, though at first there are no obvious signs of decay. As the picture emerges more clearly, however, the chest appears to be concave, and patches of fur have been ripped from the back, exposing skin the colour of porridge. The last detail to come clear is the one black eye facing up. It looks alive, but something tiny moves near it, an ant perhaps, and the eye doesn't react. Jack thinks he recognises it.

'Hard to tell if he's snarling or grinning,' says Jack, 'but that's a dead dog all right. And I think I know it from somewhere. Yeah, that day at your tea party, out back in the park.' Without thinking he inhales deeply, and what fills his lungs is like a battering ram to the chest; he staggers backwards a couple of steps, turns away, bows deeply and breathes rapidly.

When he recovers he asks, 'Who could do such a thing? That animal's been tortured before it was killed.'

'Someone as different from you as a serial killer, old buddy, that's who. Not a native Troutstreamer, I'd be willing to wager. You're just too good to conceive of this kind of thing, big guy.'

'Let's get out of this,' says Jack.

As they approach the picnic tables, Eugene zips past Jack and commands, 'Veronica!'

Jack slows down, thinking to make a joke for Veronica about man's best friend, but he thinks again when the needles of sunlight reflect wetness on her cheek, and puzzled he hoists the picnic cooler and passes on. Kids.

'See ya at work, old buddy,' Eugene calls, raising his hand limply.

He waits until Jack turns his back and takes a step: 'Jack?'

Jack turns smiling: 'Yeah?'

'You're so honest, and I rely on your forthrightness, we all do. So tell me honestly: do you think glasses would make my ears look bigger? I'm embarrassed even to be asking, but I've developed an allergy to contacts.' He smiles: 'I wouldn't admit this to anyone but you.'

'Imagine that, five years and I never even knew you wore contacts!' Jack laughs. 'But no, Gene, your ears are no bigger than anyone's else's.'

'Thanks, buddy.' Eugene turns and takes the trail.

Hangdog, Jack is still watching Eugene disappear into the darkness of the woods when Veronica emerges from the dappled shadows of the picnic area. She takes the trail without seeming to notice him, but Jack calls in light mockery, 'Goodbye, Veronica.'

She halts and stands stock still. Then turns with her arms stiff at her sides, her green book in her right hand, her head bowed. 'I hate them!' she snaps, turns and runs.

Teenagers, thinks Jack, worried for the girl, but pleased with himself that Ashley doesn't seem bent on giving them too much trouble. They must be doing something right.

THE
COMPLEX

Iris is Troubled by Visions

•

Iris is troubled by visions. Not the visions in the tea leaves, where she looks for what she suspects as much as reads the pattern at the bottom of the cup. No, Iris is seldom troubled by those visions. Only that one time she scared herself with the picture of Anne from Home Hardware in burnt tatters and blackened all over and carrying the number nine, and nine days later she lost the twins, and nine months after that her husband left her . . . But it's not even like that this time, more like with the Wier triplets last week. Indistinct, scary, no control. They've been coming uncalled for, these scary visions, and at the strangest times. Like when she was waiting at the IGA checkout, where the retarded bag-boy with the head like a square white rock had called her back to planet earth, *dummy* he'd called her and snorted like a little bull and everybody'd laughed at her and the manager had upbraided the idiot gently. Or waiting for the bus and looking down to find that big dark dog with his snout up her dress, the same brute that'd scared her at the Vietnamese's garden tea party. Or even sitting on the toilet doing her business and finding Fred'd been rattling the doorknob for ages. A lot of those times she can't even remember what she'd been dreaming, though afterwards she'd been clammy and trembling. It was two weeks since she'd had the first one she can remember. It had begun as a pleasant dream, with her lying on something warm and soft in the middle of a green field like on her father's small farm back in Depot. But her head was heavy, too heavy to raise, so she couldn't look about to be sure of where she was. She knew she wasn't meant to be in the dream, only to look on. And for the first time she understood Mavis's telling her that that was the worst part of the gift: to know, to tell, to go unheeded. . . . A beautiful dream of an emerald and golden farm, it may well have been her Daddy's, which she and Fred took over, only when she looked sideways it was greener than life, like a fake Christmas tree, and the water surrounding . . . the island was blue and teeming with fish arcing into the air like wriggling salmon set on home. Iris sighed heavily, wanting so to be a part of that beautiful island again. That wanting sigh was a mistake, for it set up a noise like a moaning wind. The white-capped sky-blue water darkened, the sword fish jumping all around seemed to be leering, the sand disappeared, and an unseen beast was eating around the perimeter of the island, snuffling like a bull, chomping off great rings with each circuit, hungry as death.

That was the way Iris had described it to Fred after he'd cupped her elbow and shaken it not so gently. She'd been standing all the while at a window facing the hedged back yard of their town house, then with her forehead in her palm. 'It was like a great moaning desire, Fred. And don't you laugh at me, this is different. A great moaning desire eating its way around that island like a starving dog working on a pistachio ice-cream cone.' Fred howled. She looked unknowing at him and looked away. He was shaken by Iris's blank look, by her voice, by the trembling hand that moved to the wattled fish-belly throat, by the way she'd turned to him and her pupils had contracted to a pin prick right before his eyes.

'A great moaning desire, Fred. And now that I hear myself say it, those were the very words Mavis used just before that boy shot all those girls in Montreal. God help us all.'

Just this morning Iris had been standing at her front window watching the garbage men collect the trash on Salmon Run, and like falling asleep to dream the surrounding noises she was watching a ghost of herself on the black shore of a black body of water. Or not so much a black ghost on a black beach as like the aura-emanating figures in the negative of a holiday photo, she and Fred visiting Cavendish, only there was no Fred and it was spooky. Still as a graveyard, until the black water began to rise coldly up around her, or she began to sink into the black sand, she couldn't tell which; at her abdomen it stopped, shooting an icicle of painless fright right up through her crotch and out the top of her head. And that distant noise like yelping pups in the air, or like a V of geese leaving, no it was . . . children, girls, squealing somewhere down the darkened beach. Then that other sound again, familiar already, the heavy breathing and quiet wheezing and moaning . . . like a fat man gorging himself in the dark. She smirks in her dream: 'Now Mavis never said *that*.' The garbage men gunned their truck and she was back at her front window. But the garbage cans were still standing full along the kerb of Salmon Run. It had been the recycling truck, what she called the blue box men. She'd dropped her jaw and touched her forehead with two fingers and a voice came out: 'The blue box . . .'

The troubling visions were getting stronger and more frequent, and now a voice only half her own was speaking from her. She had to call Mavis. It was Mavis's voice had mingled with her own.

'Oh, you know Fred, he's happy so long as there's sports-card shows on Sunday and half-dressed women calling him at all hours to fix their plumbing. He's just paid a hundred dollars for a little faded picture of Tim Horton. You know, him that started the doughnut stores. Fred says it's a steal, and I'm afraid he's right. It's the Irish in him, Mavis: they're always wanting something to make them feel special.'

Iris cocks her head like a robin listening for a worm. She smiles lightly: 'Yes, your friends the Boat People are still there, but no, Fred and I haven't spoken to them since you left, or only once. By rights they really should've been put in the Project –

'Well, yes, I suppose you are right, dear. Last I heard the old woman was warned by the Public Health not to be doctoring her countrymen or she'd find herself up on charges and on a boat *back* to Vietnam, or wherever it is they're from. I'd meant to write or phone and tell you this, Mavis, but do you know just after you left they came banging on our door one night terrified. *Terrified.* With their slanty eyes buggin' out like squeezed darkie dolls. I thought at first it was just more kids, but there they stood, all six of them waiting quietly in the cold rain, all dressed in their pyjamas, I think, and with the old woman standing down on the sidewalk with her hands up her sleeves and nodding away like the one grown-up shepherding a crowd of trick-or-treaters. It only strikes me now that I'm telling you, Mavis, but I remember a big dark dog like that one from Tackle Court that Fred says he's gonna call the dog catcher about . . . the *very* one at their tea party, now that I –

'Yes, dear, I *am* telling you. The dog came snuffling along with its nose to the ground and stopped dead in its tracks and looked up at her, and without looking she touched behind its ear, and it shook itself and bounded off . . .

'I'm sorry, dear, I'm grown addle-headed, I know. Oh, I suppose they'd come to us because you talked to the old woman all evening in her smelly little garden that last time you'd been visiting. Anyway, the young boy could just barely jabber that they wanted *me* to call the police, if you don't mind. Because *devils* have been coming to their house since sunset and banging on the door and throwing stones when they don't answer. Sure it was Hallowe'en, Mavis!'

Iris's laughter dies without dignity, her smile fades, she pinches her mouth, her eyes go tiny and shiny black.

'Well, I won't say *how* did you know, though I never thought to call till only just this minute.'

Iris smirks and shakes her head: '*She* said that. *She* said things could get worse *here*, here in Troutstream, *worse* than in . . . Cambodia? Why that ungrateful – '

Iris closes her eyes, her chin trembles and her free hand reaches for her throat: 'Yes, La Corriveau.

'Of course, you always have a room here, you know that. I'll have Fred put up the heavy curtains.

'Yes, dear, I'll try my best, goodbye.'

But even as Iris holds the dead phone to her left breast drops are forming at her closed lids like tears from a blind woman.

★

Those who know Troutstream north of Inglis only are surprised to learn that the community has a population of ten thousand. It's easy to forget that Troutstream south of Inglis is deep in rows of town houses like barracks, containing some eighty per cent of the population. Three long and winding packed streets on the southwest side alone, all with fishy names: Salmon Run, Casting Avenue, Tackle Court – or Hook, Line and Sinker, as Fred calls them for the enjoyment of Paul Arsenault at the Troutstream Arms. Iris and Fred have lived in the Complex for three years, which already places them among the long-term residents. In the Complex all are hurrying to something better or worse, to a small detached house beyond Troutstream to the east, in a new development like some Legoland uncrated on a planet whose atmosphere contains defoliant; or, if suddenly lucky in love or a lottery, to an older home in the leafy streets north of Inglis; or, if suddenly unlucky, to the subsidised housing project, or some other project. In the Complex south of Inglis families also come and go because fathers up and leave when, upon entering middle age, they see purposelessness everywhere: in their work, their children, their gadget-clogged residences, their cereal, their marriages. They leave the children who weren't reared properly anyway and the women with poor incomes originally intended as supplemental, leave for a last fling at satisfying desire. For a while diminishing support payments arrive, mortgages and Complex fees are barely made, property taxes are rescheduled, screws come loose, garage mechanics cheat, things are sold off, the kids turn nasty permanently, application is made for a place in the Project, or some other project. In the Complex the one constant is accelerating change, in the personalities of fathers, in the fortunes of women and children, in neighbours, even in the silent speed at which tv channels are incessantly switched. While the only things that really change are the objects of constant desire: yesterday for love, today for eternal youth; today for a steady pay-cheque, tomorrow for immortality; or tomorrow for a little relief, and the day after for uninterrupted happiness; or yesterday for tomorrow and today for yesterday. Desire goes round and round and round till all's eaten up, and there remains only the black hole of pitiable engorged desire itself, climaxing with a big bang into infinity again, starting over. That's often what husbands in the Complex say when they mess up their lives: 'I'm starting over.' Sometimes they add, 'From scratch.' As if their lives to that point had been an itching rehearsal. Perhaps they imagine they're living in one of those tv sit-coms that loses its comic energy and opts for spectacle, canned laughter and sentimental closings. Maybe that makes more tolerable the way desire uses them.

For someone like Iris, life in the Complex is more vividly dramatic than when she and Fred lived for a short time in the newer suburbs to the east. If her neighbours knew that she'd chosen the Complex over the suburbs, they would think her unbalanced. Iris would never admit it, but she'd be even happier in the Project. There's material enough in the Project to keep Phil and Oprah and Geraldo in business till kingdom come. And Mavis. Though Mavis would appreciate the Complex more, because there she would see played out her vision of men as the curse of the world. Of course, Fred would be there too, and Mavis never knew what to make of Fred. Iris and Fred have loved one another for forty years. Around Fred cool Mavis can sometimes be as shy and flustered as a teenage girl. And because Iris loves them both, in a half-dream she sometimes wishes that Fred and Mavis would sleep together. It's never too late. She wouldn't want to join them, or watch, or anything sick like that. She just doesn't think their love should go unconsummated. And she doesn't think God would call it adultery.

Iris and Fred had moved to Troutstream from a village of three hundred called Depot, which straddles the Ontario-Quebec border near where a tributary of the Ottawa River empties into the St Lawrence. The name of the village is a conflation of the English and French words 'deep eau', which describes the phenomenon of a commercially useless deep harbour on the big river. Somewhere in geologic time a retreating glacier had stumbled there and gouged a deep socket, and the St Lawrence had rushed in and pooled to a depth which in spots remains unsounded. Iris was born in Depot, met and married Fred in Depot, farmed with Fred near there for thirty years on what had been her own father's farm, had six children there, met Mavis Lachance there. It was Mavis told Iris that she too had the gift, if one much weaker than her own, and

Iris had tried reading cups for the fun of it. Mavis had been right, and Iris had begun reading in earnest, though she never charged and accepted no donation over twenty dollars. She'd been happy in Depot, though she'd not known it because she'd never been truly miserable. Until the eve of the day she and Fred left, when Mavis had sat all evening over pot after pot of tea in the slant-floored kitchen of the old farmhouse, and read only Iris's final cup as the air outside was turning cold and grey. Mavis had said, 'You will always be a spirit unable to occupy its body complete, Iris dear. That happens more frequently than people know. Something often goes wrong when the Divine will expresses itself in human matter, though in varying degrees. I've heard the medical word is *proprioception*. But the real trouble comes from Evil incarnate, or wanting to be incarnate. I know it, but I don't half understand it. Ultimately, though, I see, we both will encounter a severe instance, in this place you are going to. But you, Iris, are a gentle soul, a kind woman, and a dear friend. I will keep an eye on you. Please never tell Fred what I said about him, it would only make him laugh in that way that makes us cry.'

The only time Fred had ever cried, to Iris's knowledge, was when she'd told him that their buyer had resold the farm to an American developer for some big warehouse operation called a Price Club. He'd just stood there the longest while among the pale leaf-lettuce at the eastern suburb house and then, making a noise like a blender with a dying motor, gone back to thinning the poor plants. The buyer had promised a golf course. All the kids were gone, to Montreal, Toronto, and the youngest, Archie, to Ottawa, though they never see him. The money offered seemed inconceivable. Sad to learn so late in life, everything did have its price. They'd lied to themselves about the golf course to make it easier.

Standing now by the wall of windows facing the train tracks, Iris rolls her shoulders and pulls her elbows close to her sides, feeling gawky, as usual. A tall plain woman is a comical object in the city. Cigarette butts everywhere, dirt actually drifting across the floor like desert sand, and when she pulls a Crispy Crunch wrapper from her shoe she stumbles hand-first into a strange man's bum. Good God Almighty! . . . But he hardly gives heed, which may well be worse. If only there were a broom and dustpan handy. Fred says to callers she doesn't want to talk to, 'She's off riding her broom.' She should have had Debbie give her a rinse this morning. Has Mavis any grey yet? When they'd last been together . . . over a year now, Mavis had still been jet black, with her hair newly styled straight around her head then draping down the back like some Egyptian Cleopatra, as blue-black still as the wing of a crow. It was that hair more than her dead-on readings had earned her the name La Corriveau. Iris and Fred often argued over Mavis's hair, with Iris insisting that she *knew* Mavis didn't dye. Though Fred's argument was unanswerable: 'Tell me, O wise Iris, *how* can a woman who's not gonna see her sixties again *not* have *some* grey hair? Who does she think she is, Ronald Reagan?' Fred was not a believer. Fred doesn't have . . . a . . . spiritual . . . bone . . . in . . .

Iris recognises the gentle swoon, and is back on the black beach. Far along the shape of a young girl, not a child but a young woman already, is playing listlessly in the sand in that expectant unsmiling way of a world-weary girl. Iris knows the girl, not by name but by sight. The girl stands and throws her digging stick at the monstrous sun, and Iris watches the spear sail straight and true . . . but it begins to curve upwards, looping like some missile gone haywire, and it sprouts thin wings that flap frantically till they grow larger and pump languorously like black waves, and the enormous black bird grows more immense as it descends out of a burnt-orange sky, upright, its eyes twin ruby suns, its beak parting in ragged shears as it bears down on the transfixed girl. Iris tries to scream a warning but can't. Out of the hole she starts running sluggishly through the sand, it's too hard, she wants only to lie down and sleep . . . All is black, ah she's sleeping, only dreaming, hearing only her own deep breathing, that's all, and some wheezing, Fred, just the old boy's desire moaning still through a closed or full mouth. But no. It's not her or Fred. She has heard that noise before, and not in another dream-vision, in reality. Yes. And in her dream-vision she relaxes into the memory. When they had first moved to Troutstream Fred spent every Wednesday afternoon at the local bar, the Troutstream Arms. It was a way to make friends, though Fred never needed much of an excuse to drink, which hadn't interfered too much when he'd had the farm to run. One Wednesday Iris had got to feeling cooped up and gone looking for something to do. She'd never liked shopping, and there wasn't much in the strip mall anyway. And the prices of what was there! Even the Bi-Way. No wonder people're taking shopping bus-tours to the States. So she thought she might take in a movie. Before the third video rental store came to Troutstream, a Cineplex had thrived where the IGA now stands, and Iris drifted over to read the marquee. She knew all about the new movies, though they came to Troutstream late. Only three were listed. *Silence of the Lambs*, that was horror. *Cape Fear*, that was horror too. *Beauty and the Beast* . . . Hmmm? But on reflection she didn't feel like a fairy tale. She was about to abandon the idea when she noticed the small poster advertising a forth: *The Canterbury Tales*. She remembered studying it back in Depot Secondary, and though it always looked to her like somebody'd snuck into Mr Chaucer's study and switched some of the keys on his typewriter, the lessons had made her laugh and think how foolish people had always been. Though they did seem to be getting worse. But yes, a good comedy. Funny she'd never seen mention of it. And what luck, starting in five minutes!

A man in a black cowboy shirt with white piping and a string tie sold the tickets, which was odd. He frowned his eyebrows down his buzzard's nose when he finally had the courtesy to acknowledge her request. No one showed her to her seat. And when her eyes adjusted to the darkness she saw that the theatre was very small, seating no more than twenty or thirty, though there were only two other people for the matinée, both men, distant from each other. In the dark she had mistakenly sat only a few seats from one. She had no time to wonder further, the screen blazed white and both men's forearms went to their eyes. The title appeared in old-fashioned Gothic script: *Jeff Chaucer's Canterbury Tails*. Imagine that, *Jeff!* and misspelling *Tales!* She should have got herself some double-buttered popcorn and a Coke Classic, that squirming fat man a few seats along had some and he was making her hungry. Or was he drinking? Never mind him, and you're watching your weight now.

Right away she could see why she'd never heard of this movie,

not just because of the repeated errors – 'The Priest's Nun's Tail' –
but the picture looked like it was shot with one of those camcorders, and the music sounded like the dentist's office, only
blaring. The movie began with a heavily made-up nun milking a
cow in a stable that looked about as real as a *Hee-Haw* set. A
modern-day priest walked up and stood right beside her, and
when the nun turned her head the shot remained tight on the
priest's crotch, of all places, which looked exceptionally swollen.
The nun licked her lips, and Iris leaned forward, 'Good Sister ye,'
the modern priest said in archaic manner, 'enjoy you your handi-
work here amongst we men of the cloth?' You would think,
thought Iris, that he spoke through his crotch – what was that, did
he scratch himself? 'Oh yes, good Father, I haveth strong hands
for to pull.' The nun giggled, and the shot zoomed in on a pair of
hands expertly milking, then a tight shot of the nun's mouth filled
by her reaming tongue like a galvanised oyster. Those hairy hands
were not hers, thought Iris. But something more is wrong.
Another quick cut and Iris didn't know *what* she was watching, it
looked like an operation, like on medical shows with fibre-optic
cameras, of a valve opening and closing or someone being force-
fed. There was much fidgeting beside her, and Iris heard a low
moan closer than she'd thought the fat man to be. She glanced, he
was hunched forward uncomfortably, staring up at the screen with
his cheeks blown up like that negro trumpet player, while frantically trying to pull the cork from his bottle, and he *was* a seat
closer. When she turned back to the screen Iris gasped and covered
her mouth: it was like the whole wall was a penis moving in and
out of a vagina. Beside her the enormous man scrunched lower,
moaning deeply, and breathing hard like some old locomotive
struggling to get off. Trembling all the while he moved into the
seat beside Iris, groaning, 'Help m – ' And she bolted as a man's
voice whispered hoarsely, '*Good* Sister Frances, have yet ye made
acquaintance with our divinely endowed Brother Jackass?'

In her dream-vision Iris shouts her warning through the dark:
'It's the fat pervert man having sex with himself!'

But now there is no sound of a young girl, only deep adenoidal
breathing, moaning, and the slopping chops of something gorging
itself. It pauses, and the sound itself turns towards her in the pitch

dark, it and darkness one, taking notice of *her*, taking her in, it breathes closer, she cannot move –

'Iris?'

Mavis, standing close in front of her, drops her bags and enfolds the much taller Iris. Still dazed, Iris thinks to say some banal greeting, but that's not how she's being hugged. Her tears drop on the shorter woman's shiny dark hair like on a helmet, and roll off. And wouldn't you know it, not a grey hair in sight. Iris snuffles shamelessly.

'I know,' says Mavis. 'I have felt it at home for weeks now, and growing stronger as the train drew nearer. Child, we can only do what we can do. But there's not much time, maybe none. Will the police listen to you?'

'The police! No! . . . No. Oh Mavis, everybody here thinks I'm an old fool.'

'Well, I'm here now and I know different. Speaking of old fools, how's Frederick?'

'He thinks we're a pair of old fools.'

'Does he now? . . . But *blehh*, physical travel, my very aura feels . . . *soiled*.'

'Is it that bad, La Corriveau?'

'Look, we'll all go out for a drink tonight. Then you and I have some work to do.'

· 5 ·

The Needs of Others

·

They moved in next door while I was away for five weeks on Malaconsejado, that well-named hell-hole off the west coast of Mexico. And though a hell-hole was the very place I'd fancied, there was nothing Greenelandish or Lowryish about Malaconsejado. Only breathless heat stuffing the stunned mouth, dust fast filming to dirt like a second skin, excremental filth everywhere, toothlessness and thievery, foul food spiced to tastelessness, untreated well water safer than the treated . . . more heat, more filth. Fat flies would not be waved off, they had to be pushed. I lost thirty pounds the first thirty days, and knew that at that rate I'd either die of dysentery or disappear if I didn't go home. . . . Malaconsejado, poor judgement, originally christened Buenocompañía by the Hollywood mogul who'd bought and abandoned it in 1922, renamed by the deceived company of nouveau locals. Malaconsejado. Indeed.

By the time I got back to Troutstream in mid-July, Les, Linda, and Wes (their German Shepherd) had established relations with my roommate, Mike, who had agreed to hold our town house on winding Tackle Court in my name. He'd just finished a BA with a major in philosophy, and the deal was he could stay rent-free for the summer because I knew I'd be returning to graduate studies in journalism at Carleton University that Fall and idle Mike would be up and gone. (I'd kick him out if I had to.) Troutstream is some distance from the campus, but the transit system in this part of the world is excellent, the rent here reasonable, and the neighbourhood quite pleasant, with semi-mature trees and not too many low-lifes, not like the bare Project just the other side of the shopping plaza. I joke, of course, when I say 'this part of the world', as I'd never before been beyond the Ottawa area for more than a week. To this extent, though, I do not joke: Malaconsejado showed me that this part of the world – Canada, Ontario, Ottawa, Troutstream – is the true El Dorado, that even the welfare thieves thick in the Project live fat.

Ironically, the day I returned was as breathlessly hot and dusty as the days I'd left behind forever. I paused inside *my* front door to listen to the noises from *my* living room. I closed my eyes and breathed deep the clean dust streaming into my nostrils from the ragged foyer throw-rug (*ragged* by Canadian standards, I thought). As I moved along the hall I could have wept for joy over the familiar snot into which *my* dust was congealing, shut forever of that tar I'd been digging out in Malaconsejado –

A stranger sat in a loose lotus position on the living room floor at the end of the couch where Mike sat . . . rolling a joint? A large bag of dark chips of some sort lay half-spilled to the stranger's right side and a German Shepherd lay at his left. The dog lifted its head and bared its teeth at me in that smile or grin that makes a dangerous dog's intentions impossible to determine; the stranger looked up at the doorway and grinned broadly, gently placed one hand on the dog's head and with the other lifted a beer towards me. 'Good boy,' he whispered.

Mike glanced up, started, then shouted, '*Salut*, amigo!' He startled the dog, who barked once. Mike bowed his head, pouted and combed his free fingers through his sparse fair hair – same colour as mine, but thinning to premature baldness – then returned intently to the packed cigarette paper scissored in his left hand. Still grinning at me, the stranger grabbed a handful of triangular chips, got some into his mouth as he crushed most against his stubbly chin, spilling them onto his shirt front. He tucked his chin and peered down his nose, giggling lowly as he and the dog picked the bits off his chest like grooming apes.

Just what I needed, strangers in my home, and an animal.

'You're home early, and a lot thinner, wow, what happened?' Mike returned to his joint: 'The price of grass is outta sight here, but we're growing our own . . . uh, in your room for the moment, amigo. Hey, I'll bet weed goes for zip in ol' Meh-hee-co, eh señor?'

I made a pinch-lipped face at Mike's bowed head.

The dog tried to rise, but the stranger held down its haunches. 'Uh-oh,' he said, grinning broadly back and forth at Mike and me. 'Big brother's watching,' and he giggled alone like a well-timed engine.

'And a welcome home to you too,' I finally said in as relieved and friendly a fashion as I could muster. 'I'm gonna go dump my bags, be right back.'

'This is Les Mellanson, Dennis,' shouted Mike, holding me out of sight in the hallway. 'He and his wife, Linda, and Wes here, are our new neighbours! They're also newlyweds! . . . Though they've been living in sin for fifteen years.'

That last crack was a new voice for Mike, throaty, mock-conspiratorial. Midday and he's stoned: ashtray spilling butts and roaches, brown empties ringing my coffee table, Mike smirking bleary-eyed brainless as ever. Some things you can count on.

'Welcome home, Dennis!' shouted Les. He giggled, Wes barked.

'Les Mellanson, Dennis Ames, Dennis-Les, Wes-Dennis, Dennis-Wes. *There*,' said Mike, 'I've done my duty as Troutstream host, so you can all fuck right off.'

Yes, strange talk for Mike, confident, like somebody had been encouraging the crippled wit that never hobbled far from a sneering global cynicism.

'*Dennis-Les?*' said Les. 'We have been for a month now!' And the two of them howled as only the stoned do at lame humour.

My bedroom, the master on the main floor, was filled with plants like a fucking greenhouse! Like I'd been invaded by pod people who needed a daily chlorophyll fix! Marijuana plants, tall and straight like leafy spearmint, they hid everything, covering my Wyeth and Danby posters. A quick finger counted twenty-eight large earthen pots, six pale-blue wooden window boxes in green plastic troughs, and any number of tiny brown pots and

Styrofoam cups suggesting nothing so much as the tolerated participation of children. Did Les and Linda have 'love children'?

Strangers, animals, kids, shit.

But counting the pots had settled me and shown me that my initial impression of a green chaos was inaccurate. The plants were actually arranged in a kind of progressive order from tender shoots closest to the window to spiky rugged growth along the farthest interior wall. This was *not* Mike's work.

'We'll move the plants out today,' said Les from my doorway. 'It was the whole wall of windows, the great light, made us choose this room. Mike said you could be okay about things like this.' He giggled. 'Hey, Denny, you're not pissed off, eh?'

'Na, na,' I flung my arm about without looking at him. *Denny?*

He came in carrying a twelve-pack and shook my hand too firmly. The dog, Wes, followed and lay at his feet by the beer. Les stared into my eyes for too long. He was average height, my height, but powerfully built, with a craggy face that looked older even than forty, and crinkled pale-blue eyes laughing out from under a real mop of tousled dark hair. Most striking, he had a head like a buffalo's, disproportionately large and square if you thought about it for too long, but somehow fitting, noble even, if you simply noticed it. And there was something else, some suggestion of a character you'd heard legendary stories about but never met. Some ancient uncle adventurer back from the dark beyond. It was in the heavy plaid shirt (not twill), the bib jeans (not stone-washed or pre-faded, but worn down from the original cast-iron denim), the sandals without socks, his indeterminate age . . . – Hey, I clued in, is this an original hippie standing here before me? Certainly there was about him that medicinal smell I'd always imagined clings to druggies from the sixties and seventies, a fanciful tinge like tincture of iodine, as though the pale pores of their sick skin exuded the odour of burnt lobes incompetently doctored. That air of someone who was present physically but whose soul had never made it all the way back from some Odyssean 'acid trip'. Of someone not in full possession of his self's house.

He bent to pat Wes: 'Good dog, say hello to the nice man, Wes.'

Wes yipped.

'No problem,' I said officiously. 'I'll give you a hand carrying them out, right away.'

'You will, eh?' and he giggled enigmatically again, irritatingly so. 'Talk to him, say something.'

'Who? The dog?'

'Yeah, *the dog*.' Mocking giggle. Then plaintively: 'Hey, Denny, Wes'll be your friend if you say something nice to him.'

'Uh, hi, Wes, nice dog.'

'Nice dog,' spurted Les, revving up his giggle. To hide his mockery he bent and ruffled the dog's flanks: 'That's better, isn't it, old boy?'

'Sorry, I'm just no fan of animals. Uh, do you and your new wife have any kids, Les?'

'Kids?' and he snapped his head down. 'Na.' He twisted his head up like some Quasimodo: 'But that's not really any of your business, is it Dennis?'

'No?' With arms uplifted in greeting I gestured round at the plants like the Pope welcoming munchkin converts out of the rainforest, and ended with Wes and Les: 'It's just that I don't much like kids *either*.'

Les frowned and his whole face crinkled: 'Hey, Denny, that's okay. No one has to pretend. But I love animals, eh? Especially ol' Wes here. Right, boy?' Wes barked joyfully into Les's face. 'Ol' Wes and Les are gonna be together forever, right ol' boy?' He dropped to his knees and spent a playful minute cuffing Wes back and forth, as the dog slurped his whole face.

I pinched my chin with thumb and forefinger: 'You know, they lick faces only because they think you have food in your mouth for them.'

He hugged the dog's neck and looked up at me like some large-faced retarded person: '*You* know, Denny, that's just about the stupidest fucking thing I've heard in a month, and I've heard some doozies. Welcome home, amigo!' He howled, the dog joined him.

We spent too long carrying the plants to the kitchen at the rear of the house. The next step would be moving them quickly across a thin strip of back yard and into Les's house, which was a safe

enough step, since Tackle Court was the last street of garden
homes bordering the greenbelt that surrounds Troutstream. (And
now there's the added protection of the huge green plastic fence a
hundred metres to the back; semi-translucent, glowing at twilight
like a fish tank, it's supposed to shield us from the sights and
sounds of the new Troutstream Bypass. Mostly I conventionally
hated the sight of it, but I kind of secretly liked it, too, thinking it
the modern version of a medieval moat keeping all the shit out of
Troutstream.) But before taking that next step, we stopped for a
beer.

'I'll have to buy some lights now,' said Les, smirking at Mike
over the lip of his bottle.

Mike dipped his chin, Les winked at me.

'Well, I'm broke,' Mike pouted. He held his empty to the
kitchen window and swung it like a bell. He looked like he hadn't
washed his hair or shaved in a week, or changed his clothes likely.
'I supply the room. Now they're growing so well, you gotta get
the lights yourself. That was the deal, remember?'

'Don't get so worked up, Mikey, you'll get a nose bleed,' Les
grinned at me. 'I'll get 'em, *sure, no problem.*' He spoke with such
sudden intensity. 'Won't we, Wes boy?' The dog barked at Mike
till Les settled him down. 'The deal,' he smirked. 'Hey, but is my
weed any good, Mikey?'

As in my bedroom earlier when I'd asked if he had any kids, Les
had passed so quickly from solicitous humour to playfulness to
disdain, that my head spun briefly. I couldn't help laughing,
wondering, worrying. He winked at me again. It was that bushy
head like some Mark Twain or Stephen Leacock that let him get
away with winking so much.

'Huh?' said Mike. 'Uh . . . it's all right, I guess.' He finger-
combed his hair, wiggled the fingers like someone waving bye-
bye to a baby and floated some strands to the floor. 'Anybody
want another beer?' And he bent to the twelve-pack Les seemed
always to have at his feet like a smaller dog.

'*Duh,*' groaned Les for my appreciation. Wes sniffed my feet.

'Not for me,' I said. 'I have to shower and get something to eat.
I've not felt clean or had a decent meal in *weeks.*'

Mike had wandered off and said now from the hall, 'Oh yeah,

Den, I was gonna get some groceries today. Les, you got any more beer? There's only four left in the case.'

'*The* case?' Les grinned at the plants covering the kitchen table. He shook his head, then put a hand on my shoulder: 'Look, Denny, why don't you go and have your shower, okay?' He whispered like a scheming gangster out the side of his mouth: 'I'll make Mikey give me a hand carting these over to my place.' And in his normal voice: 'Then you guys come over to our place for supper. I know Linda, my wife, will be glad to meet you after hearing so much about you. We're only having spaghetti, though Linda's spaghetti sauce'll put some good ol' Canadian bacteria back in your intestines.'

'Sounds great, Leslie,' I yawned long and loud.

'Here, boy,' he ordered gently, pulling Wes back from my feet. 'Whew! What you been doin', Denny, stompin' cock-a-roaches?' He laughed loudly.

'Something like.'

'We-ess, I hear you,' a woman's voice fluted from the front of *my* house.

'Back here, honey,' he boomed. 'I'm back here with Wes and Denny, our legendary neighbour and wannabe gonzo.'

'Wannabe *what*?'

He squinted at me: 'You know, Hunter S. Thompson? . . . Gonzo journalist? . . . C'mon, Denny boy, don't make me feel ancient.'

'Oh yeah . . . I remember, sort of. One of my weirdo profs in first year was always gettin' carried away about him. Didn't he write something called *The Armies of Vietnam*, or *Breakfast of Champions* . . . or something?'

He smacked the heel of his palm to his forehead and pushed his head way back: *Wha . . .'*

'Lord, chile, you're confusing two of Mailer's titles, *Norman* Mailer, and Mailer and Vonnegut, *Kurt* Vonnegut,' said the woman who came into the room. Or skipped in rather, her long, straight, mousy hair bouncing along with her. She looked much younger than Les, more my age. But she wore sandals too, plastic thongs, and an old-fashioned blue-and-white flower print dress to her ankles that, against the light Mike had left on in the hallway, was semi-translucent. She sidled up not a foot from me and delicately held up her hand like someone passing a reception line, carrying through with the southern belle routine in which she'd softened her correction of me. And when I took her fingers she actually curtsied and gazed up at me through the lightly green-tinted glass of her large clear plastic glasses: her face, a touch too long, was pale and beautiful, and her eyes, even behind the tinted glass, were the dreamy marbled blue and white of the planet itself seen from space.

'Linda, Dennis,' and he giggled as though this were all some old private joke I'd walked into. 'Introductions,' he laughed, as though that explained it.

'Hi-ee,' she said brightly, dropping the pose. But then she looked around at the plants, tightened her expression and said, 'Les, I said – we agreed, *remember: no plants in the house this time.*' Her head had come forward, and in anger she spoke nasally.

'Deals,' smirked Les. He assumed a tone of mock-enlightenment: 'Oh, I get it, *now* I see: Mike's house was okay, but ours is *a big deal.*'

Linda pinched her mouth and waited, waited against the light from the hallway, and I couldn't keep my gaze moving from her face to her body and up and down again. I said to myself: *I gotta get out.* But it wasn't just my long absence from sexual relations with another. No, I could think of very few women who radiated Linda's charming combination of sensuality and wholesomeness, very few women as beautiful as Linda.

'Look, nice meeting you guys, but, as Wes here knows, I gotta take a shower.'

Linda blushed and laughed brightly, while Les crinkled his whole face, smirked, then laughed along as though at his own private joke. Linda caught his eye and they exchanged some visual information.

'Talk to you guys later, okay?'

From the hall I heard Linda's nasal voice: 'What!'

Linda's spaghetti supper turned out to be the best meal I'd had since long before Malaconsejado: packed salad, fresh-baked whole-wheat buns, Les's very good home-made wine, and in my honour a sauce concocted to be as gentle as Mother Nature herself. Even Mike's smoking a joint between supper and dessert – fresh strawberries and French vanilla ice cream – detracted only aesthetically from a perfect meal. Linda and Les apparently had achieved rapprochement about the marijuana plants, which were nowhere in sight. We talked only of pleasant things: the tricks of winemaking, the benefits of travel and the Troutstream Bypass, the private spiritual blessings of the age-old institution of marriage. Intuitively we knew to avoid practical matters, though I was curious to know the facts of their lives. Only once did the brief after-supper conversation threaten discomfort, when Les looked at me out of the blue and pointedly asked why I had abandoned my plan in Mexico. I didn't want to answer, I wasn't prepared to elaborate my reasons, and I suspected I couldn't satisfy Les with anything superficial. But Mike saved us, saying with the hint of a slur, 'He came back 'cause he heard Paul Anka was giving a concert at the Congress Centre and Preston Manning was gonna lead the Senate in some stage diving during "Havin' My Baby".' He stood and sang a few lines lugubriously, and I wondered what had gotten into me earlier: Mike was a funny guy, the perfect complement to me, I should invite him to stay on if he needs a place. Fine. Though it may have been the food and wine.

Later that evening I was sitting at my desk, which abutted the bottom of my bed, and reading through the mass of notes I'd written during my aborted sojourn on Malaconsejado: some connected paragraphs, but many more isolated, mostly sentences, fragments, phrases, single words. These pages were supposed to form the basis of my thesis. As I read I was overcome by a vague worry that turned into sharp distress, a distress that sighted choking desperation with stabbing despair hot on its tail. It was like a dozen different people had written these notes which, at the time of their composition, had struck me as piercing insights into the diseased heart of our continent's very own colourful Third World. But I saw now that nothing cohered. There wasn't even the weakest suggestion of the feature's *raison d'être*: a consistent point of view. No trace of a grounded perspective – *nada*.

I was staring with pattering heart at a thing that read 'Bonus!!! Title for piece on IMF – "Once Too Often to the Well" – possible sale *Economist, Business Week, Financial Times*, thesis: developed countries cannot simply throw money into the black hole of Third World problems', when a rumble sounded from the back of the house. At first I imagined, almost with relief, that they were moving the plants back (but all the noise had probably been Mike getting caught in the slapping aluminum door, kicking at it, and stumbling into the kitchen); the rumble rolled along the hall, and right into my bedroom the three of them came, four counting Wes. Les set an unopened twelve-pack of Foster's at my feet like an offering, sat himself cross-legged beside it while Wes lay prone beside him. Wearing work-boots Mike flopped onto my bed and began squirming and playing air guitar and sputtering the lyrics to some song I'd never heard, no doubt some new song on the music channel, whose only distinct phrase was the much-repeated 'When I think about you I touch myself'. Mike performed so only to ridicule the pretensions of popular songs, whining or snarling the lyrics in challenging mock-seriousness, though sometimes I suspected he thought he was pretty good. (I made a mental note: I must·get rid of this media clown.) Linda sat at the foot of my bed, half-turned to face me. With a bright by-your-leave smile she picked up a sheaf of my notes and scanned the first page, maintaining a poised expression. The bowed reading profile and falling hair gave her a look of classic modesty. But those gravity-defying kind of ample breasts. And I swear her skin was clear to translucence. God, she was beautiful. And I thought again: *I'm getting out tonight.*

'Hey man,' said Les challengingly, and I feared he'd caught me staring. But his voice turned as hushed as a priest's: 'No hard feelings about using your room as a greenhouse, eh Denny? Have a beer, let's toke.' He ripped open the case, screwed the top off a bottle, reached up like a competent child and pounded the much-needed brew onto the desk. He completed his performance by fishing from his shirt pocket and displaying to us all a joint like a tampon for an Amazon.

'All right!' Mike shouted at the ceiling.

'Why not?' said I, and drank deeply. 'Thank you. This work's depressing me. But I don't have an ashtray in here.'

'Hey, no problem,' said Les fervently to ridicule my fussiness.

He drained his bottle in one tilt, set it on my desk and giggled: 'You do now.'

'How very resourceful of you,' I said dryly.

Linda trilled a laugh and looked up from my notes: 'You should put more of that in here.'

'More of what?'

'You know, whatchamicallit? . . . Oh, I don't know, *humour*, I guess.'

'Hmph.'

Les lit the joint and we passed it around as we talked. I acted nonchalant, though I hadn't smoked any grass in years. Mike's comment earlier about the prohibitive price of weed had been bullshit. Marijuana had simply disappeared from our lives. You know how it is: you have to do other things, assume real responsibilities, fulfil worldly commitments, then the inflationary passage of time makes grass look so expensive, then you forget how good it is, till it's offered gratis. As for Mexico, who knows? *I* saw no one smoking it. And though there may well have been kilos of cheap weed around, who can think of scoring dope when everything you put into your mouth comes spraying out your asshole in a crimson skitter.

When taking the joint from me the lovely Linda would gaze deadpan through her lightly tinted shades, squint slightly, then smile with a breath-snatching brightness. But regardless of her friendliness and my hungry fantasies, I had recognised in her immediately a true artlessness about the power of her beauty and sexuality. She was genuinely unaware, that girl-woman, in a way that most men find incredible, of the gravitational force of her body, and (I must add, since many physically beautiful women are beautiful losers) of the attractiveness of the mind and spirit that housed themselves in that flesh. I caught Les frowning at us another time when she was giving me her delayed smile, though when he saw that I saw him his boisterous laugh exploded with the toke he was holding. Linda must have sensed something too because she began reading my stuff again, smiling, occasionally puffing through her nose and pulling back her head in surprised appreciation, chortling now and then, and making other agreeable noises. Mike didn't bother to rise whenever the joint came his way, simply blowing rings of smoke like some Old Faithful. Wes seemed to be sleeping. Then Mike too. Les and I sat staring into space, in silence, for quite some time, at Mike, on the bed. Only when Linda rustled a sheet of paper did we crank our heads towards her like dinosaurs.

I looked at Les: 'Did that crinkling paper sound amplified to you, Les?'

'So,' he said, wetting his lips very slowly, 'Mikey seems to be slipping into a coma since you got back, Denny. Any guesses as to why? . . . He said you want to be a writer.'

'Trying.' My modest answer, followed by my pat joke: 'Mostly I feel like a wronger.'

Linda trilled, but Les frowned so strenuously you'd have thought my little self-deprecating remark a personal insult.

'Why do you say that, Denny?' he asked with contorted concern.

'Just a joke, no big deal. I'm a wronger of the world's rights.'

'What's that supposed to mean?' he sneered. 'Is that some of your stuff Linda's reading? Gimme some.' He reached a hand up to my desk and bounced it about like a hopping spider till it landed on one of the pieces of yellow legal paper I'd over-supplied myself with for Malaconsejado.

'That there's my stuff you're pawing, pardner.'

He frowned again, compressed his lips and shook his bowed head. Then laughed loudly. He squinted at the page, his lips actually moved. He frowned up at me for the longest time, then lay flat on his back and roared, inappropriately, for I am not a humorous writer.

Wes raised his head and placed his snout on Les's crotch. From the bed Mike raised himself and said, 'Whazo funny?' and collapsed.

'Well, fuck you, Dr Johnson,' I snapped, snatching his page and the pages from Linda. Like a nervous newscaster trying to look important, I picked up and squared the whole bundle on my desk.

'Denny, Denny, stop, stop,' shouted Les angrily, and Wes alertly angled towards me and bared his teeth. 'Settle down, boy,' said Les, 'settle down.' And both Wes and I relaxed a bit. 'I don't know what's got into *him* lately . . . but *you* got it all wrong, Denny. I love it! I really do! That part about rats the size of rabbits, people keeping them as pets! Fantastic!'

'I made that up,' I grinned.

'Who cares,' Linda groaned as she leaned over to fan my squared bundle, I all the while enjoying a desiccating view of her breasts. She pulled a page and recognised it, held it towards Les: 'Read this, dear.'

Les read aloud, read without feeling, as might a child, concentrating for comprehension: 'At seven each morning I watch the unbelievably fat women of the village gather round the well where the filthy water pours continually from a brown pipe like the pissing cock of North America. I have not drunk from it in the week I've been here, a good thing too, because to slake thirst at such a spring would be to tease the anal volcano into eruptive activity for sure. It's like a town-hall meeting down there, or a wetback version of a Troutstream coffee klatsch; after half an hour or so they disperse. Every morning's the same. Oh yeah: this morning a fight broke out between two fat women, one of whom tore the other's shirt off; no bra; breasts like empty saddlebags on a swaybacked jackass. At the time I knew what they were fighting about, but now I forget. Not over a man, nothing so interesting. I think it was about some old woman, a relative of some sort, and whose turn it was to take her in. I'm dying for a beer, but I'm more determined than ever to break the back of my thesis before I touch a drop. This whole island stinks to high heaven of Death Death Death.'

Les again lay on his back and laughed till you'd have thought he'd be sick. Even Wes looked concerned. Then he whipped into a sitting position, frowning strenuously. 'That anal volcano, that killed me, Denny. But those women at the village well, what did they decide about the old woman?'

'Who knows? Probably fed her to the pet rat.'

Les furrowed, drank. Linda stared at me slack-jawed, and quite fetchingly.

'What about the water pipe and breasts metaphors?' I asked.

Les began a slow giggle that built, didn't speak till I'd stared him down. 'What really gets me,' he managed, 'is that you use all them . . . whatdya call 'em? Them semi-things? Even when you're taking notes!'

'Semicolons?'

'Yeah, them semicolons.'

I looked at Linda: 'Les prefers the full colon?' and raised my eyebrows.

'La-la, you've lost me,' she sang.

Les slid his mouth sideways and did his scheming gangster: 'It's a homophobic dig, honey. You know, *colon, full?* Funny joke, ha-ha.'

'Oh,' said Linda, drawing it out like a tune. 'But do you mean to say that the people of Malaconsejado pass their old relatives back and forth between them?'

'Did I say that?'

'I think that's sweet.'

'*Sweet* is *not* the word Denny'd use, honey.' He smothered a laugh.

By then the fat joint was down to about an inch, and time and space were pulsing. Mike had been dozing for the last while, so the three of us had been smoking even more. Without prelude Linda undid a button opening her dress to mid-breast, I shot forward and stared blatantly while she fished in cleavage then slipped over her head the leather necklace she was wearing.

'Ta-dah,' she sang, swinging an ornately handled roach clip before my eyes.

'Shit,' said I, slightly winded, 'I haven't seen one of those in a long time.'

'There's two of 'em, pardner,' said Les, giving Linda one of his furrowed secret signals.

'Huh?' said I.

'Oh,' chirped blushing Linda and buttoned up.

Les passed the joint to me. I took the warm clip from Linda and applied it, sliding its single jade bead along the nose to pinch the butt. I toked deeply now, and the joint was back to Les and on its way to me again by the time I let out my breath. Going cross-eyed through the filigreed handle of the clip, I'd forgotten how handy a roach clip was:

'It looks like the key to some old church.'

'What's that, Denny?' grinned Les.

'The roach clip. The key to some old stone church that was devoutly demolished by junk-bond salesmen in the good ol' eighties.'

'Is this stuff any good, Denny, or *what*?' Les said seriously, paused, then giggled towards Linda.

Linda blew her toke in a laugh that made Mike stir and Wes bark. 'Le-ess,' she said in a way that made me want to murder Les and marry her.

'I don't know, I guess so, when they're not fighting.'

'Uh, Denny, what are we talking about now?'

'The relatives who take care of Malaconsejado's old people,' I snapped. 'Linda asked me. *Du-uh.*'

Linda rested on me her wide-eyed quiet look.

'So, uh, Denny,' said Les, 'you quit drinking while you were there, eh?'

'Not so much quit as couldn't, Leslie.'

'It's Lester,' said Linda quietly. 'This is cooked.' She dropped the roach into the beer bottle and wrapped the leather thong around her hand.

'Lester, do *you* work?' and I tried to giggle innocently.

But there was a silence, then Les looked up with his serious face. 'No, that's okay. Sure I work, Denny. Here and there, I do odd jobs.'

'Enough to pay the bills? How do you guys get by?'

'Whew,' said Les into his bottle.

'I work too,' sang Linda with a finger in the air: Wait a minute, don't ignore me.

'What do you do?'

'Ah yes,' she said, 'the great Canadian greeting card. Hope you're not dead yet, what do you do for a living? Where's your money come from? *If* you *have* any. Well, Dennis, dear, this year I'm going to be a supply teacher right here at Holy Family Separate. And I can work every day if I want to. *If* I want to, which I don't.'

'Hey, slow down, I didn't mean all *that*.'

But she continued dramatically like someone simultaneously confessing and browbeating: 'I work with mentally challenged kids in the integration programme. Know what that is? Didn't think so. So I won't go on about it. But I'll tell you what you do want to know. Les and I pay all our bills on time, and even have some left over to treat our friends to beer and weed.' She gestured about my room: 'We don't even ask that they house our plants!'

'Honey,' whispered Les, 'you're tripping out on us.'

She caught herself with a flat palm to her chest, turned crimson, tried to trill, walked behind my chair, draped her arms around me and hugged me back against those breasts I'd been shamelessly obsessing about. Talk about putting an end to stoned rancour!

'Sorry, Dennis,' she whispered. 'I got carried away. We've been having a bit of a tough time about these things lately. Let's drop the whole subject. Okay?'

'Of course,' I whispered hoarsely.

Les managed to snort into his own chest and come up with a grin: 'Speaking of tripping out, Denny, you say on *your* trip you quit drinking, eh? What timing, eh honey?'

'Yes. I thought if I'm really going to use these two months – one as it turned out – to write my thesis, I'd better be sober. So for two weeks – '

'Two weeks!' spurted Les, throwing back his head and crowing. Wes barked and put his snout back on Les's thigh. Mike swung his legs off the bed and stumbled out of the room.

'Mikey,' shouted Les, 'come forth!'

'Yeah, well, I got sick. I got drunk at the end of the second week with the guy who owned the house – mud hut really – I rented. Drank deeply from the communal tap next morning without thinking and just managed to get to the filthy clinic that afternoon before I collapsed. They took all my money. But OHIP reimburses Ontarians abroad. Here's to Canada! *Salut!*'

'Canada!'

There was a stoned interval.

Linda summoned me to fuller consciousness: 'Money, money, money, money . . .' She continued lightly singing what I recognised as a background chorus from *Cabaret*.

'Sure they do,' said Les.

'Do *what*?' I snapped.

'Do-wha diddy, diddy dum diddy doo,' sang Linda, and Les threw in: 'There she was just a-walkin' down the street . . .'

I recognised that song, too, from oldies radio, a group from the sixties called Manafraidman, or something. Pre-punkers, I guess. But how old *was* this Les?

'But what's your book called, Denny?'

'What book?'

And they both laughed at me.

'The big book?' said Les.

'It's not a book, it's a *thesis*,' Linda said.

'Still, it's gotta be called something, and it could be a book, right Denny? Don't lots of people turn their theses into books? . . . Denny?'

'Yeah-yeah, it's got a title, a *working* title: *Who Sez Cortez was Wrong?*'

'Why not *Anal Volcano?*' He laughed, Linda sputtered.

'Not bad,' said I.

Linda scooped up a sheaf of my notes. She scanned whole pages with a speed I've envied in only a couple of other people. And she had to be soundly stoned.

She replaced the notes on my desk, carefully in some kind of order. 'I still say it'd be improved if there was more humour and more you, and less acting like some sorta wise-cracking camcorder.'

'Thanks, Mencken.'

'Who?' they both said.

'Oh, just someone from before your bozo journalist.'

They both howled in surprise, and Wes barked till Les settled him, saying '*What* has gotten into this old boy lately?'

Mike returned with a remarkably large twenty-four of Foster's and a bag of cheesy popcorn the size of a tackling dummy. He'd gone to the IGA for cigarettes and won one hundred dollars in a scratch lotto!

'*Deus ex fortunis!*' I saluted, and Les and Linda cheered.

'None o' your fuckin wetback talk around here, gringo,' said Mike, tearing open the bag and covering my floor with golden balls of popcorn.

We all, Wes included, dug in for the night, or until we slept or passed out.

I remember actually reflecting at some point that I was happier than I'd ever been in my life. But of course, you can't live like that.

I awoke alone, afternoon, and right away I wanted company. I blinked, and between my ears a headache came silently screaming into the world. The room was tidier than when I'd first sat at my desk the night before. I noticed pages of my thesis-in-progress taped to the wall, got up to check it out. They were in some kind of order, if defaced with marginal writing that would require deciphering. A neatly printed index card began the series: 'You *made* us do this, Dennis, and the revisions are mostly yours, too. Linda, Les and Wes. PS. We decided you have a potential bestseller on your hands!!!!' I turned to my whole wall of brown curtains, which were moving dreamily in a cool breeze, and as I'd been doing for the past weeks, I shifted my attention to my lower tract. I flexed my sphincter . . . ? . . . Nothing burned or itched, the demon Montezuma had left me for good. Even with a scorching hangover, the realisation gave me a rush. (Rush!) I touched my throat and in turning away from the windows saw on my desk the large glass measuring cup with its flotilla of ice-cubes. Ignoring the upturned plastic glass, I gulped straight from the cup, the cubes like grace against my upper lip . . . Ahhhhh. Canada. Ontario. Ottawa. Troutstream. *Home. Salut!*

I blinked and was barraged with stroboscopic flashes from late in the night, or early in the morning. Les is wedged cross-legged in a corner and I am standing over him: 'Fuck you and all your *bourgeois* this and *bourgeois* that. Compared to *them*, we live like bloody fucking Chuck and Di! You refugee from the Merry Pranksters! You impish oaf!' *Dear God, am I quoting myself accurately?* And Linda laughing so uncontrollably she had to run to the bathroom with a hand on her bum, and Wes barking wildly and being lightly restrained by Les. I also recall rolling an unconscious Mike off my bed, so that he clumped to the floor and stumbled off to his own bed, thrusting obscenely and twirling an imaginary lariat and wailing about trees falling in the Amazon. And taking his place on the bed with my clothes on, and Les leaning over me close-up like someone about to deliver a pummelling of head-butts, shouting, 'Why are ya kicking Mikey out, Denny? Why? Why'd ya come back, Denny? Why'd ya come back, Denny? . . .'

One other thing, though I remembered it much later. Les and Linda did a song and dance for us, or for me really, some old song about friendship: 'Friendship, friendship, when other friendships are forgot, ours will surely not . . .' Something like that. They stood in the middle of the room with an arm around each other's shoulders and marched back and forth singing and crisscrossing their interior legs – quite a performance for stoned drunks. Or for any couple.

No one reminded anyone of anything the next time we got together to drink and smoke. We all honoured that prime directive for wasted socialising: forget the past, forget the future, do and say what you will in the stoned present, report nothing afterwards. Each time we started from scratch. Over the next few weeks a good half of the marijuana crop was harvested for local consumption. I even returned a number of the struggling plants to my room, to give the striplings the benefit of my splendid light. Our new neighbours' interest in my thesis – Linda's almost exclusively – encouraged me to try whipping it into shape. *More* than encouraged me, I should admit: Linda made many valuable suggestions. Spurred by her enthusiasm, I again began to believe that I had, if not a book, a potentially publishable feature or two. (And who's to say what it takes these days for a book? Many seem pretty disjointed to me.) Anyway, we were getting on like a house on fire. True, Linda never accommodated herself to the idea of all those marijuana plants, but not because she was against toking – obviously not – or because she feared the law. She was afraid only for Les's sake.

One night towards the end of August she surprised me by coming over alone, with no beer and no weed. She had her hair tied back in a matted tail, wore a baggy maroon sweat suit splotchy with blue and black paint. I wondered if she hadn't dressed down to deny any suggestion of impropriety in her first solo visit. But no, for the first time ever she looked beat. She said

Les was doing a job for the Super of our complex development, and that she felt like working on the thesis with me. By then, that's how she put it, *the* thesis, which was accurate.

I gave her the desk chair, which had also become our practice, saying, 'Good for Les. More for Les, eh?' Nothing. 'But shouldn't you be working on lesson plans?'

'Yeah, I guess so,' she said, picking with a thumbnail at the edge of my desk. Then with a poor stab at enthusiasm: 'Fred really likes Les's work, he's even talking to the Complex management about something more permanent.'

'That doesn't seem to make you very happy.'

'Oh no, I think it's great.' She brightened a bit. 'Anyway, do you agree yet that the well scene should be the centre of the whole story?'

'Uh, yeah, but I'm still not sure. I mean, we'd risk hanging the whole thing on the metaphor of a fight, like.'

'Fight? You guys. How do you know they were trying to *dump* the old woman?' She'd never sneered at me like that.

'Hey, I was there, remember.'

'Oh,' she drawled, in a sarcastic manner as alien to her as baggy sweats and dirty hair. '*I* see. You were *there*, were you? You were *there* – '

'Linda, what's going – '

'How do you know they weren't fighting to see who would get to *keep* the old woman, eh? Tell me that, Mencken? What evidence against *that* presented itself to your omniscient peeled eyeball?'

'Holy shit, what a concept!' I recalled the whole scene at the well in Malaconsejado, remembered the way the villagers coddled their old people, and saw as clearly as I now saw Linda's eyes fill that she was right. And in an epiphanic flash I saw my thesis finished, envisioned a series of features, a book.

She rested her forehead on her forearm and convulsed slightly and silently.

I took one step backwards and waited. When the shaking subsided I asked the obvious: 'What happened, Linda?'

She gazed up at me with that long beautiful face smudged and raw, and with those planetary eyes pleading behind the lightly green-tinted shades and drooping lids. 'Can't you see?' she whispered distractedly.

'I don't get it.' Good God, did she have the hots for me?

'Everything's going right for us for once: Les will get work, I've got a job I like, and we have good friends for neighbours. We like where we're living.'

'What then?' She was in love with me?

She sat up straight and turned to stare out the wall of windows. Standing behind the chair I leaned to the left – that side of her face was aglow in the orange light of a setting sun – I leaned right – the other half in a sickly grey shadow. What did she want, this weedy flower child? This anachronism, what could she want with me?

'Nothing, really. Must be PMS or something.' She snuffled and began shuffling my papers. 'It's just . . . Well, you know Mr O'Donaghue who lives next to us?'

'The old guy who teaches at your school?'

'He's only fifty-five, Dennis. But yeah, him. I've got to know him pretty well since my interview. Well, his mother just died and he's taking it really bad, and Fred's pissed off at him for playing these old Elvis Presley records loud half the night, and . . . Oh, I don't know, because I know him Fred wants *me* to talk to him about it. Shit . . .'

'No-no, keep going, I'm with you.'

'Well,' she said evenly, 'Les would kill me if he ever knew I told you this, so scout's honour, okay Dennis?'

She glanced at me and I held up two fingers.

'That's a peace sign, Dennis.' She then spoke to the windows, her voice that throaty whisper tellers of dramatic confidential tales have learned from movies and tv. 'Mrs O'Donaghue's death has been giving Les some bad flashbacks.'

'*Les?* Flashbacks? I'm sorry but I'm – '

'*Flashbacks*, Dennis. You know, recurrences? From when he used to eat handfuls of LSD with his twin brother, way back when, like about twenty-five years ago? When mind-altering drugs were *good* for you? Only they went riding double on Wes's – that's right, same name – motorcycle and drove right into a low wall somebody was building where there hadn't been a wall, and Wes was thrown into a tree trunk and died instantly, and Les spent half a year in traction with a broken back. So he gets bad flashbacks and nightmares, especially around the subject of death. It's weird, like he's having phantom pains for some part of his psyche. They're like waking nightmares, the flashbacks, he goes crazy, mostly crazy jealous. He's always been jealous, but now, since we married this summer, well, I think he's capable of violence. I wanted to tell you about that, too.'

'Wow!'

'Yeah, like *wow*,' she said like some dippy flower child.

'I'm sorry, Linda. It must be hell for Les.'

She swung towards me, mouth open.

'Well, yeah, and for you too.'

'Look, it's Les I care about. When I first met him he was *so* messed up, but at the same time he had such a serene approach to life, like the worst had happened and the rest was Wavy Gravy. I was still a kid, my home life was shit. I took care of Les and he took care of me. But now . . . I think getting married was the big mistake.'

'What? Wait a minute, I still don't get it. You're saying O'Donaghue's mother died and Les is getting flashbacks and he's jealous and you're unhappy . . . because . . .?'

She stood, shuffled and squared my papers. 'I just wanted to warn you that Les is in pretty tender shape these days, and not to be staring at my tits when he's around.'

I laughed. I'd been staring at her face, but now I looked at her baggy sweat shirt and raised my eyebrows lasciviously. And she laughed, thank God. 'I'm sorry, I'm a total pig.'

'No, it's okay, really, I don't mind; I mean, I understand, I guess. Anyway, I can't help you any more right now. You're right, I do have lesson plans. Frank says he thinks they'll have me working the equivalent of full time now that the integration programme is in high gear. Uh, another thing Les doesn't like.'

'Hey, you've helped me, you've helped me! You'll never know how much you've helped me!'

She squinted for too long from those green-tinted glasses, almost as if *she* had reason to be disappointed, eventually smiled, and was again as genuinely pleased as I'd ever seen her. 'Don't forget the

95

humour,' she trilled on her way to the door with her old a-moment-please forefinger in the air. 'And humour, not sarcasm.'

'Gotcha, chief. But I think I can finish myself now.'

'What!' She stopped dead in her tracks and turned with her mouth agape. 'Finish yourself?'

'Well, I just mean – '

'Oh, so you don't need my help any more, is that it?'

'Linda, what the hell's got into you?'

She headed out the door: 'And stop staring at my ass, pig!'

I sat in the growing dark for a long time, and did that which is so difficult to do: thought. About Les and Linda. My thesis. My life. By the time I stood up from my desk in the little light from the street, I knew a new thing (apart from the simple matter of how I would re-vision and finish the thesis). I had seen with laser sight why a story's subjects are always wrong in their soul-stealing anxiety over how they will be portrayed. What most people know about the real story you could cram up a gnat's ass and still have room for a disquisition on journalistic ethics. Unavoidable *subjectivity* confuses their view of this and that. But *you, you* have to get off the spot of your illusory life, stand off from where you're standing and look unflinchingly into the black light. Return: see that empty white space where you were? You must fill it with the stories you invent from the needs of others. That's 'you'. Now you're the real thing: a journalist.

It was a few weeks before anyone came over, and then it was Les alone, one night in late September. Idle Mike was out looking for another place to live, and wouldn't be back till he thought I'd gone to bed. I asked Les if Linda was well, or if Mike or, uh, I had unintentionally given offence.

'Linda's fine, we're working a lot.'

'And that's all?'

'All what, Denny?' His face crinkled deeply.

'Nothing, I guess.'

'Well, okay, just between you and me, friend – and I mean that, scout's honour – one thing is pissing me off, and it's the same reason Linda's not been coming over here much.'

'Yes?'

'She's spending a lot of time with that O'Donaghue character whose old lady croaked over a month ago. He's been to our place for supper almost every night. Linda tries to get him talking about teaching, but he won't stop yacking about Elvis Presley. Then he drags her over to his place to listen to some records. But who knows what's *really* going on over there. I think the guy's going round the bend and taking Linda with him.'

He sat on the floor and opened a beer. He frowned deeply when I refused. Les took it personally when anybody refused to drink with him, and he was indulging so infrequently lately that he took even greater offence than usual. But I was consumed by the thesis.

'Come on, Denny,' he whined shamelessly, 'don't make me drink alone.'

So I didn't. Anyway, for once I was ahead of schedule, my supervisor couldn't keep up with me. I took the beer and inevitable joint and we got silently stoned for a good ten minutes.

Les blew a tunnel of smoke into the cloud, and out of the blue said, 'Shit, now Linda's saying she's gonna work full time at the school.'

'And you don't like that, Les?'

'Hey, Denny, who the *fuck're* you now, Clark Kent or Carl Rogers?'

'It's just that I thought you might want to tell me what's bugging you . . . as a friend?'

'Nothing's bugging me, Denny. What's buggin' you?'

'Me? This has nothing to do with me.'

'Yeah, *you*. You're looking like you been flashing back to Malaconsejado or something.'

'Flashing back? *I* don't get flashbacks.'

No giggle, no frown, no deeply quizzical or probing expression, just his withering stare. Then: 'Just what the *fuck are* you talking about, Denny? Let's clear the air.'

'Nothing.'

'Nothing, eh?' He spoke mincingly: 'You and Linda been having some private little chats about ol' Les and his traumatic history while you're putting your heads together over the great Canadian travel guide to Meh-hee-co?'

'Les, there's no call to ridicule the work.'

'No call my hairy ass, Denny. And did she tell you when she met me I was some burnt-out helpless babe, deeply traumatised by my brother's death?'

'Your twin brother Wes?'

He violently twisted the caps of two beers and slammed one on my desk.

'No, nothing like that. She was just concerned that O'Donaghue's mother's death was giving you fl – reminding you of your brother Wes's death.'

'And did she tell you I get crazy jealous and sometimes beat my forehead against brick walls?'

'What! No way!'

'Look at your face, Denny,' he pointed. 'Some reporter. I could tell she told you that one a long time ago, the way you two're always grinnin' at each other.'

'You and she are the ones with all the secret smiles.'

'Denny, don't you know *anything*?'

'Some things.'

With a hand covering his heart he lay flat on the floor and spoke to the ceiling: 'Linda, Linda, lovely Linda. God, I love that woman. But she's crazy, Denny. Crazy as a bag-woman with a soaked bottom to her bag. I won't trouble you with *her* history, but watch out for her, Denny. Ya gotta believe me.'

'Les, how old is Linda?'

'Forty-one. But that's all I'm tellin' ya, Woodward. How about you, Denny?'

'Forty-one. *Whew*. And where's Wes?'

'Don't know, amigo. Your guess is as good as mine. Hey, isn't that the motto of Carleton's school of journalism!'

I lay down beside him and we had a good laugh together. But I wanted to hear more: 'Are we getting stoned or what?'

Long afterwards I pieced together some of the key confrontations of that night's stone, one of our deepest, and our second to last. My hounding Les again about the wilted flower-power life he was trying to lead in the grave nineties, and insisting, on no evidence whatsoever, that Linda wanted more stability in her life now. Les sneering maniacally that I didn't know a thing, that I got everything backwards. Why did I go to Malaconsejado anyway? (I think he actually had me pinned by the twisted shirt front against my poster of Ken Danby's Goalie.) The truth!

'Fieldwork, I needed material,' I laughed, because I believed it was all a game anyway.

'And where's your material, Denny?'

'I'm working on it, Lester.'

He applied a twist and lightly bounced my head off the wall. 'Where is it, Denny?'

'Whaddya mean? Hey, ease up, my friend, you're choking me – it's here, it's right here in my room.'

'Ha!' he yelped and slightly reversed his grip on my shirt. 'Here? What do you mean, *here*? Malaconsejado and all those poor people are *here* and you still need my wife to tell you what the fuck you're writing about?'

'Not any more, my friend.'

'What really happened, Denny?' He snarled and twisted slowly, lifting me up on tiptoes.

'Nothing happened, Les. I mean it. For Christ's sake!' And he let up again. 'That was the whole problem. Nothing happened already. I had to make up most of my notes.'

'Your notes? . . .' He was startled, baffled, frowning bemusement. 'I *knew* it,' he smiled, letting go and smoothing my shirt front. He returned to his loose lotus beside the desk. 'Nobody takes notes with semicolons.' He cuffed his temple with the heel of his palm: 'Fuckin' mind games.'

I grew brave: 'You knew what? You know nothing.'

He snorted, shook his head, then returned his attention to me as if with an effort, giggled. 'I know that any writer worth shit would be over interviewing the welfare cases in the Project before he'd be off making up shit about strangers in Mexico.'

I laughed along, grabbed my beer and sat beside him. We lit up.

I slowly exhaled a long toke: 'That's right, nothing happened, *nada*. Just like nothing happened after all those summers of love in the sixties.'

'Nothing happened? Look around you, oh Denny boy. People gave a shit then, and we changed some of the things we didn't like. Look at the way women are now. Look at Linda. Look at you.'

'I like the way I am, Wavy Gravy. Look at yourself.'

'That's good, Denny. That's what I mean. That's the problem, and you don't even know it.'

'Yeah, right, you shitty hippies had all these beautiful dreams of organic equality for man and woman and all our animal companions. Trouble was, opium *was* the opium of your masses. Talk about naiveté. We have dreams of a better society, too, my friend, only we know that to be effectual you have to *work* from within the entrenched power system.'

'Denny, you sound like that jerk Jerry Rubin bad-mouthin' Abby Hoffman on Oprah.'

'So? That doesn't make it any less true.'

'Sure it does. The medium is the message. You're the reporter, you should know that.'

'We're just more practical, more *realistic*.'

He made big lips and nodded mockingly: 'That, my friend, is about on a par with your kissing dog story.'

'You've lost me.'

'Know what else I know, Denny? Something else you don't wanna know: you're giving poor old Mike the boot and that guy loves you like a brother. Shit, you guys even look alike . . . 'cept he's got more hair. But you've used him up, you're finished with him. So out he goes, right?'

'Out he goes.'

'*That's your* dream, Denny.'

And he laughed his impish laugh like a well-timed engine.

In October school shifted into a higher gear for Linda and me, and that gave all of us a good excuse for seeing zero of each other socially. One Wednesday morning about ten-thirty while waiting for my bus on Inglis, I saw Linda go into Troutstream Donuts with that O'Donaghue character. She had her left hand on the small of his back, and he had his hands crossed on his crotch, his chin on his chest, looking in his brown suit like someone being taken along quietly.

★

As events unfolded, that was the morning after the police finally found the body of the twelve-year-old girl who'd been molested and murdered and stuffed into a big blue dumpster out behind the IGA. It was the first murder ever in Troutstream. The victim had been missing for three days. She was last seen wearing a pink sweat shirt advertising the Troutstream Fun Fest. The Ottawa papers repeatedly called this last detail 'an horrific irony'. (An!) I don't remember her name. I don't mean to appear shockingly insensitive, but the story appealed to the journalist in me . . . sporadically. I was going through the horrible business of final revisions to meet thesis-submission deadline for Fall Convocation.

That Friday Linda and O'Donaghue disappeared.

Les quit working part time for Fred the Super and began drinking full time, eventually begging beer money off me. I last saw him semi-coherent in his own place. I'd gone over to see if I could recoup any of my 'loans'. It was a warm and colourful Indian summer day. Out back past the ten metres of tolerable lawn and the ninety metres of weed and scrub, the renewed sun made the plastic green wall shine like emerald, while from beyond cars could be heard zipping along the Bypass like revitalised insects. Les's interior door was open, but no one answered my calls. The aluminum door was unlocked, so I noisily let myself in. I heard a plaintive call, 'Mike?' I found him upstairs in the front bedroom they'd used as nursery for the marijuana plants. He was sitting in his loose lotus like a big lost kid among clay pots filled with dirt and flayed yellowish stalks. He said O'Donaghue had wheedled a paid sick leave and was living with Linda in a hotel in Smiths Falls. He lay, or collapsed, on his side, hugged a huge pot and sang some old Elvis song: 'Are you lonesome tonight? Do you miss me tonight? Are you sorry . . .' Then he just lay there flat on his back and laughed and laughed and laughed. His filthy toe-nails had cut through his caked grey thermal socks. He wore no shirt under his bib overalls. His chest hair was greying, his tits radiating stretch marks to his pits.

Wes lay in a corner, apparently unconscious, his chest heaving sporadically. By then he roamed freely throughout Troutstream and the surrounding greenbelt. He had all sorts of burrs and junk stuck in his hair. Patches were missing along his back, like he'd been in a scrap with a pack of badgers. Only there were no scars. The exposed skin was a smooth boiled pink, like he'd been prepped for surgery.

Then Les and Wes disappeared.

Then Mike took off, without any extra prompting. One cool morning he was standing in the living room with his duffle bag at his feet like some faithful old hound. 'Dennis,' he said, swinging the bag on to his shoulder, 'you're such a fucking asshole, I'd need a proctologist just to begin to figure you.'

Like I said, Mike was a witty guy. I may even miss him.

Postcript. My supervisor went gaga over my finished thesis. He showed it to all his colleagues, who unanimously agreed that it was better than any thesis in journalism they'd ever read. Well, not all agreed. The tearful clown who'd taught my first-year survey course, one Professor North, said I'd merely acquired the jaded journalist's trick. The only impressive thing was that I'd learned it (I heard he'd said 'been corrupted' by it) so young. The *cause célèbre* of my thesis presented him an opportunity to give fresh currency to his old coinage for this trick. I remembered it well from his survey course: 'Detached Retina'. He'd explained it was something that could happen to prize fighters after the legs go and too many blows to the head. If they were lucky it ended their career. With journalists, it was the ability to observe without seeing. Conversely, detached retina could extend a journalist's career; in fact, apart from teaching, he'd snickered, it was the only way to a long career. And when, way back then in first year, I'd asked him what all that was supposed to mean, he'd explained that detached retina was a mechanically correct – even exceptional because focusing intensely only on surfaces – eyeball without the impulse to convey meaningful messages to the brain. *Meaning*, I'd sneered just audibly (even then!). He'd held up the class for a minute to stare at me with his almighty compassionate eyeballs like he was *so* sorry for my journalist's imperiled soul. 'Or,' he announced, 'we might say instead that a journalist with detached retina is like a fighter on whom no one can lay a glove. Nor can he hit. Float like a butterfly, float like a butterfly.' A *journalist*, we were never *reporters*.

But his opinion of *Who Sez Cortez Was Wrong?* is the lone exception. (And the irony is that my thesis is pregnant with meaning, as the cliché artists say; fabricated meaning, true, but what other sort is there? Though I'm not sure about the title any longer. I need something with more spin. Juan for the Money? . . . That might do for my IMF piece.) All the other professors are stopping me in hallways and approaching me in the graduate lounge with their Styrofoam coffee cups in an attitude of supplication. They praise my work for its refusal to impose a 'master narrative' (one eager beardo even said a 'fascist point of view'), for its deceptive and actual randomness, for its salty sense of humour ('vicious sarcasm', North was reported to have said). They encourage me to do a book. They promise to use their 'contacts' in the publishing world. (These nerds would need contacts just to see to the bottle-bottom lenses of their glasses.) They ask what I'm going to do for an encore. They suggest I apply for teaching positions. But I wouldn't be a journalism teacher, I tell them. Those who can't, etc. I'm a writer.

I permitted the student newspaper, the *Carleton Banner*, to do a story on my experiences in Malaconsejado. The young female student journalist they assigned to interview me would have done anything I asked. But I've had no sexual desires since the brief period of gluttony I allowed myself immediately following my return from Mexico. I permitted the *Banner* to publish what used to be my favourite section – because the catalyst – of what is destined to be a bestseller. Here follow the paragraphs, which are atypical only insofar as they retain too much of that thing called I:

Every morning the sun like an AIDS mouth coughing blood screams down upon my defenceless head: 'Go away! Leave us alone! Go home!'

Yet each morning I am impelled by some half-understood impulse to gather with the women of the village round the communal cistern. There, brown water trickles like mock-

Hope from a rusted pipe like the spike of a contaminated needle.

Some would say there is only Death here, fat Garcia Death wearing a red-and-white tablecloth for a bib and sitting on a small stool overlooking the square, his knife and fork held like banderillas.

But the square has been alive for hours with rooting pigs and twitching chickens doing a hat dance on the hemisphere's hot stove.

Beside the stone cistern lies an emaciated German Shepherd with its tongue in the dust like some refugee from a Graham Greene story. I squat for a long time and knead the nape of his neck, ruffle his flanks. It would be the only human affection he's ever been shown. I cup some water in my palms for him.

I have not drunk from this communal tap in the week since my arrival. I had thought my resolve necessary, because to slake thirst at such a fountain would be to risk dysentery. But I am determined this morning, for I feel in a way that scorns the reported facts that if I am ever to know these people, the silent majority of Malaconsejado, their inner lives, I must allow them the privilege of sharing with me their most precious possession, their water.

It is here that the community comes together for an hour each day in a manner unknown amongst their more affluent neighbours to the north. To the careless eye every morning looks the same, but to the eye of discernment each day begins differently.

This morning, for instance, a dispute erupted between a husband and wife. My Mexican was just good enough for me to learn that the wife – tall and slim for a Mexican, though with the typical mournful face and coal-black eyes – had spent the previous night with another man, a *gringo*, for money. The husband – short and fat, but in a way expressing reserves of strength, and with a magnificent head as square and brown as an adobe – was in the kind of rage that comes and goes among the Malaconsejadones as impetuously as a dust dervish. He was enraged not because of the infidelity but because the wife, Lucinda, was supposed to have been at Malatreka on the north side of the island taking care of his ailing brother, Jesus (hay' soos).

In a careless display of outrage (for my gringo's eye perhaps?), the wife lunged and tore off the husband's shirt. In the sudden silence he stood dumbfounded, with his hands held wide and gesturing alternately at the indifferent sun and his tattered shirt (thinking no doubt that a shirt costs him a week's wages). Matted black hair brushed with grey covered womanly breasts like leather saddlebags on a burro.

Finally he glanced at his wife, looked down at himself, snorted, and began giggling. She fluted a laugh like a call to love. And the two of them walked off towards one of Malaconsejado's twelve *cantinas* with arms around one another's shoulders like children in a three-legged race.

I had been tempted to intervene, and was pleased to see confirmed how ignorantly rash any such action would have been, how clumsy must be any interference in the involved dance of others' lives. We participate by invitation only, we must be given house room.

I bowed and drank deeply from the pipe. Doubtless it was a wisp of cloud, but for a moment as I straightened there by the cistern, the sun, that wide indifferent eye, closed in a wink of approval.

Jesus, I learned later over some neighbourly mescal, was in the terminal stages of an AIDS-caused illness. I jokingly asked if the name Judas were ever used, but my friend looked shocked and blessed himself. Malaconsejadones view humour with a suspicion founded on deeply held religious beliefs.

Next for me? Oh, I don't know. I'm tempted to pay a visit to Linda and that O'Donaghue character in Smiths Falls. There's something about his story intrigues the writer-journalist in me. Why, for instance, did he choose to idolise the young Elvis? And did he *really* dress like the young Elvis when he cracked-up that day in his classroom – the cowboy shirt, the baggy pants, the two-tone shoes – or only as today's *Happy Days* crowd thinks the young Elvis dressed? And, for that matter, why Elvis? I mean, what was the guy anyway that people care so much? A fat drugged-out greaseball who pumped his voice with tons of reverb. That's why I take my lead from the costume. One thing for sure: no more Third World trips for me.

・6・

Shall I Come Back Again?

•

Indian summer and the sun is strong again. Out back, burdock is the only thing plentiful in the rough ground between our row of town houses and the new Troutstream Bypass. Walking there this morning I'd found myself squinting through a hole in the Bypass's green barrier at the workers painting lines and planting doomed shrubs along the highway. (I am not morbid. Do you know of even a two-year-old road system whose shrubbery has survived? What with megatonnage of exhaust and acid rain and . . . But let us put a stop to that line of thinking right now.) This morning I could stare through the hole, thanks to my remembering the sunglasses I bought last month at the beginning of my troubles. It was not punched out frivolously by vandals, that hole. It is a mechanically cut circle, laser smooth, with wisps of white plastic like frazzled nerves still clinging in its emptiness. To all others a mystery, that hole, like those perfectly executed circles in the grain fields of England. But to me that signal hole presents yet further evidence of the Vegas Porker's return.

The older workers putting the finishing touches on the Bypass, those who've endured decades of menial labour, are built close to the ground, with stubby legs and arms, and disproportionately long torsos. Though this morning a gangling boy slouched lasciviously beside the traffic sign he held carelessly, watching a petite

107

girl in yellow hard hat fringed by straggly red hair picking her way through the eternal mud with a cardboard box of coffee and doughnuts. Transients doubtless, the two of them. Perhaps they will find one another and run off to Smiths Falls. . . . Nothing happened. The silver-sided caterer's truck blew its horn loudly, folded up and shot off like the Lone Ranger.

The boy and girl aside, the norm for road workers remains male, fiftyish and stout, men formed along the lines of the voyageurs who opened up this great country, those top-heavy adventurers for whom long legs were a disadvantage in the close quarters of the company's great canoes, who could paddle all day at forty strokes per minute and portage for two miles with four hundred pounds on their backs, 'at a dog-trot'. So Hugh Mac-Lennan says in the essay I assign my mixed grade seven and eight class every year. (Good old Hugh. He's dead now, you know. All my life I had counted on him for reassurance and guidance. Rereading *The Watch that Ends the Night* held me together for a while after my mother's recent death. What a waste of time. What avoidance. Day and night, watch or not, the Vegas Porker was there, waiting, watching . . . acting!)

Were those voyageurs different from you and me and our road crews? You bet they were! They *had* to have been. In the wilderness they would have experienced atrocities we only read about and watch on tv today (albeit every day). But did those experiences threaten their sanity? Would they have allowed themselves even a pause at the paddle to reflect on the violation and mutilation, even the ingestion, of a brother's wife and kids at Fort Michilimackinac? Let alone grief therapy. Not likely! *Stroke, stroke, stroke,* with but a moving rest to stuff their faces full of pork fat, then *stroke, stroke, stroke . . .*

Aye, Hugh, once upon a time there was much indeed to be said for hard work and duty, those Carlylean virtues that served us well until the big boys discarded them like redundant workers in the corporate body. Aye indeed, it would seem that the collective heart has undergone a severe downsizing.

I actually used to hope with the likes of Carlyle and MacLennan that the past could live still in the present. And now? Well, for one thing I lost my tiny mind recently. For some others, I still

remember very little on my own, live wholly in the present, find
my voice only in fits and starts. I have to write longhand with an
old-fashioned fountain pen to recover even that much. Thus this,
you and I . . . Aye and Hugh – hue and cry – Ha! – the Porker is
afoot!

(These days I also derive unhealthy distraction from such
trivialities; I refer of course to the interchangeable *u* in *thus* and *i* in
this.)

Avoidance aside, the veracity of what follows relies almost
exclusively on what Linda told me yesterday on our walk down to
the soccer fields, and on what I'd managed to drag to the surface
with my therapist.

Two other caveats before we launch. For the past few weeks I
have been weaning myself from medication, mostly antidepres-
sants and global tranquillisers. As I do so I find my memory
improves; I also find that a deranging pain recurs intermittently.
It's a delicate balancing act, this reality thing. And finally: since the
onset of my illness I've displayed the symptom (or developed the
talent) of talking to myself in different voices. You will please bear
with me. Now onward intrepidly with nary a backward glance:
stroke, stroke, stroke . . . The Vegas Porker is hot on our homonymic tail.

It should come as no surprise that the author of an elementary
Canadian history textbook – *Pathfinders and Ploughers* – considered
himself a lifelong conservative. So conservative was I that I
described myself as a capital-T Tory and vehemently distinguished
my rooted sense of humanity's fallibility and responsibility from
the sorry individual of techno-mechanistic capitalism, that projection of the new breed of babbling neo-conservative, those projec-
tors who disguise their small-l liberal avariciousness, their own
unpalatable hunger for individual fulfilment, behind buzz-things
that are best summed up in their corruption of such terms as
'progress' and 'family values'. I would be lying, though, to deny
that my practical heart was briefly gladdened by the triumphs of
that troika of neos – Thatcher, Reagan, Mulroney. I was easily
fooled. I couldn't help it. All my ideas were second-hand. Thus I was
handily manipulated, perhaps because I always considered myself

immune, and was encouraged to think so by my manipulators. This is not paranoia or another conspiracy theory. 'Manipulators' refers simply to the highest echelon of the global business-military-political consortium, and to their number one agent, the Vegas Porker.

I had other reasons for thinking my citadel self as impregnable as Graceland. For example, among my fellow teachers I took every opportunity to boast of not owning a television. And now? I am the fat frenetic owner of a large-screen high-definition tv on which I can watch multiple shows simultaneously on smaller windows, a state of the art VCR, and a satellite dish that sits between my back door and the green wall of the Bypass like some laser weapon warning aliens to buzz off. (Simply a simile: I don't believe in little green men.) Still on sick leave, I watch tv all day and all night, though no show for more than three minutes. I eat round the clock, snack food, junk food, hungry all the time; I've put on so much weight that I'm comfortable only in my black velvet housecoat belted loosely. I never think of real sex.

I had feared that receiving some one hundred and fifty channels would overwhelm me with new information, but I find the deluge strangely reassuring. And I've still to hear a single memorable thing I'd not picked up from my colleagues' disjointed conversations or read in my kids' current events essays, or simply picked mysteriously from the very crowded ether. For example: I already knew exactly where I was when my gigantic hole on the world presented a pinprick-pupil close-up of flies feasting or depositing around what looked like a barely living infant girl's dark glazed eyes. I was watching a ten-year-old (!) in the Third World, Somalia or some such dreadful locale. I was tearfully watching an innocent victim of famine and drought, watching along with the misty-eyed anchorperson who'd just swung away from watching a big screen at her back. A bracing experience, we were both better for having faced it for a while. 'All the news worth watching' in three minutes or less, all from elsewhere, and all as eerily familiar as I suppose the afterlife will be to residents of Erie, Pennsylvania. . . . Sleep, mostly I sleep in front of the tv, and can't remember whether I've been watching a G-Seven Summit on Global Warming or dreamed it, or if I'm being monitored for correct behaviour.

I rise to the occasion and turn up my air-conditioner full blast. Then the tube, virtual I and reality have reached rapprochement.

Primarily, though, I purchased my equipment to monitor for clues of the Vegas Porker's movements. I stake out my big screen with a forbearance equal to my forebears' dedication to their great canoes. *Stroke, stroke, stroke . . .*

Naturally, one who misunderstood himself as I did wasted a lot of time looking intently into his past for understanding of his present troubles. I was encouraged in this vain pursuit by my therapist, a neo-Adlerian whom I was seeing once a week courtesy of the Carleton Separate School Board. (I found him sensitive and intelligent but tied to his clock and a touch Teutonic in the psychic clinches. Once when I balked at his suggestion that I visit my old kindergarten class – he meant the school I'd attended as a boy – he actually said, 'But you *vill!*' We both near died of embarrassment, he's as Canadian as I am.) But there was nothing in my past to explain my present, nothing of a pathological or even neurotic nature. In truth, I can remember only good things about my first home. My mother was loving and affectionate, highly literate, a teacher too, and the kindest person I've had in my life. I was her only child, though a twin had been stillborn (they said). Until I reached adolescence I had plenty of friends. Oh, my father had his problems, a tendency to alcoholism, uninterrupted temper, but then, who hasn't?

No. As I'd suspected all along, the present is to blame for my present troubles. That appears so obvious it rightly sounds tauto-logical. But who wants to believe *that*, that *their* time, and consequently they themselves, are responsible for the danger we are all in? Not my therapist, that blindly encouraging man of zero faith.

What I really needed was a good humanistic phenomenologist. A disciple of the late R. D. Laing would have been nice, someone who would simply have *heard* the truth of what I was saying and not have kept goading me to take control of my life. Someone like Linda. But she's gone too, to Sarnia to look after her husband. To be fair, I should add Linda's name to my shortlist of kind people. Though her kind care was not what my Adlerian friend called 'unconditional'. Besides, I'm trying to forget her, because it shames me what I did to her marriage. Not to be mysterious: she was in an only slightly less tender state than I, losing purpose and direction in her life (my therapist's words), and we found each other and ran off to Smiths Falls. It's all very embarrassing blurted out like that, especially the Smiths Falls business.

But enough of that for now. Already I'm losing my thread through this maze.

The present: when those workers on the Troutstream Bypass, those soft impressions of the original voyageurs, finish the land-scaping job, this community will be even more isolated. On a map it already appears bypassed: a green oasis surrounded by protective greenbelt a good fifteen kilometres east of Ottawa. It's laced with crescents and *culs-de-sac* within crescents within crescents, not a straight sidewalk to be trod, so that a lunch-hour walk leads me back to where I began, enclosed in a secure circuit, within a green enclosure. Marvellous! The green barrier protecting me from the sights and sounds of the new Bypass had seemed the green icing on our green communal cake. Until from my bathroom window I spotted the hole.

For ten years I wished and wished that I lived in the real Troutstream, the neighbourhoods north of Inglis, the real homes, the 'detached houses', as the real estate agents call them. On Sundays I walked dizzily around those involved verdant crescents, visiting every open house. Most of the agents came to know me as a browser only, but they didn't mind, as I offered them opportunity to ply a body with mock coffee and silly pitches. But I only worked over there, teaching at Holy Family Separate School on Izaak Walton Road. I live south of Inglis in the middle of a cramped brown row that looks like a turd from Mann Quarry surrounded by the rot of our soft age: a strip-mall, two doughnut stores, three video rental stores, an arcade, more banking machines than public telephones, numerous self-serve gas stations, a tiny library of cinder block with the weeds pressing up against its windows. Concrete and obscene graffiti everywhere.

Oh, it may well be true what the tourists say: Ottawa *is* a pretty city. From certain approaches – say, the Nicholas on-ramp heading west on the Queensway – Parliament Hill rises like Disneyland's Magic Kingdom. Exactly: Tinker Bell and Michael Jackson should be giving tours. But for most of us, Ottawa is *way* over there somewhere, a postcard inhabited by old money, senior civil servants, high-tech executives, the wannabe rich and that part of the sinking middle class still willing to slip its fiscal neck into an even more unquittable mortgage. To the sensible rest of us, Troutstream North is one of the few remaining communities that looks affordable, holding out the possibility of recovering and continuing that spankingly clean dream of the suburban fifties. That was a good dream, make no mistake. (You have a better? Both parents working for less and the kids regimented all day all year in that vision of the bogey life with which we used to ridicule the communists? Perfect.) The piled irony is that the vast majority of Troutstreamer adults, the swarming horde of us who make possible the northerners' suburban dream – we whose kids fill the rosters of the T–ball and soccer teams those north of Inglis organise for their one-child two-income families – we live cramped between Inglis and the Bypass in our very own turd-world to the south, between the dream and the nightmare. The nightmare being the Godforsaken Project east of the IGA. Forsaken not by God, if the truth be told, but by us.

Don't be misled by the 'we whose kids' phrase above. I have no family. Since graduating from teachers college I've taught for ten years each in three different cities: London (not England), Kingston (not Jamaica), and now near Ottawa (but not Ottawa, not even the real Troutstream). I'm fifty-five and already being pressured by the board to take early retirement (now more than ever). I still have hair, but not enough to hide the new liver spots on a scalp beginning to look like shitty underwear turned inside out. I came close to marrying twice, but each time the relationship was broken off (not by me).

I often used to look at my life and think: Am I one of those who has nothing to live for, potential suicide at best, serial killer at worst? Other times I would think (as I will henceforth): What a compelling dream my life is, I can't wait to see what happens next. And feel that I'm embarked on an heroic adventure – *coureur de moi!*

My therapist said I display classic symptoms of manic depression. Cheering fellow.

Analysis aside, I didn't buy the wraparound sunglasses last month to hide my eyes or to look cool, they were part of the act. And I don't say that I do look cool. My kids said it. When I entered the classroom that morning, Cash said, 'It's Michael Jackson!' And his crowd – Blake, Melissa, Ashley (the Soapies, I call them) – went, 'Ooooo, Dude-man.' I did a passable moonwalk a good three yards, snapped off the shades with my left hand and slipped the fingers of my right inside my shirt front, then shifted my legs and head robotically. (I keep in shape and up to date, I have to in this business.) They loved it. Though Christine's group – Michael Sheridan, Veronica Davies, Leslie Cameron, and the twins, Rosalie and Adrian Richards (the Desperados) – simply shifted in their seats, eager to get to work.

But I guess I looked okay, though you'd never mistake me for that skinny negro. I'll concede this much: it may not be rock'n'roll he sings, but that Michael Jackson has admirably carried on the tradition of the pure entertainer. And you can take that to the bank, honey.

Since I've already clumsily told you my age, I may as well dispense with all pretence and simply describe myself. I am exactly six foot, one hundred and seventy pounds. I have straight black hair combed in a modified pompadour, navy-blue eyes, a clear complexion. I'm ideally proportioned and (I'm being perfectly frank) breathtakingly handsome, if with lips of a voluptuousness that suggests overlong breast-feeding. Women take a second helping when they think I'm not looking. (Though I'm never distracted; in fact I see too much, one of the perils of my stint as a teacher.) My favourite colour is black. My favourite music is gospel, rockabilly and hard-driving rock'n'roll (no surprises there!): Amy Grant, Stray Cats, George Thoroughgood and the Destroyers – those three are about the best these days, though I'll still take Mahalia, Gerry Lee, Roy and Carl over anybody. My second engagement ended because of my nightly practice of loudly playing my music into the wee hours of the morning. I tried headphones for a while, but they restricted my movement. I need to feel the walls breathe, brother. And yes, dear, the sideburns *are* real.

I don't mind living alone at all; in fact, I sometimes think I'm happiest alone. Though, as I said, I loathe where I'm living, hate *how* I'm living, and sometimes dream I'm the father of a family in the real Troutstream, all boys, 'cause I like having the boys 'round. On one of my open-house walkabouts in the middle of September (about fifteen days after Momma died), I visited the home of three young fellas on Anglers Court, two of whom I'd already taught. I decided to stay. The family had disregarded the agent's advice and remained *à maison*. Bad career move. I accepted their invitation and took a seat in the family room, and chatted about teaching and how well their home was appointed (whatever the heck that means!) and talked and talked, and asked for tea, and 'Tommy, you be a good fella and bring me the paper', and kicked off my shoes and put up my feet on the ottoman and insisted they turn the tv back on the football game . . . until they had to call two other agents to get me outta there. Man, I was hot!

Don't feel too embarrassed for me, for that's only the third-to-worst thing Linda remembered for me. Above it stands what I did in my classroom and what I did to her. And who knows what else no one remembers. . . . But no, don't feel bad for me, be concerned for yourselves and your children: the Vegas Porker is at large. I have seen his hole. And his footprint by the stream.

My colleagues, my fellow teachers, are mostly in their late thirties or early forties. Each year we get one or two fresh faces in their early twenties, but there's really no more room for new blood in the cushy 'profession' of teaching. Linda was this year's token new blood, though she was not as young as she looked. Anyway, my fellow teachers all claim they want to be out of the profession in another three years, tops, always three years. Unlike me, they really have no idea what they're going to do for an encore. Some still talk maniacally of fortunes to be made in real estate; others wistfully refurbish old dreams of owning their very own wooden toy store in a small town, or a pizza franchise, that sort of thing. Anything but embrace the reality of a lifetime spent teaching at

Holy Family here in beautiful Troutstream, where many of them have already lived for years and years, north of Inglis. To be fair to my co-workers, some do see their life-writing on the wall, and have begun casting about among their colleagues for an AIDS-safe affair.

Casting about in Troutstream. Yes. And see earlier: the Vegas *Porker* is at *large*. But don't expect any more of those distracting verbal coincidences. I am also unique in that I freely admit to having no sense of humour. I say this because I believe a humorous sensibility indicates a lack of commitment, and – what must again appear pleonastic – a failure to take life seriously, *ever*. I stress my humourlessness, too, because people sometimes think I'm joking and misunderstand what I'm about.

For example, a few weeks ago I suggested generally to the yackety-yak teachers' room that they should form a consortium of chinchilla ranchers.

The room silenced, as it often does when I speak, and Principal Clint snickered into his magnum of coffee: 'Must be nice, Frank, having no family or mortgage.'

'*Nice?* . . . Hey, people, I'm serious. I saw it on the shoppers' channel last night. There's big bucks to be made, fur's making a comeback! There's gold in dem dare pelts!'

'What?' Clint grimaced. 'You don't even own a – ' He stared at me, then frowned at Julie Martin and Marge Slater like maybe they really should think about chinchillas. I figure Clint, short, fat and balding, is already stirring late-thirtysomething-and-barren Julie's coffee at Troutstream Donuts, maybe even dangling a V-P-ship (and who knows what else?) in front of her. Late-forties Marge calls all the men Mister, acts like she's everybody's Momma, because she's sacrificed her body to the great god gravity and Momma's the only role left for her. She came over and placed her chubby hand on my forearm and talked to me quietly, if inappropriately, about how upset they all were over my Momma's death.

'*Dead?*' I said loudly. 'Don't you mean *murdered*?'

'Oh, Mr O'Donaghue,' she whispered, 'you don't want to upset everyone. You're confused over . . . over Teresa's murder.'

I whispered: *The Vegas Porker.*

But she acted like *I'd* insulted *her*. She changed the subject back to my Momma, who'd passed away *weeks* before. So you go figure.

Anyway, the new blood, this Linda chick, she intervened and took me out for a walk, talking to me like I was one of her 'mentally challenged' freaks. But that's okay. If I could show you a snap of this babe, you'd understand: beautiful horsy mug, bod like a Botticelli. The way she flutes my name, giving it two syllables, puts me in mind of my own Momma.

Really, though, it spoiled one's idea of Troutstreamers, that fast-food franchises and toy shops should form the goal of their thought when, if only they'd see it, the sunlight of north Troutstream was so much better.

No, I can't see any of them making a break and a go of it in the real world. Their pay cheques are generous and bi-weekly, their families growing, and their household's second income – from moonlighting stints as carpet-cleaning salespeople, part-time clerks, fast-food slingers, that sort of thing – is either disappearing in the economic sink-hole opening beneath us all or becoming inadequate for their accustomed lifestyle: mini-vans, weekly parties, month-long globe-trotting vacations every summer, the best steady scotch, expensive clothes, and monster homes littered with enough electronic junk to mount a moonshot. Fortysomethings, they look haunted by the bone-knowledge that they will fail to keep diets and meet jogging quotas. And if they've managed so far to look on average five years younger than I know them to be, they have grown mentally and morally flabby. Like their roost-returned unemployable kids of affluence, it's come home to them: you too will die, are dying. It's sapping them.

Change? Them? They don't have the discipline, the will, only a weary old appetite that excites more jaded appetite.

Still, I can sympathise with my colleagues in their desire to get out of teaching. People think it's a cushy job: short hours, two weeks off at Christmas, two months every summer. But in addition to the tedium of teaching the same thing year in and year out, and the realisation that in early middle age one is advancing nowhere,

in addition even to the infantilism of always having a principal –
in addition to all that and much more, the job is made unbearable
by the pervasive stink of kids. Man, *nothing* smells of fetid
humanity like a room full of twelve-and-thirteen-year-old bodies
cooking on the hormone burner in late June. Boys with ferocious
BO and other odours attesting to hurried shaking and wiping,
unprepared girls menstruating right in class (two or three per
year), all stirred into a mixture of drenched penny aftershave (!)
and perfume and wafted up front on the nausea-inducing warmth
of an open beauty-salon door darkened all morning by fat hags.

Imagine the sort of pervert who could tolerate such a stench!
. . . But perverts do, regularly these days. And now even right
here in green, secluded Troutstream. That's the kind of world we
live in today, the larger world to which I will soon be revealing
myself big time.

So, some ingrates complain about the way adolescents smell. But
these kids are great, I love 'em. There's not a one of 'em I don't
love, even blind Michael Sheridan, who would like nothing so
much as to see my guts trailing from the jaws of one of those
heavy-metal beasts he's always writing about.

Here's another way of saying what's happened to my trapped
colleagues: their desires have become needs. And when that
happens you're finished. Not that I still can't sympathise. Because
this all goes back to your Momma, and no one loves his Momma
more than I love mine (though she's long dead, almost two
months ago now, God rest her soul). We never get over leaving
our Mommas, or their leaving us. We spend our lives trying to fill
the hole left by that loss. With food, with love, with work, and
some with perversity. But that hole could swallow the sun and
still be as cold and dark and hungry as death. The big money boys
have always known this. The Colonel explained it to me this way,
the one time he told me what we was really sellin'. You see, the
big money boys convince us if we buy this or that we'll be sexier
or happier, or whatever, that if we throw bigger houses and better
Nintendo into the Momma hole we'll begin filling it up. Hogwash,
he spat. Then winked: But damn sweet-smellin' hogwash far as

you an' me are concerned. You see, the magical thing about the Momma hole is it has no bottom. Colonel said it's just like Jesus' basket of loaves and fishes, only in reverse. Colonel knows Momma and me are very religious. He's very religious too, he said, the Colonel. An' he told me to eat whatever I want, 'cause I got a high metabolism. I love fried chicken, the other Colonel's.

An' then, at the end of a lifetime spent tryin' to fill the Momma hole, you die. Like the bumper sticker says, man: 'Life's a bitch, then you die.'

If I could just talk to the Colonel again for a few minutes, instead of that quack, he'd know how to vanquish the Vegas Porker, he'd help me . . . But the Colonel's gone too, long gone. Everybody's gone.

You *see*? It's happened again: the occurrence within a few lines of the two Colonels, fried chicken, and my quack, all associated with different kinds of nurturing and nourishment. *Something* is definitely controlling this, a *thing* that cares only for sick puns and not a piffle for humankind. Perhaps if I just let it all come out, serve as its medium and let it exhaust itself through me, perhaps then it would leave me alone. Or I would die. But I must find out what it is, what it wants. Maybe it's chosen me for something special, some noble purpose. . . . Heaven forbid the Vegas Porker is behind *it* too. *Or*, what if this *thing* is behind the Vegas Porker? . . . What a thought to conjure with.

For a while there people – shrinks, neighbours – persisted in asking me how I knew Elvis was alive. Had I seen him? Talked with him? Did I know someone who'd seen him? Had I too spotted the King at Burger King? Look, honey, it's not that easy to explain. I'd never believed in anything before. I don't think I ever really believed in Santa Claus. As far back as I can remember, I remember doubting everything mysterious. But with Elvis it's different. I know he's alive. And I don't mean alive in the spirit of his music or his legend or the good influence he's having on ordinary people. I mean alive and walking sleekly upon this earth in a black leather outfit like the one he wore for his '68 comeback special on tv. (As though Elvis had to make a comeback.) And of course I don't mean anything blasphemous, like Elvis has become some new-age Jesus Christ. Look, you can believe all you want about miracles and mysteries – virgins having babies, a man being God, *life* after *death*, whatever – and I won't contradict you. I just never could believe any of that, though Momma was devout. Elvis is no God, and Elvis would be the first to sneer if you suggested such a thing, if he didn't have the boys throw you right out of his Graceland pad. All I'm saying is that Elvis is alive. Proof? I don't need any. I know Elvis is alive as surely as I know I'm alive. I can't prove something like that. Knowing *is* the proof. *You* prove you're not dead. Do you think Elvis knew he was Elvis? It'd be like Glenn Gould thinking about each note as he played the 'Goldberg Variations'. For God's sake already. It's called keeping the faith, sonny boy. Case closed.

. . . A little grey about the sideburns no doubt, and perhaps a little shorter due to the contraction of the spine that occurs naturally with the erosion of discs, but a-l-i-v-e. Hey, and I'll take Elvis's shorter spine any day over Michael Jackson's lengthy flexible one.

After Teresa's funeral, I was raring to restart the school year. My second day back I'd been in class no more than fifteen minutes when Principal Clint came to the door, tapped on the glass and signalled me into the hall. I dipped my chin to the left and smiled knowingly, figuring he'd heard about the load of chinchillas I'd ordered to be delivered to his house (I'm a great practical joker). I raised my right hand to the class, with pinkie and forefinger extended like a Texas longhorn, said, 'Now, you maniacs be good, we'll be right back after a short pause for the cause.' Some still looked alarmed, some frightened, some howled, some heckled, your typical stadium audience. They'd been like that the whole day before when we planned the comeback as a special unit.

In the hall Clint went bug-eyed at my shirt (black velvet) and leathers. He insists that his male staff wear ties, though he's lenient about jackets. Sweaters are okay by Clint, who thinks nothing of steaming into the teachers' room of a Monday morning and shoving Roger Whitaker into the communal tape player. So I turned down my collar only because I felt sorry for the little guy.

I mean, what could he do? Fire me? I'm about to blow this pop stand already.

But he gripped my forearm like he'd pull me down the hall, looked kind of misty-eyed: 'Please, Frank, just come with me.'

'Hey, lookee here, little man, I really gotta say goodbye to my kids. The line-up starts to the left.' I chucked him under the chin. He's only about five-and-a-half feet, too short for a man, too tall for a voyageur.

'*Please*, Frank, think of the kids.'

I shook him off easily and wasted him with a wink: 'Hang tough, little man.'

Applause at my return, I knew I was doing the right thing. I just stood majestically before their bright pink faces and listened to their little minds buzz like a blossoming cherry tree full of bees. God, I love children. *Think of the kids.* Sheez. What else do I think about! But then a cloud must have slid in front of the sun, because the room dimmed slowly, and their faces reminded me of the fields of purple flowers I'd passed on the way to Teresa's funeral. (I've since learned that those plants are called purple loosestrife and that they're new to this part of the world. Also, they're taking over everywhere, like zebra mussels and perverts.)

My Momma had a hard life, a life of thankless work and worry, a mean drunk for a husband. In my life she was like a sun, and without her my world has grown darker and colder, and I'm hungry all the time. *All the time.* Like, I could barbecue squirrel! And I mean road-kill, man.

About six weeks after I returned from Momma's funeral in Toronto, the police found most of Teresa in a green plastic bag stuffed in the big blue dumpster out behind the IGA, naked, like a dead dog that's been mauled by some wild beast, a human being couldn't have done that, a human should never look like that, human beings shouldn't show each other such pictures in their newspapers and on their high definition tvs. . . . But I don't mean to focus on this one scene, because, well, because it's not the point of my story. . . . Though I too easily see her dark eyes staring vacantly (thank God), unflinching from the touch of flies.

He'll pay for this! He'll pay! He will! I'll strangle him with his own fucking cummerbund!

In the classroom I tucked my chin, raised my arm and pointed: 'Tell me, blind Michael Sheridan, who invented rock'n'roll?'

'Uh, my dad says Chuck Berry.'

'And your daddy's right, boy. Always tell the truth. Leslie, who brought it – or wait, all together: *Who brought it to the people?*'

And they all shouted at me: 'Elvis Presley!' And commenced poundin' their desks: 'Elvis, Elvis, Elvis . . .'

Talk of a rush. Man, I was ridin' a rocket to Russia.

I first blew my cover on the evening of the day they found Teresa. It began harmlessly enough in my own living room, with me humming along to my original seventy-eight of 'Are You Lonesome Tonight?'. Then I started singing. I could tell from the way Linda looked at me without any expression on her face that she found me convincing. So I stood and began slouching back and forth in front of the couch like I was playing to fans at the apron. By the time I threw my head way back and hit the line like a pure thought, 'Shall I come back again', Linda was crying and I was executing some devastatingly accurate (if inappropriate) karate kicks.

When I caught my breath and towelled off, I started crying too. I wasn't thinking of my Momma, or of anything, far as I can remember. It had been twelve hours since Teresa was found, and I guess the two of us had been bottling up a lot of feelings, for Teresa, and for each other. At the Troutstream pool that summer Teresa had shattered the adults' record only her second time doing the butterfly. Linda had told me swimming was *her* favourite sport too. And, you know, chicks can't get enough of my stuff. I tossed Linda the tea towel.

She stood and took my hand loosely, gazed at me through her green shades in a way that let me know she recognised the real me, then moved in to kiss. But I whispered, 'No, I have not yet gone to my public who made me.'

She stared vacantly at the fairly accurate reproduction in velvet that had pride of place in my dining room over the buffet, and whispered without hurt, 'I understand.'

I said, 'That's right, honey: never, and I mean *never*, forget the little guy . . . or gal.' I chucked her under the chin.

Even some of the Desperados finally joined in: 'Elvis, Elvis, Elvis . . .'

From the farthest reach of my big toe-nail to the tip of my modified pompadour, I vibrated, hummed like His own tuning fork. I slipped to the side of the room and hit the switch on the deluxe ghetto-blaster I'd bought at Home Hardware that morning. (Anne, the chick who works there, Leslie's Momma, was on the yackety-yak phone before the door had shut behind me. You can guess what she was so excited about.) The opening slide of 'Jailhouse Rock', C to D (people still think I can't play, though anyone who watched my '68 tv special saw me pick out a boogie on the big semi-acoustic with the best of the boys), and I work my way back to the centre doing my stiff-knee jitter, right upper lip arched like a hissin' cat, and stand there shakin' and syncin' the song. (Hey, I'm not singin' for real without my charts and good equipment. And by the way, it's true what you've all been sayin' about the big number in my one decent movie: I choreographed it.) At first they're stunned again, and I can't say as I blame them: *me* giving my first comeback special backed only by a Canada food-guide poster and surrounded by blackboards crammed with math problems I couldn't figure for the life of me. But in a minute they're all right back into it, snappin' fingers and swayin' like in all those other dumb ol' funky movies I made. (I know, I know: bad career move. Colonel, what were you thinking?)

God, I love these kids.

Look, don't mistake me. I'm not saying Teresa was the most beautiful twelve-year-old girl I'd ever taught. I had her for both grade seven and what she did of eight. She had what my Momma called a handsome face, with bluntly defined cheekbones and a squarish jaw. She was physically precocious, with disproportionately long limbs, powerful thighs and thick calves, a too-short torso with sloping shoulders, a coarseness to her jet-black hair, a bit of down on the upper lip and alongside the ears – all of it portending homeliness for her teens. She was also potentially an Olympic calibre athlete. I've coached extramural long enough to recognise the truly gifted athlete immediately. In thirty years I've seen only two or three such, a couple of NHL hockey players and a world-class downhill skier. They win two-hundred-metre races by fifty metres, with a smile; over a fifteen-hundred they lap the others in two laps and are just breaking a sweat; outdoors their breathing sounds like a compact locomotive, you look around wondering . . . then amazement. I recognised Teresa the previous Spring when I saw her pick up a javelin for the first time and throw it in a perfect arc way over my head where I'd safely stood to mark the class's fumbling throws. I whipped back my head and watched it cut like one pure thought across the peacock blue sky, then had to hide my tearing eyes, couldn't even say good throw because of the gagging lump in my throat. As a witness said who first heard Mozart play: I was listening to God speak. And I'm not even a sports fan.

As amazing, at the age of twelve Teresa could write better than I could when I was writing a lot at university. Her home had no tv. During Free Fall English second day of class this year I assigned the topic, 'Good and Bad Habits'. All the other kids wrote the standard barely literate clichés about smoking and drinking. (Though Michael Sheridan typed a doubly punning little piece called 'Cross-Dressing Nuns'. He's a spooky kid, I tell you.) I've kept a copy of what Teresa wrote, which I reproduce here, though the original was written in exquisite longhand with a fountain pen using turquoise ink. Read and weep:

The Habits of a Lifetime
The rhythm of daily life can accommodate interruption. In fact, the breaks give life's rhythm its strongest illusion of permanence, as variations in the metre of a poem make iambic pentameter seem natural to daily speech (or so Mr O'Dona-ghue says!). But these variations, whether in poetry or life, also run the risk of drawing too much attention to themselves, until attention becomes fascination, and variation becomes a kind of peephole on a frightening reality. Then you sense

most strongly that the man-made rhythms of permanence play upon a constant bass that is truly eternal – the monotonous rhythm of the universe, space without sun and stars, darkness without light. Interruptions carry echoes from that permanent state into this transitory one of light and life. They are not, then, 'interruptions' as we commonly understand that term. No: what we think of as the established rhythm of daily life is more truly an interruption in the permanent state of things. Stars interrupt Mother Night. Thus we crave signs of life from elsewhere, from out there in that sparking darkness that may well prove to be no more intelligible than the random electrical charges in an idiot's brain. Thus this: you and I desire to create meaning everywhere (unless we are idiots ourselves!!).

I suggested a couple of paragraph breaks (at the first 'Interruptions' and the first 'Thus') and changing the 'you and I' and 'yourself' to 'one' and 'oneself', with requisite changes in verb tenses. I also questioned the lugubrious use of double exclamation marks and the unavoidable facetiousness of parenthetical remarks, especially that concluding clause; in fact, I questioned the need for the final sentence. (Overwriting is the vice that began as a virtue.)

I carried that essay around in my breast pocket, unfolded and refolded dozens of times, till the ink washed out and I had to make a facsimile from memory. I found it more comforting than MacLennan's *The Watch* so soon after my mother's death.

Teresa's funeral was in Smiths Falls, where her grandparents maintained a large family plot. It was a morning service, so I left my apartment at seven o'clock determined to ask permission to read her essay to the assembled (the family refused). A picture-perfect day, with Highway 7 sweeping westward through low-lying fields brushed completely with the pale blush of purple loosestrife. I pulled onto the shoulder, got out and stood there staring at a violet field for who knows how long. And came to conceive of the sky as a peacock-blue lining to the black cloak of space, of the earth as a swelling belly, of the field as a purple cummerbund, and of that fucking Vegas Porker. Look what he had done now. That made me think of how much the real Elvis loved his Momma and all children (Priscilla, you will recall, was only thirteen when he met her in Germany), and how religious he was. And that made me think of how the statuary in church is draped in purple during the Lenten season. At Easter the purple veils are snatched away and – presto! He has come back again! Rejoice! Rejoice! And for just the briefest moment I reflected, Am I losing my mind? . . . Perish the thought!!

I squelched into the field and gathered armful after armful of loosestrife, thinking as I filled the trunk and seats that purple flowers would not go unappreciated at a funeral. Perhaps I should have taken the time to scrape my shoes and tidy myself up some, but the picking made me rush in late as it was, hugging a double armful of loosestrife like a violet stook and shouting, 'Message from Teresa Archer! Message from Teresa Archer!'

Now, I can just barely remember doing that. And I may well have dreamed some or all of it. But after that, nothing. I rely on the memory of others, especially Linda's. I can only imagine how I must have been feeling.

Before I finish 'Jailhouse Rock' Clint is back outside the door. He holds up a cue card: 'If you don't come out we'll come in and drag you out.'

The little guy knows I'm driven to give one hundred and fifty per cent. (The little guy *should* know he requires a comma after a protasis.) That's just the way Momma and the Colonel brung me up. So I hit the off button.

The experience of me come back to my full glory has been understandably overwhelming. The Desperados are crying, even blind Michael Sheridan rolls big tears from behind his own shades. But I tell them all not to worry, that it feels right to be back at last. And to remember, at the very worst, it's better to be alive than not, and always to love your Mommas. 'When I get back, we'll slow things down a bit with a perennial and, I might add, a personal favourite, "Are You Lonesome Tonight?" We'll send it out to Teresa, wherever you are, darlin'.'

Some wail and cover their ears, but I was prepared for that. On my way to the wings I wave and make reassuring eye contact with as many as I can.

Clint is flanked by the same policemen who'd confiscated my piece the night before after I shot out Madonna on one of my smaller tvs. Then they'd plied me with a lot of yackety-yak questions, but Linda'd saved me with some incredible story about Teresa and Momma. Now, they tell me not to try to speak. Good advice. My throat is a little sore and awful tight. They must know I've still got the big gig to do.

Finally I'm in the back seat of the limo and being escorted to Ottawa International. I can just hear Clint on the PA: 'Quiet, people, quiet please. I have an announcement to make: Elvis has left the building. I repeat: Elvis has left the building. Will the oldest child in each family please come to the office before . . .'

I feel a bit scooped out as we leave Troutstream behind forever and swing onto the new Inglis – what was actually the first completed stage of the Bypass – and . . . slow down at the Regional Detention Centre? Lordy-lordy, they want me to clear up that silly business about the gun before leaving the country.

I've been abducted. The Colonel has been sent a ransom demand. (I wonder what I'm worth?) But that's all my night guards will reveal. They laugh in my face when I remind them the Colonel has long gone to his just reward. During the day I keep my own counsel, no matter what ruse they use.

Now the story is there's been a murder. *I've* been arrested!

I tell them I can't remember everything I did. I lie that I've been on a lot of medication that confuses my senses and memory. Someone or something else was controlling me. I had to fake my death. The pressure got to be too much for that character. All day every day buy this buy that give to this give to that. The show just got too big for a good ol' boy from Tupelo. Nothing works. They grill me. What about this? What about that? The essay in *my* handwriting, obviously written *by* me, but signed with the murdered girl's name? (But I've *explained* that!) Why the detailed model of Troutstream North on the card table in my dining room? (*And that*. The real estate agents!) My basement full of purple loosestrife? (What *else* was I to do with it? They refused it!) And on and on and on it goes, yackety-yak, till *I* almost don't know who I am any more. (A cool billion? Sure, at least a billion in bullion. Shucks but don't that sound good. A billion in bullion for me from the Colonel . . .)

Oh, I know their game. They want to keep me off the streets. They're blunt about that, the night guards anyway. Would the streets of Troutstream be safe with someone like me at large? No, I agree. The streets would never be the same again were I to be recognised. When the people see me come back again in full glory, the entire global business-military-political consortium will be brought to its knees . . . in a manner the Vegas Porker could execute only with the aid of a winch!

They roll their eyes, put their hands over mine on the bars and crush my fingers, then shove me backwards.

This piss-soaked cell is closing in on me. For some reason I keep missing the toilet. I all but straddle it, let go, and the piss goes whizzing all over me and the walls and the floor. It's the erection! What can I do? Stand on my fucking head! I scream and scream that I can't *move* in here. Man, I gotta *move*.

They laugh, say 'Shut up, Porky.' They really know how to hurt a guy.

I sleep and dream and freeze and wake and sweat and shit the bed and get my face pushed in it like a dog.

I ask for a copy of *Seven Rivers of Canada*. They pretend they don't know what I'm talking about. We strike a deal. They will accede to my demand if I give them what they want. Which I do, desperately, weepingly, eagerly (I could have been a great actor – ask Preminger!): I didn't do it! I didn't do it! But I know who did! Yeah, that's right, I know who and *I'll* sing for ya. Porky did it! The Porker did it! Yeah, that's right, the Vegas Porker did it. . . .

By then it was all like someone else's bad movie anyway – Don't say it, man. I puked at the rushes of *Kissin' Cousins* too.

They gingerly wheel a tiny portable into my cell, deposit it among my excreta, and tell me Joan Rivers is on at four. Very funny. Ha-ha-ha.

Another girl in a new development east of Troutstream is murdered. Same modus operandi: the battering, the light burn marks, the selective dismemberment, the mutilation of the sexual apparatus, blah-blah-blah, et cetera, et cetera, thank you ladies and gentlemen. I am transferred and more deeply drugged.

My flesh is a senseless sopping sponge I would tear off in fistfuls. If I could move. I will die of hunger because I cannot part my jaws. I must concentrate forever just to lick my lips. When I open my eyes again it will be for the last time. When I do, a light like my Momma's own cool fingers on my temples draws my head to the bedside chair, and I behold myself sitting apart in glory and aviator sunglasses, and he smiles that boyish smile and says from behind his magnificent shades, 'Hang tough, man.'

And I will. I am at peace now.

I'd been in the historically present-tensed Ottawa Psychiatric Hospital. Linda says *all the time*, and that she'd stayed with me, sleeping in the lounge, then on a cot. She finally got me released to her care. On medication I managed fairly well for a while, though that didn't stop us from taking off together to Smiths Falls. A week or so into our farcical elopement Linda grew deeply depressed and began sharing my medication. Then I took the dope only when I felt like it and got manic-bad again thinking I was King Shit Creole, while Linda slid precipitously into an even deeper hole. Eventually my prescription expired and we returned to my place in Troutstream. Her husband was gone, her dog was gone. Man, never return to a place that's gone.

Then two days ago we heard through Fred the Super that Linda's husband, Les, had written from an address in Sarnia, Ontario, requesting that his mail be forwarded to a place called the

Bluewater Hotel on River Road and asking if anyone had seen Wes, their dog. That jolted Linda off the bottom, and melodramatically she said she must go to him, he needed her.

Drug free and itchy hyper we had grown shy with one another anyway. Each morning had become waking up to a different stranger in the same celibate bed. With the goal of her trip to Sarnia before her, Linda was better than I and growing stronger by the hour. I was stretched face-down on the bottom of the deepest ocean, waiting for that bottom to open up. I was useless. I was purposeless. I was hopeless. I was going fast.

The day before she left we took an aimless evening walk along some cross-country ski trails in the greenbelt. Or rather, she took me, loosely holding my hand out of habit. It was as hot as a high summer's day, though around us the very last leaves were detaching and arcing, spinning and plunging headlong. With sweet halting concentration she filled me in on events of the past weeks, and I was a sick kid being told a story of someone else's madcap adventures. (She said Michael Sheridan had visited me in hospital a number of times. And that he'd spelled her by my bedside for hours. She said, in fact, that it was after his longest vigil I began to come out of it. Sheridan! Imagine that!) We ended up in a thinly wooded picnic area near the Troutstream soccer fields. We could hear and glimpse children playing, but the sounds had no effect on me. We remained hidden among the pines down by the foul creek that gives this place its name, staring at the stagnant water and waving away insects as the afternoon stalled in its slump towards evening. I thought: Why is even the ugly world always so good and I here to foul it further? I smiled slightly: I would kill myself when Linda left. At last, something to look forward to.

Linda heard it first, cocking her head and opening her mouth in an unspoken Wha . . .? Then I heard it, coming not from the soccer fields but from the Troutstream side, a smothered sound like a child whining in a bed on another floor.

Together we moved into the more thickly wooded area on the left. There was a thud like a swatter hitting a carpet, a yelp, and the whining grew momentarily louder, subsided. We stepped into the overgrown brush and were startled to find ourselves only a few metres from a dark figure bent low over a . . . a dog. Linda screamed. The figure straightened to an enormous size and stared at me out of the dark, his teeth flashed. He was wearing a black high-collared cape. The dog began dragging itself towards us like a dying soldier through a no-man's land. As the figure turned away he punched a fist into the air as might someone after a successful performance, and slouched noiselessly into the darker woods.

'It's Wes! It's Wes!' screamed Linda running to the dog. She knelt beside it and her hands, as if afraid to alight, hovered about its head. She cupped its snout in two hands and rested its head on her thighs. It breathed heavily once, shuddered, breathed no more.

Linda went to pieces for a while kneeling there, then turned catatonic. I had no trouble leading her back to my place, where I administered some sleeping pills, a triple shot of brandy, and put her to bed.

Dozing off she whimpered, 'Who could do such a thing? Who could do such a thing?'

'You saw him.'

'Yes.'

I said I'd go back and look after her dog.

'Close his eyes,' she murmured. 'Promise me you'll close his eyes before you bury him.'

I promised, and sat by the bed till she slept. I'd close his eyes all right.

For the first time in weeks I felt in full self-possession. I took one of my other guns and a flashlight, though at eighteen fifty there was still enough light to see by. I marched through the greenbelt with senses on full alert. It was still where we'd left it. I played the light across the body: head looked fine, but chest and rib cage had been battered in with blunt instrument, so skin folded where it shouldn't; streaks and patches of hair had been shaved and torn from back. I recognised the modus operandi, did not bother inspecting sexual apparatus.

Without warning I threw up, and continued heaving away on all fours till bloodied bile slithered like a sweet organ from my mouth.

131

Exhausted I prayed: Momma, make him go away. I can't do it, I can't. I'm weary of this ol' world.

Yes, Momma, if it be your will.

Despite what I'd promised Linda, I picked the dog up by his hind legs and dumped him in the blue oil drum used for picnic garbage.

That was yesterday. I've been fine since, now that I understand why I've been put through what I've been through, and know too the Lord's purpose in placing me on this good green earth.

Who could do such a thing? To Momma? Teresa? Linda's dog? I know. Who else could punch such a large perfect hole in the Bypass's green barrier? I would know that shape and those sounds anywhere: the swollen size, the adenoidal breathing, the peacock-blue cape, the hulking movements in retreat. As I tried to tell those guards, he's here now, the Vegas Porker, right here in Trout-stream, and killing indiscriminately.

Oh they'll think I'm crazy again, I know, but it's my self-sworn duty to inform the authorities. First things first though: I must warn the crowds of endangered children on Troutstream's playgrounds. Then clean all my guns and begin my patrols.

THE
PROJECT

Troutstream Arms

·

Paul Arsenault must input a complete draft of his editorial before the bumper happy-hour crowd arrives. Then it must be printed, photocopied, distributed, all before sunset. The Master is expected at sevenish. Sitting in his windowless back-of-the-bar office, he clenches his fists over the keyboard and springs the fingers – Yes! . . . Nothing. Thank God anyway for the miracle of computers, they make this writing business so much easier. If not for Desktop King with Mighty Mouse and Windows, *Current Affairs* would never have developed beyond grassroots bar talk to become the professional four-page newsletter it is today.

He eliminates from consideration the GST, yammering French-Canadians, the triple-E Senate, various affirmative action pro-grammes, and narrows this month's topic to a difficult choice: either the Project people again (now they're demanding free taxi rides to doctors and hospitals, *and* dentists. Dentists! Where next, the Brewer's Retail?) or a welcoming profile of Master Aaron, who was paying his first visit to Ottawa – to Troutstream! to the Arms! – this very day in history!

But Paul is distracted again by the television screen that covers one wall of his office (he'd wrangled a two-for deal on large screens), and he wonders fleetingly what it would be like to compose on a screen that big, to transmit instantaneously to like-minded citizens. Hypertext!

Master Aaron's first visit to Ottawa had inspired Newsworld to compile a half-hour documentary on his life, thereby scooping Paul and *Current Affairs*. Paul already knows the details of that life better than those of his employees or regular customers. More than that: Paul had written to the Master, the Master had corresponded with Paul; Paul had invited the Master to drop in to the Arms for a pint of genuine bitter, the Master had accepted. Paul must do both Master Aaron *and* the Project. It is an historical moment not to be missed. He drags his attention from the bigger screen. Point of view would prove decisive. The image of the Master always gives him a tickle down the length of his tract, which makes him worry if maybe he's not one of those latent homosexuals. If he ever finds out that he is, he will do the honourable thing and kill himself. He wipes a palm along the top of his head, crown to brow, and it slides before his eyes wet and trailing strands of alfalfa-like hair. Damn Newsworld! He turns back to the tv.

The file-footage sign has disappeared and a live interview is taking place in the clacking lobby of the Chateau Laurier. That cute female reporter with big head and hair holds a microphone up to Master Aaron, who wears an expensively cut plain black suit. The Master is quite tall (six foot four inches, Paul knows), with just a hint of farm boy gawkiness, a lingering impression that he'd not grown into his body till his forties, and had suffered for it till then. He wears large wire-rimmed glasses that magnify his small sad eyes. But as the reporter asks her question, the Master's eyes crinkle and he smiles warmly, as though on a genuine impulse he might put his large palm on the small of her back, bow down and say something encouraging. When he does speak it's with a slight drawl, and the effect is of a young Jimmy Stewart come to tangle with the powers of corruption.

First he grins down at the reporter, as if to say, You little dickens, what a perky question that is. Then he purses his small purse of a mouth and speaks directly: 'Well now, I wouldn't exactly put it that way, Brenda. You see, Brenda, I come from poverty, a poor but fiercely proud people. My Daddy was an itinerant farm labourer, my Momma took in other people's washing and sewing and the like. So I know from experience what these unfortunate people being left out of the so-called recovery *feel*. I *know* what's in their hearts. And it *ain't* one-way charity, if you'll pardon my French. Whoops, shouldn't say that, should I, Brenda. But the point is, these people *want* to work. They want a better life. They want to *earn* the respect of their children, and their children's children. What they *don't* want is more handouts from big government or being told to learn French like they were a bunch of schoolkids. No thank you, Ma'am. That is why we simply *must* introduce both a means test for those who can pay their own way, and a system of work-for-assistance for those whom big government has been pushing down into that welfare hole for generation upon generation. The good Lord helps those who help themselves, Brenda. Pay as you go, that's the Change Party motto: no more deficit, no more free handouts to the able-bodied. And no more official bilingualism shoved down the throats of law-abiding Canadian citizens!'

The reporter pulls the microphone down to her own weakly grinning face; she cringes slightly as though perplexed, a signal to the nation that she is about to pounce: 'But, with all due respect, sir, your father became a wealthy man, and you *are* a wealthy man. What do you *really* know about the *disadvantaged* in this country?'

Master Aaron looks hurt: 'Young woman, today I shall be with those so-called disadvantaged in a development on the margins of this thriving capital.'

Paul swallows. Is that you stirring down there, Roger?

'I don't see how that answers my question, Mr Aaron,' Brenda smiles.

'Brenda, don't be suggestin' to the good people of Canada that I intend to bust the deficit or the recession, or whatever you media people are calling it this week, on the backs of the poor. Or on the shoulders of the weary middle class – they've been burdened long enough, and *enough's enough*. Or, for that matter, don't blame this mess on those who earned their wealth through hard work and frugality – the old-fashioned values that built this country we call Canada, and home. Let me tell you something, young lady, something you're probably too young to know: this deficit and this depression are the end product of big liberal government and outrageous Tory taxation at all levels. *That* is why it is time for a new broom. And *that*, young lady, is why it is time for the Change Party. Enough *is* enough.'

Master Aaron stares straight into the camera, a small apologetic smile puckering the corners of his small mouth. That smile says, I'm sorry to have to be like this, like a politician. You can trust me, believe you me.

The unflappable Brenda is momentarily flapped . . . though she soon returns to her aggressively condescending style with a statistical question about regressive taxation. But who is listening? Not Master Aaron, who is smiling broadly off to his right and waving, perhaps enjoying with a handler the clinching of an airtight news bite.

And not Paul Arsenault. He's been trying to concentrate on an imaginary cricket match played in Antarctica. Satisfied, he turned off the tv, clamped his right hand atop his glistening head and stood like a man who'd had a hand in the selection of genes that had dictated his growth to six foot six. Towards his balding, though, Paul had a different attitude. As he infrequently said near closing time after one brandy too many: tired time had carelessly cut only a mower-wide swath across that most important part of his public property, abandoned the job and gone for a pint. What he didn't say was that he sometimes felt like a towering clown, and in this respect alone he allowed himself to claim victim status. To compensate he had cultured a handlebar moustache and greying lamb-chop sideburns brushed backwards like Mercury's dashing wings. He believed that smoking a pipe helped, though since January he'd kept his resolve and simply worn it unlit in his mouth.

But Paul knew whereof the Master spoke when the Master spoke of a poor upbringing. Like the Master, he had come up from poverty, a bombed-out slum in Coventry. And now, tall, distinguished, virile, Paul had realised his dreams: he looked like the brainy editor of some classy magazine in the Edwardian epoch, at fifty he owned a mock-British pub in – well, *near* – the capital of a Commonwealth country, he had women whenever he wanted them. He must do his bit to help the Master realise *his* dream. Down, Roger, down, boy.

He picked the pipe from the large brown ashtray on his desk, caressed it with full lips prehensile in their desire to draw smoke, and exhaled like a stoking Mencken through his large nose. He reached to the wall behind his desk and like someone running up a keyboard drew the back of his fingers along the spines of the single row of paperbacks: the complete works of Evelyn Waugh, Kingsley Amis, Mordecai Richler, and Martin Amis. 'Well well well, we shall see, shan't we,' he mused aloud in a nasal voice. He reached further up the wall and touched the loaded shotgun, an uncle's fowling piece which had been presented to him for his protection when the family remnants learned he was immigrating to Canada. Inspired, he sat rigidly, pretended to brush back the tails of a tux, and positioned his clawed hands over the keyboard.

Courage. The Master still championed Cruise Missile testing, and not just for over tundra either, for anywhere in Canada, down Bay Street if necessary, up Parliament Hill preferably: that would confirm Canada's commitment to NATO and peace through strength. Never mind the break-up of the Soviet Union and the disintegration of the Warsaw Pact; through it all the Master had bear-hugged a pro-nuclear position, both for domestic energy needs and weaponry. The Gulf War had proved him supremely prescient! Courage. In *How to End Poverty Once and for All*, the Master had argued that money currently being thrown into the Calcutta of state-sponsored welfare programmes, like the Project, could be more gainfully spent employing the willing poor at minimum wage in a made-in-Canada defence industry. Courage. Paul swooned inwardly: it was like Master Aaron sometimes took his lead from *Current Affairs!* Which wasn't as absurd as it sounded, since Paul regularly mailed him a copy. Yes. Courage. Paul had a title for his editorial: 'Arsenault on Arsenals'. If well begun is half done, spendidly titled must be . . . splendid! He reached again and touched his paperbacks. The rest would come easy. King, Paul commands, it's show time! *Clickety-click-click-click* . . . *Clickety-click-click-click* . . .

★

139

Officially, Troutstream's subsidised housing project was now called Piscine Court, though it had begun life only a year before as Sea Breeze Estates. It had the look of newly dilapidated Mediterranean villas which even the sea had left high and dry: three storeys of box-like pastel-coloured apartments at odd angles, bracketed on the west by the one-storey strip mall and on the east by rows of town houses. Already it had acquired the run-down appearance with which hopeless renters imbue a hated place: cloudy plastic covering thin windows here and there, whole corners of screens hanging from aluminum doors like something flayed, the odd interior door kicked in, so that the fractured wood around the knob looked as freshly pale as bone, even the siding slacking like a leper's jaw from one outside corner of a third-floor apartment. The colours remained garishly bright, but the effect was of an unwashed coal miner in a new suit. True, a fair number of residents resisted the tide of resignation with neat flower beds and well cared for units, but that tide was tireless, and they were not.

The Project people have proven to be somewhat less grateful for government subsidised housing than ex-Alderman Callwood had secretly assured the Troutstream Community Association they would be. (It was rumoured throughout Troutstream that Callwood had traded the Project for the Bypass, and profited thereby.) In fact the Project people are clamouring: more daycare, more benefits, more attention, more money. Alderman Hilton had unseated Callwood on Foster City Council with the promise of greater municipal assistance and a commitment to change the Project's official name from the dehumanising Sea Breeze Estates to Fisherperson's Cove. The Project people were convinced that the change would indeed signal at long last their arrival in the greater Troutstream harbour. That campaign had shown that the Project vote could decide an aldermanic election, which more truly signalled their arrival. But by then those living in the Project were referred to by most of Troutstream simply as 'cast-offs', a name given them by Paul Arsenault in *Current Affairs*. When for the second time the Project was officially renamed – Piscine Court (again through Hilton's efforts, though now at the request of the Project's newly formed Tenants Association, or the names caucus thereof) – Arsenault had headed his feature editorial 'Pissed In

Court', and written about how 'these Project people are given taxi vouchers to attend their day in court on charges of so-called "domestic disturbances involving alcohol" meaning, my friends, that they use *our* tax dollars to get all boozed up – not in the Arms, mind you – and then go home and beat the wife and kids. And get off with a lick and a promise, you can bet *your* hard-earned dollar.' That was getting on to half a year ago now, and though Arsenault still referred to the place as Pissed in Court or Pissing Court, to everyone else in Troutstream it was simply the Project, and its residents Project people.

Despite Arsenault's insistence to the contrary, the arrival of the Project in Troutstream doubled his receipts, making possible the purchase of the big screens and the time he devoted to *Current Affairs*, not to mention the sponsored soccer teams, the darts league, the periodic car rallies, and, most recently, the plans for a hot air balloon club, balloon to be piloted by Arsenault. Every Wednesday now brought mid-week happy hour at the Troutstream Arms, which carried over into 'Carry On Night', when all evening the big screen showed twenty-year-old movies by the British 'Carry On' team.

Anne Cameron from Home Hardware lives in the Project now. Because she enjoys spending the whole weekend with her twelve-year-old daughter, she likes to drink a few beers in mid-week, a few too many most weeks, and likes to drink it in company, likes to walk home, so has no choice but to drink at the Troutstream Arms. Paul Arsenault she dislikes, him and his *Current Affairs*, and she's had more than one run-in with him. She knows from Jane at the Arms that it was Arsenault put the authorities on to her for leaving Leslie alone on Wednesdays, if *alone* is with Joan right next door. That was after the Oka issue of *Current Affairs* – Wagonburners, Homohawk Warriers, Chief Cheap Cigs, Tax Squawbbles – and the near-successful prosecution of Arsenault for publishing hate literature. So this afternoon Anne has had to ask Joan to meet Leslie at the bus and sit her, and because it's a formal request Joan will not do so for less than three dollars an hour. Which means no Chinese and a video instead of taking Leslie to the movies this weekend.

Yas pays fer yar sins, thinks Anne in her old-tar voice as she

141

pulls open the door. Though Rick the prick hasn't paid, and Arsenault gets away with murder. She stands inside waiting for her eyes to adjust, though her nose is stung instantly by the stink of piss that settles in any popular bar not regularly scrubbed. Pissing Court is right, she thinks, though not for us. Maybe nostrils adjust, too, contract or something, because after a while you don't notice the reek. The boys never learn to keep it all inside the bowl. She should give the Health an anonymous call, Arsenault doesn't have separate Women's and Men's, only two 'heads'. When Rick lived with her he sometimes didn't bother lifting the seat, and she couldn't tell till she stood and her ass peeled off it like plastic wrap. She nagged and nagged, and towards the end she's sure he purposely wetted the whole thing down. There's only Jane behind the bar and two swollen skinheads at a table to the right, slumped towards a pitcher and snickering like anyone in the whole world gives a red rat's asshole what the fuck they think. Oh it's early, Annie me girl, too early in the day to be drinking. Maybe they're laughing at her in her Home uniform. Fuck 'em.

'Hi ya, Janey. A couple of your coolest, *s'il vous plait.*'

From behind the bar Jane, pretty and sinewy, but even more heavily made-up than usual, and with blonde hair the texture of a doll's, says, 'Hi, Anne. How's Leslie?'

Strange, an old disco ball hangs in the middle of the room, with red, white and blue streamers twirling into the corners like the fourth of July. She chooses a table away from the large dead screen tilted like a lidless clouded eyeball looking down at her, and shouts back: 'Okay. Wants to hang out at malls. Talkin' boys boys boys. Scares me. But she's with my friend Joan today.'

'Send her to us,' one of the skinheads snickers.

Anne stares hard at them, but their heads are bowed again. 'Pigs,' she says just loud enough, and thinks she hears 'Bitch'. But why not her? Is she that unattractive already? *Not that she would.*

'Hey, Janey, what's going on here with the disco ball? Arsenault gonna do a *Saturday Night Fever* revival? Hasn't anybody told him, karaoke's the big thing nowadays, everybody wants to be Elvis.'

'I'll tell him,' Jane shouts. Grinning, she arrives with the two draft and offers to run a tab, then whispers out the side of her mouth like a thug: 'King Chrome-dome is in the back. Look, everyone around here, and you *know* that includes yours truly, thinks he's a fucking jerk for what he did about you and Leslie. Try to ignore him, don't nag him about his stupid paper.'

'Yeah-yeah, blah-blah.'

'And don't worry about Leslie, she's only about the sharpest kid I've ever met. Relax, you've earned it.'

'You on all night?'

'Yeah, just about everyone is. That politician guy from out West Paul would like to blow is supposed to be paying us a visit. Big time, big crowd, maybe tv.'

'Maybe it'd help him give up the pipe.'

'You are a *bad* woman.'

Jane turns to leave, but Anne hurries: 'Hey, did I ever tell you that while this place was being turned into John Bullshit on the Stream your boss used to come into Home for small supplies. Used to flirt with me, though he knew I was married, asked me out. Never came back. Then tried to get me fired.'

Jane says, 'Fuckin' guys,' makes a face and leaves.

Within half an hour the room has filled up, with standing room only along the bar. Her old neighbours Iris and Fred and a friend of theirs are sitting with Anne. The three are well past retirement age, though Fred is part-time Super on Salmon Run immediately back of the Arms, where Anne and Leslie lived before Rick left. Fred has insisted on buying all the beer, so Anne works to keep the table, and those nearby, in light spirits. An uncharacteristically nervous Paul Arsenault appears before the big grey screen to announce that, in view of the impending visit to the Arms of Master Conrad Aaron, Carry On Night has been cancelled. Everyone cheers, Anne carelessly fires a cardboard coaster which nails Arsenault in the abdomen. On his way back to his office she sees him point at her and whisper to the Arms' one bouncer, Hughie, who also doesn't like Anne because she'd refused to go out with him too.

'What a stinking dickweed that guy is,' Anne says to the table. 'Have you ever seen his head shine like that, he beat the disco ball.'

'Now, now, Annie,' says Fred, jiggling with laughter. 'Don't get started on him. Mavis here knows nothing about you and our gracious host. Don't get started.' Fred has to lean far to fill Anne's glass, the belly buttons of his plaid shirt straining.

'Good advice, Fred.' Anne swings her glass towards the back of the bar, says loudly, 'Here's to ya, Arsehole!' and empties the slim draft glass to laughter, cheers and whistles from the neighbouring tables. Hughie glowers and takes a step towards her, but thinks better of it, leans back against the bar and pushes the chest of his white T-shirt up around his huge neck like a fat lineman compulsively adjusting his shoulder pads. Hughie had in fact passed one hellish day at an Ottawa Rough Riders' rookie camp twenty years before.

'You tell him, Annie,' says Iris, tightening her lips and nodding sharp approval.

'What's in the leaves lately, Iris?' Anne asks.

'Well, it's not the leaves that's worrying me, but as I've been explaining to Mavis, I've had a bad feeling for weeks now.'

'Haven't you been to the doctor lately?'

'Oh, it's not me, Anne, it's much more important than that. It's a dream I've been having, only not at night and I'm not sleeping. I don't want to say *vision*, because, well, I know Fred'll look disgusted and you'll laugh. But I keep seeing this black beach, and then black water rising up out of the ground, flooding Troutstream and covering the schools, and then they're talking about it on the tv and we're big news. It won't go away, the *dream* I mean. That's why I called Mavis.'

Mavis, who'd been introduced to Anne as Mavis Lachance from Depot, still nurses her first glass of beer. She has convincing neat black hair and lively grey eyes, and, but for a jaw that seems forever set on edge, she looks hardly worth looking at. Though her hands, too, as she curls the left about her glass, present unnaturally long fingers, at least as long again as Anne's. With pink nails so extended they funnel under, she picks at nothing on her glass, either out of embarrassment or simple shyness, Anne cannot tell. Presently she addresses her glass: 'This . . . computer course your're taking, Anne, what sort of job will it get you? Do you expect it will get you out of the . . . the Project? In *this* economic climate?'

Anne makes to answer, hesitates, stares at Mavis with narrowing eyes. Her whole body relaxes and she smirks at herself, tightens her grip on her glass and speaks calmly: 'Iris told you that.'

'I didn't,' Iris says.

'You did,' Fred sighs.

'I did not, Fred.'

Mavis smiles: 'Don't fret so, child. In time you'll be happy enough.'

'Never would've landed in the Project if Rick hadn't left us high and dry in our town house over on Fred's block. Or if he'd pay the fucking support he owes. Excuse me.'

'And how did you meet Rick the prick, dear?' Mavis asks.

Anne snorts as she tilts her head in slight withdrawal. She looks across at the curious face framed by the surprising jet-black hair. 'Okay, Iris and Fred know the story, or part of it, so here's the shortened version. I met him on the Victoria Day weekend at a camp called the Pines. I was like seventeen, like twenty years ago. He was so thin, and with his strawberry hair down to his shoulders he looked like Robert Plant. Twenty – '

'Who, dear?'

'Good for you, Mavis,' says Anne lifting her glass, 'make me feel young. Robert Plant, he was a rock singer with a band called Led Zeppelin.'

'Oh yes, I know them. Whole lotta love, right?'

'Yeah. Anyway, twenty years later he looked and acted like his old man, gristly and mean. And he began asking me to do strange things.'

'What kind of things, dear?'

Anne looks at Mavis, at Iris, then back at Mavis: 'You sure you're up to this, Mavis girl?'

'Anne, dear,' says Iris, 'Mavis has been married four times, once to a Frenchman, and her third was a negro, a big black man from Milan, an *Italian* negro. And she's very special.'

'Oh well then, I'll only be boring you.'

Iris laughs, Mavis smiles, Fred drinks.

'But like I was sayin', strange things for me, anyway, like sit on it backwards, or him standing up behind me – ee-youch. Once he rented one of them camcorders, that's when I put my foot down. I tell ya, I felt pretty silly doin' some of that stuff, though I didn't let on, and, well . . . kinda unprotected like, like you feel walking to the can in a hospital gown. I dunno. In bed, someone on top, someone on bottom, or rolling side to side for all I care, that's my style.

'These men and their cocks – excuse me, Fred – the men I've known anyway. Imagine if women sat around braggin' about how tight they were, or who had the biggest tits? Imagine – '

'Some do, dear. But what happened between you and Rick?'

'Mavis, I honestly don't know. He stopped talkin' to me. He watched tv all the time he was home. He bought Leslie a mountain bike and disappeared. She worships him. Cries all the time when she thinks I can't hear, at night. He lives in Hull now. And there's nothing I can do.'

'She worships *you*, Anne dear,' says Iris, who reaches across and with her large hand pats Anne's. 'You should see the two of them together, Mavis, it would do your heart good.'

'I think she's sweet on a boy in her class, a blind kid, believe it or not. Uh, Mavis, are you . . .?'

Mavis has placed her hands flat on the table, holds her head poised, closes her eyes, and quietly draws a long breath through her elegant nose. 'M,' she says the letter. 'M, mmm . . . Michael. A special child of rare gifts, capable of breakthrough.' She continues speaking as normally as if she were confirming a hair appointment: 'Yes, Iris, I see something now, of all times and places. You were right, it is a huge black shape . . . with blades. It cannot help itself, it doesn't know its own body any longer. And a spear shooting through the air, but not its. And young girls, schoolgirls, you were right, too, about that, Iris dear. You must tell parents to be especially careful over the next while, until it reveals itself more safely . . . yes, with an animal, a dog. But I cannot tell if its male or female, beast or human.'

'You are one spooky girl, Mavis,' Anne says. 'Michael, that's good, but safe. What *are* you drinking?'

Mavis opens her eyes and turns her head like a turret: 'I do know now. It is a man, but a man of indeterminate size.'

'Hey,' Anne snickers, 'maybe it's this Master Aaron guy.'

'It may well be,' Mavis smiles. 'Only I sense strongly that it's a local disruption.'

146

'Mavis,' Anne says, 'seeing as how I've been so personal and all, would you mind telling me something: how old are you?'

'Seventy-three.'

'You're lying.'

Iris is shaken, and says whimperingly, 'Anne, dear, one thing you *must* know about Mavis: she *never ever* lies, *never*. She's always had a crush on Fred, and that's never come between us. Oh but from *here*, Mavis? Oh Fred . . .'

'She doesn't look ten years older than me!'

Mavis allows a tiny smile and takes Anne's hand, which rests like a club foot on her fingers: 'And don't you worry your head over Leslie, Anne dear. She is going to make you one of the proudest mothers in Canada some day. I knew that the moment you spoke her name. But this boy, Michael, could you tell me where he lives? He may well be what's attracted this . . . evil.'

'You're scaring me, Mavis.'

'He is a *very* special boy, dear. Never have I sensed such self-possession, a soul so at home. He is close to the one who made us all.'

'I really should be getting home,' Anne mumbles, taking back her hand.

'I feel I must come down and see where you live before I go home, if that's all right with you, Anne?'

'Sure, Mavis, sure it is, not much to see, though.'

'It's where you live, dear. But I have other reasons, too.'

A threateningly depressive silence sneaks up on the table. Until Iris speaks rapidly: 'I did a reading a while ago for three sisters who live together over on Anglers Court, all three of them got agoraphobia bad now, and the youngest, Maya, had only recently had dentures bolted right into her lower gum, not plates like what Fred has upper and lower, but bolted right into the gum. Thank God I still have my own.' Iris smiles around the table in that way that once led someone to define smiling as a baring of fangs.

'Does she have any idea what that does to her aura electromagnetically?' Mavis asks rhetorically.

Anne comes fully to herself and says, 'Sorry ladies and gents, but I think I'd really better call it an early night while I still have my wits about me.' She slides the full glass towards Fred and smiles weakly. 'Thanks for the brew, Frederick.'

'Oh, come on, Anne, it's just after six.'

'No, no thanks. It's Leslie. I really shouldn't be leavin' her like this. Thanks again.'

'Any time, Anne,' grins Fred. 'I'll call ya when these two old witches are out flying some night.'

A weaker smile: 'I've been up nights myself dreaming about it, Fred. Bye all.'

She has to squeeze between a table of skinheads and Hughie the bouncer. The skinheads have started a chant that no one picks up, but for a while they lightly pound the table with their bottles and grunt, 'Mas-ter, Mas-ter, Mas-ter . . .' And as she squeezes past, Hughie sneers down at her, 'Nice outfit, Orphan Annie, going somewhere fancy tonight?'

She stares at his stretched T-shirt and thinks to ask when he's due, but can't raise the spirit.

Then, just when she alone can hear, he whispers harshly, 'Scuzzbucket, who'd fuck ya anyway.'

Evening washes the world in an underwater glow, a drowned feeling. Her brown uniform is the colour of dead wet leaves, the pants are cut too high, flood pants they used to call them, she smirks, and the wide lapels of the dun-coloured jacket seem designed to point to her protruding abdomen. Kids, men, nature, they use your body and turn it into shit. She's looked like her old lady since she lost the twins. *Why* are we here? Now I know. Women anyway. But what's she thinking. She loves Leslie. *Love*. The word strikes her as inadequate, silly. Loves Leslie? It's unfair the claim that kid has on her heart. And now she'll be angry with Leslie. The very worst time to quit drinking, after only a couple of shared pitchers, the very worst time to go home, she'll be overly polite to Joan and sharp with Leslie. As bad as Rick the prick. She's heard he's living with another woman, a single mother like herself. He won't stay with her either for long. Mr User, no responsibilities, just like he always must've wanted to bolt while she was pinching pennies for a down-payment on a real home. She'd lied to Mavis: he's still handsome, and she misses him enough to cry, and she will tonight after she's put Leslie to bed.

Fucking Project. Useless scags like herself and old people too poor and healthy to get into a good home, just about all women too. Life's shit for women. Men are such fucking assholes! They just don't give a –

Forced to stop for a red light at Inglis and Izaak Walton, she pulls herself up short, she's growing hysterical, talking to herself like that, half-drunk. Kitty corner rests the two-storey old folks home, Safe Harbour. Condom Flats, Arsenault calls it. Too tony for anybody she knows. Across the road to the right lies the short L of the strip mall. Sunlight reflects off the store windows, then dazzles her. When she breathes it's as though the air continues up through her shoulders and lifts her slightly, or maybe she's just drunk and tipping forward. But no, her head's suddenly clear, clearer than ever, and light, the light, it turns the entire mall into a brilliance that makes her widen her eyes rather than squint, all of it seems to bounce off the stores and find a focus on her, and warms her. She says aloud to herself in a voice hardly her own, 'You're doing just fine, dear.' If not for the ballast of beer in her belly she could rise off the ground like a brown hot air balloon. If only she were younger . . . She drops back on her heels, and what light's left in the day darkens as suddenly as if someone had turned a dimmer switch. The windows look like the sunglasses of thugs. No one will ever make love to her again. Fit only for fucking. For raping. She'd been tricked by the light, mugged. And all the dead world around her makes her feel deader still, and lost, as if she's been taken from her home, her real home in Sandy Hill, and plunked down here in the middle of a concrete waste that was farm land and bush when she was a girl. The light's green, and the walking figure looks like it's wearing the wide-legged Home Hardware pants suit. She can't move. Where is her home? . . .

A car has stopped at the green light. 'Hey, Anne?'

Dear God, no – But it's big Jack Kavanagh, who regularly chats her up in the store. She thinks she grins at him, holding the strap of her black purse high against her chest like some doddering old douchebag.

'Anne, it's me, Jack, Jack Kavanagh. Can I give you a lift? I hear from the radio there's big doings down at the Proj . . . at Sea Breeze.'

'Oh, hi Jack. No, no, I was just daydreaming, I've only got a short ways to go. We've moved, you know, into . . . the Project.'

'Yes, I know. Hey, Sunday my nephew's coming over for a barbecue. Wife died a few years ago, two kids, boy and a girl. Why don't you and . . . your daughter come over for – '

'Leslie,' says Anne, letting her purse down and stepping towards the car. 'But I don't think so, really, Jack, though it's awful nice – '

'Come on, Anne, don't give me that crap. We've been friends for years. My kids know Leslie. It's high time you came over. We'll burn some beef, have a drink, no big deal. How about it?'

'Jack, you're a nice guy, but – '

'Anne.'

'Oh, why not?' She smiles weakly: 'Haven't slummed north of Inglis since Rick left. Thanks, Jack. And please tell your wife – '

'Marla.'

'Please tell Marla I'm bringing enough potato salad to feed a pack of ravenous dogs.'

'All right! Sunday then, around four, it's supposed to stay hot.' Jack looks painfully pensive, then plunges: 'And you know of course I'm doing this just to see you in shorts.'

Anne squints indulgently, as she does in the store when Jack pretends to know something: 'Same here, Jack, and make sure it's your skimpiest speedo.'

Jack howls in relief and waves her off: 'Take care, Anne.'

He must wait to turn left against oncoming traffic onto Izaak Walton. What a nice man, thinks Anne, and remembers her father teaching her to cut angles on a mitre box when they built the doll house that still sits in Leslie's room. Leslie. Too old for dolls now. She swings her head away from Jack's winking tail lights and sees the crowd and flashing red lights at the entrance to the Project. Leslie! Something's happened! Suddenly clear-headed again, she clutches her purse and runs, thinking, I deserve this, I deserve this, dear God, take me instead.

A black stretch-limousine is parked illegally across the entrance, with a police car behind it and another in front, and a couple of police motorcycles leaning like toughs at a bar. One policeman, looking threateningly overheated in high boots, tight-waisted jacket, helmet and reflecting shades, stands near the limo stiffly spread-legged and with hands behind back. Some in the crowd she recognises, though none lives in the Project. There are long saw-horses across the entrance and another policeman checks the identification of those from the Project wanting to enter. Pulling her wallet from her purse and her driver's licence from her wallet Anne hurries to the makeshift gate, continuing her prayer while asking, 'What's happened? Has anyone seen Leslie?'

Ignoring her flipped plastic, the policeman says, 'It's nothing to be alarmed about, Anne. You have a celebrity visiting today, that's all. Mr Master Conrad Aaron, the guy from out West. Relax.'

'Huh,' she says, distracted, peering into the tacky courtyard of the Project, picking out the knot of people moving along the walk in front of her place and wondering about the odd nimbus of light that surrounds them. Project people crowd the margin around the dark central figure and his knot.

'Anne,' says the policeman, 'it's me, Mark, Mark Fournier from Salmon Run. Hey, do you guys sell dog leashes at Home? We've been getting tons of complaints about dogs running loose here in Troutstream, packs of 'em. I know for a fact that that old hippie on Tackle has been letting his Shepherd run free, and I think he's been beating that dog pretty badly. And you know that Vietnam-ese family two doors down from where you used to live? Well, someone, or some*thing*, mangled *both* their cats just a couple of nights ago.'

'Yes, officer, of course we sell leashes. Excuse me, please.'

'Anne?' He watches her walk away and smirks in disappointment.

The small crowd has paused at her door! As she hurries forward she registers that the bright light is artificial, and that the knot of people, like the lights above the two tv cameras, is focused on a tall man in black. She has trouble pushing through: 'This is *my* house, this is *my* home, if you don't mind, please. My *daughter* is in there.'

A tall boy smelling of body odour keeps his elbow in her face and says, 'Lady, they're the CBC, if *you* don't mind. Settle down. The Master's answering now, watch him wipe the floor with that little bitch.'

Anne jams her heel down on his toes, his eyes bug like a choked frog's and he's easily shoved aside. When she reaches the rim of the inner circle, her own eyes widen: Leslie in faded black jeans and blue plaid shirt with sleeves rolled to the elbows stands alone beside the tall man in black. Anne cannot step into the lighted circle. It's as though something has captured Leslie, or consumed her whole and is displaying her live but inaccessible in its belly like a huge fish bowl. Anne focuses on her face, Leslie's yet not Leslie's: staring straight ahead but unseeing, then with the slightest of anticipant smiles. For a fleet moment Anne recalls the face of Iris's friend Mavis. The man nervously snorts a laugh and speaks into a bouquet of microphones, but Anne doesn't hear. The mikes drop down to Leslie's face, one brushes her ear, another clips the side of her head, she says 'Ouch!' and rubs her head, making a mean–little–girl face like some kid in a tired sit-com, like the girl on that *Full House* who's learned to act like she's acting cute. Leslie pouts, the reporters laugh while cameras whirr, and the tall man puts his hands on his knees and bends down: 'Now, sweetheart, is Mr Aaron's answer good enough for you, dear? Will you soften your position on the Change Party? Do we have your vote?' Everyone laughs again, the BO boy whistles and claps his hands above his head.

A young woman reporter tilts her microphone towards her own impatient mouth and asks, 'What *do* you think of that answer, Leslie?'

Leslie composes herself in a way Anne has never seen before, and speaks without hesitation or shyness: 'Are you kiddin'? This guy doesn't care about us at all. Let *him* try living here for just a month, *then* I'd believe he cares. Let *him* try working as hard as my Mom works, take care of a house and raise a kid by himself. *Then* I'd believe he knows how we feel. He just wants to get elected, just like he said, *that's* all *he* wants, that's all *any* politician wants.'

Breathing hard through his nose, suddenly ashen about the gills, Master Aaron straightens, moves in front of Leslie and walks towards the entrance; unsmiling, he signals to others in the crowd like he's twirling a lasso.

Anne reaches and takes Leslie by the upper arm, stoops and gives her a long hug. 'What was *that* all about, young woman?'

'I've seen that goof on tv,' says Leslie, unsmiling herself now. 'I can't believe anyone believes a word he says. You shoulda heard the crap he was saying about this place. He even talked about that guy you hate who owns the bar, what a great Canadian he is. But I gotta see him leave, I'll be right back.'

Leslie runs after the entourage. Anne straightens, and beside her the gawky kid is waving a piece of paper and desperately asking the people surging towards the entrance, 'Do any of you people know where there's a place called the Troutstream Arms? People, please, do any of you know – '

'I do,' says Anne. 'Why?'

The startled boy drops his arm. 'Uh, I have a note here from Master Aaron for the owner, one . . .' He unfolds the slip of paper and reads, 'One P. Archembault . . . I think.'

'Yeah, you got that one right. So what?'

'Well, I gotta run, lady, or they'll leave me behind. Supper at the Press Club! Look: I'll give you twenty bucks if you'll deliver this note for me.'

'Make it forty and you gotta deal, Junior.'

The boy takes out a thick matted envelope and fishes for two twenties, which he hands to Anne with the note, and runs off.

Anne unfolds the paper and reads: 'Dear P. Archembault, I am so sorry to have to inform you that I will not be able to visit your premises on this trip to Ottawa.' The note is typed lightly, with the addressee's name, the word 'Ottawa' and some others written in green ink. 'I will make it a point, however, to visit your establishment the next time I'm in Ottawa, which I trust will be soon. I look forward to your continuing support, P. Yours for a Changed Canada, Master Conrad Aaron.' It looks like a genuine signature, but the ghostly border of blue ink proves it a stamp.

Anne feels a rising giddiness as she runs after Leslie. At the gate the boy who'd given her the note gets into the back seat of the limo, which is already rolling. Motion in the upper periphery of her vision, a white blur, which she follows as it lobs over the crowd to splat on the hood of the car. An egg. A resounding cheer. A stone or piece of gravel follows, then others in a light hail. The police do nothing.

She finds Leslie giving her name and address into the woman

reporter's tiny tape recorder. When Anne comes up, the reporter flashes a smile: 'Is this your mother, Leslie?'

Leslie turns, 'Hi, Mom, I'm gonna be on tv!'

'What's this all about?'

'*This* is about this remarkable daughter you've got here, Mrs Cameron. I think this young woman was born to be on television.'

'Huh?'

'*Really?*'

'I'm sorry,' the reporter says, 'but we've gotta run. It's six twenty-two now, and we promised live feed to the local affiliate for their evening broadcast.' With a forefinger across her throat she signals her crew and moves off, shouting over her shoulder, 'It should be on before seven, then maybe again on *Prime Time* with Pete. Hurry home and shove a tape in the VCR. And Leslie, please call me sometime soon, I'm serious about the tour of our facilities. You're a natural, kid!'

She gets behind the wheel of a red, white and blue station wagon bearing the blurred CBC logo and, as the other doors are still shutting, shoots away, spraying a few bystanders with kerb-dirt. Some people clap lamely. The thinning crowd inside the gate are subdued after the violence against the Aaron entourage, wearing the drained look of the media-blitzed: life in the Project suddenly feels even shabbier after the bright lights, impossible to believe in.

Anne has hustled back to her door. 'Joan,' she says to the plump and pasty woman standing in the door not three feet from her own, 'would you please look after Leslie for just another half-hour or so? *Please?* She can stay by herself in our place.'

'No problem, Annie. I wasn't expecting you till a lot later anyway. Hey, but you shoulda seen that kid of yours askin' questions! And answerin' 'em too!'

Leslie is already deep in the corner of the dark interior, kneeling in front of the bright tv and loading a tape. She shouts without turning, 'Mommy, I've decided: when I grow up I'm gonna be a tv reporter like Brenda!'

'Honey, you can be anything you want!' It's been a long time since she's said that and believed it. 'I'll be back in fifteen minutes, okay, Leslie? . . . Leslie?'

'She said I'm a natural!'

At the entrance to the Project Anne is startled to find Iris and Fred and their friend Mavis talking to the cop . . . Mark, her old neighbour from the Complex. But this time it's Mark who doesn't notice *her*, and even when she speaks he only glances, giving his full attention to Mavis like someone being told a rumour about himself.

'Iris, Fred, back to the Arms! You don't wanna miss this!'

But Iris and Fred only smile at Anne like shy people passing along the reception line at a funeral home. Anne doesn't pause, and just as she's passing out of earshot she hears Mark say, 'A blue box, you say, *a large blue box*? Somewhere near *here*. But how do you come to know this, Ma'am? And besides, no one's reported a missing person, man, wom . . .'

Paul Arsenault stands in his office with his left foot forward and his right arm cocked in oratorical appeal, its thumb and forefinger like a starter's pistol, with a film of perspiration evaporating on his dome, and with draft one of his *Current Affairs* editorial in his left hand. He glances at the clock – eighteen thirty-two. Twenty-eight minutes to the absolutely grandest moment of his life, thus far. Of course, he could never get the newsletter copied and distributed in time now. . . . Inspiration! He would stand before the big screen in the bar and read the editorial aloud to the Master! . . . *Easy, at ease, Private First-Class Roger.* At the noise from the bar, a noise that usually makes him jingle the change in his pocket, he strains to ascertain that it is not *the* arrival, then wishes he'd simply closed the bar for the day and held a private party for the Master. He smirks and imagines that it's Hughie throwing out that scag-bag troublemaker from the Project he'd snubbed.

He collects himself and reads aloud:

Arsenault on Arsenals

It looks like nuclear weapons are much out of fashion these days with the Big Brains up on Parliament Hill, when it's unfashionable to think of national defence and the future of our kids' kids, while popular to spend billions housing indigent bums and so-called refugees such as them who dwell in the Project, otherwise known as Pissed-in-Court. (Yes, why not call a spade a spade!) But as Martin Amis (son of Kingsley) writes in *Einstein's Monsters*, 'They squat on our spiritual lives.' By which he means that nuclear weapons keep the countries of the world from acting like tired brats at a kids' party. Amis, Jr: 'Nuclear weapons deter a nuclear holocaust.' And it's true, of course, believe you me. For centuries the idea of God (still more than an idea for me I don't mind saying!) and the Devil and the threat of hell kept us in line. (The great Stephen Leacock, he and Mordecai Richler being Canada's best writers, has an essay about this very subject called 'The Devil and the Deep Sea'. Read and weep my friends.) And the Bible forecast of an Armageddon that would make any mere nuclear holocaust a weenie roast by comparison. Yes my friends and faithful clientele, the threat of instant annihilation was always there, because people believed literally in God and Armageddon (Arm-a-geddon warmed up now, Master – pun intended! **Wait for laughter**). But seriously folks, if you give it a long and hard think: that's what made life worth living and meaningful. And when they (God and Armageddon) were taken away (like half your pay-check – oops, sorry, *cheque* – by the Brain Drain on the Ottawa River), we missed them. That's why history from about 1850 till about 1945 was so crazy, because there was nothing to keep us in line after we killed God and cancelled Armageddon. We thought we could keep ourselves in line and found out we can't, we made a mess of things, like a whole planet of Sorcerer's Apprentices. And why did history begin to get better after 1945? Need I spell it out? Because we invented nuclear weapons to take the place of God, the Devil, and Armageddon. (And we rid the world of a questionably large number of shall we say *undesirables*.) And for close on to fifty years now those warheads have been doing a good enough babysitting job at the brats' party. How else can you explain how we learned so quickly to live comfortably with the idea that there was enough firepower in the world to toast it ten ways to hell? That's easy too: because we'd spent centuries living with the idea that God could do the same thing, and would some day. So we'd better be good. With the invention of nuclear weapons, the human race was open for business as usual with a huge sigh of relief.

Now a lot of politicians and unbeknownst-to-themselves warmongers want to do away with all nuclear weapons and start spending the so-called 'peace dividend' on those poor oppressed Canadians who have nothing to do all day but drink, smoke – not in the Arms, mind you! – and beat the wife and kids, and demand free taxi rides to their legal-AIDS lawyers and Brewer's Retail. Right, just what this country needs: no nuclear weapons and even more Projects. Ottawa's Shangri-la! More layabouts you can't do anything with but send off to a war, and no *real* reason *not* to start wars. Hump-jockey and Hymie will be tearing at each other's ragtops and dragging us in. What's to stop Pat and Mike from launching an all-out strike on Buckingham Palace? Hung Thin and his hoards would surely launch Pearl Harbor Two. And don't you think for a minute that Fritz isn't eager to shine up his jackboots and waltz across Europe (though with some modifications that might not be such a bad idea!). Don't kid yourselves. I'm not kidding myself.

Friends, neighbours, fellow Canadians, and faithful clientele, I come now to the second major point of my editorial. And that is to welcome to Troutstream and the Troutstream Arms the one political leader in Canada who sees clearly the dangers of nuclear disarmament and a growing welfare state, not to mention open-door immigration and bilingualism. I am talking of course about the leader of the Change Party, Master Conrad Aaron, who is paying his first visit to Ottawa today and, at the request of your humble scribe, has deigned to drop by the Arms (we trust it won't be the last time he drops in – to the Arms or Ottawa, if you know what I mean!).

Roger, down boy, down. At ease, sir!

Master Aaron, Welcome! We've been hoping you'd visit for a long time!! We need you, Master Aaron!!! Canada needs you, Master Aaron!!!! Master Aaron *is* Canada!!!!! Canada *is* Master Aaron!!!!!!

Perfect, perfecto mundo, no call for other drafts . . . '. . . such proud Canadians as dwell here in Troutstream,' that voice, congratulating him, comes from within Paul's office. 'Even we Canadians who suffer the consequences of big government and are forced to live in subsidised housing should yet feel proud to be Canadians. As I, born in poverty, am proud to be a Canadian.' It's like surfacing breathlessly from a dream filled with dark naked girls lusting for him. He'd not even known his big screen was still on. He glances at his watch – eighteen fifty already! – and returns to the screen. The Master again! On . . . Inglis! *Ro-ger, you traitor!*

To drown the commotion in the bar, Paul hits the volume on the built-in control on his desk. The scene cuts from the Master to that cute reporter with the big hair Paul would not mind diving into a dream with. And she's married to a bald guy, too. Her serious face fills the screen: 'Earlier today, Change Party leader Master Aaron arrived for his first visit to Ottawa. At that time he assured this reporter that his visit was not going to be spent among the rich and powerful only, but that he would be visiting some subsidised housing projects in the Ottawa area. However, it has been discovered that this was not originally on the itinerary, that in fact the visit to Piscine Court represents a change in plan following repeated accusations that the Change Party not only has no intention of including a *real* social contract in its platform but would vigorously resist any such clause in a revised Constitution.' That condescending smirk: 'Damage control, I think the spin doctors call it. So the impromptu visit to Troutstream, a suburb of Ottawa – '

A shout from the bar, 'Foster!' which Paul hears but doesn't react to. Moisture is draining from his mouth, small stars are flashing in his peripheral vision, he grows light-headed and steadies himself on the desk edge.

In the bar Anne stands close to and facing the big screen, which she'd insisted be turned on, hurriedly convincing Hughie that Master Aaron is talking about Paul on the local news. Leslie's small face fills the big screen, and the whole bar is hushed by those who recognise her. Just to the left of her face there is a black line, which Anne knows to be Master Aaron's leg. At first Anne does not hear what Leslie is saying, because again it's like watching her daughter trapped in some alien space. With a heart-swelling recognition of permanent loss, she knows that this time she cannot touch her. She thinks again of Mavis and smirks slightly at what the witch did not know about her good news. She listens almost indifferently to the unfamiliar voice of her child:

'. . . I don't know *why* he likes that guy that owns the Troutstream Arms. That man is always writing this stupid newsletter that my teacher Mr O'Donaghue says is badly written – *propaganda*. Full of these stupid jokes about new Canadians, but especially about all the people who live here. Like we *want* to live here, right? *Duh,*' as she twirls her forefinger at her temple.

The mike shoots up to Master Aaron's tight smile, and the reporter asks, 'Well, Master Aaron. Why *does* your party attract so many loonies from the fringe of the right?'

The shot pulls back, and Master Aaron places a large palm on Leslie's head. She swipes backwards knocking it off. There is a moment of silence, even on the screen. Then the bar erupts in cheers and whistles, and a chant begins at the table where Anne had sat with Iris, Fred and Mavis: 'Les-lie Les-lie Les-lie . . .' The Master's answer is lost, though not the stunned look that preceded it. His response trails into something about 'good people and hard work' and 'thank God we *still* live in a country where dreams such as this . . . little girl's can *still* be realised, and where these Project people can work their way up and out of these subsidised – *substandard*, Brenda – ghettos.'

Close-up on Brenda's face, the sound and light are slightly different, and her hair is combed; she twists her mouth ever so slightly: 'These *who*, sir?'

The mike is back at Leslie's face and Brenda asks, 'How do you like being characterised like that, Leslie?'

Leslie's eyes roll upwards for a second showing whites only, and Anne gasps. Leslie remains without expression for a moment, and the black margin disappears from the right side of the screen.

Then it pours out: 'Look here, my Mom works hard all day over at Home Hardware, and she's the best Mom in the world, and I love her more than anything.' *Don't cry, honey.* 'My Dad, Rick Cameron, just left us for no good reason, and he pays no money to help Mom, he just takes advantage of other women like he did my Mom and me. And that ugly goof who owns the Troutstream Arms just hates everybody and wants everything his way, and always makes fun of people like my Mom, and always writes about what a great guy this man is and how he would run Canada the right way.' Leslie compresses her lips and looks delightfully impish: 'My Mom calls him Master *Error*.'

Who is that young actress?

Brenda snickers: 'Well, Master *Aaron*, how do you respond to this young Canadian?'

The Master is stone-faced, but paler: 'Brenda, as I've told you before, the Change Party is doing its best to dissociate itself from those on the lunatic fringe like the sick and twisted owner of this Troutstream Barn, or whatever it is. There will always be nutcases, and this fellow sounds like his own cluster. But you would be wrong, *and* unfair, to confuse the principles of Change with the self-aggrandising desires of some demented farmer.'

The Master's smiling face appears beside Leslie's and asks, 'Now, sweetheart, is that answer good enough for you, dear? Will you soften your position on the Change Party? Do we have your vote?' And the reporter's voice asks, 'What *do* you think of that answer, Leslie?'

But Leslie's answer, which Anne has heard already, and which will be broadcast later on Prime Time, and for weeks in every piece about Master Aaron, with the name Master Error prominent, is lost in the sound of a thunderous blast. Everyone silences, lights flicker, the screen goes blank with fizz and pop. Only the ceiling lights come on. Plaster dust descends upon the disco ball as gently as first snow. Hughie is crashing through people to get to the back-of-the-bar office. Anne follows in his wake, holding high the note like a mockery of truce.

From the doorway she watches Hughie reach around Paul, grab the gun by its hot barrel, take it away in two pieces and set them on the desk.

Facing the demolished screen, Arsenault says, 'Forgive him, Lord. That brat drove him to it.'

Wary of the shattered glass, Hughie takes Arsenault by the elbows and turns him. Anne gasps.

The fowling piece has misfired, blackening Arsenault's face so that his eyes look bloodshot and wide awake, and his long side-hair, where it hasn't been scorched, is swept into twirled points like some bozo's.

Hughie grins: 'Are you okay, boss? You . . . you look like a nigger!'

Arsenault doesn't move a muscle: 'Get, that, woman, out of here.'

'Just a sec, Hughie boy,' Anne smiles when she sees Arsenault recovering. 'Don't shoot the messenger, eh, 'cause I've got a message from *the* Master for *the* Arsehole. Here.'

She holds the paper at arm's length. Arsenault brings his arm up stiffly like it's hinged only at the shoulder. He unfolds the note and reads, then commences quivering. As he is enfolded by Hughie in a manly hug, Anne turns and walks through the bar, where the chant has grown raucous and universal – 'Les-lie Les-lie Les-lie' – pushes out the door and into the warm autumn evening.

· 8 ·

The End of Jokes

·

Know what Shitbag did today? I mean, different from his regular doings? Such as: conversational nose-picking and ear-auguring, or leaning across my desk to explain my work and displaying fresh angles by which I can confirm again that his scalp is as unavoidably flaky as a two-day-old turnover, or closing his eyes and tipping back his head and saying Ahhhh like I really could have explained myself better, then batting his lashes as he chirps No-no-no and asserts the opposite to what I've suggested, or plucking his underwear from the crack of his ass when he turns to leave, shaking his bag off his leg as he walks away laughing like a revved-up Elmer Fudd, splay-footed.

I know, I know what you're thinking: *no one* who behaved like that could hold a job holding the spit bucket at a fight. And normally you'd be right. Thing is, abnormal Shitbag behaves this way only around me. To his superiors he is a flatterer of the first hole. To secretaries and janitors he is simply the curt superior. Only to his equals (perceived) is he the essential Shitbag, brazenly displaying his *raison d'être* as fleshy container of fuming excrement. Meaning, only *I* get to see him as the true *sac de merde*, because there are only two technical writers in this pod of the National Research Council's Division of Laser Technology – Shitbag and I, together forever in a windowless corner with just a baby-blue barrier diagonally between us, I and Shitbag, like two wedges without a door.

But yes, I'd almost forgotten: What did Shitbag do today?

He gave me a gift. In congratulation for completing my probation period here at the NRC. And as he handed me this gift, Shitbag said, 'No hard feelings about the review, eh Mark? I was just doing my job.'

The accompanying card, larger than the actual gift, displayed one of those Gary Larson cartoons, not one of his best, though I find his work not to my taste in any case. Perhaps it's a generational thing, though I think he's closer to my age than the NRC losers, young and old, who titter daily at his endless takes on the one anthropocentric joke. I all but immediately threw the card in the garbage, but I can describe it from memory. Three wolves crouch behind a tree at respectful distance from a cave where three cavemen stand around a fire. Another wolf sits on his haunches by the cave scene, tongue lolling and eyes as vacant as a beaten dog's. Back at the tree one of the wolves is saying, 'It's Bob, all right . . . but look at those vacuous eyes, that stupid grin – he's domesticated, I tell you.' Admittedly there's something humorous about the wolf on his way to doghood, but otherwise this kind of joke does nothing for me, it has no point.

The gift was one hundred business cards with my name embossed in fourteen-point bold, 'Dr Mark Macdonald'; below that and two points smaller the title 'Technical Writer'; our division, 'Laser Technology'; then the address of the National Research Council of Canada, phone and fax numbers.

'Thank you, Sh . . . Sherman,' I drawled carefully like the brain-damaged. 'No sweat about the review. If I'd been fired, dismissed, terminated, declared redundant, hung out, kissed off, downsized, depersonnelised, or whatever the hell they're calling *betrayed* these days, you'd've unintentionally done me a big favour. Hey, funny card, like I'm suppose to be the domesticated wolf now that I'm permanent, right?'

'Or me,' Shitbag smirked, sliding round to his side of the divider, head tucked and shaking.

I called across the hollow divide: 'These business cards look like my tombstone.'

And Shitbag fluted his favourite refrain: 'A job's a job, Herr Doktor.'

At my probationary review Shitbag had questioned, not my actual work – a failing grade twelve English student equipped with the Style Sheet could do the work – but what he called my 'attitude', the 'sincerity of my commitment to Council objectives', my 'interpersonal skills'. He said all this in my presence, no doubt confident I was gone anyway, though he was not so damaging as that lard-assed Jack Kavanagh, head of our 'team', who said he had no complaints about my attitude but wondered how long someone with a PhD would be happy correcting his illiterate scribbling (his words). Eugene Davies, the other senior engineer, sickly slim and with ears like some innovative wind machine, seemed to sleep through the whole rigmarole. When startled into response, he referred to me as *Dr Macdonald*, said that he was sure I'd work out just fine, said in fact that it was an honour finally to work with a technical writer with a PhD. *Work* with me? Shitbag and I spend our days mopping up the mess Kavanagh and Davies make of the language, and it's like cleaning up a battlefield where both sides died of heart failure, crapping themselves copiously.

But the whole performance review was *pro forma* anyway. What those assholes don't know is that Division Supervisor Peter Donovan and I share an alma mater, the University of Waterloo, where we both received our undergraduate degrees in engineering. That was over twenty years ago. We were co-conspirators in the radical student movement of those times, protesting the Tricky Dick regime in beards that suggested hormone imbalance more than Che, denouncing Trudeau's invocation of the War Measures Act in tattered jeans that need concede nothing to the human belly. (Do I have to explain those 'historical' references? Please, no.) Pete, who always refused the soft drugs I ingested regularly, went on to do his doctorate in bio-medical engineering at Texas A&M. I switched to English and beer for an MA at the selfsame Waterloo, then took ten years to complete a doctorate and a lagoon of cheap scotch at Lakehead and Memorial. But no university or college in the mid-eighties would hire a recent PhD already in his late thirties, not according to the inequitable affirmative-action policies of politically correct academe. Strangely enough (because I can't stand 'irony' in my life), I was being thwarted by some of the very political principles I'd midwifed in the sixties and early seventies.

After about a half dozen years of doing this and that here and there, I ran into Pete Donovan at the Troutstream Arms, the local bar in the neighbourhood where I now rent a government-subsidised apartment. I'd come to watch a darts tournament final, having developed a taste for darts and dark bitter while at Memorial U. Pete also lives in Troutstream, in the better neigh-bourhoods north of Inglis, as do half the people who work at the NRC. (Some place, this Troutstream. Remember the Monkees? The so-called Pre-Fab Four? Remember their song, 'Pleasant Valley Sunday'? This was a long time ago, I know, but you must remember: *please* don't make me explain everything, it's too painful. Suburban sameness? Barbecued boredom everywhere? Pleasant Valley? Remember now? The Monkees were an imitation, and their anti-suburbia protest song was an imitation, and the situation they were protesting, middle-class complaisance, was, *ironically*, the very thing that made the Beatles exciting, the Stones dangerous, and the Monkees possible. Anyway, that's my private name for Troutstream North: Pleasant Valley. A long way to go for a poor joke, I know.) Half-drunk, Pete told me about his job, that he made eighty thousand a year, with great benefits, and that he could get me started as a technical writer at forty grand. *Starting* salary, mind you, for as Pete stressed: in a Crown corporation there are no limits for a motivated white man with a PhD in *anything*. I was currently teaching English as a Second Language for part-time peanuts to a motley crew in a smelly old schoolhouse in downtown Ottawa. I hadn't a friend in the world but this dwarfish welfare bum at work, Nigel, who regularly lies to his case worker and pulled strings to get me a hole in this housing project. So I leapt at Pete's offer. Pete saluted with his pint of genuine dark bitter and ordered me to sing our old fight song. But I didn't remember any old fight songs from the numerous schools where I'd learned defeat. Luckily, sloshed Pete's fight song had something to do with longhorns and cowboys, so I mooed along.

From there it was an amnesiac night. Smoky images: of the darts tournament winner, a wiry little Scotchman, being presented with a trophy that was a mounted dildo, of a fat and putty-fleshed

waitress running through with her top undone and play-scream-
ing, then back the other way and really screaming with a dart
embedded in the ample flesh of her ass, of the bar's owner, Paul
somebody, sitting at our table and he and Pete reviling immigrants
and Jews for the state of the Canadian economy . . . clouds of
confusion, thunderous bad jokes, torrential laughter . . . a back-
of-the-bar office and a big bottle of Bushmills, and Pete and Paul
talking of neo-Nazism and the KKK, a girlie magazine showing
hairless adolescent females, Oriental looking, and Paul somebody
literally drooling on a centrefold. Or were some of them
photographs?

Next morning I was shocked only to recall Pete's behaviour,
but I guess the American South can do that to even the most liberal
of us. I also remembered the promised job.

That was four months ago. I am currently preparing to move
out of the Project and into my newly purchased condominium on
Casting Avenue in the complex south-west of Inglis. Pete Donovan, still smitten with some old integrity and loyalty, now phones
me at home and whispers that he's working on my promotion to
editor. Then, who knows? Senior editor? Director of publishing
operations? A wife, kids, a real home in Troutstream? Why not? I
am, after all, the only one in the Council's publishing programme
with a PhD (thus Shitbag's envious 'Herr Doktor'). And I'm
motivated. No longer the self-styled buccaneer, more and more
I've regretted missing the boat of conventionality. I want to board
that social ship now. And I will, by hook or by crook.

While pondering problems such as the deployment of 'bullets'
and 'boldface' in a report on experimental polishes for telescope
mirrors (I don't have to understand the subject), I still sometimes
ask myself, Why am I here? Mundanely such questioning is
inspired by some noise from Shitbag on the other side of our
'soundproof' divider, like he's hung his face, loosened his jowls
and rapidly shaken his head, making a sound like Donald Duck.
(Really, he does that frequently, as an antidote to fatigue.) But I
don't always mean my question specifically. My philosophical
speculations can run from conceiving myself as the Big Bang
evolved to self-consciousness, to viewing myself as a divinely
designed producer of shit. I mean, the only things that make my

life bearable are cigarettes, beer and marijuana, jokes, and *The Tonight Show* starring Johnny Carson. But I can't smoke in the places where I used to smoke, much beer leaves me liversick for days, the price of weed has gone through the roof (though the roof's been raised a few feet since I landed this plum job), and Johnny's been replaced by Jay (even the name signals diminution), a guy who looks like he's permanently wearing one of those Mulroney masks you can buy across from Parliament Hill. I read an interview with Leno where he happily says he just doesn't *do* offensive material. So this marks the end of jokes.

Speaking of jokes, the Herr Doktor of Shitbag's refrain actually refers to a couple of things, the most obvious being his envy of my PhD. (He has only an MA, or have I said that already?) But the Teutonic address has at least one other significance.

Early on here, I did an uncharacteristic thing and had Shitbag and his wife, Sara, over for a barbecue. 'Charcoal burning everywhere . . .' We Projectiles (as Nigel calls us) share a barbecue pit. Shitbag no sooner slid his baggy ass into one of the plastic adirondacks than he said with all the whining volume ever at his beck that *he* could never live in a place like this.

'But it's so *pleasant*, honey,' Sara smiled at me, handing over a screw-top bottle of wine imported from Brobdingnag. 'Mark'll soon have his own condo, and there's so much *space* out here.'

'Oh, I didn't mean to imply anything but,' Shitbag hurried in mock-amazement. 'I was just saying what suits me.'

Yes, Shitbag.

'Hey Mark, what'd you think of those women on the Hill yesterday?'

A number of women had demonstrated topless on Parliament Hill because men can go bare-chested and they can't. Shitbag was baiting me, Sara must be militant. This is how gentleman Shitbag puts new acquaintances at ease.

'I'm behind them all the way, Sherman.'

Sara smiled warily.

'And if the law gets changed, I want to get in front of them.'

Shitbag revved up his Elmer Fudd, while the smirking Sara, a dark beauty, helped us all to more wine. Strangely enough, we were off to a good start. Till Shitbag added: 'Someone said in the paper today that he was against it because there were already enough *boobs* on Parliament Hill. Get it, *boobs?* Heh-heh. That's better than yours, Marcus.'

I said, 'Sara, what do you think?'

'I think these women want one law to permit baring and another to prevent staring.'

I laughed. 'Hey, that's pretty good . . . for a feminist.' Did Shitbag know his own wife? He was capable of any misreading, that steaming pile of ego.

'When did feminism come into it?' she said.

It had clouded over, so we ate supper around an arborite table in my 'living room'. They both ate bowls of salad and potato salad and coleslaw, not even touching their burgers.

'Aren't they cooked to your taste, or are you guys vegetarians or something?'

'Something like,' Shitbag snivelled. He hurriedly added that Jack Kavanagh had to be at least fifty, and Sara said he didn't look *that* old. They caught themselves and grinned sheepishly at me.

'I'm forty.'

Sara did a comic startled face. She complained that Shitbag worked too hard, that he was doing more than his share and others weren't carrying their load. Shitbag condescendingly explained that, *Honey*, Mark and I are our pod's whole team of technical writers. The situation was teetering when out of the blue tipsy Shitbag gave it a running kick by revealing that for over a year they'd been trying to have a baby. *His* sperm count was *way* off the chart, needless to say. Sara must be the problem. (The worst legacy of the sixties: the licensing of such abrupt personal revelations; these twentysomethings just don't have the conditioned restraint we always felt, even at our most liberated.) In *his* family children were *everything*. *Everything*, he insisted, as though Sara and I were arguing the contrary. *Really*, why else *are* we here if not to leave offspring? he asked, sneering about my lowly quarters as though *here* might just have to do as proving ground for his and Sara's existence.

Sara excused herself and spent more time in the washroom than it would take to kick the shit out of Shitbag.

I must confess, though, the *faux pas* of the night belonged to your gracious host. Not long after Sara returned from weeping for the children she didn't have despite Shitbag's chart-topping ejaculations, and because she'd been sitting morosely, I thought to retell the innocuous joke I'd heard the proprietor of the Troutstream Arms tell quietly across his bar a few evenings before.

'Why don't Jews drink?'

Maybe I should have noticed how the question immediately got Sara's attention: 'We – '

Or perhaps I should have wondered why Shitbag shushed her with a flapping hand, or why his thick black brows crinkled his rat's face in an expression of bemusement as foreign to Shitbag as goodwill: 'Why?'

'Because it would interfere with their suffering.'

'That's good,' said tight-smiling Shitbag. 'My old man would love that one, he tells the best anti-Semitic jokes I've ever heard. We're Jewish, you know.'

'Yeah, I know.'

With a palm pressing her abdomen Sara again felt along the wall to the can.

And I, with sweat now splashing down the small of my back, grinned at Shitbag and tipped my head at the bathroom: 'Might be a good sign there.'

Shitbag pursed his lips and shook his head rapidly. He raised the bun of his burger, peeked under and said in a comical voice, 'Hello, hello, anyone ta home?' Then spoke deeply out the side of his mouth: ''S'all right.'

Three months after my probationary review an editor in our division fulfilled a life's dream by quitting to open a sports card store in Smiths Falls, a town about an hour west of Ottawa. His wife would have to remain a full-time nurse at the Ottawa General, commuting daily, shift work. Shitbag fired in his application for promotion. I submitted mine the day the process closed. At quarter to five Shitbag asked if I'd bothered applying.

'Sure, why not.'

He stood before me jiggling like someone riding a freight car, with one finger auguring his ear and the other hand plucking at the ass of his pants: 'Hey, that's great, smart move, shows you're

169

committed, motivated, just don't be too disappointed when – *if* you don't get it.' The Elmer Fudd laugh. 'You'll be taking over as senior technical writer.' There was no such title. 'Then you'll be the next editor when I get booted upstairs, Herr Doktor.'

Shitbag, where does the kicking line form?

Next day I received a call from Pete Donovan to come up to his top-floor office suite in Tower One. Eugene Davies, Jack Kavanagh and two top brass were there. Kavanagh was admiring Pete's panoramic view of the Ottawa River some distance to the north, while the others were lounging around Pete's desk twisting stir sticks or poking them through Styrofoam coffee cups. I waited in the doorway feeling strangely short of breath.

'Come in, Mark, come in,' Pete said. 'Informality's the rule up here. Of course you already know Jack Kavanagh and Eugene Davies.' Davies stood and pumped my hand once, collapsed back in his chair; Kavanagh threw a tight smile over his shoulder and returned to his view. 'And this rotund gentleman is Bradley MacKenzie, Senior Personnel Officer, and this hyphenated lout is Victor Arthur-Gladstone, *Vag* we call him in private, V-P in charge of our division, the whole shebang.'

Pleased, pleased.

'Mark,' Pete continued, 'we want to make this short and sweet. By a majority vote we have decided that you're the man for the editor's job.'

He dropped his voice: 'Now, I don't anticipate any problems but we do want your promotion to go as smoothly as it should.'

And down to a whisper: 'Normally, you see, the position might have been offered to your associate, Sherman Wills, but we have decided this time to bypass conventional channels and simply offer the job to the best man.'

'Thank you.'

A noise like a snort of laughter from Kavanagh at the window.

'Jack?' said Pete.

Kavanagh turned and looked only at me: 'Look, Mark, I have nothing against you personally. In fact, I always find you good for a laugh, even when the joke's publicly at the expense of me and my poor writing. But you may as well know, the one dissenting vote was mine. Because I still don't see why we're *not* following established practice . . . though I have my suspicions. Sherman Wills has been with us longer. *And*, PhD or not, frankly I think he's a better writer and he'd make a better editor. That's what I said in this room this morning, and now you've heard it too. Nothing personal, though, and no hard feelings, I hope.'

He stepped over in three strides and shook my hand vigorously. Foolishly I held on when he tried to withdraw and managed to say steadily, 'Of course not, Jack. I appreciate your candour, though I cannot concur with your view, needless to say, *I* hope.'

Jack laughed and slapped my shoulder, said to the others, 'See what I mean?'

The personnel guy tried to jolly him: 'That's the spirit, big guy, no big deal, and remember our agreement, eh?'

Jack turned, his smile fading to non-committal: 'What agreement was that, Brad?'

No one spoke.

'Yeah well look,' Pete finally chuckled, 'I'm sure *everyone* has a valid point of view but we did sort of agree that Sherman Wills hasn't the interpersonal skills a management position requires.'

'We did?' said Jack. 'Then I'll say it again: he'd mostly be teaching a bunch of fresh-faced college kids how to make our scribbling readable. He can do that, and plenty more, and he's got seniority. And, if we are going to get personal, I think Sherman and his wife have a child on the way.'

'Who's getting personal?' Eugene Davies drawled. He pursed his lips and examined the back of his right hand, grinned: 'Besides, Jack, if we promote Wills he becomes responsible chiefly for recommending future hirings of writing staff. And you know what that means, loyalty to the tribe and all that.'

'When did *that* come into it?' Jack asked.

'Easy, big guy,' Pete yawned. 'It was mentioned informally during a preliminary discussion Eugene and I had with Vag. Anyway, Gene's just joking. Anything wrong with that? A little joking among friends? Lighten up a little.'

Jack snorted, stared at MacKenzie, the personnel guy, and waited. But the guy, intent on shredding his cup, said nothing. Jack said he had to get back to work. After an uncomfortable silence, Pete pulled a bottle from a container disguised as an old book and they all welcomed me aboard with a relieved drink. Bushmills neat, the poison of choice, I guess. Abruptly the meeting broke up.

The thing was, it had all been so unreal. It had that atmosphere of false silence that immediately follows an accident. Or the unreality of being stoned on grass on a Sunday morning and walking north through a bright cool Troutstream October day and hearing that noise like raucous complaint in the air and looking up into a washed-out sky to spot a V of Canada geese heading south, and turning north again to confront a dark hot air balloon suspended menacingly close up like a hole in space. It was like we'd just been *pretending* to be doing the thing we were really doing. Playacting, imitating some imitation.

Shitbag seemed to take the news well enough, though after he received Pete's memo I thought I heard him heaving in his waste basket. There was no congratulatory gift this time, and in the weeks preceding my move up and out he began popping these thin black pills like triangular licorice from a circular dark green tin like a snuff container. Nerve pills of some sort, I guess. His hands trembled, and his ratty look seemed to grow even rattier in observance of a paranoia that is, as the old joke has it, but true knowledge of all the facts.

As Jack Kavanagh had suspected (or did he *know*, were he and Shitbag in cahoots?), it turned out my little joke at the barbecue was prescient. Sara Wills was indeed pregnant. I ran into her only once again. I was leaving work, heading out of the parking lot as she was driving in. She was sitting in their old maroon Reliant and jamming at the card machine that operates the single barrier which lifts automatically in response to pressure on the inside. She'd have been using Shitbag's card. I pulled my car to the side, got out and was at her door before she noticed me.

'Uh, uh, uh . . .' she said as I took out my card and inserted it. Nothing.

I smiled, raised my eyebrows and nodded at her swollen abdomen, said congratulations, but she didn't return my smile.

'No,' she protested as I walked to the barrier and with right hand lifted it above my head. I stood there in the Indian summer sun with a few late yellow leaves arcing down like feathers in a cartoon about some bird that's been gobbled whole out of sight. And as she passed just under the barrier, gripping the wheel and staring straight ahead, she said through her teeth, 'Who said I wanted to be pregnant . . . fascist prick.'

I started drinking and smoking once I got home. While still sensible I slipped in the tape of Johnny's last week as host of *The Tonight Show*. I fast-forwarded to Thursday, his last real show. The monologue is vintage Carson, with some jokes designed to flop so Johnny can make better jokes about his bad jokes. Mel Brooks, who was a guest on Johnny's very first show (no one saved those early tapes, as Johnny complains yet again), comes out and tells a series of Jewish jokes – anti-Semitic jokes in any non-Jew's mouth – that makes anything I've ever said seem a stump speech for militant Zionism. Mel looks like a computer-aged version of what I remember him as, and his jokes, once risqué, are now passé.

Then the event I've turned on for. Mock-solemn Johnny says that in memory of the highest-rated *Tonight Show* ever, he wants us to watch this clip from the 17 December 1969 show. It's the wedding of Tiny Tim and Miss Vicki. Unrestrained distant laughter from the current studio audience infiltrates the tape and mingles like ghost laughter with the nervous laughter of the original wedding audience. (Seeing the wedding now, you wonder why the astronomical ratings; but I guess the promise of the weirdest man who'd ever been on tv marrying an innocent girl had an anything-goes appeal for that age of Happenings. For the equivalent today you'd have to have something like Princess Diana eloping with Vegas Elvis's love child by a Sasquatch.) But the ceremony proceeds with surprising due solemnity for an event that had begun as a joke, and you can still see it was the weird sincerity of Tiny Tim himself that wouldn't let them make a total joke of his wedding. When the tape ends the most striking thing is the change in Johnny. It's like he's faded or something, worn thin, and I'm always jolted by the discovery. Then the real Tiny Tim, who probably hasn't been under tv lights much in recent decades, lopes out looking exactly as he did all those years ago. Mel Brooks notices this right away, says, 'So and tell me already, how is it I'm

173

looking like the portrait and you still look like Dorian Gray?' It's a tony joke for Johnny's show, but the audience seems to get it, or doesn't care.

Tiny Tim, still taking everything dead seriously, doesn't laugh; he places his hand flat on his chest and waits. When the laughter dies he trills, 'Oh, Mr Brooks, I've always been a strict vegetarian, and I'll bet it's all those animal fats you consume, Jewish or not.'

No one speaks.

'Well, Tiny . . .' says Johnny in his Jack Benny voice, doing that perfect collar-fiddling impression of Benny's version of someone who's both slightly hurt at being left out and a touch shocked at what's been said: 'I've never really thought of my tenderloin as *animal fat.*'

That gets a big laugh, even Tiny Tim giggles. It's the word *tenderloin* that makes the joke, three syllables, a suggestion of sexual playfulness, Johnny's a genius.

Hurried conversation reveals that Tiny Tim has reunited with Miss Vicki, that sweet and simple girl he'd married on national television way back then and subsequently been divorced by. But time is fast running out, you can see it in the way Johnny keeps looking off to his right where director Freddy de Cordova has stood for thirty years. So without further ado, Tiny Tim agrees to sing a song. He takes his ukulele from a paper bag at his feet and remains seated, the lights go down and he's spotted. He tinkles the strings and launches into the old Elvis Presley song, 'Are You Lonesome Tonight?', sings it not in the famous falsetto like your fussiest aunt gargling but in a startling voice as resonant as Elvis's. At the talking part he turns and addresses a shadowy Johnny. When he finishes the house is dead silent, then thunderous applause that lasts till Tim himself puts an end to it.

On the Wednesday, Bette Midler had sung a song to Johnny that had made him and me cry, though I can never remember its name, something about Johnny having been her hero. But with Tiny Tim now, ever-alert Johnny recognises a happening of a whole different order, and he smiles his rare smile of genuine concession: 'You know, Tim, you never had to look forever young, did you? Elvis, Marilyn, Ali, and just about everybody else in this crazy business, we weren't supposed to get old. Forever young and sexy, that was never your bag. And you know something: you were right all along.' Johnny reaches and clasps Tim's forearm, gives him that perfect wink.

'Oh, Mr Carson!'

Laughter.

(The next day I would call Shitbag up on the carpet over his increasing dereliction of duties. The man had lost it, he was a wreck. He should quit and emigrate to Israel already, start up an editorial service, become the Goebbels of the kibbutz.)

'We'll be right back . . . *not*.'

Laughter, fade.

Peeking Man

·

Big Jacques

More and more as I sit here in the dark waiting for the show to start I find myself imagining how it unfolded for Big Jacques at the beginning of the end. The planet's pelt would have rippled, naturally, and the ground eventually have shuddered beneath Big Jacques's *pieds*, and the vibrations have ridden the spine stairs to his alleged pea brain (oh, he was not so stupid as you imagine). Then the first lasting change, the dimming of the light. Though such a practical brute as Jacques would no more have noticed changed lighting than I understand symbolism in non-representational art (texture I understand). Still, the light would have changed, coldly, as at a partial eclipse of the sun, as at the dim realisation of yet another lover's rejection, as at being discovered sitting in the dark waiting for the show to start.

Some hours after impact, say at three post meridiem, Big Jacques would have looked up ponderously from his interminable munch and 'thought' like an old seventy-eight record whose plug is pulled, *What . . . was . . . tha-at? . . .*

That, big guy, was the earth moving. That, *mon semblable*, was the beginning of the end: our beginning, your end. That, you brute, is that.

But for a while there the sun still shines as stupidly as John Lennon's eyes after he'd been shot. Yes, for a time that old reliable sun shines off Jacques's pink slab of a head like an uncovered (because not worth protecting, relatively speaking) brain; shines off the underside of his endless orange neck like some ringed eternal flame; shines past his absence of shoulders like a few ton of pale shale and off his dun-coloured forelegs like millennial-old pillars. And the big guy ruminates like Elvis's last thought: *Huh-uh?* And relaxes his thirty tons of insatiable hunger, unfazed, in blissful ignorance of the cataclysm, and continues consuming.

(You may wish – oh, I know you – to think that Big Jacques was rutting at the moment of impact, your image as of some pioneer sawmill mechanically shoving an ancient oak trunk back and forth and back and forth with all the self-consciousness of a meteorite attracted nowhere in particular. Don't bother: Jacques'd have been grazing at the moment of impact, the big lug, always more interested in eating and sleeping than in mating. So keep your filthy imaginings to yourself.)

At five the following afternoon he lumbers like a moving hill towards the watering hole, where he pauses in mid-slurp and looks out on the wet green world, and the light is . . . he certainly can't figure it . . . dirty?

Back to where he was gorging last, and he feels that the gigantic ferns against his face are strangely drooped . . . a new weight in the world. While unbeknownst to Jacques – but isn't everything? – wisps of dark cloud like smoky floss scout playfully below an easing black line of sky. Oh well, eat, eat, ees good for you, beeg boy.

Next morning (and here we must play a bit with the facts), poor old Jacques actually notices the change in the light before feeling its absence. (Such *noticing* is as revolutionary as are the geophysical changes occurring. And who's to say what the big guy would have become, left alone for a few million years more? In the Museum of Nature I have seen a sculptor's conception of what an evolved dinosaur would have looked like, and he doesn't look half bad; somewhat exposed and flayed, true, because the artist didn't allow for the dinosaurian discovery of three-piece suits, but gentle certainly, upright, and touchingly vulnerable in his stripped-down,

ET-ish, polio-armed, sensitive-guy kinda way; though a beast still, make no mistake.) But *night*? When Jacques's stomach says *day*? And hey, there's something furrier about the frond brushing his tongue resistantly when it should be sluicing home to that personal primordial soup in his swamp of a gut.

But Big Jacques can think only like Ali on a drug-balanced day: *What . . . the . . . hey . . .*

He summons all his famished energy and perishing nascent promptings to self-consciousness, and thinks again like a falling Tyson: *Ah-dah . . .*

And thinks again for every shocked cell in his mortal dress: *Wah . . .*

It would be tragic, or at least laughable, if it weren't so pathetic: furry food for a herbivore-by-choice. Indeed.

(Ah, the suddenly senseless world. It makes one almost . . . young and powerful again!)

And then a new sensation in this twilight of morning: conscious panic dancing like a freed imp up and down Jacques's staired spine to that knot of reticulated nerves passing for a brain: *His* world is hot, dazzling, green, wet, global aquarium, undifferentiated womb. Now all is grey and . . . what *is* that thing?

Cold?

Cold, you say?

Cold!

. . . Cold.

His world fast become contracting pangs of hunger, Jacques eats continuously, per usual, like some unmindful dick ignorant of Nature's and God's second great commandment. Per usual, yes, maybe, but also with a new urgency in the world, an (as it were) Thoreauvian quiet desperation.

It *is* enough to make one cry, or laugh, or both. It's like reading a favourite male writer straining now to please the preponderantly female readership.

And then? (I mean, for Big Jacques.)

Oh, a little more dust in the diurnal chomp and grind than the old reptilian palate is accustomed to, a touch too much grit on the fronds'n'kelp, liquid refreshment sucked through muck more than drunk. And the recently dulled air even duller than it was only the last time he lifted that head like Fred Flintstone's dragline bucket. (All the consciousness in Jacques's world just to lift that proportionately dainty head a smidgen above subsistence, and *such* relief to drop it back to chomping along his infinite salad bar. . . . A gentle creature, really, you must concede, the brontosaurus, and harmless too, despite looking like a fearlessly and permanently exposed knob, like the severely circumcised member of a molester too lazy to act. Oh, my pre-fellow creature, whose face displays an expression as if having just been thwacked between the eyes by the spiky tail of some butchy steg. O who would not sing for simple Jacques?)

Big fella, Jacques, my man, when you mounted languorously for the last time – when was it? Who knows? Or cares for that matter. Sometime between eats – unknowing as in everything, all exquisite bruised mouth and member, Jacques, señor, when you went off upon entry like the primal insult to considerate foreplay that you are, Jacques, amigo, when you dealt with her abruptly in your beastly way, did a spark in your one-watt brain leap the gap and prod you consciously into the cold breeze of changes blowing in the granular wind? Did you, old Jacques, Big Jacques, the Jacquesman, did you know it was all over? . . .

Silence, dark dark silence, dark and bottomless, and a cold black wind a-blowin' across the world. Is it not what awaits us all? All of us, women who will have become Masters of All Matter, gone with the solar wind. And men so sensitive they refused to mate any more, gone beforehand. And who will rebuild from nothing? Without the jizz? Without the Big Guy? Go ahead and laugh if you want, but you just try it, Missy.

Day two post-Impact turns into day three, the outer and upper leaves of the ferns turn grainier and grainier, and it's like eating cheesy popcorn spilled at the beach on an overcast day, with Dad saying, We may as well go home, and day deepens unnaturally in the early afternoon. Day three and the mulch oozes only to Jacques's stumps of shins, as he stands with his befuddled delicate head in a once-nurturing green world, acrid now, while his tail like a hundred black boas anxiously flays a trunk three trees distant. More and more dust irritating the big guy's blinking eyes . . . or no, not dust, something soft and black: soot. Soon a burnt mud clogging the nasal passages and sludging his throat, the once luscious fronds pasty now, no question about that any more.

Time passes, deep night falling far too early on sunless days. With his belly but half full. And with most of that being irritant. Too early to drop down again into near inanimacy, with room still for another ton of salad, or for two dozen sickly rats the size of thin pigs (a taste he's suddenly acquired). Too early, yes, but better to sleep than to suffer this hunger for . . . For what?

And the great and colourful Jacques simply collapses onto his side, his neck whips, his head thuds, bounces once in slow motion, comes to rest. The gentle giant sleeps, never having awakened, really, to any but the basest of appetites.

Perhaps one last dull throb ripples his hide like something escaping its skin, and he ejaculates an eggwhite bathtubful. It used to be thick as mayonnaise! It used to send up its own steam cloud in praise and glory! It used to . . . It used . . . But why go on? It's all over, Jacques. *Buona notte . . . il miglior osso.*

Good God. I'm actually fucking crying! If the show starts now I won't even be able to see.

No more of this . . . this simpering self-indulgence. No more. What would my friend Nigel say?

My Friend Nigel

When he was twelve my friend Nigel startled himself with a growth spurt from which he never recovered. Not to say that Nigel suffers from gigantism or even gawkishness. Quite the contrary. It was only in the last two years of elementary school that Nigel found himself grown a good head above the rest of us, which placed him just below five feet two inches, where he stopped, in shock, or so I've always suspected. It's not easy, you see, to be a giant among men when the men are boys and your spirit is destined to animate a short adult body. By high school the rest of us were squirting past Nigel like tumescent zits, and it was too pathetic watching him try to adjust his large soul to an unaccommodating, prankish body. Most noticeably, he began carrying himself somewhat obviously: straight up and down, so rigid in the reaching carriage that his back grew slightly concave. He was willing length into his bones, you see, and is trying still, a good twenty-five years post-pubescence. I sometimes imagine that my friend Nigel is straining to turn himself into a bow for the Supreme Archer. And Nigel being Nigel, he would doubtless conceive his dick as the tip of an arrow destined for an eternally orgasmic black hole.

As recompense for its somatic practical joke, Nature blessed my friend Nigel with wit and a special sensitivity (in a manly kind of way). And though I would very much like to convince him that he constitutes a compelling compact argument contra whatever prejudice against shortness people hold, I won't. I have my reasons. In any case, the way the Cosmic Archer has arranged matters, old ironist, this essential element in Nigel's make-up – his failure to crack five foot two – is the one subject we never talk about in an otherwise liberally contrived catalogue of topics.

Or only once. We were cruising from a closing Troutstream Arms, rosy with beer and buoyed from knowing there was more at my place, when a toothless mouth said clearly from his dark hole in a field of sagging grey stubble: 'That one's suing the city for building the sidewalks too close to his arse.' The joker lowered his pig-bristly chin further into the mouth of his empty draft glass and mugged expectantly, awaiting rewarding laughter. But his two ratty friends only snickered.

My brain was suddenly infiltrated by the room's ages of piss-soaked linoleum and concrete, piss-cured cigarette filters and perfumy traces of stripperstink. I turned on the nasty joker, who'd been unable throughout the evening to keep the verbal pace set predominantly by Nigel's banter with the 'exotic dancers'. But Nigel's hand gripped my forearm, and when I looked he was in profile grinning at the exit. His head was held even more unnaturally, his colour was a shining apple's, his back a taut bow for the Devil's fiddle. From my height – six feet two inches – I observed that his tonsure was spreading.

'C'mon, cowboy,' he squawked like a nasal New Yorker, doing our *Midnight Cowboy* bit.

Outside Nigel merely nodded to a plump middle-aged woman – a sober stout immigrant type, a janitor heading home perhaps – who snorted like a deranged rocket, propelling her kerchiefed head backwards and her chest forward as she hurried off in fear and loathing. Said Nigel normally to her back, 'I could give her more pleasure, I tell you, than is dreamed of in her soaps. And I would ask for nothing in return. Nothing! . . . But will she let me?'

'Injustice, Nigel, it's everywhere. Now don't give yourself a nosebleed, and tuck in your shirt tail.'

Nigel's shirts, for example, I don't know where he gets them, but they have to be tailor-made. No real business would mass produce such torso-coverings. Below the waist he wears only blue jeans and sneakers (with the choice of thin-soled sneakers saying much about Nigel's relation to vanity). He may well have only one pair of jeans, or ten identical scruffy pairs, I don't know. But oh, my friend Nigel does drape his trunk in such a variety of brightly coloured materials as would make a gathering of hot air balloon or tall-ship enthusiasts grin sheepishly at their rigging. His sleeves are so amply accommodating that Nigel literally billows in the slightest breeze rippling across his furry nipples like a warm wind in the sea's ear. A veritable pocket Errol Flynn is my friend Nigel, a promising swashbuckler of heterosexual fucking – *if* they would only give him half a chance. Which they, being women, won't.

One other telling thing: Nigel's shoelaces. I learned at six to tie my shoes, and since then I've not given a thought to the matter of secured footwear. A standard crisscross technique terminating in a large loopy bow suited me fine then, and such still keeps my shoes – size twelve – from flying forwards and shooting backwards when I walk. But post-pubescent Nigel took the trouble to invent other ways of tying his tiny sneakers. Early on he mastered that most popular alternate method: that arrangement whereby the lace is threaded from top to bottom on the right, and then . . . God-only-knows-what-else then. I've never learned. But Nigel soon disdained such a popular alternative, seeing it as conventional in its pat unconventionality. *Nigel's* shoes I have seen tied with the laces threaded through the four corner holes only and bowed at tongue-centre. I have seen bottom and top holes tied only to each other, with a bow apiece. The very punk of grunge, he once fashioned a miniature affair involving tiny locks and near-invisible keys, even petite combination locks. I record how with telephone extension wire he once tied the right flap of his right shoe to the left flap of his left shoe, and vice-versa for the interior flaps, thenceforth slinkying from bar to bar like some accordion *à pied.* Fish hooks, paperclips, plastic snaps off bread bags, large staples, nuts and bolts, twist-ties, pipe-cleaners and dental floss, and for the ultimate in lacings, braided strands of his own abundant hair.

So don't think I exaggerate about my friend Nigel, his short-comings and gifts.

Or perhaps I might add something about Nigel's abundant hair. Wherever Nigel has been, there you will find two things: the at-once organic and mechanical trace of patchouli oil, and hair. Hair sticks straight like broom bristles from Nigel's nose, shags his chin and cheeks, tufts his ears, and even flops like a few wayward lashes from the bridge of his nose. 'Hirsute' is too exotic for my friend Nigel, *beastly*'s the word. He never trims, seldom bathes, con-vinced that these two things, patchouli oil and hair, will one day click in the better collective female consciousness as the irresistible allures he believes them to be.

On post-insult Inglis at two a.m., with sickly fluorescent lighting displaying only a disaster of dead and dying dragonflies deceived by Indian summer, and Nigel's impeccable teeth, he pleads: 'Look, I'd get a *doctor*'s certificate to prove I don't have AIDS or anything. But would they let me then? No. They'd *still* rather dream about the pointed red dicks of Great Danes than permit me to do them as the Laplanders do. Why? What *is* it with women?'

'As Freud said.'

'That crazy fucker? – Hey, look, there's Arsenault waving us into the back!'

'Are we up to it?'

Nigel goes dead serious and reaches a hand to my shoulder: 'What I want to know, my friend, is what have *you* been up to lately? . . . That *was* you on the news, wasn't it? You know something you're not telling me, you old peeper. . . . I *knew* it.'

'You know nothing.'

And so – my brain suddenly alert with all mixture of legally bought and self-produced alarming chemicals – back into a pissier part of the bar than the part we'd just floated from.

But what is it with women indeed? Why won't they, or a lot more of them than the sorry young street types who do, permit my friend Nigel to pleasure them in certifiable physical safety? Knowledgeable Nigel, who delicately pinches thumb and forefinger together like a spicing chef and speaks only of *pudenda* and *bindus* going into *yonis*, or something like that, instructing me in the *Kama Sutra*? Nigel, whom I once failed to surprise kneeling up between a woman's – well, she looked legal age anyway – legs in a posture of genuine adoration? Nigel *loves* heterosexual sex, and women, and the women into whose charms he insinuates his scented hairy self love him. So why *won't* more decent (older, and regularly housed) women have my friend Nigel?

I know why. Only it has little to do with the reality principle. And it has nothing to do with morality, for women are, as you know, romantically free these days to do what they will, sexually speaking. So you well might wonder why, friend Nigel.

More to the point, though: why do you ask *me* such a question, friend Nigel, testing our friendship so? Why is your seeming bafflement accompanied in this smellier hole by your head bobbing away like a pigeon's, your perfect teeth set in your perfect grin, your hand soon squeaky on the sweating surprise of another draft glass? Nervous, Nigel? Are you double-daring me to respond particularly, friend Nigel? *Et tu*, Nigel? Insisting upon some woods-drumming male intimacy?

Or is it a moment of mutual recognition you have pressed upon us?

Okay, then, I will answer you here, and only here, and only this once, and have done with you before you have done with me. So listen up, you patchouli-exuding hairy devotee of Oriental technique.

'You see, Nigel, decent women in suitable numbers will not have you because they are women of our world yet, products of millennia of history and culture, civilised social beings more than we guys are. More directly, beautifully middle- and upper-class women will not *let you*, Nigel, because heaven is high and hell is low. Which is to say, Nigel, they will not admit you in the class you lust after, even for their purely private frictive pleasure, because, Nigel . . . *because* Nigel – because you are too short, Nigel.'

It's as if someone has butted him between the shoulder blades with a baseball bat. Then only his small-toothed grin in the dim: 'It *is* you, isn't it?'

'Is that clear now, Nigel? Need I sketch it out?'

'Yes? Not quite clear yet? I will explain, then, in a way that will both confirm your narrow understanding of the unfair sex and titillate your disintegrative sensibility. But after this, friend Nigel, query me no more, please.'

'*You* fucker. You sick, sick fucker. Women love me.'

'Yes, yes, they love you, Nigel, and they should love it *with* you, about that you are bang on. But yes also, they do not let themselves love it with you, do they, my friend? *Why?* . . .'

'Here, then, Nigel, for your edification, follows the triangular key to the tricky trinity w/hole. (I insert a slash there, Nigel.)'

'You sick, slimy fucker.'

'Tall, dark, and handsome, Nigel. That's about the size of it.'

'The day you crawled under my door with your red-rimmed eyes . . .'

'But let us take them up individually, in reverse order.

'One. *Handsome* is as handsome does, Nigel. You have heard that one, have you not? Handsome is in the eye of the beholder, Nigel. Handsome is (I must mouth it silently I see) *relative*, Nigel. Handsome can be stood on his head, Nigel: which is to say, he can be so ugly that he slips through the aesthetic membrane and becomes . . . handsome. And you are, in an at once hawkish and worming way, handsome in, as some say, your own way (on a bus I have overheard one of your own adolescent sperm-buckets apologise to her friends thus).'

'You sick, lying fucker. Forget reporters, I'm going straight to the cops.'

'Two. *Dark* we can dispatch with a bravado, if for the sake of philosophical reliability we bracket off the fact that all women are themselves quite dark, broodingly narcissistic black holes. *Dark* must have its messy historical origins in the silly troubadours or Byron, or in the squelching nightmares of the Brontë sisters. But you can be the blond stud of a realised fantasy as well as the dark beast. So your ample fairheadedness is no explanation, Nigel, for your multiplying rejections.'

'You are a slimy, lying, sick fucker who knows nothing about love and healthy sex.'

Was that a hint of a whimper?

'But Nigel, the one jewel in the triple crown of fantastic stud service with which today's worldly women will not part, and never will part either, no-never, not in the most sordid conjured scene of man or beast (they are *Great* Danes, after all, Nigel), the first and biggest diamond of the triad, the most elongated and engorged, as it were, the unalterable in that tried and true trinity *i-is* – TALL. Numero *trois*. For which I have used caps, Nigel.'

'First, I'm going home to watch a *Nature of Things* on Arctic sovereignty.'

Oh, what a hollow voice of ineffectuality have we here!

'Nigel, Nigel, Nigel: at no time in the written or oral history of love and lust have women preferred short men. Ugly? Yes. Fair haired boys? *Mais oui.* Short? *C'est incroyable! Short*, dark and handsome? Need I say more, my friend?'

Even the grin is gone.

'Napoleon? you say. Well, go say it on the mountain, because nobody shouts such nonsense from a hole.

'Oh, there are psych cases, Nigel, granted, weird sisters who fantasise getting it off with husky puppies or seven lustful dwarves, but such Snow Witches, however intriguing, do not constitute a contradiction.

'So there you have it, my friend. The real ineradicable inequality of the sexes, from a simply sexual perspective. For women can be all three – short, fair and ugly – and still be of invaluable service to men. As you know. But women themselves continue to suffer chronically from heightism, and understandably so, since they are shorter than men . . . well, most *real* men. Women can wear heels and shoulder pads till bulls give milk, and still look no better than cross-dressing coal miners. And they will never be truly liberated until they are freed from this hypocritical, self-defeating prejudice regarding height.'

'Look, micro dick – '

Ouch.

'So query me no more, friend Nigel, about the cunnilingual conundrum of offering yourself up to Woman in self-effacing oral delights. Offend no more with your suspicions and disingenuousness, and our lifelong friendship remains intact. Do you understand me, Nigel? Do we have a deal? . . . Nigel?'

Nigel's Pensées

Nigel lives in the unit across the hall from mine in this Project. This Project: like some movie set built for a brief tryst on the French Riviera, location shot conceived by Ronnie Howard after touring the set of *Popeye: The Motion Picture* with Stephen Schlockberg, and brought in way under budget. This Project: pastel-coloured ersatz chateaux so crammed together that simultaneously opened front doors bang into each other. Everywhere you look in this poor Project new things are freshly broken, or new things are already peeling, everything smaller than life. *The Return to Munchkinland* – I mean, *Munchkinland: The Return* – as cinematic offspring of a liaison between David Cronenberg and David Lynch. There are even some genuine false fronts – chimneys but no fireplaces, dormer windows but no *dormeurs*! Like rust, which we also will always have with us, the poor must never sleep.

Nigel faces the front court (a parking lot centred on a collapsing brand-new jungle gym) and Inglis Road, while I nightly experience the one glaring design flaw in this Project. You see, in the effort to cram in the required number of units, the builder broke faith with the architect and wedged a couple of units right outside my back window (a suit for damages to the architect's reputation is before the courts). The single-mother family-of-three who used to live in my unit raised low-rental hell (we have much free time, we Projectiles, to litigate in the Civil Courts of Self-Loathing): their view of the Troutstream Bypass had suddenly been blocked by the new units – the very view we'd collectively been complaining about at the previous tenants' meeting. I volunteered to trade units with those victims of an uncaring patriarchal system (as I called it, standing at my folding chair and trembling with my you-can't-take-away-my-dignity indignation, Nigel nodding purselipped

and making a fist, because a sixteen-year-old daughter was num-
bered among the oppressed). And it was true, I saw upon moving
into my new digs. The view had been occluded. Tch-tch. Jeepers,
just as I'd suspected, I couldn't help but look right into our newest
tenants' bedrooms not ten feet from my own. How could the
Tenants' New Members Caucus – Nigel, Nutcracker Sweet, *et moi*
– not have foreseen this indelicacy? Or, to be precise, how could
two-thirds of the committee have been so blind? No privacy either
for the impoverished, that's all there is to it.

Like mine, Nigel's unit is a single, with a galley kitchen, a main
room, a bathroom and a bedroom. Execrable Housing (I won't
risk a suit) says we have six hundred square feet of living space per
single unit, but Nigel has measured with his industrial tape and
insists that his is five hundred and thirty tops, and he encourages
others to measure. (Nigel's relations with tapes and measurements
are, you will readily understand, legendary in the Project: the
depth of bathtubs, the volume of washbasins, the circumference of
toilets – 'What's this, the poor man's training seat!' – the space
between bricks, triangulations involving plumb bob, landscape
features and Nigel straddling a dormer as he sights across his
thumb, the width of lines marking parking spaces, and the like
calibrations of various thicknesses.) All of this preparatory liti-
giousness despite the fact that Nigel's needs are readily satisfied by
enough space and energy to soft-boil his smelly eggs, toast his pre-
mouldy white bread, drip his tap-hot water through a large Melita
filter packed tight with coffee picked from around Juan Valdez's
outhouse and, of course, power his twenty-eight inch tv, VCR,
and ancient little record player.

Nigel loves tv, or 'the tv', as he calls it. Just about all his time at
home is spent watching the tv. When I visit, simply walking in on
him, he is just about always sitting in the full lotus position not six
feet from the screen. If the tv is in rare standby cool-down mode,
Nigel will be grooving to the one and only record he ever plays,
'Satisfaction'. My friend Nigel has no truck with tapes or CDs,
remaining loyal to the foot-square red and white record player his
high-school sweetheart gave him when he turned sixteen. (She
gave him the forty-five of 'Satisfaction', too, and a social disease
that broke his heart.) Nigel concedes that 'the shits' is too generous

a word for the sound this machine produces at top volume, but argues that no digital-laser-fibre-optic dildo could ever evoke the terror he gets from his player when he drops the needle. I agree. *Only* at Nigel's and only with that one song can you still experience the dark soundspace of a manly needle edging towards engagement with the first groove, the building *woo-woo-woo* and hiss and spit and crackle of blackness itself crowning for the Big Bang, the air galvanised by pungent patchouli; then that dirty driving guitar, Jagger's obscenely plaintive whisper, and bristly Nigel in his breezy silk paisley housecoat shuffling like some almost-life-size question mark across the thin carpet, lips imperceptibly pursed in fine thought more than grossness, head moving minutely like a pigeon's, joining in, 'I can't get no, do-do-DO, Sa-tis-fac-tion . . .' hitting air-drums on the do-do-DOs. No one ever complains about Nigel's little machine cranked to full volume; in truth, you'll often recognise 'Satisfaction' whining from some hundred-year-old geezer in the laundry room.

But most often my friend Nigel is to be found 'scoping Tombstone', as he describes his viewing life. Often there will be a viewing companion – a female friend – stretched on the ratty brown couch at his back, either plucking her eyebrows or picking at the exposed cord trim of the arm, or simply propped on one elbow and watching with that piercing intelligence the tube cultivates in its devotees, her homework ignored. Nigel is talking nonstop, and whether to the girl or to me who wasn't there a moment ago, or to the tv itself doesn't matter finally. For my friend Nigel is most truly addressing his own best self and the conducive ether, piggybacking his observations on the radio waves that come and go willy-nilly between his mind and the farthest reaches of space. He pauses only to draw breath and pick his next cue from the screen, where tapes are often playing at fast foward.

What's on?
The Nature of Things (live). An underwater shot of a steamy ocean floor, a voice-over talks of something called 'pillow rocks' and our being privileged to witness the actual creation of new earth. It's an undersea volcano. Something like toothpaste is being extruded from the ocean floor, squeezed out like the most regular of turds,

then a tumbling forth like nothing so much as a birth (in other films I've seen). And Nigel gasping, 'I have nothing to say,' as he dashes from the room with his hand to his mouth. Retching sounds.

What's on?
The Ascent of Man (live). 'Piltdown Man: an ape's jaw fused to a man's skull. And they call *that* a hoax!'

What's on?
TVOntario's Imprint (tape). 'These middle-aged writers do like to rewrite their roles in the sixties. They're ashamed, you see, because they once thought better of humanity, and themselves. They're just like those American communist writers of the thirties who euthanised unpromising careers by writing scripts for *Father Knows Best* in the fifties and sixties after kissing Joe McCarthy's hairy ass.'
'It's *Paul* McCarthy, Mr Know-it-all. And look who's talking about hairy asses.' She giggles.
'Oh yeah, thanks, sweetheart. You've got a lot going on up here.'
Nigel makes to tap his temple but shoots his hand to clasp the back of her head, drags it to his lap.
I try to stand quietly but am signalled by Nigel's eyebrows to leave similarly.

What's on?
Venture (live). Nigel, *sans* bimbette, lies curled on the floor in his dark paisley housecoat, holding a dessert spoon like a pen in his right hand. Before his face sits a baby-blue egg cup containing a gutted shell with yolk plastered to its sides: 'Global economic growth can no more continue indefinitely than can bone-growth. I know. This "sustainable growth" thing is like foreplay as an end in itself. The feminisation of economics, that's what it is, and it won't work, my friend. The bigger the better, that's what I say, and that's what capitalism says. This is no time for a failure of Western nerve. Take it to the max, find out if there is a limit!'
Inspired, Nigel sits up and strums air guitar to a poor Dylan imitation: 'The bigger the better you better believe, the bigger the

business the bigger the sleeve, the bigger the lover the better conceive. Megalomania running wild, bigger the future, bugger the child. Thank you, thank you, thank you.

'You didn't know I was a poet, did you?'

'It's as good as Leonard Cohen, my friend.'

'Now *there*'s a guy who's managed sustainable growth.'

'You think he's been in it just for the chicks?'

'Uh, duh, no, he's like on a fucking spiritual quest with his latest Hollywood bimbo, eh man?'

What's on?

Masterpiece Theatre (live). This evening Nigel lies staring at the pimply stippled ceiling, his arms out like some pocket Christ. The sound is off and the large screen shows a bunch of svelte bumboys smoking cigarettes, picking tobacco from their lips and mouthing snootily in a panelled room – probably one of those cheap mostly-interior-shots Forster 'dramas'.

Nigel: 'Routinely at work our colleagues sit in the small room adjacent to my smaller shared office and – thinking who knows what? making what faces? – are daily betrayed by their bodies: assholes blowing raspberries, inadvertent grunts and groans and sighs, an opened door that wafts smells foul enough to fill Swift's out-tray for a decade. Oh, we are an admirable animal indeed!'

'My friend, heterosexuals engage in sodomy too.'

'What? Not as a *modus operandi* they don't.'

'And when it comes right down to it, no heterosexual act sounds too picturesque reduced to graphic physicality.'

'No? You have problems, my friend.'

'And you're homophobic.'

Nigel does his Peewee Herman: 'I know you are but what am I? . . . Hey, I don't phobe them, they just disgust me, I find them repugnant, and I don't go looking. As they excuse themselves, I was *born* this way. Besides, the vagina evolved through hundreds of thousands of years for various purposes, one of which is to accommodate penises. Colons, for other purposes.'

'Yeah, yeah, and now we've got divinely retributive AIDS, right?'

Nigel smiles. 'A toilet is also an echo chamber, that was *my* point.'

'Poor old Alistair Cooke, maybe you should apply for *his* job, Nigel.'

'Are you listening to me? Something *bothering* you?'

'You could do it, piece of cake.'

'One of my thuggish Arab stars said that learning English was a piece of chicken. Despite my best self's efforts, somehow these leeching pricks pick up and fuck up the idiom. Piece of chicken.'

My friend Nigel owns an MA in English literature and teaches part-time for peanuts, English as a Second Language, in a former elementary school in our old lower-town neighbourhood, a mouldy wreck which serves also for poetry readings and aerobics classes. Nigel teaches his students to speak Elizabethan English. He's been doing so for two years now, has taught dozens of classes, and has never been found out or even inspected. There are numerous sweatshop workers spreading through this great land who, when they sew their thumbs to a zipper, exclaim, 'What ho!' An expression which might well offend some neighbouring woman of colour, thereby setting in motion a harassment suit in one of our human rights tribunals.

Nigel again says, 'Piece of chicken.' We snicker, then catch the kind of laughing fit that makes us such tolerable friends, that makes our lives tolerable. When Nigel pulls himself together, he stares at the screen, speaks solemnly, a catch in his voice:

'This was Alistair's final show, his last words in close-up were: "And now, sit back and enjoy John Henry Cardinal Newman's recently discovered monody, *Fudgepackers in Tight Jeans*".'

That wastes us, though normally I don't enjoy homophobic jokes.

What's on?

MuchMusic (live). 'Turn it down!' I shout.

'Tombstone as it was meant to be!' Nigel overshouts as the volume decreases. 'But no comparison to a ride on the dark needle, eh?'

He is sitting on the floor in his black speedo underwear, with his back against the couch and the remote on his crotch. He is one hairy human, my friend Nigel, a lick from a cow would put a wave in his back. On screen an attack of blacks in spandex dance spastically like Egyptian stick figures walking across hot sand. The video ends and the host, an older white guy who has made no effort to look young, does a parodic dance as might your bellied uncle at a wedding. In a growing ecstatic oblivion he undoes his shirt and undulates his gut. The guy must be drunk or stoned, or he learned comedic technique from Jerry Lewis movies of the early sixties. But Nigel's interest is piqued, soon he's intrigued; a *pensée* is a–whelping; he slithers right up to the screen and kneels there, his fingertips resting on the screen as on a sill, like someone peering at his own nightlife through a lighted window.

'Old men, even older men, say fifty, and this guy's fifty for sure, such men should not bare themselves to young women who have been deceived by power dressing, for there is ineluctable disillusionment in all that thin skin the colour of a finished lily.'

'But Nigel, we have grown a culture that leaves us no choice but to compete with dancing blacks on *their* terms.'

'We should stick to things like clogs and reels and square- and line–dancing, dancin' for white men, goddamnit.'

Nigel switches channels: '*Musique Plus* doesn't do so much rap. Though I was thinking more of the ravages of time.'

'What's wrong with nature's love handles?'

'Loves Handel, hates Hammer.'

'A poet, my friend, you are.'

What's on?

The Oprah Winfrey Interview with Michael Jackson (tape). 'The most important show since the Sermon on the Mount! Listen to this part.' And he speeds through pictures of Jackson standing back with arms crossed and head held in profile, looking like some decadent *fin-de-siècle* cameo sniffing tailwind *à* Liz Taylor, who herself looks like reconstituted shit desiccated in a microwave. Nigel slo-mos and freezes on a close-up of Liz's face. 'Now you have to understand that old Liz has been dragged on stage and propped up to offer testimonial to Michael's humanitarianism. Look at him! The very fucking Gandhi of geeks! And look at her! A face like on the guy they thawed out from the Franklin

Expedition, only without his expressive elasticity. I tell ya, one more facelift and old Liz'll be wearing a goatee!' Fast forward with Nigel's mincing voice-over: 'Oprah and Michael have already discussed his crotch-grabbing. It's something, you simply *must* understand, that he spontaneously choreographs. The poor little darkie, he's like a caged monkey that jerks off all day, only in a big luxurious cage. And if he bleaches his skin occasionally, well . . . *Bleaches* his skin! Jackson cried poorly and said he was undergoing metamorphosis into a new kind of human being, an albino Pied Piper of all the hurt inner children victims of the Big Daddums world! But shut up and listen to this.'

'Look who's doin' the talkin'?' the bimbette whines.

Nigel hits the pause. 'Get out.'

She clamps her translucent red plastic lighter on her Players Light and heads for the bedroom, naked under her pale-blue housecoat. My heart is a fibrillation in my throat at this window of opportunity. I backstep to get an angle on the bedroom, but she's out and slamming the apartment door behind her.

Nigel has the remote against his cheek: 'I should go after her.'

'Oprah's looking again like she's yarding down all that lard during commercials.'

'. . . Yeah, right, listen.'

Nigel hits play and Oprah brazenly asks Lizless Jackson if he's a thirty-four-year-old virgin, the implied question being, Are you boning Brooke Shields? Jackson squirms and smiles petitely like a Victorian bride eyeing her first marbled dick, and says in that copyrightable choirboy's voice, 'Call me old-fashioned if you want, Oprah, but I think these matters are private.'

Nigel accidentally presses fast forward as he curls foetally, laughing and whimpering: 'Old-fashioned and private, old-fashioned, the very thing I was beginning to think he was!'

What's on?

The Fashion Place: Back-to-School (live). Designer Larc Alemahn, a disease accessorised with colour-coordinated cigarette holder and champagne-tinted glasses, with all topped hopefully by a grey mushroom cut, intentionally lisps about how fashion designers can no longer tell women what to wear. He used to be able to dictate, but that was yesterday. Today he's giving independent co-eds what *they* want. And the obviously queer host, who nonetheless looks like a linebacker beside Larc, asks his guest if he set out to deconstruct the basic white blouse, pleated plaid skirt and knee socks. Larc answers, 'Tcz-tcz-tcz,' bringing the tip of his forefinger to his lips. Cut to this season's assertive sorority flaunting down the runway like heavily made-up Dachau survivors in green garbage bags.

Nigel, livid, bounces the remote off the thin carpet: 'Oh, I guess girls don't *have* to wear underwear to school any more!'

'The truly liberated sport jockey shorts now, my friend.'

'Fine, show me.'

He has a point.

What's on?

W5 (live). A segment on the Los Angeles riots of 1992. Blacks run wild because the cops had beaten a drunken violent black man viciously. Not many of the jackals doing the rioting could care less, but in interview they all take it personally. Why does *W5* care? Because it's America, and it's there, and we had our own little sympathetic riot in Toronto, thank you. A poor overhead shot shows a truck driver being dragged from his cab and beaten savagely. We are told that this time the victim is white and the beaters black. As the victim struggles on all fours, one lanky fellow goes over and bends down as if he might help him with a hoisting human hand in the armpit, but instead he throws a brick right in the guy's face. The guy collapses in what has to be death, since he looked near death before this. And as disturbing as all that is, what the assailant does next is even worse: he dances ecstatically. No other adverb would do justice. He claps his hands high overhead and, beaming to the sky, lifts one knee in an expression of overbrimming joy, like some Shiva's jig.

Nigel non-committally: 'There is no way to prevent that violent joyfulness. No way, not when someone takes that much pure pleasure from doing evil. Batten down, my friend. The jig, she is up.'

'I was just thinking the same thing, my friend.'

'Bullshit.'

★

195

What's on?

The Tonight Show (tape). I arrive late after an exciting night alone at my place, eyesored and drained. Nigel is again playing his tape of Johnny Carson's last week of *Tonight Show*s. A spotlit Bette Midler is singing 'You Are My Hero'. Nigel in ritualistic housecoat, his arms outstretched like a mostly plaintive worshipper, kneels amongst a litter of beer bottles and eggshell, his face lined with tears, and wails: 'Johnny, don't go, don't go . . .' He means it.

What's on?

Sunday Morning, Various T-Vangelists (live). 'I have been working on a concept for a movie of the week. Working title: *The Evening Jesus Heaved*. Christ and the inner circle have come to rest for the night beneath a stone bridge. The day has not gone well, the timing of the last miracle was not sharp, an angelic tuberculoid girl fell off her pallet, *et cetera, et cetera*. Before they can settle down Christ must banish an ogre from under the bridge, which manages still to carry off their prettiest groupie. Cut to later, sitting amongst a mess of spat pits (all the supper they've had), Christ asks Peter if he loves him, not once but three times (you know the story, blah, blah). At first Peter shoots goofy eyes side to side in embarrassment and says, "*Je-sus* . . ." And Christ thrice responds to the eventually affirming Peter, "Then feed my sheep." But after the third time, Peter throws a fit: "Sheep? Do you see any *sheep* around here, Lord? I don't see any sheep. Johnny, do *you* see any woolly baa-baas? Rocks, yes. Shit, yes. Oh plenty of shit, some of it the flyblown slush of young Mark there, who can't seem to hold water, but will you *cure him?* . . . But sheep? No. Now I might be wrong – God knows I've made some *big* mistakes in the recent past – but we don't even seem to know where our next *meal* is coming from, oh mystical one, magus, and former shavings-sweeper to one journeyman carpenter named Joseph. *Sheep?* I'll sheep you, you sonofa . . .?" But Christ is leaning across a rock and throwing up till only air comes. Cut to desert remote, where the ogre's mother is slouching towards vengeance. In the climactic battle Christ turns her into a leg of lamb, which they barbecue, and all is atoned for.'

'Stick to poetry, my friend.'

'Stick it up your ass.'

'Nigel, these homophobic tizzies of yours.'

'I know you are – Shut up, here's the man.'

'Who?'

'Remember Oral Roberts? It's his only begotten son, Tactile or something. But watch this guy perform, a real lip off the old mouth.'

Nigel turns off the sound, lies flat on his back and stares at the ceiling: 'It's too much, I can't watch, tell me what's on.'

'Well, he's got some old woman in a sari indicating pain in her neck, he touches her forehead, she's down, flat out. Wait, she's up, and sashaying like some obscene runway show. Now it's a real babe in a short dress pointing to her lower back, he touches her, she's down – and a guy who looks like Elvis is covering her legs with a towel, I can't believe –'

'That's it, they always do that. Olfactory Roberts doesn't want us looking up the skirts of the jockey-shorts-challenged!'

'What's with the Elvis character?'

Still on his back Nigel plays air-guitar and sings: 'Elvis is everywhere, man. Elvis is everywhere.'

'He seems to be, but why?'

But Nigel is jiggling silently with a satisfaction only he can appreciate. And I can't help thinking how easy this is, what a wasted life Nigel is living. One of these days I just might give him the sort of personal critique he dispenses so freely. I just might have to.

The sound comes on, and the Elvis impersonator – if he is that – a mid-career Elvis type in big belt, bigger buckle and sequinned sky-blue body suit, is singing one of those soppy gospel numbers with which the real Elvis – a religious boy, a good boy who loved his mother – repeatedly blackmailed the embarrassed faithful: 'There will be peace, in Graceland, 'cause my Quaaludes have arrived. . . .' That sort of sheep shit of a song, Jesus as the last big Daddy defender of pastoralism.

What's on?

The Learning Channel (live). 'Really, what is the use of learning post-1800 English? Why set my charges down the disintegrating slide we're on? Though I'll grant this: the way the Romantics began to feel – i.e. learned from the Germans – that there was an ideal meaningful existence back of the apparent, a refitted personal God, that's how I feel about the lives of others. And that's why you *must* let me come over to watch the show at your pla – '

'Shut up, Nigel. I mean it. Just shut, the fuck, up.'

He must be silenced.

What's on?

CBC Prime-Time News (tape). Nigel kneeling back on his heels like a gliding canoe paddler silences my greeting with a raised palm. Reporter Brenda Cawsley is standing in front of a large blue dumpster: 'In this small suburb of Ottawa a most grisly crime has been enacted, the sexual murder of a young girl.' The shot pulls back and with a rush of prickly heat I see that Brenda is standing on familiar ground: out back of the IGA just down the street.

Nigel freezes the picture and scuttles on knees to the screen, points: 'Provocative Brenda, big blue dumpster, various officials, scraggly trees, Bypass sound barrier . . . and this, what have we here?' He fingers a shadowy figure beyond mid-ground.

'A man?'

'A man. And he's pointing to . . .' Nigel draws a line farther into the background. 'A man's best friend, I believe. A dog.'

'So?'

'And looksee here, just above the dog's head, that blemish, I'll bet that's a hole, a hole cut in the barrier. But by whom?' He drags his finger back to the shadowy man: 'There's something about this guy . . .?'

'What? Could it be you, Nigel? Have you finally achieved apotheosis and made it onto the *small* screen? Where's your tape measure, my friend? It's difficult to gauge the shadow's length, or lack thereof.'

'My friend, you are sweating bullets. What have you been watching?'

'It's fucking hot in here.'

'It's *freezing* in here.'

'Your point?'

'Oh, no point, just that I might phone Ms Cawsley. I think I may be able to throw a little light on this dark mystery. Maybe Brenda and I can cut a . . . a *deal.*'

'My friend, just what the fuck are you implying?'

'Dum-dee-dum-dum-dum.'

'You've lost it, Nigel. You know that?'

'You're getting shrill, my lanky friend.'

'Or is this a confession? Is that what it is, Nigel? A confession? I mean, it *has* been proven statistically by criminologists that the vast majority of criminals are short men. You didn't know that, did you, Nigel? *Did you?*'

'You are shouting.'

'And hairy too. I've read that hirsuteness is a symptom of sociopathology. Doubtless patchouli is the scent of choice for – '

Nigel purses his lips, shakes his head and hits play. As we watch officials load a green body bag into an ambulance, Brenda Cawsley does voice-over: 'Police are releasing no details other than that they believe her to be the adolescent girl who went missing from the area three days ago. The murder has rocked this quiet community – '

'Couture by Alemahn!'

'Alemahn?'

'Alemahn, all coordinated mushroom cloud and mirrors! *Alemahn*, who passively demands svelte pubescence from our suppressed sisters, and bums and boobs and lips pumped full of enough silicone and collagen to raise the dead! *Larc Alemahn*, the chick-plucking, bum-fucking liberator of well-turned-out schoolgirls in garbage bags everywhere! Alemahn! Alemahn! He's our man, *he* did it . . . with a little help from his friends.'

I don't find that at all funny. I can no longer put up with this secret sharer. One must draw the line somewhere.

What's on?

The Nature of Things (tape). I enter a touch reluctantly and find him lying buck naked before the big screen. The windows are wide open and he's shivering. No wonder, Indian summer is over. On screen an icebreaker bearing the Maple Leaf is slowly cutting a black line through a solid white field. The volume is low, but I

199

can just make out David Suzuki's scolding voice: 'Territory is *not* the issue. It's *how* the Arctic will be used, or *not* used rather. For hundreds of centuries in the North . . .'

'The Arctic, whose sea is frozen silent.'

'No hard feelings about last night, eh big fella?'

'Whose *c* is silent, asshole. It's a homonymic pun. As it was in the beginning, so too in the end, the pun. As friend ends with end.'

'A poet, my friend, you are, yourself the Holy See. . . . Nigel?'

'Father, end this.' He turns onto his side and curls into a foetal ball, his shaggy rump towards me, and mumbles, 'I will go there.' Or 'I spill no hair.' Or 'I fill nowhere.' Or 'That wasn't fair.' Who knows?

But yes, I almost forgot. This was the day after my little talk with him about heightism, which talk I misrepresented (sue me). My friend Nigel had actually had the last word.

'My friend,' he had whispered, 'I saw it, with some difficulty, true, but I saw it, that time I surprised you standing starkers at your darkened window, your ninth micro-wonder of the world. They *can* do things surgically.'

Oh, such sincerity, such *concern*. I relay this now only for the sake of reliability and trust (and to have the last word? Perhaps).

But let me explain myself.

Sneaking In

Once upon a time, a long long time ago, before we had rung our changes on the social ladder (welfare fraud) and climbed to this eyrie Project in Troutstream, Nigel and I were poor boys in Ottawa's Lower Town. Quietly desperate we would sneak into anything going: hockey games, baseball games, football games, hotel swimming pools, company Christmas parties, and many's the foreign embassy lawn party, where, buying time to gulp pink lemonade and wolf down numerous triangular egg salad sandwiches, we faked ignorance of any language addressed to us: *Zo zorry, no spekazee* . . . Mostly, though, we snuck into movies, at that time a shared passion.

Our favourite target was the nearby Capitol Theatre on Rideau Street, a big old brown brick movie house with a monstrous yellow beak of a marquee advertising in blue icicles like stalactites its air-conditioned interior. We approached from the rear, through a long alleyway between the Capitol and the Colonial Hotel, an alleyway filled with stinking building exhaust, intermittent shrieks that sounded human, lipsticked butts and occasional puke, an alleyway so narrow you could touch both smoky brick walls at once, which only Nigel was brave enough to do. The ticket wicket was right in the middle of the frontage, with four glass doors to either side, a shallow foyer behind, then eight rose-coloured ancient wooden doors that swung outward only, one of which stood open to admit the ticketed blessed to the softly shadowed lobby with its lighted candy counter like an altar. Deeper still, behind the swinging doors to either side of this counter, waited plush violet seating and the hushed anticipation that really was matched only at church, while up front a gold-tasselled green velour curtain draped a huge screen, beyond which no one had ever gone and come back to tell the tale.

Customers purchased their tickets and lined up outside on the right, while only one usher stood inside the open interior door on that side. This arrangement left the whole left of the foyer unsupervised. The trick was to slip into the foyer on the left of the ticket-seller (easy enough as she was always distracted from our purpose), wait until about half the line-up had filed past the usher, who kept his head down tearing tickets, slip your fingers under the farthest-left interior door, pry it open a crack, ease it a little further, then simply curl gracefully into the lobby and walk directly to the deeper interior seating, one sneak at a time.

Nigel was bold and slick, I was timid and clumsy. Nigel always had to convince me. Nothing to it, nothing compared to climbing the slippery iron fence of the French embassy, whose fleur-de-lis spikes were sure to impale soft wrists. Sometimes at the Capitol, my nerve having frazzled, I would wait for two hours across the street in an itch of self-loathing. Other times I would panic and walk briskly in with another, thereby doubling our chance of drawing the attention of the usher or the candy-counter girls. Even when the sneak went smoothly – with no ticket-holding customer suddenly recognising us and shouting our names into what should be empty foyer space, and with no slipping resounding doors splitting fingernails – even with a slick sneak I would suffer, sitting there in the attentive dark, suffer more than any show on earth was worth. The physical jolt of making the sneak ruined every-thing for me: the envisioned public humiliation of being taken by the scruff of the neck and tossed to the sidewalk in front of the citizenry – there he lies, oh honest Ottawans, cast your gaze upon his Lower Town wretchedness and feel free to spit. Or worse: being held for the police in some tiny fluorescent-lighted office. Adrenaline pumped by the sneak and unable to turn off fuelled such imaginings, and I couldn't breathe easy until we were again a block behind the theatre and headed for home turf. But even when the sneak went *splendidly*, when the deaf and blind old fart was ushering and six of us could whistle in, even when I was sitting safely in the protective dark, heart tripping to the deeply resonant thump of those ancient speakers like the oldest log drum pounded in the deepest drumming Congo – even then, fear of humiliating exposure *still* kept me tensed in my seat as though in the next moment Maureen O'Sullivan would turn and point, 'Oh, Tarzan, it's him, he snuck in to steal a look at me, him and all his wretched little Lower Town filth.'

Also, there was Smiley.

Smiley, a huge woman of eternal late middle age, was manager of the Capitol. That was her real name, Hanna Smiley, and she went simply by Smiley. Smiley: feet in blue plastic-mesh sandals with holes cut to accommodate her naked bunions, calves and thighs that long ago had run out of nylon and looked to be running out of skin, a spread of high-riding ass that made the front of her dark skirts a good six inches longer than the back, torso like some beast that had to be caged anew each morning after a night of unimaginable indulgences, a butcher's arms always akimbo in readiness to grab a poor boy running by, a neck that had suffered compression between that body and that head – that head like some cross between a goat's and a buffalo's, because Smiley's block had a hugely square shaggy presence, and because Smiley had a wispy blonde goatee like cornsilk. Smiley also had eyes of a dumbfounding alarm, beady eyes ever bugged with newfound capacity for prying shock at the criminality of Lower Town boys.

You got the feeling Smiley hated all boys, only poor boys especially, because even as paying customers we Lower Towners would be unaccompanied by an adult and more likely to bring our own jam sandwiches than to buy from the lucrative candy counter. Still, to paying parent-escorted children she could manage a smile, could Smiley, and when they'd escaped her smile you could see even the youngest of such children themselves smile pityingly for her, that inarguably ugliest woman in the world. A widow, rumour said, whose husband had been executed for harbouring Jews during the war (executed by SS agent Smiley herself, we said, cannibalised). But Smiley recompensed her forced smiles for rich kids by focusing a yet more intense hatred on about six of us boys whose names she had somehow found out, and to whose houses she occasionally dispatched threatening police without even a scrap of legal evidence. Nigel's hungover father had been paid one such visit and, in gleeful relief that the cops weren't after him, had beaten Nigel with a belt till he'd bled.

To complete the picture, or slash it, Smiley had serious trouble with English, even after who knew how many centuries in Canada. (Nigel, artistically talented, inserted good likenesses of Smiley into his Canadian history text's few iconic pictures: a sputtering Smiley sideways on all fours behind an eagle-feathered Indian talking to Cartier, who with hand up in greeting is really about to shove the chief backwards; a straining Smiley giving Wolfe a leg up the Plains of Abraham; a leering Smiley applying bullwhip to the back of a pathetic Acadian mother and child; a bearish Smiley with popcorn and peanuts slouching through the crowd at Riel's hanging; a beaming Smiley beyond the beach waving the boys ashore at Dieppe; a tongue-wagging Smiley with huge dildo about to sodomise Queen Elizabeth at the opening of the St Lawrence Seaway.) So Smiley seldom spoke at all, preferring what she must have thought her communicative smile (imagine a balloon of Uncle Sam inflated to bursting point). But it wouldn't have been only the Shultz-like command of the language that made Smiley shy of speech, it must also have been her dim recognition, signalled by her auditor's furrowing reactions, of her misconception of certain English words. To take but one pertinent example, she called 'tickets' 'stickers', and not just 'stickers', but *schtickers*, schlobbered forth in a bombs-away of thicklipped foaming spittle. So that it was almost normal of a quiet summer's evening, or at least it had become a common sight, to see this unsexed monster hulking along the line-up for that evening's movie, barking, 'Got your schtickers? Got your schtickers? Got your schtickers? . . .' with the line waving away from her and shielding itself with forearms.

Nigel and I would lurk across the street among the crowd coming and going from Nate's Deli until Smiley had consummated her one public-relations act. Then we could safely initiate the first stage of the sneak – into the foyer on the left – knowing that Smiley would hole-up in her tiny office and not sally forth again till the schticker parade had firmed up for the evening's second performance. We had to be very careful still, Smiley knew our names and faces. Only a week before she had caught three of our friends in headlocks, cracked all three heads together at once, and given them the shakes so bad that for days Norm, the youngest, was found sleepwalking each night in his bathroom, tearing off single after single of toilet paper and eating it, whimpering, 'My schticker, my schticker, my schticker . . .' Nigel said Norm'd have to be sent to a mental hospital for sure.

So I especially didn't want to risk the sneak that last evening Nigel and I watched Smiley lurch along doing her schticker bit. And the movie, a re-release, *Tarzan's New York Adventure*, was not one I cared to risk my head for so soon after our friends' capture. But Nigel would not hear of our trying the pool at the Chateau Laurier, though it was a hellishly humid evening.

'Chateau,' he sneered. 'Like I really want to stand around watching you file fat jack-off material – it's so *embarrassing* the way you just stare openly at *any* woman – when we could be in air-conditioned comfort collecting a free ticket.'

The Capitol had begun advertising a policy whereby any child under thirteen presenting twenty-five empty popcorn boxes to the candy counter would receive one free movie pass. Nigel and I were only a year too old.

'C'mon, with a free ticket we'll be able to walk in like everybody else!'

'Yeah but, we'll miss the movie that's on now.'

'So? This show's crap. We'll be able to *choose* the next one.'

'Will we collect boxes for another free ticket during that one?'

'Sure, then we can walk in like everybody else again!'

'But we'll miss that one too!'

'So? What's your point, goof?'

'We'll never get to see the show!'

'But we'll be going in just like everybody else!'

'Like Norm?'

'Norm? . . . Okay then, wait here and watch if you want.'

So in we snuck. Nothing to it. A fair crowd had been attracted by the novelty of air conditioning and the mystery of whether Tarzan could still swing in the Big Apple. We sat in the empty last row with our heads against a carpeted wall. Usually we hid ourselves as close to the safe centre as we could get, because periodically the usher would step inside and stand at the back, either as part of his duties or to pick up the movie in pieces. The rules published in the *Citizen* made it clear that the empty popcorn boxes were only to be collected between shows. But Nigel and I knew that that was *way* too risky, maybe even a trap, and that's why we sat dangerously alone at the back.

According to plan we waited until the movie was about three-quarters over before making our move. We got to the floor and on all fours crawled to opposite aisles, Nigel left, I right, turned towards the screen and, in the flickering dim, began working the rows. People may well have thought we were some sort of ridiculous promotional stunt, or workers for a conscientious maintenance company that hired the outrageously deformed. Whatever, when I tapped the first man's shin, turned my head slightly leftward and upward and whispered, 'Got any empty popcorn boxes,' he startled, and the row startled, but a scraping sound followed and with his right foot he eventually kicked into the aisle a flattened red and yellow box bearing the face of an inhumanly smiling clown. 'Got any more?' A whisper went down the row, more scraping cardboard, sounds of *shshsh* from other rows, but three more red and yellow boxes were kicked gently into the aisle.

On to row three, same thing, but only two boxes. At the next row, gripping the accumulating boxes in my left hand, I pressed its middle knuckle on a burning cigarette ember on the concrete floor (only the middle of the aisles being carpeted); the gum I next squished relieved the burn somewhat, and what later felt like hocked-up phlegm made me forget the pain entirely. At about the tenth row, my question was answered by 'Sure kid', and out of the corner of my eye I watched as the teenager bent and picked up his box, heard it torn into large bits, felt it snow upon my head and back. As I knelt upright to curse him, the air was shot through with light from the front left exit, a few voices shouted protest, and I ducked. But by then I had counted some twenty-eight boxes anyway and, hearing the film winding down – 'Oh, Tarzan, I should never have asked you to leave our home in the jungle' – I turned and crawled up the gentle slope to the back row.

One row from the last I raised my head above the armrests, but could not spot Nigel. On all fours I turned into the last row and moved towards its middle – *Someone had left the theatre, that's what the exit light had been . . . before the end of the show?* – glanced up and thought some of the seats had tumbled over . . . or something. Then that bundle of seats came hustling towards me like a burrowing beast and not six inches from my own I was looking into the ecstatically mad face of leering Smiley. A thin beam of screen-light through the backs of two seats played in the fine golden silk of her goatee as she whispered wetly into my face like the building itself:

'Got your *schticker*, boy?' And commenced moaning, I swear it, like the muffled drone of a dervish.

There was some cheering from elsewhere.

I dropped my boxes and turned in that tight space but my scooting toes slipped on the cardboard and I fell flat. I felt myself hoisted by the belt and curled downward in as helpless a position as there is. I was swung along the row, and repeatedly kneed hard in the ass by Smiley's battering knee.

Some scattered applause. Why the hell *do* people clap at movies?

I was stood up, shoved through the swinging door to the lobby, and by the scruff of the neck flung into Smiley's tiny fluorescent-lighted office. With meathook hands on my shoulders she slammed

me onto a wooden chair before her desk and sat on the corner of
that grey Formica marvel, her knees unable to close.

She leaned down: 'So, you *another* boy who likes to watch show
without schticker?' She let her knees drift a bit. 'That is *schtealing!*'

'I-I'd pay if I could.' My God, don't let me wet myself, *please.*
Please God, just let me die now. Please let me die and go to hell.
Or purgatory, *please?*

'Oh, tch-tch, but you vill pay, bad boy, you vill pay.'

She walked round behind me, took a fistful of hair at the nape
of my neck and yanked my head back against her Sherman chest.
'You *have* money.'

'Not on me but I can get it at home!'

She twisted: 'Where is home?'

'I'm an orphan, but!'

'You lie!' and shoved my head forward so that my forehead
almost bounced where she'd sat, held it there, the warmth of
which spot I could feel on my eyes, and imagined I could smell.
Don't ask me why, but with a secret smile I wondered: What does
Smiley wear to bed? A flannel nightshirt and sleeper's hat? A damp
silken tent? Nothing? Poor woman.

Smiley whispered: 'Maybe when the *paying* customers leave,
Schmiley will take you up behind the screen and show you what
happens to schtealing boys. You would like that, schtealing boy?'

No. I would not like that. I would prefer death from exposure.
Then swallow your pride and cry, or whimper at least, why not?
'No, please, I really am an orphan. My parents were killed in . . .
in the war, and eaten by Russians.'

'Liar! You are too much boy!' She whipped my head back and
poured schlobber on my face: 'Schmiley already knows you *and
your parents* live at 171 St Patrick Street, schtealing boy, and where
your little friend Nigel Withers lives too. Schmiley had him by the
ankle but he kicked and got away. Kicked Schmiley in the – ' But
wait, she was rubbing my head against her chest, or rubbing her
chest against me . . . she really was. And her voice had softened:
'But Schmiley knows everything, Schmiley had a nice long talk
with your other little friend, Norman Levesque, schtealing boy,
and he promised to come again for another little talk mit Schmiley.' She was stroking my hair, cooing: 'You think you can schteal

from Schmiley, see show without paying and – ' She crushed my
head against her and stiffened for a long moment . . . let go. I
pretended to faint and fell off my chair, collapsed onto my side,
my head thudded, bounced once in slow motion, came to rest. I
may well have ejaculated my first thimbleful.

I blew small bubbles of saliva from the corner of my mouth,
and as though at a great distance heard *Oh, oh, oh*, and smiled
secretly knowing it was Smiley chirping, no more Gestapo voice,
more like your sister upstairs when she finds her diary open on her
bed, or you faking surprise when you perfectly time your barge
into the bathroom, or you in her closet, or you sitting in a
darkened room staring at a neighbour's lighted window, or maybe
I really had fainted, or maybe God had granted my death-wish, or
maybe Smiley then sat me up and apologised and gave me a whole
book of free schtickers and made me promise not to tell any of this
to my cannibalised parents, then filled my lap with candy, closed
the venetian blinds and turned off the light. On dimpled knees she
climbed onto her desk and spotlit herself with the conical desk-
lamp, growled Dietrichishly, 'Showtime, boys!' and struck a pose
like a daintily dressed vaudeville card-turner. Then she stripped
and performed unimaginably inventive intimacies with mundane
office accoutrements, singing huskily: 'You schticker here – *oooh* –
you schticker there – *aiii* – Schmiley schticks it anywhere! . . .'

Eventually I found myself flat on my back in the alley between
Colonial and Capitol, clammy, a spread-eagled *ecce homo* touching
both brick walls, with a burnt knuckle, but none the worse for
wear.

And the way I figure it, *that's* why I became a daring voyeur,
intrepid voyageur in love's sick lane.

I mean like, I been victimised too, eh?

Show Time

A force to be reckoned with still – *c'est moi*. One of the lower
powers, granted, but a powerful force nonetheless. Ah, there you
are, old guarding friend, blue T-shirt, old navy chum, obscurantist
pale-chest-cover, dark-on-dark, I want my baby bark, ow-ooo,

ow-ooo. A force akin to collective unconsciousness, am I, a noospheric foreskin protecting priapically the global show, valiant last bastion of man's divine right to lookism, a tour de foreskin, I reckon, Ma'am, ah reckon. Si-si, señor, jew haf a beeg one, none of zee girls can handle jew, jew must pay double, and only with Granda Wanda. Come here, my canyoned señorita and I'll show you some probing lower powers . . . O what a filthy pervert I am. That's what I am, truly, with a lower-case t and that rhymes with me and that stands for mule tool. A filthy little (though quite tall for all that at six foot two) lower-case pervert gladdened by his darkest shirt, is that what I've come to? . . . Oh yeah, sez who? I mean like, relative to whom, to what? Like, am I hurting anyone, eh? No one's been or being harmed, keep in mind, it's a victimless . . . bit of fun. So what filthy? Who pervert? Come-come, my forward upper lobes, my superior ego, let us lance your moral-ethical boil with a tip of the old deconstructionist's cap. Let us hear it from your clean-shaven shadow. Put 'em up, put 'em up, I'll take ya wit one hand tied behind me back, I will. You and your hairy little friend Nigel too. To wit: everything you know is wrong. Better yet: there is no *you*. It's been proven, by guys and gals who read a lot and wear lab coats, the quantum verbalists, all those rejected nerds you went to high school with, those weasely guys and pasty girls who wore black armbands when some student radicals died elsewhere, those marginalised zit-kids, they're the ones – they've scientifically proven that you don't exist! The sixties liberals have come home to roast, to spit Mom and Dad and the kids under permanent erasure! . . . There now, I can do whatever I want. Nyaa-nyaa-nya-nya-nyaaaa.

I mean, look at Heidegger! Look at de Man! But then, why should you, when you can schtick with me and look at de Woman.

Or perhaps I should just lie down for a while?

Naaaa.

Powers of darkness, stand by me, prop me up, now and forever. Ancient lightning rod, do not forsake me now. I go forth for the one hundred and thirty-seventh time this year to . . . well, not quite to encounter, more to sneak a peek at my near neighbours – Wait a sec: didn't the younger Molly Bloom once entertain a peeper? Yes, I'm sure of it. And I feel even more noble now in my culture of complaintency. That's what much secret reading does for the highly educated poorly employed.

Let's see now, to the business of in-ness. Yes, the navy blue tonight, mein sweet, for mine suite, no gaudy piping or stitched penguin begging attention, no-no-no. My subconscious desires are all quite conscious. Nutcracker Sweet. Oh how we danced on the night she was wed, we danced and we danced till she . . . And for pants? *Pants?* I'll show you pants: hu-hu-hu-hu-HU! Not that I ever expose my lower regions to light (but for that one alarming evening when the dwarf barged in). But the pants, the pants, my behind-the-arras life for some pants for my arse-arse! Can I get no rest anywhere! . . . Purple gym shorts? Hmmm. To complement the honourably engorged member for Troutstream South, itself soon arcing like a sexy salmon into the strange element? And now – lights out! Curtain wide on a benighted screen windexed in the full light of day. I have nothing to hide but hiding itself! My chair, sir. Thank you. No, no kneepads, thank you, I'll not be collecting popcorn boxes this evening. One cannot eternally defer encounter with the show.

Wait and see.

Before I draw deep breath, Clyde is displaying in her light-flooded room, with that plodding grace only Clyde commands in our selfless moments alone. Her tank-top whips over her head, her shorts and underwear are kicked off into her hands, her feet snapping up to her face like those of a female primate instructed to punt her own tits backwards into my end-zone. Then Clyde, her ass and thighs like cottage cheese on a cellulite bed, belts a quilted housecoat and clomps off to the showers. Good game, big girl. Her lights go out, with Clyde, as it were. And O to be water, what e'er, what er you want, Popeye? Everything, matey, every-thing, *c'est tout*!

The good news is that I love Clyde just the same, come light or come darkness. Across our shared and narrow abysmal back yard, and the unconscionable chasm that no words or actions could ever bridge in this verbally meaningless world (is there another?), I love her: her comings (*pace* girls), her goings, her utter absence of . . . Oh, how shall I put it? I mean, apart from her clothes . . . Defences?

But I do love you, Clyde, all passé irony aside. No one will ever love your private faceless weightless moments as I do, your thighs like two belugas frolicking at whalelicking foreplay, your chest like wannabe tits on a white air-mattress, your bluntly ugly face like every Swiss's nightmare. O Clyde, I am touching my temples (with my free hand) and sending a telepathic message: if you are in the shower now, with one hippo-hip actually distending the curtain, Clyde, even if, *especially* if your sad downward gaze has further foreshortened your front, Clyde, I am empathetically rubbing my telepathic temples: I do love you, Clyde . . . in my own small way.

No answer? Oh well, I can wait. Oh yes, we are PhDs at wait and see we wee peepers in darkness.

With me the first movement always excites a sympathetic reaction of the bowel, unfortunately explosive. Like many a devoted patron of the performing *ars*, I duck into the hall to light a cigarette. With the ember shielded *à l'homme au pissoir*, I hurry back to my place, breathless: Have I missed anything? (I mean, other than a healthy normal life?) I bow deeply to puff spurtly between my knees like a little choo-choo, unavoidably cooking the heater. Wait and see, wait and see. I must have it chiselled into my tombstone, an epitaph carved by laser-concentrated testosterone: Wait And See. RIP.

Memo: Clyde (not her real name) lives with two other women also in their mid-twenties. And a husky bunch of broads they are. Big young women, you see them everywhere these days, smoking their tits off. Must be all that growth hormone farmers feed cattle. I suspect my three large ladies of latent (perhaps punctual) lesbianism. That's all right with me. Unlike my friend Nigel, I'm non-judgemental in such matters. Judge not lest ye . . . and all that intolerable liberal shit. Though I've never actually seen them perform in concert, the thought of their good quarter-ton of pale flesh . . . *Gulp*. There, a dried throat at the thought. But I mean, they have to be queer, eh? Not one of them has made a move on me – Dear God, there really *is* something wrong with me, isn't there? Seriously. I mean, talking to myself like this? Wrong? Something wrong with *you*, oh flower of my firstmoistest creation? Thirty-eighty years old, well fed, solid, single, and leading a virtually rent-free full and active social life here every night between nine and eleven. A rewarding life, surely, a life whose span is a hymn of praise to the Begetter of the Big Bang. But surely, *surely* there must be *some* little thing wrong with me? I mean, uh, like this peeping tom thing I'm kinda into? (*Voyeur* is too good for me. Sounds like something Freud dignified with a treatise, as were all his fetishes. *Voyeurism and its Relation to Benighted Hand-Eye Coordination. Peeper* really sounds too sweet. *Filthy little pervert?* Ah, there's the schticker. How could I have missed it?)

But where was I? . . . Ah yes.

Memo: To members of the responsively sympathetic reading
       pubic
From: The Narrator
Re: The Subject(s)
Date: To be determined
Place Up yours (I will not supply the colon)

Clyde lives with Butch and Steg (not their real names), and here follows a word-picture sufficient unto all three: *Aaaaaaaagh.* Clyde I've named for the drawers of beer wagons, with the significant difference being behavioural: the other beasts don't drink numerous cans of their fare and stumble about a lighted blindless room in pastel drawers and no bra on New Year's Eve. (Though make no mistake, we genuine filthy little perverts would wait to see even one of our animal companions cavort so. *Comprenez, mes lecteurs semblables*: the species is irrelevant, if anything is.) Clyde is raven-haired, square-headed, with foreshortened torso and tits, and with legs . . . but I've mentioned her kegs, haven't I? Poor Clyde. A body that just won't quit . . . grotesquely parodying the form God gave to Eve.

Of the two who periodically perform aerobics for me – Clyde and Butch – Butch is the better looking. (Har! I'm sorry, a private joke: Butch might have made an acceptable man, in the eyes of a woman with a taste for the stout and crop-haired, the pugnosed –)

Clyde's back, shut up. (Look who's talking! Get out.) Time's up, sorry. Look: Steg is mousy-haired, long-nosed, tall (for a woman) and skinny, with hip bones jutting like a skeleton's pelvis and with something of a humpback. (As if any of this matters.)

There used to be a fourth, Nutcracker Sweet, who let down the side and married . . . another woman! (So *there's* my evidence, Your Honour, the stroking nun, as it were; and I might add that I have taken deep offence – deep, yes, but in other dimensions as well – at these repeated innuendoes regarding my alleged homophobia. And what, Your Honour wonders, *is* the innuendo? . . . An Italian enema!) Nutcracker Sweet's spouse, Sergeant Butko, is past President of our Tenants Association. Together the Sweet-Butkos hump happily ever after in the Project's one three-bedroom suite, which they finagled between them. Isn't it nice when things work out for good kids?

Clyde now wears a blue towel upon the head and her quilty bathrobe around the body. A suggestion of bounce in her boulderish clumsiness suggests bare feet. She removes the towel, bows deeply and shakes out her hair, gives it a preliminary comb with her fingers, uh-huh uh-huh, unties her bathrobe and lets it drop to the floor, emerging like a wingless white pig from an unbecoming chrysalis. The large thing does have its gravity-defying moments of lonely bounding grace, yes . . . indeed yes. My heart soon outpaces my breathing, and I can only keep my hands to myself, but I must remain calm. Lately I've had to fight the impulse to bang on the window, or to put my fist or face through it, or to take a running leap, my very body a feminist grapple: Clyde, my love, I'm coming over! I'm coming across! . . .

She clomps in beauty to her window and stands looking out on fast-fallen night. It's Friday, but there will be no heterosexual date for Clyde tonight. Perhaps the game plan's as usual: to go drinking with Butch and Steg and roll home around midnight to denude the fridge and cupboards. (And I can derive almost as much pleasure from watching that scene, happy for them.) Regardless, Clyde turns away and walks to her closet, opens the unpainted folding door and stretches up on tiptoe to the shelf, displaying to this artist's appreciative eye the ineffable loveliness of a bilateral arrangement of furry-based bifurcated globular ass, a mass that draws the desiccated oesophagus from me as the maiden moon herself draws whole oceans. She thumps down on her heels, *ca-chung*, puts her robe back on. Exit with hair blower, morosely. Lights out. Curtain.

I close my eyes in vertiginous swoon. O female shape eternal,

O perfect refraction of divine light onto my darkness, O pale body of ample flesh promising immortality, *ora pro nobis*, flesh of ages, s/mother me, let me hide wee things in thee, O me, O my . . .

What? You had assumed that I thought Clyde, Butch and Steg beneath contempt and me? Merely because Larc Alemahn would stick his cigarette holder down his throat? Tut-tut. That just goes to show how wrong *you* really can be about Troutstream's furriest. And if you can be so wrong about this essential fact, this Truth, imagine all the other things you could be wrong about? (Boy, you better re-read.) Be that as it may, let me, like the late Richard Nixon, make one thing perfectly clear: we live, my lovelies and I, in the midst of a miracle, a *miracle* I tell you! We co-exist in an undeclared marriage sanctioned – nay, sanctified – at heaven's convenience counter: voyeur meets and falls madly in love with three exhibitionists.

But let me entertain the practical prosecution.

Do my lovelies know I'm over here in the dark? I would have to say they must have a pretty damn good idea. I would say, mmmm – Yes! Mine is the only window facing their two bedrooms. Yet neither Clyde nor Butch and Steg has a blind. They show, I watch. No one tells. We honour social and domestic convention: I keep my lights off, my curtains wide, and my viewing clothes dark; they never enter or leave their rooms naked, and never remain clothed while *in camera*. No one is hurt. The perfect victimless crime. Though I do worry about my eyesight, having been drilled throughout childhood about the dangers of watching tv in the dark, which I always did anyway, the only way. No big deal, I was beaten savagely about the buttocks and small privates for much lesser transgressions. (I firmly believe that's what stunted its growth; *stunted*, I say; there is no justification for the dwarf's demeaning *micro-*.)

Oh yes yes, I see your impassive pathetic puss pushing its stupid objection about behind your eyes like a tongue at Finn's loose tooth.

Why do *I* do it? What drives *me*? Is that it? Is that *all* you care about? *That* old cause-and-effect cost-effective fiction?

Oh you, you analysts. Do you still think there are other than material-biological answers for the likes of me? A faulty sense of proprioception, my proprioceptors skewed chemically, with consequent failure to appropriate my personal property, my proper person, fully. You see, I have lived always at a great remove from my own body, unhoused at home, like an artist disconnected from his sensory material means, with my God's prank of a cock like a snail's horn. One of these nights I'll do myself real damage (I threaten Him). I'll hack it off with nail clippers! Or worse! You know what I mean! . . .

Easy, big guy, easy . . . See what you've driven me to? You analysts, you pseudonymous scientists, you buggereyed cowards, you wouldn't know Truth and Beauty outside a magazine. *You* make me sick. Did you not read the preceding section of this *apologia*? Tch. You should be ashamed to show your vicious little vicarious mugs to these pages, you . . . I'll bet you eat as you read, since your lips are moving anyway. And come to think of it, just what the fuck *are* you doing here? Who asked *you* to sneak in here, with your greasy chops and buttery fingers peeking into *my* life, eh? Like, get your own fucking window! Look up, look out: there's a whole real world out there, mein literary voyageur, *mon semblable* voyeur. Close the fucking book already!

Okay? Get it?

No, not yet?

All right. But this must mark an end to your investigations, then Sherlock must fuck off.

I do it because it has nothing to do with me, you silly twittering deerstalking fuckhead! . . . Sitting here in the dark, waiting for the show to start, or post-show, or watching others so completely other they're not even their miserable social selves – my God, I feel so . . . so . . . They remind me of me, and I do it because it has nothing to do with me. And I have only to do with nothing now. *It*, has nothing, to do, with *me*. Oh why don't you all just *leave me alone*! I didn't do it! I didn't! He did it! He did! The . . . nothing, to do, with me. Nothing, because me, to do is . . . nothing. No

Troutstream Fun Fest

·

Saturday morning, and sunshine brightens the world, strikes past the blinds, renews a small smile on my forgetful face. Saturday morning, and an odour of dead leaves rides the sharp autumn air, while Martha, rump towards me, slumbers in bedsmelling warmth. Saturday morning, and a pot of strong coffee and the *Citizen* and *Globe* to look forward to (two papers this one day a week and none the others). Saturday morning, and the Troutstream Fun Fest to look forward to this afternoon. An Indian summer Saturday morning. There is no lovelier time, not by my lights.

From the sounds of things, or the lack, the girls seem to be sleeping in too. But tinny music from Michael's room, music as from an old transistor radio, means overflow from headphones. If he keeps that up, he'll eventually be deaf too.

The girls' rooms are disorder bordering on chaos. Three-year-old Marion can always be found with her bony ass – remarkably bonier since she outgrew the diapers – tented and her face crammed into the crumpled bedspreads as if she's dropped from some height . . . from clouds, from heaven. Ten-year-old Margaret's is a wasteland of artwork and ugly dolls called trolls. When Michael tries to impress upon his younger sisters the benefits of order, they always snap back, 'At least our rooms don't stink.' Which is true

216

and unfair, because they can leave their windows open, while allergic Michael cannot.

I stand in his doorway uneasy at the odour and order of his room, not odour of leafy humus but of fetid growing boy. And the order: Batman stuff fanning from one corner, from monstrous and menacing black poster backdrop (he used to be a good guy, with a Boy Wonder), to dangerously finned Batmobile and mid-size villains, to tiniest figures in foreground; squared away desk centred hugely by a computer he's named Cyclops; even his bed in the morning is envelopish instead of scrunched by adolescent heels. I still hope he's passing through a compulsive stage, though he's been like this for a year now. He's a worrier, is our Michael, about the weather for Fun Fest, his own mortality, his sisters' safety. And with better reason lately, given Mr O'Donaghue's breakdown right in his class. How long had *that* being going on? And, of course, the girl, Teresa Archer, was one of his few friends.

There *is* something definitely boyish, though, furtively adolescent male, in the lurking odours of his room. Perhaps it's a difference in the material of boys' and girls' clothes, the dyes and softeners, added scents, whatever. Certainly the girls' rooms have instead a fruity and musty smell reminiscent of baby shit from the breast-fed, where Michael's is of freshly cut metal, ferruginous, smouldering. Or is it hormonal? A difference between prepubescent oestrogen and pumping testosterone? That sort of thinking is very much in the news these days. Or is the difference in my nose, odour in the nostrils of the sniffer? Whatever, this nose always leads me to Michael's room, where I feel more welcome than in the girls' rooms, or at least less of an intruder.

Tiny Bare Naked Ladies are tinnily singing 'Lovers in a Dangerous Time'. I must tell Michael it's a Bruce Cockburn song, and that the original's much better than the novelty cover. I'll wait, though, till the song's over, but on my way to his blindless window to look out on this promising day he says,

'I know you're there, Dad.'

He distinguishes vibrations, the kid's like an organic seismograph. I stand in the middle of his carpet and stare at his light fixture:

'How many surrealists does it take to screw in a light bulb, Sherlock?'

'To what?' he says taking off those wiry headphones that always make me think of language labs and UN translators; his sunglasses slip and he all but smashes them back against his head.

'I said: how many surrealists does it take to screw in a light bulb?'

'How many *what*?'

'They're a kind of artist who do very weird things with shapes and colours.'

'Is Mom up?' He paws about on his bed for . . . what? A gun?

'A fish.'

'What?' He's irritated now.

'That's the answer. How many surrealists does it take to screw in a light bulb? A fish.'

He snorts and shakes his head, lies back on his knitted fingers in phony comfort. Then he remembers, finds his white wand on the night table and relaxes.

Fooling myself that I do it for him, for us, but knowing I do it mostly for myself, I press on: 'Oh, I see surrealist humour is not your cup of eyeballs.'

'We're going to Fun Fest today, right?'

'I've been unable to sleep all night thinking about it.'

'Da-ad! You promised we were *all* going!'

'We are, we are, and I'll bet it was the mention of fish made you think of Troy the Trout.'

He smiles. 'How many *flies* does it take to screw in a light bulb?'

'Beats me.'

'Only two. But how do they get *in* the light bulb?'

I laugh: 'Where did you – '

'What's that?'

'I don't hear – '

'There.'

And I hear it, a sound like a hinge in the wind, louder and it becomes like dogs barking . . . dogs barking . . . in the sky?

He says, 'That's geese, I'll bet, Canada Geese heading south.'

I go to the window.

'Can you . . . see them?' He props himself on both elbows behind, a boy again.

I search the perfect sky, and though the sound has grown louder I can't spot them. The trees are nearly bare, some from disease and acid rain as much as from autumn, so there's more light everywhere. A woman down the street with her hand in a plastic bag stoops to encase dog shit. As the sky-barking recedes I lie:

'There they are, a large flock too, upwards of fifty I'd say. They spend their winters down south.'

'No kidding,' he says sarcastically. 'They're flying in a big V, right?'

'Yes, our very own avian pharmacologists.'

'What?'

'Nothing, a bad joke. You know, the Big V drugstore?'

'That way the leaders make it easier for the ones behind and the weaker ones. The guys at the front provide updraft for the ones behind them, and they take turns leading. That way they increase their range by up to seventy-four per cent.'

'Impressive.' That memory of his. He'll need it.

'We did them in environmental studies. And if one of them gets injured two others accompany her to the ground and stay with her till she's better.'

'Who're the stronger flyers, males or females?'

'I dunno. The males, I guess. Aren't they always?'

'Not always.'

'Mrs Manning would say that's irrelevant.'

'Is it?'

'I say nothing's irrelevant.'

'Smart boy. Want some maple waffles for breakfast?'

Sniff-sniff: 'Da-ad, did you fart?'

'No way.' It wouldn't have draughted a fruit fly. But *quel nez, incroyable!*

'Then what's that stin – Uh, sorry, it must be the pulp mills.'

'Waffles?'

He's out of bed and dressing. At twelve he's as tall as his mother, but delicately so, with proportionately long pale arms and legs signalling that he'll easily break six feet, unlike all the males in my family.

'I read an essay last week called "Why the Sky Looks Blue", by a guy named James Jeans. Do *you* know why it's blue, Mr Environmental Studies?'

'*Duh* . . . what's blue, Mr Wizard?'

'That's my point. It's simply a matter of the shorter-frequency light waves reaching our retinas through a mine-field of dusty deflectors. The sky isn't really blue, it just looks blue.'

'You liar. That is *definitely* a daddy fart.'

I sing to the tune of a band he likes: 'It ain't smelly, it just smells that way.'

'You said waffles? *Whew!* I'm outta here.'

After lunch the five of us take the good walk to the playing fields at Holy Family Separate School. We live in the northernmost reach of fishy Troutstream, on Jonah's End, in one of the seven new single-family homes that were grudgingly permitted a year ago by the reactionary Troutstream Community Association, and only then in the hope of stopping the subsidised housing project to the south. Margaret skips ahead of us, Martha pushes Marion in the stroller, and Michael loosely holds my right forearm, which feels a bit awkward, I prefer him to walk on my left.

Martha, who's been uncharacteristically quiet, is suddenly talkative again: 'I had a dream last night that I was in Michael's room and I heard a barking noise outside, and when I went and looked out, Margaret and Marion were on the porch roof and acting so silly, it made me so mad at them. It was winter and snow was falling heavily. I was scolding them through the glass and they were laughing and making faces at me, making *fun* of me, then Margaret slipped, and little Marion went and looked over the edge and came back right up close to the window with the most horrible look on her face.'

'I think you had that dream this morning, dear. The barking was geese.'

'What's it mean, Dad?' Michael sniffs the air and adds singsong: 'Someone's breaking the law-aw.'

It's a running family joke that I interpret all dreams. 'I don't know what it means.' But he would have felt something in my arm, probably before I did.

He says: 'Well *I* think it means that subconsciously Mom wants to throw Margaret and Marion to the wolves. I don't waste dream time on perfectly acceptable stuff like that.'

We all laugh but Margaret, who turns and thrusts a wrinkled nose and rapidly shaking face at Michael. It's just as well he doesn't see it.

'I had a dream too,' Marion hurries. I don't think she knows what dreams are, but simply understands the phrase as license to make up a strange story. 'I dreamed I was on the roof with Margaret and Mommy was in Michael's room, and . . . and . . . and we fell and Troy caught me and gave me candy.'

Troy the Trout, Fun Fest mascot: an eight-foot plastic fish with a man's head in his mouth and a small fan for inflation at his ass, who walks among the crowd dispensing candy and balloons. Troy is all Marion remembers of the preceding year's Fun Fest, but that's something, that's the beginning.

'Dad?' says Michael.

'What?'

'Marion's dream about Troy the Turd – I mean the Trout – what's it mean? C'mon?'

I assume a deeper voice, fatherly comic: 'Well, my son, you see it's like this.' Margaret has dropped back to listen, they all wear smiles now. 'Since olden times the fish has been a sacred symbol. I refer here to such documented facts as the early Christians' fondness for tinned sardines. . . . Uh, but the trout, the trout especially has been the conveyor of magical abilities, such as a lifetime of cavity-free dental health for the Irish, a concomitant curse upon the teeth of the English, and the ability to see through clothing for the French.' I gently elbow Michael: 'If you know what I mean.'

'Da–ad,' Margaret and Michael say, and are echoed by Marion: 'Da–dee, that's grotesque. That's not being nice to Michael.'

A moment of discomfort.

Michael laughs at bit awkwardly, 'You be quiet, Marion.'

I hurry on: 'It's a fact of Hiberno-Gallic myth and legend. Anyway, be that as it may, in Troy the Trout we see the sacred fish once again elevated to its ancient place of veneration. The word IGA emblazoned on Troy's back is the Latin acronym *Nord*

Inglis gratia Dei amoritoriumque, meaning, For the love of God let me live and die North of Inglis. The candies dispensed by Troy, the holy lifesavers and such, symbolise the sweet present moment that we should all enjoy, the inspired balloons the inflated value accorded the thin skin of human memory, and the fan up his butt the divine afflatus – '

'*John.*'

'By such means, my children, the wizards of consumer capitalism intend to cook, cool, and consume our consumerist goose, on the hermeneutic principle that what's good for the goose is goods for the gander.'

'Consume our Canada Goose?' Michael asks. '*Then* who will lay the golden egg?'

'Ah, good point, my son, a very good point. I must rethink my theory.'

'Oh, Michael,' Margaret snaps, 'don't try to be like Daddy.'

'You just don't know when to stop,' Martha chastises through her teeth.

'Be that as it may, my son, Marion here, in taking the sweet opiates from Troy the fishy king is, as youngest, subconsciously revealing to herself something of what the global economic future holds for . . .'

I don't know what it is, the day is made to order: the last black and bright yellow leaves arc and spin through the air, friendly neighbours are out and about tending garage sales or enjoying the walk down to Holy Family, smiling and greeting one another with admirable Canadian reserve. And someone in Troutstream is indeed breaking the law, it's in the air, the perfume of burning leaves cueing childhood memories for the middle aged, of the world in a pipe and cardigan scratching its back with a rake, even if only on tv. Perhaps it's Catholic guilt at this unearned October light, or the way the light's absorbed by the concrete sidewalk that looks especially unforgiving of a fall, but as I ramble and we saunter on I grow deeply uneasy. Or maybe my joke about sardines subconsciously reminded me again of the newspaper's detailed descriptions of the state of the girl's body, which was found finally in a dumpster out behind the IGA. It had been the frenzied obsession with that particular horror story which convinced us we'd done right cancelling daily delivery. The killer makes the kill and the media pick the corpse clean, and more, some throwing of the bones. And now that story's 'long' over. Though no one's confessed, no one's been arrested. I guess no one did it, twice. But I'd grown anxiously weary anyway of explaining all the paper's inexplicable atrocities to my children, of seeing in Margaret's face the unspoken 'That could happen to me', of being depressed at Michael's fascination, of reading the age 'eighteen months', 'the father is being held for questioning', and watching Marion stomp bowlegged out the door like some dwarfish wrestler in a sopping diaper like some bug's tux. What was as bad, I'd begun to suspect my neighbours of all manner of criminal behaviour, mostly psycho-sexual perversities. Every other father was molesting his daughter, and every other one was looking the other way for an uncle's sake. By the time I interrupt my fishy nonsense to look up at the barking sky, I am toppling with foreboding.

'John?' says Martha digging her nails into my tense left biceps.

'Nothing, it's nothing.'

'Look,' Margaret points, 'Canada Geese.'

'Dad and I already saw a big V of them this morning,' Michael says angrily.

An erratic V is heading more southerly than South, when the western arm breaks off, pivots on what had been the point, and the whole formation begins to lose definition, swerves westward, northward, all over the place. In the southerly distance I pick out a few dark dots . . . hot air balloons, and wonder if they've confused the geese, and if I should draw attention to the possibility. Michael. No.

Margaret says, 'Well this big V looks like a big U, smartass.'

'Margaret,' Martha scolds.

'A-big-a-me?' Michael says. 'Thank you, but why are you speaking like an Italian?'

Michael's joke gives me a rush and I sputter laughter, as does Martha and a reluctant Margaret.

'What's a bigamist?' I ask and don't wait for guesses. 'An Italian fog!'

That gives them pause, then cranks the laughter up a notch.

Hopeless Marion complains rapidly in two voices, 'I know a joke, I know a joke *too*. Listen Daddy, listen, Knock-knock, who's there, boo, boo who, you don't have to cry all the time.'

It's especially the way she says 'all the *time*', as usual misplacing stresses, so that a stranger might think she's cleverly riddling something profound. We all howl, and people warily give us room. Hey, what's the problem? Why should our expressed happiness elicit such wariness? Obviously we're not a family of maniacs. Or is domestic happiness so prevalent as to be boringly avoidable? . . . Can't be, we all have to work so hard at it, *all the time*. Why do we seem only to be attracted to the things that kill us, from bacon to stories of battered babies? Next time we're alone I'll ask Michael: Did the dinosaurs worship meteorites? See where that leads him.

A banner across the entrance to the school parking lot shows two Troy the Trouts arcing like apostrophes around the sign TROUTSTREAM FUN FEST. In someone's harebrained application of comedy and tragedy, the Troy on the right smiles while his counterpart pouts.

Michael draws audibly through his nose and says with ironic gusto, 'Ah, IGA jumbo dogs. The dog-catcher had a good day' – *sniff-sniff* – 'I detect German Shepherd.'

'I wanna jumbo dog too,' Marion whines.

'Marion,' Michael says, 'when you bite them they squirt.'

'Yuck!' says Margaret.

We push politely through a large and roving pack of unsupervised kids. Martha waves to three identically dressed old women – neat perms, dark buttoned cardigans and stretch slacks – biting into jumbo dogs by the IGA trailer on the right. Two of them wave back, while the third cringes as though she's been squirted in the eye.

'Have fun, girls!' Martha calls.

'We're not staying out!' the squirted one shouts back.

'Do you know them?' I say into my chest.

'The Wier triplets, I'm surprised they *are* out.'

From behind the trailer Troy the Trout manifests in all his lumbering swollen glory. The triplets freeze in chomping approach to their dogs. Troy takes the reluctant one by the elbow, but she fights to disengage, and a scuffle breaks out. She sounds as if she's actually crying: 'Leave me alone, leave me alone . . .'

'Troy?' Michael asks.

'Troy,' I say.

'Troy!' Marion squeals.

The large fish releases the Wier morsel and turns our way, but I usher us off.

To the left Mann Quarry has set up an information booth, with a sign bearing its name and the news 'Gravel courtesy of Mann Quarry. Making Troutstream a Better Community'. The parking lot has been freshly covered with powdery white gravel, stones that have not been ground small enough, for Margaret's ankles twist and the wheels of the sticking stroller dance to some tune other than Martha's, as if the ground were vibrating.

'What's that whirring?' Michael asks.

An adolescent girl with a camcorder has come up on our right. 'It's me, Michael, Leslie Cameron.' But she doesn't remove the camera from her face. It's like she's been waiting for us, or for Michael.

Anne Cameron, the saleslady at Home Hardware, shouts back as she walks off towards the other end of the grounds with two men I don't know, though the older one I've seen around: 'Now, Leslie, you ask your friend's permission before shooting him, okay? We'll be in the beer tent. Okay, honey?'

'I hear you, Mom,' she drawls. 'I'm sure Michael doesn't mind if I film him and his family at Fun Fest, do you Michael?'

'What?' he says tightening his grip.

Before turning away Anne shouts at someone behind Leslie: 'I'm sorry, Dennis, but I really can't allow Leslie to help you out. You'll have to ask Mr O'Donaghue yourself. And good luck . . . you'll need it.'

The young man seems to have been waiting as eagerly as Leslie for her mother to leave. He steps forward and without touching anything moves his open hands around the camera like one of those psychic healers, drops his arms and smiles. There's something irksome about the way he stands off and grins at the girl, though recent events may have me imagining dangers where they aren't.

225

He says, 'Perhaps if you retracted the viewfinder a centimetre or so you'd appear that much more *less* intrusive to the subject. One often notices – '

'Huh?' Leslie removes the camera to expose a pinchlipped look: 'You heard my mother, Mister, and I told you too, I can't help you, and *I* don't need *your* help. So go bug somebody else.'

He smiles sheepishly at me, shrugs his fists into jacket pockets, and walks off towards Inglis, a sorry individual if ever there was one.

Leslie smiles and frowns: '*Please*, Michael, I'm making the official record for the IGA. It's my very first assignment as a film-maker. Can I, *please*?'

'Sure, sure . . . if my Dad says okay.'

I don't know, but I don't like to interfere with any friendship of Michael's. 'Okay, but only for a while.'

'Thank you, Michael's father.'

'Shoot away, Fellini.'

'Huh?' she says, never lowering the camera, so making me self-conscious that everything I say and do is being recorded for the eyes of strangers.

'Okay, Bergman.'

'*Try* not to look at the camera, *please*,' she says.

'Fellini,' says Michael like a carnival barker, 'the Italian cat woman, and Bergman, the cold Swede, fire and ice, together again for the very first time ever. Step right up, for only one dime, one tenth of a loonie, a thin piece of silver.'

'Huh?' she says, and I see that I've further hurt his chances of a normal life.

'Shoot away, Spielberg,' I say, and turn us into the grounds proper.

'What about Spielberg, Michael?' she asks, walking steadily sideways through the few who don't respectfully give way to a camera.

'He who speaks only for cool millions.'

Leslie laughs, a flirtatious laugh, and I feel Michael's confidence in his loosening grip.

We move up a rise to the left, and stand on a stout hill beside the queue that has formed before a booth garishly painted orange and black, with crude white lettering and logo.

'Iris Tells Fortunes for a Loonie for Charity,' I read aloud. 'So it is written beneath the divinely triangulated eye.'

'Gee, like I wonder if that's her real name,' Michael drawls in Leslie's direction.

'Don't look . . .'

Nothing is done secretly. We walk up to a counter where two women also stand sampling the reading in progress. Iris, whom I've heard about, is an older woman dressed no differently from those in the line-up – and they're all women. She sits under a canvas awning holding the hand of a lone man who neither talks nor smiles as his feet scrape each other like the feelers of a fly fresh from shit. One of the women ahead of us touches her mouth and points into the left corner, where a boy with a two-foot plastic Troy in his lap sits cross-legged, perfectly still, staring at the southern sky. I've heard of him too, from Jack Kavanagh: the Burroughs boy, who for mysterious reasons hasn't spoken or expressed much at all in six years. The two women go and line up.

We have arrived at a prolonged silence. Finally Iris pats the man's hand and says: 'You would like to make it up to your friend the . . . the manure . . . man?' Some laughter, and the man snarls over his shoulder. Iris continues: 'Really I *am* more at home with tea, and I don't want to deceive anyone. Still, I'm afraid I do see clearly that you will remain uneasy in your heart until you do make it up with your friend. But the baby will be all right, I just know it will be.'

The man pulls his hand away: 'Don't give me any more of your crap, you old shitbag.' He stands and kicks back his chair: 'Someone told you to say that stuff. It was Jack Kavanagh, wasn't it? I saw him leave here just ahead of me.' He stomps off, shouting, 'What *a* joke!'

Iris smiles at the Burroughs boy: 'It's no joke, I'm afraid, is it, Paul? But don't *you* worry, child, your daddy and mommy said they'd be back this way to pick you up. You just sit there and watch that sky to your heart's content, and you tell Iris if you see anything coming. Next, please.'

Regardless of the long line-up, Martha and Margaret decide to stay for a reading, so Marion remains with her mother. Leslie follows Michael and me down the gentle grade.

'Ah,' Michael inhales, 'universal midway: diesel and burnt sugar and' – *sniff-sniff* – 'cooked dirt.'

'Michael,' Leslie trills, lowering the camera to show him a lovingly knowing smirk. He knows it too, for his hold on me is now mere formality. I easily remember that same smirk from Martha, and how it deepened in time into her smile of loving wisdom. Thank God.

At the bottom of the hill we finally run into someone I know, Jack Kavanagh from work, and his wife Marla, who are easy to spot in the chaos of kids. They're talking to a woman who looks like Eugene Davies' wife, though I've met her only once and this woman, if it is her, is flustered in a manner I'd not have thought Alice Davies capable of. As we approach them I turn and, unbeknownst to Michael, signal Leslie to hang back.

'Dad? . . .'

'*Please*, Jack,' and it is Alice Davies. '*Please* come. He'll listen to you, I know he will.'

'I am sorry, Alice,' Marla says, 'but there's nothing we can do. I mean, it's not like we've been that close lately.'

I shout, 'Jack, Marla, how are you? And it's Alice Davies, isn't it?' Clearly I'm not stopping, only making a slow sideways pass.

Alice Davies nods and turns her worried face away while Marla smiles slight acknowledgement, but Jack is relieved.

'John and . . . Michael, isn't it?' Jack points at Michael and raises his eyebrows.

'Take care now,' I say and keep moving. 'Kids here?'

'Here and there,' he gestures.

Jack's face returns troubled as Marla takes him by the biceps and pulls him after us. He halts her, takes her hand, says something, she wipes her eyes with his knuckles, and hand in hand they return to Alice Davies, who still stands hugging herself.

An assortment of booths with crafts and games winds down the left-hand side: chattering adolescent girls wait to be dunked by a rowdy line of boys, boys shoot pellet guns at crudely painted metal female figures, older girls face-paint younger ones like toddling tarts. Nothing there for Michael to see . . . nothing there for Michael. The paved parking lot of D. C. Scott Elementary covers the back of the grounds. A petting zoo crowded with squealing little kids and spooked lambs occupies the pavement before the farthest left corner, the perfect spot for lambs, while alongside a flurry of prepubescent girls vie shyly for the touch of a labelled Connemara pony named Stormy. Michael of the appreciative *nez* would enjoy a quick tour, but I won't embarrass him by suggesting it. As we pass he sniffs twice and smiles. Two wooden tables with metal legs square the deep left corner, an ASPCA booth. The Society operates the petting zoo, and I think to get some fun for Michael out of questioning its location. But when we stand at the tables I ignore the middle-aged woman whose eyes sparkle through masquerade-style glasses.

'What is it?' Michael asks, grip tightening.

'Well, these look like a bunch of eight-by-ten black-and-whites of an injured dog – '

'A German Shepherd,' the woman says.

'In a *can*?' I ask.

'Yes, he was found just weeks ago in a garbage can right here in Troutstream. It's bad enough when people buy cute little puppies and then ditch them when they grow up, but to torture an innocent – '

I escort us towards the right-hand corner, our camerawoman in tow.

'What's wrong, Dad?'

'It's nothing, son, nothing.'

'Nothing is irrel' – *sniff-sniff* – 'diesel.'

'It's the firemen's cherry picker, they're taking kids up for an aerial view.'

'Fire*fighter*,' Leslie mumbles.

'Can I go up? Can I, Dad, please?'

My heart was still fluttering, Michael's request, that dog in the can . . .

'Maybe later . . . with your sister.'

He grips my biceps.

'Hey,' says Leslie, lowering her camera, 'I've always wanted to go up in one of those things, but I'm too chicken. If you go up later, Mike, can I go with you, *please*? I'd get some great shots!'

'Sure,' Michael smiles towards her, voice dropping. 'No sweat. Heights don't bother me, I keep my eyes closed.'

Leslie trills, raises her camera, and now I couldn't look at the camera if I wanted to. 'We'll see,' I say.

'You mean, *you* will,' he whispers.

In the opposite corner two more tables, beneath a banner. We sidle up and stand alone in front of the bulky man I recognise as a bouncer from the Troutstream Arms.

'The Change Party is recruiting,' I whisper, deepen my voice and read the banner: 'Are you ready for a change? Change to Change.'

'Well,' says Michael, 'my socks *are* a little ripe.'

Leslie giggles, and Michael loosens his grip so that he's all but let go. The bouncer places both palms flat on the table and leans forward, stares deadpan at me.

'I'd heard your boss had fallen off the Change Party bandwagon after Aaron's visit here?'

'He's back on, buddy. Master Aaron handwrit him a letter of apology.'

'I believe,' says Michael in Leslie's direction, 'the correct verb form is hand*rot*.'

Leslie snorts uncontrollably, lowering the camera, and the bouncer, in a crouch now, says, 'Hey, ain't you the kid – '

I bump Michael along: 'What're you trying to do, get me *killed*?' But he's basking mutely.

We move onto the grass on the right side, onto spongy ground that is sopping in spots. Right off the corner sits the large canvas beer tent run by the Troutstream Arms, at a considerable profit, I've heard; the owner, Paul Arsenault, makes a generous contribution of proceeds to the Fun Fest coffers, thereby assuring a Fest the following year. The tent, a monstrous army-green awning dropping only to within three feet of the ground, faces Izaak Walton Road and is entered by a blue and white pavilion. Extending from its right side is a stage, on which stands a green classroom board with swirled white lettering.

I read aloud: 'Karaoke Elvis Competition at two thirty. Costume essential.'

'All right!' says Michael. 'What time's it now, Dad?'

'Two,' Leslie says, hanging the camera at her side.

'Just enough time for Leslie and me to take a ride in the cherry picker and get back to help revive the king.'

'Uh, okay,' I say, 'but only if the man lets me – '

'Leslie and me,' Michael whispers emphatically.

'Oh c'mon, Mr Michael's – Mr Sheridan, we'll be careful . . . promise.'

Regardless of my facial efforts, she won't plead or deal conspiratorially with me. She looks only at Michael, tentatively touches his left arm. He flicks a smile her way and returns a knitted face to me. Such an old mystery reworking its expression.

'All right. But you two be back here as soon as the ride's over.'

Michael takes her arm and they walk off. With my eyes I follow them through the swirling kids. They take their place at the end of a good ten-kid line-up. I squint and see that Leslie is talking and smiling and tossing her head, and a lump rises foolishly into my throat. Foolish, yes, just the thing. So I stand smiling foolishly in the sunlight.

I turn away and find I'm alone for the first time that day, in front of an empty stage awaiting the arrival of Elvis impersonators. I look towards the fortune-telling booth but cannot spot Martha or Margaret. Why not? Worry is suddenly upon me again like the large dark head of a pit bull. . . . The beer tent, yes, just the other thing to sink that foolish lump and tamp paranoia.

Mouldy damp canvas – Michael's influence on my olfactories – dank dimness. There's the swell of Elvises, all dressed in some form of Vegas show gear and swilling beer together at two contiguous picnic tables. I count nine. As he sets another pitcher on the table the tall, bald and British owner of the Arms shouts, 'Free suds for anyone taking part in the karaoke Elvis competition.' And in mock-whisper: 'And for anyone showing a Change Party membership card.'

Three large boys in leather, looking all the more tumescent with shaved heads, slap cards on the bar, and Arsenault double-takes with his handful of empty sudsy pitchers.

'Only one pitcher?' a big Elvis complains. 'Arsenault, you cheap cocksucker.'

'Almost show time, Mr O'Donaghue, and I think you've had quite enough, sir. And watch your language, please.'

O'Donaghue? I'd hardly have recognised him if he'd introduced himself. He rises to teeter awkwardly between the top of the picnic table and its bench as he addresses his fellows: 'Whaddya say, Elvii? Is that not a contradiction in terms? Can an Elvis ever have enough?'

'No!'

A very short Elvis in full baby-blue jumpsuit with rolled pant legs hops on to his bench, shoots out his right hand in a longhorn formation and freezes in an Elvis finale pose. 'No beer, no show,' he says in a good imitation of Elvis's mumble. 'And you can take that to the bank, man.'

The Elvii bang the table and, led by the short fist-pumping Elvis, chant, 'No beer, no show, no beer, no show . . .'

Arsenault lopes back of the bulky bar and begins pulling pitchers for the skinheads and Elvii.

O'Donaghue smiles and frowns and cringes in blinding succession, flutters his head and says to the short Elvis, 'Congratulations, Nigel, a task well executed. You would have made an ideal voyageur.'

'No,' says Nigel, looking even sillier talking down from the bench, 'you want my friend.' And he hops down.

'Can he be *shorter* than you? Shall we say, *under* five three?'

'What the fuck're you talking about, O'Donaghue? *I'm* not the pervert. You want pecking man over there.' He points to a lanky balding man, a sullen version of Arsenault himself, sitting alone with his hands clasped on the crown of his head, tilting it slightly downward, and his long legs stretched and crossed under a table containing two empty pitchers. The guy looks dead to the world . . . or preoccupied by the legs passing below the awning.

'Whoa there,' the Elvii intervene. And a red-haired Elvis from about slick mid-career leans forward patting the air: 'We're all in this together, fellas, remember our deal?'

'*What deal?*' snaps Arsenault retracting two fisted pitchers.

The bouncer appears beside me at the mouth of the tent, bobbing slightly, his muscled arms at the ready, barely moving his thick neck as he surveys the scene.

At a centre table an angular woman with red pageboy hair sits opposite a man with messed-up hair and beard-shadowed face. The guy needs sleep, not his own pitcher of beer. But she radiates energy from behind her long pink drink. As though to prove her appetites, she performs a daring and offensive act for the middle of the afternoon at a community affair: she raises a limber leg, kicks off its thong, inserts the ball of her foot into the man's crotch and swipes vigorously, ruby toe-nails flashing. He looks up startled, grimaces. She lifts the tiny sword impaling a cherry and sucks off the fruit.

He points a limp finger at her mouth and says drunkenly: 'The red planet.'

Back of the bar Arsenault does a silently mouthing over-the-head point towards the farthest corner. The bouncer tenses and follows the point to where a burly man sits peaceably in only a denim bib overall, even his feet are bare.

The bouncer stalks over and grabs a handful of crossed back-straps: 'Okay, buddy, your fun's over.'

The man giggles: 'What about my fest?' But as he's pushed towards the exit he shouts angrily and repeatedly, 'That's *my* dog in those pictures,' nodding in the direction of the bar. 'Ol' Wes,' he whimpers, 'the best goddamned friend – '

'Out,' the bouncer shouts and shifts into the bum's rush, past me and up towards the Change Party table.

No beer for me, not in this place – when from behind someone says, 'Looking for a friendly face?'

It's Anne from Home, sitting beside the younger guy I'd seen her with earlier and across from the older one I'd recognised but still can't name.

'Sit down, John, sit down, we've even saved you a clean glass. . . . C'mon, our kids are off together, we may as well be, relax already, you've earned it. You know Fred here, Super over on Salmon Run? And this tall, dark and handsome man is Dave Kavanagh. I think you know his uncle, Jack Kavanagh? C'mon, slum for a bit, only Fred here bites.'

Greetings are exchanged and apprehensively I sit to be sociable. I'm passed a beer by Dave, who then tops up Anne's draft glass as they smile openly at one another in a way that fills me with fondness.

I do relax, and only then notice Eugene Davies sitting by himself one table over, with nothing on his table but his left elbow supporting his forehead in his palm.

Anne leans and whispers: 'We've invited him to join us too, but he doesn't even respond. I dunno, too stuck up, I guess. You know him, John? Isn't he the asshole runs the Troutstream Gestapo with Arsenault there?'

Arsenault clangs an old-fashioned school bell, only Davies doesn't look up.

'Showtime, Elvii! Follow me!'

Clanging the bell he goes to the mouth of the tent, turns and waits. When the Elvii awkwardly disengage from their picnic tables and slouch towards him, he goes out, clanging the bell.

'I think this will be a show not to be missed,' I say. 'Thanks for the beer. I'll have to return the favour, Anne. *If* you can squeeze me into your whirlwind social life? A pleasure to meet you, Dave, see ya round, Fred.'

'Oh you,' Anne waves me off, but I can see from her blush and Dave's smile that I've managed the right tone. 'You'd better beat it before your wife hears and wonders where this sudden energy's come from.'

A big laugh.

At the mouth of the tent Jack and Marla Kavanagh and Alice Davies walk past me without noticing me or Dave Kavanagh. They go to Eugene's table, where Alice sits beside him, with Marla opposite and Jack directly across from Eugene.

'Gene?' Alice says.

With both hands covering his ears, Eugene looks up basset-eyed: 'Can't you hear it, big guy? Don't tell me you can't. Night and day, just now! Boom, boom, boom!' with his head wagging like the clapper of Arsenault's bell.

Alice looks at Marla, who looks at Jack, who compresses his lips and takes Eugene's wrists in his hands, pries down his arms.

I clear my throat twice at my table, who are staring openly at their neighbours, but they catch themselves, get up and follow me out.

I take up a position not fifteen feet from the middle of the low stage. The Elvii congregate on the right, now an intensely serious swell quietly composing themselves, all but the short one, Nigel, who is feeling his beer, cavorting and literally ribbing his co-contestants, but not getting the response he wants. Troy the Trout manifests from behind the Arms tent and shuffles towards centre stage, flinging candy into the gathering crowd. At the microphone he gestures for applause and gets some. Troy never speaks. He turns to his right and vigorously waves Arsenault to his side, drops to his knees and pleads, with fishy mits in prayerful attitude.

'Thank you, Troy, thank you,' Arsenault says to the retreating back. He reads from a poorly palmed card: 'By the way, there's a cat named Achilles at the bar looking for you.' Pause, silence. 'Too tony for this crowd, I see.' Sweat visible. 'But thank you anyway, laddies and gentiles . . . Yes, well, I'm pleased to announce that we have enticed nine performers to participate in our karaoke Elvis competition. The prize, I remind you, is a one-hundred-dollar gift certificate for the Troutstream Arms and free membership in the Change Party.'

Nigel megaphones with his hands and shouts, 'What do the losers get, *two* free memberships?'

Loud laughter.

Arsenault gestures calmingly to the cross-armed bouncer at his feet. 'So, without further *adieu*, as we say at the Troutstream Arms, where fun is our business, I give you Elvis number one.'

An exceptionally fat man, even for the latter Elvis, in pink cowboy boots, white pants that look like spandex about the thighs, Hawaiian shirt, peacock-blue cape and pompadour wig, thumps across the stage and hands a cassette to Arsenault. The music blares background to 'I Can't Help Falling In Love With You', so loudly that even the Elvii cover their ears. Number one starts to shout the lyrics, but Arsenault stops the tape, fiddles self-importantly at the controls, and finally starts over at a lower volume. Number one still sings in a shout, battering the ballad, but he finishes big – down on one paddish knee, longhorn point – to generous applause.

We're off and running smoothly, but for the hurdles of Arsenault's bad jokes.

Number two is as thin as Elvis's remains. But despite the visual incongruity, he performs a passable 'Return to Sender'. The audience nods smilingly to one another, and when he finishes with

235

a splits, however inappropriate, some girls mock squeal. He is transported, or he should be.

Numbers three, four, five, and six all sing 'My Way' with a confidence that suggests much practice and absolutely no self-consciousness.

Arsenault checks his notes: 'Unreal Troutstream, I had not thought that life had said *no way* to so many.'

Nigel megaphones, 'Prick!' And when the bouncer takes a step towards him hides and peeks from behind Elvis number one, to much laughter.

Number seven is O'Donaghue. He looks ridiculous in his wig like a fallen nest, baby-blue cape, three-piece grey business suit, and with a child's tiny plastic guitar. Many recognise him, there is much shuffling embarrassment. And he sings a song I'd never heard Elvis or anyone do, in a tone-deaf falsetto that sounds more like Tiny Tim's helium-boxed warblings than Elvis's echo chamber:

> *If you're looking for trouble*
> *you came to the right place*
> *If you're looking for trouble*
> *just look right in my face*
> *I was born standing up*
> *and talking back*
> *My daddy was a green-eyed mountain jack*

Before this point his pelvic thrusts and crotch grabs had become so lewd that even more people were looking away while others were actually leaving. Arsenault, on his knees fiddling with control knobs and causing drum-rupturing squawks, has stopped the tape but can't cut the mike. O'Donaghue continues a cappella:

> *And I'm Evil*
> *My middle name is Misery*
> *Yes I'm Evil*
> *So don't you mess around with me*

Arsenault twists from his controls and sics the bouncer on O'Donaghue, who keeps his grip on the live mike and dodges the bouncer about the stage like Elvis doing musical slapstick:

I never looked for trouble
but I never ran
I don't take no orders
from no kind of man . . .

At stage right the bouncer finally lands a clamp on O'Donaghue's shoulder, just as breathless O'Donaghue returns to the chorus: "Cause I'm Evil, my middle name is Misery . . .' O'Donaghue glances at the other Elvii like a horse facing fire, and they look grimly embarrassed. In a flash the bouncer has thrown a headlock on him and is dragging him off the stage and towards the Arms tent. In his bowed posture O'Donaghue throws up his arms as best he can, and the bouncer looks like a skidding cowboy grinding a steer to earth as O'Donaghue shouts, 'The fix is in, the fix is in . . .' So much for Evil.

The thinned post-accident atmosphere – the sudden unreality of violence like an anticlimax – remains tense until number eight, the short Nigel, re-inflates spirits with a surreal rendition of Elvis singing the Rolling Stones' 'Satisfaction'. The relieved crowd goes wild and grows again as he shuffles and pouts about the stage like a cross between Elvis, Jagger, and Yoda. Acknowledging the riotous ovation, he holds a draped bow.

Arsenault: 'A scintillating performance, I'm sure.'

'It was, you jerk!' a woman shouts, Anne Cameron.

Number nine, Elvis with freckles and a red natural pompadour, shakes his head after Nigel then launches into 'It's Now or Never'. But no one is paying him much attention, for at side stage Nigel, still Jaggered to the nines with his wrists folded backwards on his pelvis and his shoulders pinched forwards, is scratching back and forth like a pouting rooster running the other Elvii. Red Elvis signals Arsenault to stop the music, taps the mike and says, 'Hey, man, can I get a little more reverb and action on this thing.' Head-drumming castanets, and sounding like the bassest of baritones at the bottom of a well he roars back into 'It's Now or Never'. Even Nigel is stunned.

I am turning away from the vibrating stage when a cloud reminds me that this time of year is not really as warm as the gracious sun can make it. Understandably the organisers had postponed Fun Fest to late October this year. A wind blows up, a powerful wind. Michael? I protect my eyes but can't spot him in the line-up for the cherry picker. . . . Leslie Cameron at its head, pointing upwards with her camera, and I follow its line of view to where Michael stands alone in the bucket. I hold my breath and squint. He holds his cane outstretched like he's casting a spell, his face is like two black dots on a pale page.

I feel the vertigo, gasp. I cannot watch, sometimes it's better not to see. And the overcast deepens as I turn away, the dark wind strengthens, people blinker their eyes, women tuck their dresses, children cry for their parents.

The wind dies as suddenly, the sun turns on, and all is as still as a dream.

On stage an Elvis who looks exactly like pre-Army Elvis is standing at the mike with his head bowed and his hands crossed at his crotch. He wears a black shirt with white piping like lasso, loose black pants, high-top black and white sneakers. The other Elvii stand gawking from stage right, there is much awakening commotion in the audience.

'He looks exactly *like* him!' a girl shouts.

'He does!' a man answers.

'I *bet* it is him!' a boy gasps.

'It's Elvis!' cries someone. 'It's *really* him! It's Elvis!'

'Elvis! Elvis Presley!' someone wails. 'It's . . . *him!*'

He waits expressionless, eyes closed, cupid lips pursed. When the audience silences he raises that beautiful face and those generously lashed lids like curtains on a generation's undying desire for . . . For what? The song begins:

> *Are you lonesome tonight?*
> *Do you miss me tonight?*
> *Are you sorry we drifted apart?*
> *Does your memory stray to a bright summer day*
> *when I kissed you and called you sweetheart?*

Like an angel he sings, like Lucifer before his fall warbling a song of self-aggrandising praise. Space is that brilliant stage, time apart has mercifully stopped, only he is present and mobile, coming to the edge of the stage, on one knee cradling the mike like a lover, crooning to the girls up front:

> *Do the chairs in your parlour seem empty and bare?*
> *Do you gaze at your doorstep and picture me there?*

As he moves along, a good dozen people, girls and boys and women and men, faint like a falling picket fence, even Arsenault is down on one knee with his forehead in his hand as if soliciting a blessing. Elvis rises to a magnificent height, reaches for the booming sky:

> *Is your heart filled with pain?*
> *Shall I come back again?*

And in the smallest of inaudible voices, the sweetest of unheard pleas:

> *Tell me, dear, are you lonesome tonight?*

. . . When I return to myself groups of three or four in the audience are administering attention to the reviving, others stand dumbfounded, many weep openly. My own face is wet for the first time since Michael's diagnosis. Elvis, his arms again draped before him, his head slightly bowed and his eyes shadowed by his forelock, slowly raises his black left arm and points to the southern sky. All turn. Nine hot air balloons hang surprisingly close up, as unnatural in their hovering immensity as an alien invasion, sporadically breathing flames into their openings like huffing athletes. A tenth arises back of the unnaturally colourful nine, black, even more gigantic, at once ponderous and rising like a moving hole in space.

When terrified I again face the stage Elvis is gone.

I turn towards the front entrance/exit but am stopped by Martha coming through the crowd wearing her tolerant smile, carrying Marion uncomfortably in one arm and awkwardly pushing the stroller with the other.

'I can't find Margaret anywhere,' she says before she's gotten close enough for conversation. She stops pretending to smile: 'And I've looked everywhere.'

'Oh, don't worry,' Leslie says from behind me. 'I think I saw her heading towards the cherry picker with some guy.'

'You wouldn't *believe* what just happened here,' I say.

'Balloons,' says Marion pointing upwards.

'Where?' Leslie says.

'Are you still here?' Martha says distractedly to Leslie. Then firmly: 'Margaret's only ten. Would you please stop filming, this is private. Oh, John, what'll we do?'

'*What* just happened here, Mr Michael's father?' She hugs the camera to her chest.

I look calm, I know, and know too that Martha knows differently. Marion is squirming to slide on her belly down Martha's side. Martha jerks her still like someone snapping a neck, and Marion cries quietly on her shoulder. My heart is tripping and I taste metal in my throat, melting metal, what dissolving solder looks like. I know that the whole thing, all we have worked for together all this time, is coming apart, disintegrating, crashing down upon our heads. I know it, I don't know what to do, I can't pull it off this time.

I feel the tap of Michael's cane on my right leg, it slips between my legs and *wham* against my scrotum. I sicken and taste bile at the back of my throat, but I learned long ago not to startle at his mistakes.

His hand lightly clasps my forearm and he says with quiet urgency, 'Can I go to Leslie's tonight, Dad? *Please?* Her Mom's letting her have some kids over to watch the movie she's made about us here today. *Please?*'

Martha spots a neighbour up by the stage: 'Jessica, have you seen our Margaret?'

'Why yes, now that you mention it, I saw her talking to Elvis just now, she walked off that way with him.' She points behind the beer tent.

'Oh John,' is all she can manage, about to cry audibly.

And I know now with dead certainty that it *has* come. Or we have met it, we have arrived as a family, in ignorant repulsion that is all knowing desire. Once we had thought that Michael's blindness was our catastrophe, and Martha and I had talked like living clichés about the miraculous way in which it had drawn us together as a family. But I see now as clearly as I see Martha's foolishly wet face that if you live long enough catastrophe is an incremental thing. And the next worse thing is here now, a patient, loving disaster that has awaited the silly dodging dance of our lives, a touching horror that no amount of real family planning could have avoided. A black enfolding evil billows down upon our family, and we will now have to survive inside it for the rest of our unfeeling lives. And the shorter that time the better, so as to be spared the worse next.

Michael cocks his head.

'What – '

'Sh-sh,' he warns, and there is no contradicting that concentrated face.

'There,' he says, raising his cane towards Scott Elementary and twirling it. 'O-ver . . . there!'

'Dad! Dad! Mom!'

Margaret appears where he's pointing, grinning guiltily, but whole and sound, no torn clothes, no bruised and bloodied face, just skipping towards us waving a piece of paper. Michael steadies me with a hand in my armpit. I hold a palm to my clammy forehead.

Brooking no word of defence, Martha hotly scolds Margaret for taking a cherry picker ride without asking permission. I tell Michael he can go to Leslie's. Goodbyes are exchanged, and I see Leslie squeeze Michael's hand.

'Okay,' Martha orders, '*everybody* stay together, single file, and let's try and worm our way outta here.'

'Good idea.'

An even longer line waits at Iris's tent. To the right of her table Paul Burroughs now sits facing inward to the fairgrounds, and as we pass he raises his toy Troy and points to the northern sky. But, superstitious me, I will not turn back for one last look at the hot air balloons receding spectacularly. I don't deserve this – who could? – but I will shoulder my lot of happiness and keep on straight ahead.

The front entrance/exit is jammed with unsupervised kids, and when we push our way onto the sidewalk of Izaak Walton it's like being vomited forth from a smelly belly.

'Whew!' says Michael as we turn towards home.

Margaret stops behind us on the sidewalk, her fists at her sides: 'But I didn't take a ride on the cherry picker! *That's* what I've been trying to *tell* you!'

'Margaret,' I say, 'don't lie.'

'It's *not* a lie! I was right behind you all the time, Dad, watching the Elvis show. I went to get the last guy's *autograph*.' She unballs her fist and holds out the piece of paper.

'Autograph,' Marion says.

'I didn't see you there.'

'You were half asleep, Dad. I had to run after him behind the tent.'

'That was a very foolish thing to do, young lady,' Martha says.

As I take the slip of paper I say, 'He was unbelievable, wasn't he, a dead ringer.'

'It's funny, but up close he didn't look at all like Elvis. He was short, he had a big nose. He didn't even *sign* Elvis. And look at the stupid thing he *wrote*.'

I read the autograph aloud: ' "You're a good little character, pretty too. Now tell everyone it's time to go home, honey. Show's over, Jake." *Jake?*'

Everybody laughs but Michael, who turns back to the school grounds. His cane quivers like a witching stick: 'Dad? . . .' Fear, but I know from the few other times this has happened that there's nothing I or anyone can do.

'It's here *again*, Daddy.'

I so desire to sense what he senses that I try anyway: 'Is it good or evil, son?'

Surprisingly he smiles like some Lazarus: 'That really *is* irrelevant. It . . . wants – Wait. Give me the note.'

I take it from Margaret, who tries to smirk, while Martha watches and Marion buries her face in her mother's neck.

He fingers the note like a rare coin, smiles. 'Material evidence,' he says. 'This has . . . passed over.' He smirks embarrassment, then hurries: 'Dad, can I go back and talk to that Iris?'

242

'Oh Michael,' Margaret says. 'Will you just stop it.' But she's faking.

'Michael,' I say, 'it does say we should *all* go home.'

'Why should we do what . . . *he* wan – '

He stiffens, elbows pressed to his sides. With a struggle he raises his cane like a haywire compass needle and points towards the northern sky. I look finally and see that all the balloons have disappeared, all but the distant black dot.

'I defy you,' he whispers in a voice that is changing. 'I know you're up there, out there, and I defy you! I refuse to do these things you make me do! I want . . . I want to be . . . I want to be fr . . .'

I know to catch him. He remains limp for a moment, then his strength returns. He brightens, smiles familiarly: 'I think I saw a spot of light there.'

'Oh *sure*, Michael.'

'No, really. It looked like . . . like Marion felt when she was born.'

Marion comes off her mother's shoulder. 'I saw light too, Daddy.'

'Oh, Michael, you're always showing off. Give me back my autograph.'

He grins, crushes the paper and pops it into his mouth, chews and swallows.

'Da-dee!'

'Michael,' Martha says, 'that was a mean thing to do.'

'Material evidence, Mother. I don't think we're ready for it.'

He takes my arm and turns me: 'Like the man said, let's all go home and, as we say in Troutstream, batten down the' – *sniff-sniff*. 'I smell a surprise.'

A stout old man in dull-green worker fatigues is coming along the sidewalk carrying a fishing rod and net in his right hand, and in his left a . . . no, it can't be a –

Sniff-sniff. 'Fish,' Michael grins.

And a fish it is, a big grey flashing fish being held aloft for our amazement like some tenth wonder of the world, and as the old fisherman comes alongside he smiles maniacally and passes cackling:

'Troutstream! Troutstream!'

L'Envoi

And as the cry grows fainter in my ears, I find that my sense of doom has vanished into thin air. Disengaged, with his fingertips just touching my elbow, Michael walks easily on my left. Marion lolls in her stroller. I put my arm around Martha's shoulders, rest my hand on Margaret's crown, and we head home.

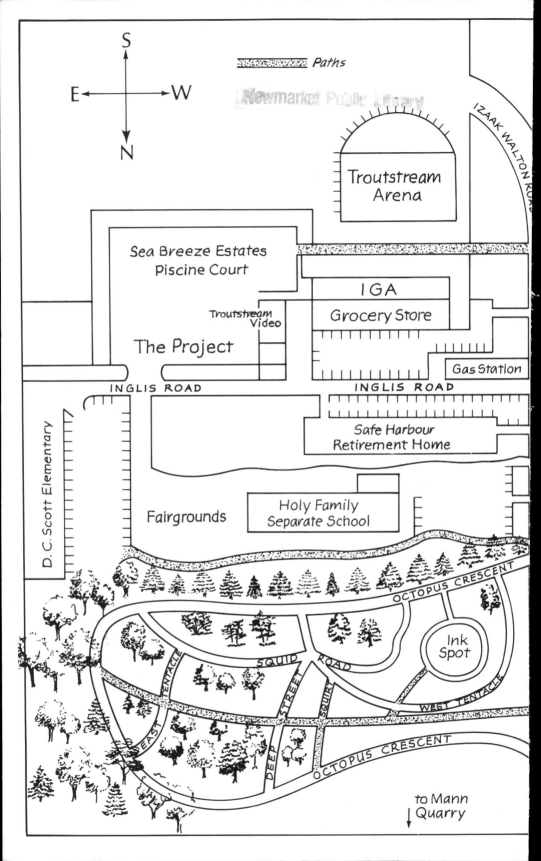